"Whimsical, darkly c[...] [...]'t
fantasy satire for anx[...] [...].
I'll read anything she[...]

OLIVIA [...] [...]t

"*Harry Potter* meets *Gilmore Girls*... Seriously, what's not to like?"

TOM HOLT, World Fantasy Award-winning author

PRAISE FOR *DREADFUL*

"An absolutely magnificent comedic fantasy with a hint of bite. This book was a witty, empathetic, and genuinely funny meditation on the nature of good and evil. It was easily one of the best books I've read this year."

OLIVIA ATWATER, author of *Half a Soul* and *The Witchwood Knot*

"*Dreadful* is pure fun. Caitlin Rozakis delivers a (loving) send up of classic fantasy tropes alongside a compelling redemption story and plenty of quirky humour. The Dread Lord Gavrax (or Gav, as his memoryless alter ego prefers) is a fantastic character, alternately chilling and sympathetic, and readers will also love the cast of seemingly stock fantasy characters with endearing hidden depths. Highly recommended."

HEATHER FAWCETT, bestselling author
of *Emily Wilde's Encyclopaedia of Faeries*

"It was very kind of Caitlin Rozakis to write this book for me. Sure, the rest of you should like it too, but it was clearly written for me, with all the elements I love: fun and humor, breaking fantasy tropes, interesting and complex questions about identity and redemption, and some delightful goblins!"

JIM C. HINES, author of *Goblin Quest*

"Outrageously funny and self aware, *Dreadful* is perfect for fans of *The Princess Bride*. Rozakis blends wit and whimsy with a deft hand in this charming debut that had me laughing with every page-turn. A vital addition to the cozy fantasy genre."

ROSIEE THOR, author of *Tarnished are the Stars*

Also by Caitlin Rozakis
and available from Titan Books

Dreadful

CAITLIN ROZAKIS

TITAN BOOKS

The Grimoire Grammar School Parent Teacher Association
Print edition ISBN: 9781835411407
E-book edition ISBN: 9781835411414
Broken Binding edition: 9781835414828

Published by Titan Books
A division of Titan Publishing Group Ltd
144 Southwark Street, London SE1 0UP
www.titanbooks.com

First edition: May 2025
10 9 8 7 6 5 4 3 2 1

A CIP catalogue record for this title is available from the
British Library.

EU RP
eucomply OÜ Pärnu mnt 139b-14 11317
Tallinn, Estonia
hello@eucompliancepartner.com
+3375690241

Typeset in Albertina 10.4/12pt.

Printed and bound by CPI Group (UK) Ltd, Croydon, CR0 4YY.

*To my child's amazing teachers and school administrators—
whenever these fictional characters are wise and kind,
know that you were the inspiration. When they're not…
it's because plot needed to happen.*

1

Maybe it was the bite-sized gingerbread man that waved
merrily at her from the half-eaten tray of its fellows, or
maybe it was the impossibly elegant woman with the
delicate gills at her neck, but as soon as Vivian arrived at the
Grimoire Grammar School Back-to-School picnic, she knew
bringing the brownies had been a mistake.

Daniel had teased her, both about making something so
whitebread American and about making it from scratch instead
of using a box mix like a normal person. He'd voted to buy a

box of Entenmann's chocolate chip cookies and call it a day. But Vivian was already feeling insecure, and she'd wanted to make a good impression. She'd thought brownies were the perfect compromise—down-to-earth enough not to be ostentatious, yet homemade with high-quality ingredients to show she'd made the effort.

But, just as one should not bring a knife to a gunfight, one should not bring brownies to a magic school picnic.

"Oh," said the woman behind the table. Up close, her skin had the faintest touch of shimmer. Her voice held haunting resonances that Vivian would have happily listened to for hours. "Brownies. How… quaint."

It didn't matter how gorgeous the voice, Vivian knew a slight when she heard one. Her cheeks warmed but she soldiered on anyway. "Well, it wouldn't be a potluck without them, would it?" she said cheerily. "I'm Viv."

The elegant woman left Vivian's hand hanging in the air. "I suppose you can put them over in the corner."

Vivian lowered her hand, blushing harder. She edged over to the Corner of Shame, and wedged her knockoff Tupperware where it wouldn't stand out too much. She'd just abandon it, she decided. She certainly wasn't going home with a full container under her arm, and as Daniel kept reminding her, it wasn't like their daughter could have chocolate anymore. Next to it was a plate of iridescent cupcakes that were literally glowing and a container of what looked like raw meat carefully cut into hearts. The shape, not the muscle. Although, come to think of it, if someone had cut heart shapes out of cow hearts, she wasn't sure she would be able to tell. No one was going to notice the brownies.

"Are those brownies?"

Vivian's ears were hot now. She turned around, waiting for another condescending look.

But the smiling white woman with the mass of brown curls peered around her, eyes lighting up. "They are! No one ever brings chocolate to these things—the werewolves always complain too much. I say, if your child is going to throw up if they eat chocolate, maybe if they throw up a couple of times, they'll figure out they should stop eating it. You're very brave. I think I'm going to like you."

Vivian had not meant to be brave. "Crap, is it that much of a faux pas? I mean, I knew about the werewolves not eating chocolate—my daughter can't have it—but I thought as long as we stayed away from nuts and alliums it was allowed?" Aria also couldn't have eggs, according to the last allergy test they'd been able to do before everything got turned upside down, but these weren't for her. Vivian had a vegan carob thingy in a baggy in her purse for Aria. It was also organic, Fair Trade, sweetened with applesauce instead of sugar, and tasted kind of cardboardy, because apparently people who bought egg- and chocolate-free desserts expected them to be penitential. But she'd also discovered the hard way, with the first round of allergies, that if she brought desserts Aria could eat to a potluck no one else ate them, and she hadn't had time to make two batches of brownies.

"Most people won't mind, but you won't win any friends with the militant crowd." The other mom's eyes twinkled. "Tell you what, you and I will disappear these and no one need know about it. I'm pretty sure I can find them a home. I'm Moira, by the way."

"Viv," she replied, a little overwhelmed.

"New to the neighborhood, are you?"

"Last week." It wasn't proving to be the friendliest of places. "What class are you in?"

"Uh… Mandrake Room?" Vivian had gone to public school, where her classes had been called the teacher's name, the room number or the grade level. She'd remembered some of her friends, from before, who had older children in Montessori schools cooing or laughing over classes named after plants or animals. She'd thought it was charming, if a little twee. She didn't think twee covered this.

"Really? You're a kindergarten parent?" Moira lit up. "My daughter Cara is in Mandrake, too!"

"Really?" Vivian echoed. Oh, thank god. No one had talked to her since they moved, and she'd started to believe that their little family were going to be total outcasts.

"Oh, this is perfect. Cara will be delighted. She's known most of the class since they were all born, and she'll be so thrilled to have a new friend. Where's yours? Boy? Girl? Something else?"

"Oh, ah, girl, Aria. I mean, her name's Aria," Vivian fumbled. She hadn't been this nervous since freshman year. Frightened, yes, terrified, definitely, heartbroken and lost, too much. But not nervous. Nervous was almost a relief. That the worst to be scared of was what other parents thought of her. "She's over there, with my husband. Daniel. Is my husband. I mean."

Moira looked over where Daniel was standing near the playground, a surprisingly normal-looking assortment of twisty metal bars and platforms and plastic slides in primary colors, in the shadow of a school that looked less like the medieval castle Vivian felt a magic school should resemble, and more like the gray stone neo-Gothic of an elite American university with an endowment and a desperate wish to cosplay as Oxford. The sun caught on his raven hair and gently tan skin, and Vivian had the familiar astonishment that someone so dashing could be hers. Aria was peering longingly at the other kids from behind his legs. She had Vivian's reddish-brown hair and heart-shaped face, but the same eyes she'd seen in photographs of Daniel's own father.

"So she's…" Moira trailed off, fishing. A little boy with an Elmo guitar swung over his shoulder beckoned to Aria. She shook her head and ducked farther behind Daniel's legs.

Same question as every time. "Quarter Japanese, yes."

"Ooookay, that's nice," Moira said. "But, uh, what I meant is, you guys are…?"

Oh. Even better. "…married?"

The Elmo-guitar kid had wandered closer, leaning around to see Aria. Aria yelped and jumped back.

And abruptly rippled, whining in the back of her throat. Her back arched and her knees cracked and there was a weird shiver in the air around her and suddenly instead of a little girl there was a reddish-brown wolf pup sitting in a puddle of shredded clothing.

"Oh," said Moira. "That answers that. Going with the chocolate so you're not tempted to break your diet?"

And that was why they were here, at Grimoire Grammar. Because the looks the other parents were giving Daniel were the same kind you'd give the parent of a kindergartner who had just wet themselves—pity mixed with condemnation. Judgment, and relief that the judgment was being rained down on someone other than them. But not horror, or screaming, or fainting, or throwing up, or calling animal control. All of which had happened before. Vivian felt somewhat inoculated to "*my kid would never*" and "there but the grace of God go I" looks, as long as no one called her child a demonspawn or ever tried to run her over with a truck again.

But. There was another misapprehension there. And as much as Vivian wanted the safety of being accepted in the community, it wasn't like she could keep up the pretext long. Better to nip this in the bud. She said, dragging it out over her reluctance, "I'm not. And neither is Daniel. Just… just Aria."

"Oh." That was what it took to finally dampen the ebullient Moira. "Huh."

"It was nice to meet you," Vivian said mechanically. She should have known it would be too much to ask to make a real mom-friend. What did she have to offer anyone? She started to go help Daniel. Aria was cowering behind him once more, now with a literal tail between her legs. Tonight was a full moon, after all, and she seemed to have even more trouble than usual turning back the day of the full moon.

"Let Dad take this one," Moira said, surprising her. "Hon, you need a drink."

"Here?" she asked, startled. "I mean, I couldn't, I should…"

Elmo-guitar boy had settled down on his haunches, holding out his hand like someone familiar with dogs. Aria peered around Daniel's legs and tentatively took a sniff. The boy waited patiently, as the wolf cub shyly took a step towards him, and then another.

"See? She'll be fine. Evander's charming with animals, he had half the birds in the neighborhood following him around by the time he was three. C'mon, you need to hit the wine and cheese table. And maybe skip the cheese." Moira grabbed her arm and steered her around.

Vivian managed to catch Daniel's eye from across the milling field of kids and their grown-ups. He nodded with his chin.

He had this. He was the one with the backpack with the two changes of clothes, anyway.

"So your daughter's a shifter," Moira said and left a little pause for Vivian to explain exactly how that had come about. She didn't. Moira continued as if nothing had happened. "Well, you're in good company. We're selkies, by the way. I mentioned Cara, my youngest. Ewan's my husband, and Cara's older brother Rory is finishing up middle school. I know, quite the gap, what can I say. Time and tide wait for no man and all, but sometimes the tide catches up if you know what I mean."

Vivian had no idea what she meant, but she could tell innuendo-tone when she heard it. Selkies were, what, wereseals? Something like that?

"Let's see, who else do you need to know? They're mostly mages, of course: there's always been a lot more of them than us. The Cunninghams are nice enough, Mother Ocean knows they've got their hands full with twins to begin with, and it looks like the girl's going to be a pyromancer." Moira indicated a Black couple, the mother fruitlessly trying to remove something sticky from her fidgeting daughter's mouth, the father gesturing broadly as he talked with a slim redhead with very fair skin and curls piled just so. They stood under a dogwood tree blooming out of season next to a flaming red sugar maple, both of which shaded the promised table covered with wine and semi-fancy cheese and olives and other things kids generally wouldn't touch. "Cecily's a bit more prickly, tends to go on and on about lineage. She's from one of those old mage families, seems to think we're all a touch gauche. Don't let her get to you."

Wonderful. Her mother would have been thrilled, if she were still talking to her mother. All through her childhood, she'd had the importance of making friends with the right crowd drilled into her. The careful dance of favors granted and owed. She'd tried to leave all that behind. But then, where had it gotten her? Maybe if she'd been a power player, she wouldn't have ended up a pariah when things went wrong for her family.

But maybe things would be different here. Moira seemed nice enough. Vivian just had to make a good impression. In a town where she was by definition an outsider, in a culture she couldn't hope to join, with nothing less than her daughter's entire future riding on her success. She swallowed, her mouth gone dry.

"Who's manning the dessert table?" she ventured.

Moira rolled her eyes. "Oh, Raidne. Speaking of cold fish."

"Is she a…?"

"Siren? Yep."

"I was going to say model."

"Raidne? Take directions from anyone? Oh hell no. She's the one who tells the models what to do. Well, not directly, she has people for that. Runs some ad agency in the city, one of the big ones."

Of course a siren would run an ad agency. It was probably restful, luring consumers to their doom instead of sailors. Less dead fish smell.

Somehow, Vivian found herself with a plate of cheese in one hand and a clear plastic cup of cheap chardonnay in the other, facing the age-old cocktail party dilemma of how to get cheese into one's mouth when the other hand is full of wine. She awkwardly balanced the little paper plate on the cup. The redhead, Cecily, raised one elegant eyebrow. Very deliberately, she made a tiny motion with her wrist, as if there were an invisible table immediately beneath her own cup. Then she released the cup to float, motionless, where she'd left it, selected a piece of cheese and a cracker from her own plate, popped it into her mouth, and retrieved the cup from its non-existent perch, without ever breaking eye contact.

Vivian gave up on balancing her cheese and took a bigger gulp of wine than strictly necessary by polite society's rules. She herself found it completely necessary. Who was she kidding? She was never going to fit in with these people.

"I know changing the bylaws are a pain, but the increase in transparency would be worth it," the Cunningham dad was saying.

"Steve, you and I know that, but a lot of parents seem to think that with Ms. Genevieve being so new to the role and all, it's more important to preserve a sense of stability. We wouldn't want to complicate things now, that would hardly be kind to her when she has so much to learn." Cecily switched her attention back to Steve Cunningham now that Vivian had been properly put in her place. "Not that I would ever dream of saying something; you know I hate to raise a fuss. But don't you agree, Sasha?"

Sasha Cunningham looked like she wanted to talk about anything else, but the familiar way her head kept turning told Vivian she was too busy keeping half an eye on the twins to force a subject change.

"But with the logistics required now that Banderbridge is no longer keeping things running smoothly, is it really the time…" Cecily had the bit in her teeth and was off to the races.

Vivian smiled and nodded through the continuation of what was clearly a tense-but-civil debate between the other parents clustered around the wine table. As far as she could follow, they were arguing about how often the Parent Advisory Council treasurer needed to present the books to the association, as opposed to the parent board (which was something else entirely?). She recognized the name of Ms. Genevieve, the headmistress, but not Banderbridge, who seemed to have been the former headmaster. She wasn't sure why people would have preferred the latter to the former—Ms. Genevieve had seemed like the very image of an efficient administrator to her. Maybe it was just resistance to change? This didn't seem like the kind of place that liked change very much. They bemoaned other departures over the summer, some whose kids had graduated and some families who had moved. Regardless of the parents' positions on Team Give-Ms. Genevieve-a-Chance or Team Banderbridge-Can-Never-Be-Replaced, it seemed everyone could agree that they were relieved to no longer have to deal with one of the previous Parent Advisory Council members, although no one wanted to talk about why. Vivian nodded and drank probably too much wine, because she wasn't on Team anybody; fear that that was going to hurt Aria's social standing was sending her anxiety into overdrive.

"But then, it's all for the good of the children," Cecily said for at least the third time. Vivian wondered if she ought to make bingo cards. Steve would play, she guessed. Sasha probably wouldn't because it would require listening too closely to Cecily, but she'd probably be willing to bet on the outcome if her husband played a card on her behalf.

Was there some way to get caught up without reminding everyone of how very much she didn't belong here? Or at least show that she was willing to learn? Most of the parents here seemed to be human mages; the cryptid community was small, she had been told, and apparently the number of non-humans capable of procreating with any regularity was smaller still. Vampires didn't have kindergartners. But the casual use of small magics she saw—a garden outline sketched in the air with colored light, a spilled ice cream resuscitated from the grass to fall upwards back into its cup—made her acutely aware of how very mundane she might be considered even by the non-cryptids. Moira the selkie felt more relatable.

"—and with Brunnhilde's youngest graduating, she'll be leaving the Parent Advisory Council, too, and while it looks like I'm going to be pressured into being president and we've lined up a volunteer to take my old spot as secretary, I don't know how we'll replace… I mean, how we'll fill the vacancy for treasurer," Cecily was saying.

"I could do it," Vivian blurted.

Cecily raised her eyebrow again. There was no way Vivian believed that anyone was pressuring Cecily into taking the president position, other than Cecily herself.

"I was an accountant before Aria," she said, hating how defensive she sounded. "I was going to go back, until, uh, until. Anyway, I've got the time—I'd love to help."

"It's a very important position," Cecily began, "and an extremely demanding responsibility—"

"Excuse me," Vivian cut her off. She was willing to be talked down to over baking, and not understanding the social mores of the community she'd unwillingly joined, and her own inability to keep her daughter from shredding her clothes in public. But not about accounting. "I was a senior manager on an audit team from one of the biggest firms in the world. I think I can manage the PTA funds."

"Parent Advisory Council. Not PTA." The temperature plunged. Vivian was pretty sure it was not her imagination, and would not have been surprised to see literal frost on the grass stems.

"It's a PTA, Cecily," Moira butted in, deftly refilling Vivian's cup. "And I think it's a great idea." She gestured the wine bottle in Cecily's direction, but the mage swiveled the hand holding the cup to cover it from refilling.

"Go for it," Steve chimed in. "We could always use a little new blood."

"Excuse me, folks, but I'm afraid I have to steal my wife back." Vivian nearly spilled her wine. Daniel had come up behind her without her noticing. "Nice to meet you all."

Never mind he hadn't met any of them. He steered her away from the group, her elbow in an iron grip.

"What's wrong?" she whispered. "I was in the middle of something."

"What's wrong is that I can't find Aria."

Vivian's heart plummeted into her shoes, and she forced it back up. They were on school grounds. There were dozens of parents milling around. She'd been assured that the grounds were warded and no one from outside the community could even see past the wrought-iron fence, let alone cross the barrier. Aria would turn out to be playing with some of the other children. Hide and seek, or tag. Nothing could have happened to her.

"I thought you were watching her," she said tightly.

"I was." The look in his eyes mirrored her repressed panic and she immediately forgave him. How could she not, when she was guilty of so much worse? "She was right there, and then she darted around faster than I could turn, and she wasn't."

"Alright." She needed to stay calm. It would turn out to be nothing. She raised her voice. "Aria? Aria, sweetheart, where did you go?"

Without needing to confer, they split off.

"Aria?" Daniel called.

Vivian saw the kid with the guitar. What was his name? Evan? No, something weirder than that. "Excuse me, have you seen the little girl who turned into a wolf earlier?"

The guitar boy shook his head, suddenly shy.

"If you see her, can you tell her that her mother's looking for her, please?"

He nodded, and then gave her a radiant smile that left her nearly dazzled.

"Everything alright?" Moira ambled up.

She didn't want to admit that they'd screwed up, yet again. Great first impression they were making. And everything would be fine. Aria couldn't have gotten far. But. What if something *had* happened?

"My daughter managed to wander off while Daniel's head was turned, and now we can't find her."

Moira shrugged. "This place is crawling with kids. She'll turn up. Don't worry about it."

"I can't not worry about it," she replied, trying to keep her temper. She was only angry because she was scared; that's what her therapist had told her. "She's new to this, this world. She doesn't know the rules, she doesn't know what's safe. And she can't... she can't control her change very well yet."

Moira studied her closely. "I think you're worrying more about this than you need to. But if you want help looking, I'll rustle up the other parents."

Vivian nodded, embarrassed but relieved. "Would you?" She didn't want to show weakness, to start off looking like an irresponsible idiot. But they already thought it anyway, and Aria was more important than anything else. The last six months, she'd had to force back panic every time Aria was out of her sight. She wasn't weeping. That was appropriate. It meant the medicine and the therapy were working, and she'd paid a lot of money for those, so it was good to get some kind of return on investment.

She headed for some likely-looking bushes. What was it about bushes that was so appealing to kids, anyway? Aria hid in them like she was going to conduct drug deals. Maybe she'd find her daughter crouched behind a holly bush, oblivious to scratches, offering another child grubby handfuls of hard candy stolen from Mommy's purse in exchange for a turn with a plastic dinosaur. Not that any of these kids would have plastic dinosaurs. They probably all had whimsical marionettes handcrafted by pixies that had been bought at the Goblin Market or something. She was babbling in her head, she knew that, but the running monologue helped keep darker thoughts at bay. For the moment.

She was already that mom. The mom other moms were going to whisper about, the one whose house no one was going to be allowed to go over to. The one who would get the condescending advice, and know she needed it. Like her own mother had said she would be.

The woman from the dessert table, the siren, what was her name, glided over. Raidne, that was it. Her feet moved, she took steps like a normal person, but somehow they were far more elegant than anything Vivian had ever managed. "Would you like for me to call for her?"

Vivian did not want the siren to call her daughter. She would have rather eaten ground glass, or maybe those raw hearts on the dessert table. Part of being a good parent was doing things you really, really didn't want to do. She nodded.

"Aria, her name is?" At Vivian's nod, the siren closed her eyes and took a big breath. Her gills fluttered. She sang out Vivian's daughter's name, turning it literal. All around the shady lawn in front of the school, heads snapped around. Vivian wanted to throw herself at Raidne's feet. It was a promise of everything she'd ever wanted, if only she came over. It wasn't for her—the message was clear—but she couldn't help wishing it had been her name. She couldn't imagine what it would be like if it had been. Several of the men and one or two of the women took an involuntary step towards Raidne. One woman stomped her husband's foot as he lurched towards the siren, snapping him out of it. Steve put one hand on his wife's elbow as she staggered a little. Moira smacked the redheaded man next to her as he took a step.

Daniel took two.

Raidne sang out again. Several of the children came pelting over, gathering around her. But no Aria.

"Maybe she didn't hear you," Vivian said, her voice wavering.

Raidne shook her head, lips thinned. "Believe me, anyone in a two-block radius heard. If she couldn't hear, it's because she isn't here."

Or she was unconscious. Or dead. The siren was looking at her with genuine pity, mixed with faint condemnation. Vivian tried not to panic. Should she go to the police? Did they even have police in this town?

Daniel was coming across the lawn towards her, his face a frozen mask. Other parents were gathering their children, lest whatever misfortune had befallen her family was catching. She looked around wildly.

Someone threw up on Raidne's designer shoes.

The air rippled a little, and there was her daughter, naked and shivering, crouched in front of them. Aria looked up, a little greenish. "Mommy?"

She threw up again. The siren stared at her feet in frozen dismay.

Vivian crouched down, rubbing her daughter's bare back. She would have clutched her daughter to her if the kid hadn't been actively vomiting. Oh, thank god. She didn't know what had happened, but she didn't care that Aria had wandered off or that everyone thought she was the worst mother in the world or that Raidne would never, ever forgive her, as long as Aria was safe.

She took a look at the sticky vomit covering shoes she probably couldn't afford to replace. The texture was familiar, especially to someone who had become a connoisseur of effluvia.

"Aria Akiko Tanaka, did you eat chocolate again?" Vivian stood up, outraged.

"No," Aria said. She turned away from the mess. And promptly threw up again, like a rotating sprinkler of destruction. Another parent leapt backwards, but not fast enough to save her expensive-looking sandals. "Maybe."

The damn brownies. Of course, it would be the damn brownies. She was the worst mother in the world.

"And where have you been? Didn't you hear us calling for you?"

Daniel was hurrying over, the backpack slung in front of him as he dug for the emergency towel. Raidne's lip curled. She stepped out of her shoes to stand barefoot on the grass. One of the other parents hurried to bag up the shoes and offered the bag to the siren who gestured imperiously towards a trash can, leaving the volunteer to dispose of the offending objects.

"But I was here, Mommy," Aria protested as Vivian mopped at her face with the wet naps she carried everywhere these days.

Wet naps could clean everything. Even poop out of curtains. Vivian was far too experienced in bodily fluids.

"She was invisible." A little Black boy who looked suspiciously like the girl peeking from behind the Cunninghams spoke up. "She was nakkie and we're not supposed to be nakkie outside, so I made people not see her anymore. And then she got us all brownies!"

His sister surreptitiously wiped at her own chocolate-covered mouth.

Daniel took the opportunity to wrap the towel around their wayward daughter.

"You cast an invisibility spell?" Steve and his wife exchanged the classic "we're in for it now" look every pair of parents perfects.

"I just did what Daddy does when he's eating Mommy's chips," the boy said guilelessly.

"Well," said a thin young woman dressed entirely in black, from soft swishy pants to a stretchy turtleneck to black leather gloves, so that only her face from chin up was exposed. She held a black parasol over her head. Her welcoming smile included a pair of prominent fangs that somehow didn't reduce the air of comforting competence she projected. "I can see Mandrake Room will have a very exciting year! I'm Ms. Immacolata, and I'll be the kindergarten teacher. I can see we'll want to review the school rules on bringing extra clothes, and allergy protocols, and the use of magic on school grounds. Please do read the school handbooks and don't forget to sign the form in the parent portal. We look forward to welcoming you!"

2

Sep 7 11:32 AM
We'd like to remind all parents that Grimoire Grammar School
is a nut- and garlic-free facility. For the safety of all our
students, we must insist that students not bring silverware
or any other non-ritual silver materials. In addition, please
refrain from bringing food containing garlic or nuts of any kind,
including peanuts. May we suggest sun butter and marjoram
as delicious alternatives to explore?

Sep 7 12:05 PM
Thank you for the many concerns raised about the previous
notification. As a clarification—sun butter is made from
sunflower seeds and does not involve solar properties of any
kind. We regret any perception of insensitivity and assure
you that we take the needs of our solar allergy population
very seriously.

"I'm just saying that, given how much this school apparently
costs, you'd think some of this stuff would be included,"
Daniel said, frowning at the list.

"It's not like we can complain, under the circumstances," Vivian said. She couldn't entirely disagree with him—the list was ridiculous. Colored pencils *and* pastels seemed excessive enough, but where was she supposed to get papyrus? And herbs? Half the list could be found in the spices section of one of the better supermarkets, but the other half sounded like something from a botanic garden. Some she'd never even heard of. Was verbena a thing you could actually buy? Monkshood? Why was a Belgian Coticule whetstone preferred over Belgian Blue and why the heck did a kindergartner need a whetstone at all? Ms. Immacolata had said something about "food preparation works," but Vivian had been picturing something like banana slicing, not knives sharp enough to need whetting.

And the volunteer list—they had to sign up for at least two weeks of providing class sacrifices? The asterisk on that one did helpfully remind them that animal sacrifices were not on the approved list which had been more alarming than soothing. But if they weren't supposed to supply a biannual goat, she had no idea what would be considered a suitable sacrifice. Wheat? Wine? Copper the parents had personally removed from the earth by the light of a full moon? It all seemed terribly presumptuous. Oh, and look at that, they also had to bring in flowers for the classroom at the same time.

But what were they going to do? Complaining about it wouldn't change the school's requirements, it would only get them singled out as the ones who didn't belong. *And now that Daniel has started grumbling, I'm going to have to be the reasonable one,* she thought with a little resentment. She knew from experience that if she joined in, he would get wound up. "I guess this way we can pick out our own blank grimoires or whatever."

"That means we have to figure out which one's the right one," he said, rolling his eyes a little. "Whatever the magic spellbook equivalent is of buying jeans from Walmart when all the cool kids are wearing Abercrombie. Everyone knows that unicorn hide is so last season, or whatever. Sweetie, I know that you're trying to make this work, but you don't have to jump to defend every decision from an authority figure, OK?"

She didn't love defending them, but she also wanted to move past the part where they got upset over something they couldn't control, and get to the part where they figured out whether Whole Foods carried henbane. Surely they didn't need the full kit on the first day?

"I'll text Moira," she said, trying to end what was brewing into an argument.

"Selkies text?" Daniel asked, raising his eyebrows. "You mean we don't have to train carrier seagulls?"

"Hey," she said sharply. "She's the one person who's been nice to me so far. Don't be a jerk."

He stopped. Closed his eyes, breathed through his nose. Opened them. "You're right. I'm sorry."

He opened his arms and she stepped into them. He nuzzled the side of her head, breathing in the scent of her hair. She let some of the tension drain out of her shoulders.

"Sorry," he said again. "It's just... I've been this kid, you know? I mean, not like this, obviously, but I've been the scholarship student. And it doesn't matter how much you try, you'll never belong. Your clothes won't be quite right, and your references won't be quite right, and you'll never be able to ask people to come to your house because your house is absolutely not right. And even if people are nice, even if they want to be nice, you'll never really fit."

26

"You're saying I should just give up?" she said, trying to pull away a little.

"I'm saying you shouldn't worry so much about what they think of us," he said, pulling her back. "She's an awesome kid. You're an awesome mom. They should have to prove they deserve to hang around you, not the other way around. So what if they can start fires with their minds or something."

"You're biased," she said, letting him fold her in. It didn't work like that, but for a moment, she could pretend.

"I can be biased and be right at the same time." He nuzzled her neck and, despite her worry, she felt a flush of heat race down her spine. They didn't get nearly enough time alone together these days.

"We need this to work," she mumbled into his chest.

"Do you need help? With the school supplies?" He stroked her hair, trying to soothe the tension he probably could feel radiating from her.

He didn't need another thing to deal with, not with the longer commute and the bigger mortgage they'd had to take on with the move. She should be able to handle this: that had been the deal when she'd decided to stay home, even before the complications. That she'd caused. "No, I'll figure it out."

"I still think we should consider homeschooling instead of throwing her in with a bunch of wand-waving snobs." His hand paused as her shoulders knotted up again. "We know she does better when she gets a lot of exercise, and adding more red meat to her diet helped a lot. I mean, other than the one night a month."

They both glanced at the old-fashioned paper calendar pinned to the wall, the day in question circled in bright red where all three members of the family could see it.

The sound of four sets of toenails skittering across the floor echoed back from the foyer. Frantic barking indicated that the mail had once again arrived.

"Don't scratch the wood!" both parents shouted at the same time.

"You think diet's going to help with that?" Vivian muttered as they disentangled themselves.

Aria had managed to change herself back by the time her parents reached the front door. She had even remembered to pull on the bathrobe they'd started to keep on a hook. She hadn't remembered to tie it shut, though.

"Aria, pumpkin, we don't open the door naked," Vivian reminded her once again.

Her daughter stared uncomprehendingly for a moment, and then a light went on in her head and she clumsily pulled the robe shut. Vivian tried not to sigh. No one wrote parenting manuals about this, but the books that were closest—and several puppy training manuals—emphasized the importance of reinforcing the behavior you wanted to see instead of punishing the problem behavior. Aria got an extra half hour of screen time each day she managed to get through without wolfing out during Human Time. Daniel had promised her the deluxe Lego castle she'd been begging for the first time she managed to go a whole week. Vivian didn't foresee them ordering it any time soon.

"Is there anything for me?" Aria asked hopefully. There was something weird going on with her butt, Vivian noticed. With some dismay, she realized her daughter was trying to wag a non-existent tail.

Daniel pretended not to notice and retrieved the mail. "Bill, bill, charity I've never heard of, cruise catalog, same cruise catalog but with Mommy's name on it, even more charities who hate trees and want our money, apparently chupacabras are endangered and the magical community charities also want our money, oh hey, here's something for Aria after all."

Aria squeaked with glee and grabbed at the whole pile. Daniel handed her a cruise catalog and the chupacabra rescue charity envelope.

"Daddy!" she protested, managing a remarkably world-weary exasperation for someone whose voice was an octave higher than an adult's. "You're being very silly."

"You don't want to donate two hundred dollars and receive a free enchanted umbrella?" he answered, pretending to be surprised. "Actually, that might not be a bad deal."

"Daddy!" Aria stomped her foot.

"Oh, wait, you couldn't possibly want this boring old envelope?" he said, revealing the envelope addressed to Aria. "Instead of sixteen new Mediterranean routes?"

"Mommy, Daddy's obstructing the mail again."

Vivian loved when Aria parroted back the ridiculous formalities of adult language. She'd never believe in talking down to her child, and Aria's multisyllabic vocabulary made her feel like maybe there was one thing she'd done right. She wasn't a stupid child, for sure. Just not an easy one.

"Who's it from?" she asked as Daniel handed the envelope to Aria, who promptly ripped into it like a feral animal. Vivian would have seen it as another distressing indicator of wolfish behavior, only she herself hadn't figured out how to open envelopes without completely destroying them until she was in her late teens. Why couldn't they all come with little pull tabs like FedEx? She bet Cecily didn't have this problem. Cecily probably waved her hand and watched the envelope open itself, then maybe fold into a little paper swan or something.

"Birthday party!" Aria's eyes grew wide and she clutched the invitation to her chest. "Mommy, can I go? I can go, right?"

Sudden tears pricked Vivian's eyes. The last birthday party Aria had been to was more than six months ago. After the Incident, they'd started declining invitations. Then, as rumors had started to fly, the invitations had stopped coming. By the time it had escalated to potential vehicular manslaughter, Vivian had been desperate to move and leave no forwarding address to which the monster and her parents could be traced.

This was why they had moved—why it was worth any amount of ridiculous shopping lists. Because people here would still invite Aria to birthday parties. And because they didn't have to say no.

"Can I see the invitation, princess?" Daniel gently extricated it from Aria's grip. "October. These people seriously plan ahead. Elowen Dragonsbane? Do we even know her?"

"She's going to be in my class," Aria said. "I met her at the picnic."

Dragonsbane? What kind of person had a last name like Dragonsbane? And who named a kid Elowen, anyway? Vivian snagged the mangled envelope from the ground and held the pieces back together to read the return address. Cecily. Gareth and Cecily Dragonsbane. Wonderful.

For a moment, she thought about that raised eyebrow and the hovering wine cup and almost said no, but Aria was looking up at her with shining eyes. So the mom was a snob. She was exactly the kind of person her own mother would have made a beeline for; she could hear her cultured voice in her head, reminding her that some families were simply more consequential than others, and how important it was to mingle with the best if one wanted to be of consequence oneself. Well, she didn't want to be of consequence. She'd turned her back on her parents and their snobbery, and had never wanted that for Aria.

But just because the mother was a snob didn't mean the daughter was. And how could she say no to the first invitation to anything that Aria had received in months? Aria deserved friends, and making nice to the local Queen Bees was the quickest way to social acceptance. That was why they had moved in the first place, wasn't it? To find somewhere Aria could be accepted.

"Of course you can go, cupcake." Now she had to text Moira about presents, in addition to school supplies. She wasn't showing up with another tray of brownies, that was for sure.

Driving through the Village, Vivian would never have guessed it held more than picked-over antiques and overpriced coffee. The town's name, Veilport, seemed a little on the nose, but wasn't as bad as Mystic, the tourist town a little farther up I-95 from them whose theme was less around mysticism and more around fish. Moira had informed her that everyone called the Main Street area "the Village" and had done so since it was first founded in the 1630s. Now it had just enough quaintness to charm daytrippers passing through from New York on their way to Newport but not quite enough distinctiveness to cause them to stop. There was a bookstore that had a few first editions and a lot of well-bound novels everyone had forgotten and didn't want to remember; a clothing shop whose windows featured the kind of expensive but shapeless gray tunics favored by older rich women, accessorized by a rainbow of tasteful silk scarves; a toy store whose contents would be cooed over by great-aunts and ignored by children in favor of something plastic; and an ice cream parlor which surely made the bulk of the street's revenue because everyone genuinely likes ice cream, even werewolves.

Vivian turned at the parking sign, certain that this was a fruitless endeavor. The little municipal lot held five spaces, which were always full, which was why despite three tries she and Daniel still had not managed to walk down Main Street since moving here. Now Daniel was at work and she had to navigate the ridiculous parking situation without a copilot. But Moira had insisted. Vivian positioned the little cardboard placard Moira had given her with its printed symbol that seemed to twist as she looked at it on the dash. In the process, she nearly knocked her right front wheel out of alignment lurching over the viciously high stone curb cut. She cursed, yanking the wheel harder than she'd meant to.

"Mommy, you told Daddy he wasn't allowed to use that word anymore," Aria lectured her from the booster seat in the back.

Vivian muttered another of the forbidden words under her breath. She looked up.

The tiny lot was somehow now easily the size of the lot of a suburban Walmart. Which was just as well. It was, at most, a quarter of the way full, but only half of the vehicles could have been considered cars. There was a miniature steam engine, parked neatly next to a very large rolled-up Persian carpet. A black-on-black-on-black carriage decorated with funereal plumes in more black, with a little purple, had two black horses (also adorned with black feathers on their harnesses) stamping at the blacktop. Many of the cars were weird on their own. A 1950s mint-green Cadillac with chrome and fins was skewed across two spaces, seaweed dripping from its tailpipe. A fire-engine-red motorcycle gleamed. Two electric cars sulked side-by-side in their designated charging stations.

Of course they had their own magical parking passes. What else did everyone else take for granted, and she didn't even know enough to ask about?

Vivian couldn't decide whether to park on the other side of the lot (What happened if one of those massive black horses kicked? Their hooves looked wickedly sharp and could surely dent a door.) or if that would be even more conspicuous. She slid her beat-up Volvo in next to the electric cars, hoping that her anthropomorphization of their sullenness was strictly in her head and not actual attributes of the machines themselves.

"Can I pet the horses, Mommy?" Aria breathed, eyes wide.

"No, sweetie," Vivian said, casting about for an excuse. That carriage looked far too hearse-like, and at this point she wouldn't be surprised if a flame or two came from the horses' nostrils. "They're working animals, like guide dogs. And we don't distract working animals, remember?"

Fortunately, Aria had spent two whole weeks obsessed with guide dogs (including trying to convince Vivian to make her a vest to wear so she could be a dog in public and still count as being dressed). She quickly moved on. "Is Cara meeting us?"

"Her mom said she would," Vivian answered. Vivian hoped Moira would hold to her promise. She hadn't been at all confident about this shopping expedition to begin with, and the parking lot wasn't helping. It had never looked like this before. She stared at the edges, which somehow felt indistinct, like they were graphics that weren't rendering properly. It was a similar sense of vertigo as the parking pass gave her, only larger. Maybe it was like seasickness, and would go away when she got used to it? Could she get used to it?

She wished Daniel were here, if only to have someone else to experience the weirdness with.

She clutched Aria's hand a little harder than absolutely necessary and dragged her back to the sidewalk at the front of the lot before she could demand to examine the locomotive.

One goal, she reminded herself: get the rest of the shopping list, and take the opportunity to try to learn a little more about how this all worked from a friendly local. Two. That was two goals. OK, two goals: shopping list, information, and make sure that Cara and Aria actually ended up making friends. Three.

To her immense relief, Moira and Cara were loitering in front of the toy store. (The fact that Cara seemed only vaguely interested in the tasteful hobby horse in the window reconfirmed Vivian's suspicion that the only clientele of the shop had to be maiden aunts and collectors.)

Moira waved cheerfully. "So, tell me what's still on your list."

"Basically, all of it," Vivian admitted as the two girls squealed in recognition and then stopped to admire Cara's new shiny bracelet. Both the list of supplies and the list of questions. What was a Babylon candle and why was it banned from campus? What was going on with all the PTA politics and why were people so upset that a headmaster who was apparently old had retired? What was no one telling her that she didn't know enough to ask? What did she need to do to get people to like her? But she barely knew Moira. She stuck to the basics. "I managed the salt and rosemary, but I don't even know what rue looks like. Can you get it in town?"

"Oh, I order it on Etsy." Moira waved one hand dismissively. "There are some weird gardener hobbyists out there, they're not even part of the community. You can get almost any kind of herb if you don't mind buying it in seedlings. I'd recommend a dehydrator, it'll pay for itself before they're in first grade."

"Oh," said Vivian. She hadn't thought of Etsy. Did they sell grimoires? "Then what do we need here?"

"Well, you can get almost everything online these days, but I figured the girls would want to pick out their ritual daggers themselves."

"So about that. I don't suppose we're talking 'Fisher-Price My First Sacrifice' playset here?" she said, without much hope.

"Nope, full-on athame," Moira confirmed with a sympathetic smile. "Traditionally silver, but for the kids they usually go with steel. Less sharpening, and less chance of accidents with the shifters. When they hit middle school, the mage kids will switch to silver, but I imagine Aria will stick with the steel. Unless you want to get fancy with obsidian or titanium or something."

"What are kindergartners doing with sharp objects of any kind?" Vivian protested.

"Everyone gets at least basic magic lessons, even if they're not mages," Moira said, starting to drift down the sidewalk, herding the girls in front of her. "It's like, I don't know, what do they teach in mundane schools? Like how barely any adults use geometry and we still make them learn it. Except almost nobody needs geometry—but no one here, whether they're a full mage or a cryptid, can get away without knowing at least the basics of magic. It's more like, I don't know, etiquette? Civics? Do they teach those?"

"Not really."

Moira shrugged. "Explains a lot. I get the impression mundane schools spend a lot of time on *Moby Dick*, but ours tend to be a little more focused on real-world skills. Fae Court manners, Aramaic, shifter genetics. Stuff they might genuinely need. Anyway, there are a lot more mages than shifters, so it's important to get a good grounding in the basics, and half their social rituals involve at least a tiny amount of blood."

Vivian couldn't imagine where they were headed, unless it was to get ice cream. But here was a good chance to get that information she was looking for. "So the mages dominate things?"

"'Fraid so," said Moira. "Probably because mages are straight-up humans—aptitude runs in families, of course, but it's mostly just early training. Any human who's stubborn enough could learn at least a little magic. Think of it like a foreign language. Super easy to learn as a small child, much harder but still possible as an adult if you get the exposure and put in the time. You might want to pick up a book or two yourself, so you know what Aria's talking about."

Vivian had already let magic destroy their lives: she was not about to try to perform it herself. But she kept her mouth shut. She was also not going to risk offending someone willing to help.

Moira snagged her sleeve. "Wait, you're going right by it, turn here."

There was a little gap between the candle shop and the coffee shop, barely wide enough to walk through. Moira was rummaging through her purse. She pulled out a juicebox, a sunglasses case, a plastic baggie full of sea snails, then finally a gleaming dagger of her own. Hers looked ancient: it was bronze, with greenish tinges in between the whorls of the heavy Celtic knots. The blade was nearly triangular. She made a couple swishes through the air that looked lazy, but Vivian sensed they had their own kind of precision. And then Moira reached out with the dagger, caught the tip in the air like she was lifting a latch with the blade, and opened reality like a door. The alley swung open on a hinge. The dappled shadows, the drainpipes, the empty Coke bottle on the ground, all moved towards Vivian as if it were a flat-screen TV, but without any width. Just an image hanging in the air. The morning glory leaves moved gently in the breeze at a right angle to the street. Behind the door, the alley opened up into a new lane of shops.

If she had been warned ahead of time, she would have expected something more fantastical. She'd been to Prague once and seen the tiny stone cottages in the castle that were now filled with puppet shops and beer-based cosmetics. She would have expected a magical hidden alley to be like that, maybe with witches striding about in pointy hats or people in medieval garb.

Instead, it looked like the mundane street. Tidy, quaint but modern stores. People wearing Nantucket red shorts and poking at iPhones. Although the shops did have cauldrons and neat, branded bottles of eyeballs in the windows, and the lady walking by in the Lilly Pulitzer dress had a doe's head. Not carried under her arm or something, poking out of the collar of her dress instead of a human one.

"If we can get everything on our list with no whining, we can stop at the candy store on the way out," Moira told the girls.

Aria looked around with wide eyes, but Cara quickly captured her attention again with an inquiry about ponies.

"Most of the cryptids run in families, too, so it's all very insular," Moira said. "And kind of inbred. Besides, most of the non-human folk have some kind of weakness. Mercifully, pure silver or cold iron are a lot less common these days."

Vivian was glad she'd been cheap with the wedding registry and asked for stainless steel flatware; they hadn't had to dump their forks, just a few necklaces.

"Anyway, it's a human world, we just live in it. Here we are!"
Moira held open the door of a store and the girls rushed in.

It was an armory. There was an entire suit of armor right
at the door (although it held out a little tray upon which was
perched a note about keeping your children close and not
touching things, which made the whole effect less menacing and
more twee). There were two or three greatswords hung on one
wall, surrounded by an array of more kinds of knives than Vivian
could have possibly dreamed existed outside the old SkyMall
catalogs. There were racks of staves, ranging from lightweight
collapsible hiking poles to seven-foot hunks of oak topped by
faintly glowing crystals. There were cases of wands: gnarled
driftwood wands, twisted horn wands (which she hoped were
narwhal, as she was not ready to tell Aria that unicorns were
real), delicate golden spindles, lengths of sleek ebony edged with
tiny rubies, and white plastic wands rimmed in chrome that
would not have looked out of place in an Apple store. There was
a rose-gold one that screamed "millennial aesthetic" that had a
matching phone case next to it emblazoned with *Live Laugh Love*.

Cara and Aria went straight for the wand whose handle was
some anime character Vivian did not recognize but the girls
clearly did.

"Now, girls, we're not here for wands, we're here for daggers,"
Moira said. "Over here, please."

Vivian took a discreet look at the price tag hanging from one
of the daggers and winced. "They aren't going to need laptops,
are they?" she whispered to Moira.

"Screen-free classroom until fourth grade," Moira whispered
back. "Also, for an extra twenty dollars, they'll put a locator
spell on it so you can find the darn thing when it gets left in
the laundry."

Somehow, they managed to work their way through the list. Moira sent her a couple links to buy the items they weren't able to pick up in town. She also convinced Vivian to grab a few books on basic rituals for herself. "After all, you're not going to be able to come back unless you nail the opening spell at the gate."

"How do you know where to get this stuff?" Vivian asked.

"There's a class WhatsApp group," Moira said breezily. When Vivian gave her a look, she shrugged. "Look, there are magic mirrors and carrier pigeons and all, but they're a pain to operate. The mundanes made some stuff much more convenient, of course we're going to use it."

An invite from Moira popped up on Vivian's phone, and Vivian accepted membership into the group.

"It's super useful for organizing class events and asking for recommendations for hex tutors, but it's also the predictable raging hotbed of drama," Moira warned. "Now, where did the girls go?"

Before Vivian could even start to panic, Moira waved her hand and a tiny little firework of silvery blue popped up over her head.

Cara came running, Aria in tow.

"There you are," Moira scolded. "Don't make me use the sigil in stores, OK?"

"The what?" Vivian asked as they shepherded the girls down the sidewalk.

"It's another little cantrip almost anyone can cast. Most families have one, so you can signal your location to each other from far away. It's a lifesaver in the school pick-up line."

"What's ours going to be, Mommy?" Aria asked hopefully. "Can it be purple?"

"Mommy can't make magic fireworks, sweetie," Vivian said, trying to conceal the wince. "You'll have to stay close to me, that's all."

Aria looked crestfallen. The fact that she didn't seem disappointed in Vivian, just sad, made it worse. But Cara whispered something and then they were both all giggles again, disappointment forgotten. They stopped in the promised candy store, and Vivian insisted on buying a treat for both girls. It seemed the least she could do in gratitude, and a little bribery might help get the Cara–Aria friendship off to a good start. She didn't recognize any of the names of the candy on display, but they both seemed pleased with their self-twirling oversized lollipops that slowly changed color whether or not anyone was licking them.

All along, Vivian kept her gaze carefully in front of her, trying not to goggle at the bits of random weirdness. She didn't want to be rude. Nor, she had to admit to herself, did she want to stand out. It might have been easier if the entire experience had been more fantastic, but everything was just normal enough that she kept being surprised. The woman with the purse owl caught her particularly off guard. She'd never understood how little dogs were happy riding around like that, but she certainly hadn't expected a bird of prey to submit itself to such an indignity.

She was so very carefully not looking at the owl swiveling its head to look at her, that she nearly ran into the woman in front of her.

"Ah yes, Mrs. Tanaka," came the voice that she still heard in her nightmares.

The first impression Vivian had had of Helene Fairhair was steel. That had never changed. Steel-colored hair, steel-colored eyes, steel-colored suit on a street where no one else was wearing a suit. Impeccable posture with a spine of steel. An aura of absolute control and dignity that she projected in a five-foot bubble around her body. Vivian was acutely aware of the tiny coffee stain on her shorts and of the red candy dye Aria was licking off her fingers.

"You are settling in well, I presume?" Mrs. Fairhair asked, her inflection implying that a negative answer would be an unacceptable disappointment, if not an unforeseen one.

"Finishing up some back-to-school shopping," Vivian replied, trying to sound casual and carefree. No one particularly bought it.

Aria gave a shiver like she was about to transform right in the street, and Mrs. Fairhair caught her eye. She didn't say a word, but even Vivian could nearly hear the command. *Stay.* Aria froze, but remained human.

"Of course," Mrs. Fairhair said, turning back to Vivian. "You'll let me know if you need anything."

It was not so much a question as a command, but Vivian would be damned if she accepted anything more from this woman. "Of course."

The older woman nodded, once, and then continued down the street. When she was well out of earshot, Moira turned to Vivian. "You didn't tell me you knew the Fairhairs," she said, sounding half-irritated and half-impressed.

Vivian wished with all her being that she did not. She debated how much she wanted to say. Some of it was public record, and would be well known soon enough. "She sponsored Aria's entrance to Grimoire Grammar."

"Oh." Moira looked satisfied, as if that had answered some questions. And raised others, Vivian was sure.

"You know her?" Vivian asked as they got the girls started down the street again. Aria kept casting glances over her shoulder, torn between trying to hide behind Vivian and running panting after the older woman.

"The matriarch of the most influential werewolf pack on the Eastern Seaboard?" Moira said, sounding a little shocked. "I know *of* her."

Vivian had realized the older woman was powerful, but had thought it was simply the authority of old money.

Moira was clearly being eaten alive by curiosity, but Vivian was not particularly interested in talking about it. Not about the worst day of her life, not out here in the sun with the kids and any passersby in earshot. She liked Moira, but not that much.

"So," she said, changing the subject as they reached the parking lot. She felt like she should have guessed the seaweed-strewn Cadillac belonged to Moira. "What's the etiquette around mage kids' birthday parties?"

3

Sign-ups for extracurriculars are still open until Friday. Some classes still available: Fitness Ferocity, Hiding in Shadows, Pottery, Yoga, Urban Beekeeping, and Intermediate Mind Control. Please check the recommended age range before applying!

Vivian didn't know how she was going to tell Aria that she couldn't have a unicorn at her birthday party next June. Because Elowen had one at hers, and there was Aria riding around on it.

Aria had never been particularly princess-oriented, at least not in preschool. She'd been solidly into dinosaurs for a while, to the point that she regularly lectured adults on getting their dinosaur nomenclature incorrect. (In Vivian's defense, apparently an awful lot of dinosaur facts had been discovered since she last played with plastic T. rexes. She'd been corrected for labeling an Apatosaurus as a Brontosaurus, for calling pterodactyls and megalodons dinosaurs, for not realizing that Dimetrodon was actually a precursor to mammals, and for drawing a Velociraptor without feathers. *Jurassic Park* had lied a lot, but then again so had most books she'd read about parenthood.)

Since becoming friends with Cara and Elowen, though, it was all tulle and pink and tea parties. Vivian had not expected to miss the dinosaurs so intensely. If nothing else, plastic dinosaurs made much better chew toys. The dinosaur/princess dichotomy made the whole thing feel so very normal, when the knowledge that any of the parents she kept having to talk to over plastic cups of wine might be able to reanimate a dinosaur or could personally know (or be) a princess was anything but normal. The preschool routine had inoculated her to the repetitiveness of the birthday party circuit. But unicorn-themed birthday parties were not supposed to have actual unicorns, and it was deeply unfair to introduce literal pearlescent horns to the mix.

"Please tell me the fairy lights aren't made of actual fairies," Daniel muttered to her.

Steve overheard. "Shhh, don't even suggest something like that. The Fae are really sensitive, you definitely don't want to offend them, and I'm pretty sure Rhiannon's on the guest list. Anyway, I'd guess will-o'-the-wisps."

"Too easy for Cecily," Madhuri muttered. Steve had introduced them; she was a short Indian woman with a long braid, a gorgeous bangle in the shape of a snake, and gold eyeliner that betrayed a much steadier hand than Vivian would ever have. She didn't even have a kindergartner; her daughter was in eighth grade, but Cecily had apparently invited all the parent council members whether or not their kids were in Mandrake Room. "I took a look. Trained fireflies."

"That's our Cecily," Steve said, with the tiniest eye roll. "Vivian told us you used to play soccer?"

Daniel didn't blush easily, at least not without a glass or two of wine, but he did look abashed. "Well, yeah, but not since college."

"How do you feel about coaching?"

Daniel perked up. "Soccer?"

"Well, not exactly. We signed the twins up for skirmedge, and they could use another coach."

Vivian and Daniel exchanged a glance. "Uh," Daniel said, when the silence had become a hair too long, "I don't actually know what skirmedge is."

"Well, it's a little like soccer. There's a ball, although the ball transforms, and depending on if it's in *sphera* or *avis* form, you can either hit it or catch it, until more than half the team crosses the *patriam* line—" Steve said, enthusiastically.

"It's wizard soccer," Madhuri cut him off as she looked up from her phone.

"Oh, like—"

"Nope, don't say it," she warned them. "We don't speak those names. And it's not like that game at all. No broomsticks, for one. And people get very touchy about the comparison. Around here, people have been playing skirmedge for more than a hundred years and they will remind you of it at every opportunity."

"OK," Daniel said slowly. "But I'm not seeing how much help I can be as a coach. Since I played, well, regular-people soccer."

"Mundane," Steve reminded him. "Anyway, they're five. Pipsqueak skirmedge resembles real skirmedge about as well as I imagine pipsqueak soccer resembles FIFA. You don't have to teach any skills: the other coaches can help with that. Mostly we need another adult to set up cones, hand out juiceboxes, and apply poultices to skinned knees that may or may not show any visible sign of injury. The kids mostly wander in circles and kick the ball in random directions and get distracted by caterpillars."

"But it's great exercise," Madhuri added. "Wears them out, they'll sit still for maybe even tens of minutes afterwards. I don't even like sports, and we still got into it when mine was that age."

Vivian and Daniel exchanged another look. Good exercise and wearing kids out sounded great, whatever *sphera* forms might be.

"OK, I'm in," Daniel said. "As long as everyone knows I'm not casting any spells."

"Fantastic. I'll email you the registration form." Steve smiled, and then his eyes widened a hair. "Oh crap, the twins are headed for the cake."

Madhuri's phone buzzed. "Sorry, I have to take this, it's work. I'll see you at the PTA meeting?"

Vivian nodded as if the meeting hadn't given her literal nightmares every night this past week. Dammit, she'd handled board meetings. She'd handled real emergencies with blood and screaming. She was not going to be intimidated by a bunch of other moms. She was going to charm the pants off them and make sure no one ever told her daughter she didn't belong somewhere again.

Raidne glided by, towed by Evander, who never seemed to take off the Elmo guitar. They were followed by a shorter, bosomy woman with a faintly blue cast to her skin wearing an honest-to-god cat sweater with no trace of irony. They were heading for the illusionist's table, where the kids were getting adorned with butterfly wings that opened and closed, and little spaceships that orbited their shoulders, or copyrighted cartoon character heads overlaid on top of their real ones. To think that at last year's party for Aria, Vivian had bought a face painting kit and had been proud when she'd turned out a half-decent cheek rainbow.

"Daniel," Raidne acknowledged, nodding as she went past.

"Hey there," Daniel responded.

"Since when were the two of you friendly?" Vivian asked, a little startled.

"Turns out we're on the same train into the city in the morning," Daniel said.

"Why didn't you say something?" Vivian asked, trying to sound casual and not like a jealous harpy. She wasn't jealous. She was a little confused, that's all. Really. Why Raidne, of all people? She bet Raidne was friends with harpies—real ones.

"You wince every time her name comes up. I mean, I get it, she's kind of cold. But we've made small talk a couple times when the train was late, that's all," he said. She tried not to wince again. Her first interaction with other parents, and she'd botched it. It shouldn't have still stung, but it did. "Hey, I'm going to duck after Steve. Looks like the twins have been successfully diverted, and I wanted to ask him about those weird bat-like things that keep getting stuck in our chimney."

Vivian drifted over to the beverage table, trying to not feel too abandoned, and grabbed another water bottle to nurse. It made sense to divide and conquer. It still felt lonely. Aria was eagerly trying to join in some kind of figure dance that the other girls and a few of the boys were doing. Vivian could only hope she made up with enthusiasm what she lacked in precision. Even her flower crown was askew, whereas Cara, Elowen, and the others all looked like something out of a picture book. Where did these kids even get dancing lessons? Was that another thing she was supposed to have done in preschool? Aria stumbled into Elowen, who gave her a withering look, but Aria gamely tried again and Vivian reluctantly decided to not be that mom and to let Aria figure things out herself.

She had to do it at school anyway, and Ms. Immacolata hadn't indicated any major social problems yet.

"Viv!" Moira waved her over, and she tried not to look visibly relieved. "Have you tried the little fruit tarts yet? Trust Cecily to get Goblin Market berries for a five-year-old's birthday party. They're amazing, I've had three."

Crap, so books about magic schools were a sore point but the Goblin Market was a real thing? She could have handled all the fiction being offensive stereotypes, but the mix of accuracy and inaccuracy was a field full of landmines. "No, I'll have to swing by the dessert table."

"Do it soon, or they'll be gone. By the way, I wanted to catch you—any chance you could pick Cara up for me on Wednesday? Ewan's having some kind of crisis with one of his captains and can't do pick-up, and I was hoping to not have to cancel my yoga class."

"Sure!" Inwardly, she warmed. Moira trusted her enough to pick up her kid? Take that, Raidne. Someone here liked her.

"You're the best!" Moira brushed crumbs off her fingers on her slacks. "So, who have you managed to meet so far?"

"Well, Steve introduced me to—I think her name was Madhuri?"

Moira rolled her eyes. "Oh, Madhuri's here? Wow, Cecily really went full Queen Bee on this one."

"Is there a problem with Madhuri?" She'd seemed nice enough.

"Oh, no, she's fun and all, just doesn't usually come to this stuff. She's a Career Mom, all busy busy busy, she's usually on her phone for half of any given event. Same with the Cunninghams—Sasha's some kind of fancy surgeon and she's always on call, and Steve works from home but always has his hands full with the twins. 'Cause they're a handful. So they're impossible to get ahold of. But a Cecily party is the event of the season, so everyone's here." Moira toasted their hostess across the yard with her plastic cup.

Vivian thought yet again about her mother's insistence on the importance of moving in the right social circles. She had never particularly wanted to move in her parents' social circles. And she was pretty sure someone like Moira would never have made the cut. But looking around, her mother had not been completely wrong—some people were the entry points into a particular social world. Moira seemed to know everybody; Cecily seemed to be able to influence everybody. Vivian knew whose company she preferred, but she couldn't afford to turn down opportunities right now. Clearly, she'd have to at least make nice to Cecily. Besides, it was pretty ungrateful to take advantage of the woman's hospitality and keep making nasty comments about her in her own head.

She wasn't quite ready to face Cecily's particular brand of condescension quite yet, though. "Who's the woman with Raidne?" she asked instead.

"Oh, you haven't met Orphne yet? She's Raidne's wife," Moira said. "She's a trip, isn't she?"

"What do you mean?"

"Well, who would expect a chthonic nymph to embrace the Lands' End catalog? Hardly the right aesthetic for Raidne the ice queen, but people are funny."

"…chthonic?"

"Uh, something to do with the underworld, blah blah. She talks to dead people. You'd expect her to be all goth or something, but she says she did gothic back when there were raiding Goths and then again when there were Victorian goths and then again when there were mopey goths, and now she likes flowers and kittens. And Raidne can afford to buy her all the tacky sweaters she wants, so I guess they're happy." Moira leaned in. "Word to the wise, though, never accept a party invite from Orphne."

"Why not?"

"She's one of those multi-level marketing scheme moms. You think you're coming over for cocktails and the next thing you know, it's a hard sell for ritual crystals or something."

Vivian winced. She'd made that mistake once before and had three overpriced scented candles gathering dust in the closet. It had seemed a small price to pay to escape. One more reason to avoid Raidne, then.

"You want a refill?" Moira asked. Viv shook her head. "OK, thanks for taking Cara—I'll pick her up at six, OK?"

Viv took a deep breath. She couldn't put it off any longer—time to make nice to the hostess. She reminded herself that this was for Aria's sake. She could be polite to anyone, no matter how supercilious.

Cecily was bustling around straightening water bottles, because heaven forbid anything in this party be slightly out of alignment. Vivian had never seen such a symmetrical living space, from the immaculate Tudor-style house to the formal garden with its topiary rabbits who waved as she passed and pale gray fine gravel paths that reminded her of pictures of Versailles.

"It's a lovely party," Vivian offered.

"Why, thank you," Cecily said, smiling warmly. Vivian resisted the urge to look over her shoulder for someone Cecily liked better than her. Why was she suddenly being so nice to her? "I heard Madhuri mention the Parent Advisory Council—you're still planning on taking the treasurer position?"

"That's the plan!" Vivian wasn't sure if the fake cheer in her own tone was meant to reassure Cecily or herself.

"No one would think less of you if it were too much. I'm sure this has all been rather overwhelming," Cecily said, leaning in conspiratorially. "But then I suppose Helene Fairhair has been helping you adjust."

Ah. Moira had been a gossip, then. Vivian fought the sour feeling in the pit of her stomach. She didn't know that, she reminded herself. Her conversation with Mrs. Fairhair had been out in the street in broad daylight, where anyone might have seen. It explained Cecily's sudden enthusiasm for her, though. "Not exactly," she said.

"Oh, you poor thing!" Clearly Cecily did not believe that. "Well, if you'd like to sit by me at the meeting, I'll help get you caught up."

Which was worse, sitting next to Cecily or earning Cecily's enmity? "You're very kind," Vivian said carefully. "I don't suppose you have the records from last year? I'd love to get familiar with them ahead of time, so I know what to be looking for."

"Oh yes, I'll dig them up. Do let me know if anything is too confusing for you—I know this is all very new."

In another tone of voice, it might have been a nice offer, but Vivian had a sudden wave of sympathy for Aria's desire to bite people.

"So what does Aria have planned for the Talent Show?"

It took her a moment to even figure out what Cecily was talking about. She'd seen the email, decided that she didn't have the energy to deal with it, deliberately didn't mention it to Aria, and promptly forgot about it. "I don't think she's ready to get up in front of everyone yet. She's still adjusting. Maybe next year."

Cecily's eyebrows rose to her hairline. "Really? How bold.

When our eldest, Cornelia, did her kindergarten Talent Show act, well, I think we must have practiced for three months! You can always tell the parents who have lost their nerve, they're the ones who hire the consultants."

Vivian had the sudden sickening feeling that she'd missed something terribly important. She should ask, she knew, but she couldn't bear to show her ignorance in front of Cecily. Instead, she made polite noises and let Cecily bustle off to oversee some other overly elaborate party element.

"Mommy Mommy Mommy!" Before Vivian could make it to the desserts, Aria darted through the crowd, mercifully human. "Something's wrong with Rhiannon!"

There was a stir over by the cake table, she realized. What had been a background child crying, a sound which had been occurring on and off throughout the party, was rising into hysterical child screaming. She started towards the hubbub.

A little girl sprawled on the ground, hair the color of starlight spilling over pointed ears to pool on the ground around her. With her left hand, she clutched the wrist of her right, which was purplish and swelling horribly, a vivid welt across the palm. A woman with matching hair and ears crouched next to her, eyes frantic, murmuring in a silvery, liquid language. Her father was tracing a door-shaped rectangle in the air, equally frantic. As Vivian watched, purple lines crawled up the girl's arm, the swelling growing. Even from here, she could hear the girl's breathing grow labored.

"Oh, stars," Steve breathed as he came up beside her.

"What's wrong with her?" Vivian asked, pushing Aria behind her, partially so she couldn't see and partially so she'd be between them if it was somehow catching.

"Gotta be iron poisoning," Steve said, pulling out his phone.

"It's like an allergy to the Fae, they can't touch it. But cold iron's almost unheard of these days."

"I'm sorry," Elowen was crying. "I just wanted to show Cara Great-Grandmother's necklace. I told her not to touch it."

"I told you not to bring it out," Cecily hissed, looking horrified.

"Isn't there something we can do?" Vivian grabbed Steve's arm. The purple streaks had reached Rhiannon's throat and the girl's breathing had thinned to a rasp.

He shook his head. "If they can get her back to the Fae Court, their own healers can halt the reaction, but…"

The rectangle her father had sketched in the air shimmered and went black. Lightning crackled across the doorway as he chanted, but from his panic, it didn't seem like the door would be complete in time. Rhiannon's eyes rolled back. It was like watching one of her own nightmares—one of the ones she had been having ever since Aria had been diagnosed with the egg allergy. Vivian gasped and fumbled in her purse, crouching next to the keening mother. "I have a kids EpiPen! Would it help?"

"Leave your mortal devices aside," she snarled. "Haven't you humans done enough harm this day?"

"No, wait," Steve said urgently. "She's right. We used to carry them for one of the Fae guys in my unit—it buys you the time to get to the healers."

The Fae woman hesitated. Rhiannon's head rolled back, and her mother nodded. Vivian fumbled the safety release off and pressed the EpiPen against the girl's thigh, pushed until she heard the click, and then counted to three out loud.

For a minute, the crowd of parents and kids froze, watching. A few kids were whimpering. The father kept chanting. Then Rhiannon took a breath.

The crowd exhaled as one. Slowly, some of the purple tendrils receded. The mom sobbed in relief. A thunderclap echoed across the backyard, and suddenly the rectangle carved from the air opened onto a path that arced behind a waterfall lit with golden sunlight. Beyond the curtain of water, a valley shimmered, impossibly green.

"We shall not forget," the mother said, looking straight into Vivian's eyes. Then she stood, gracefully sweeping her daughter into her arms and rushing through the doorway. In the distance, figures in robes came running to help. Then the doorway slammed shut, leaving nothing but the lingering scent of flowers.

"Wow," said Moira. "You seem like a handy person to have around. Come sit down."

She caught Daniel's eye—he looked torn between coming to her and chasing after Aria, but she nodded at him and he took over getting their kid a distraction cupcake. She let Moira lead her over to a chair and collapsed gratefully. Her pulse pounded in her ears as her body tried to decide what to do with all the leftover adrenaline.

"Gutsy, too," Moira was saying.

"What do you mean?" Vivian said. "I did what anyone would do if they could."

"Interfering with the Fae?" Moira raised her eyebrows. "I mean, not really. They don't tolerate mistakes. You mess with them and it doesn't go off like you planned, and you end up getting oathbound to work off your debt to them for a hundred years, or your memories destroyed, or something."

"Oh." She swallowed. Daniel didn't need to know this part, she suddenly decided. He was already freaked out enough, she wasn't going to tell him that she'd once again endangered their entire family.

She was breathing much too quickly, she realized. Moira sat down next to her, more slowly, and gently stroked her back. "It's OK, nothing happened. Here, eat a cupcake. You're probably about to have an adrenaline crash. The sugar will help."

Vivian took the cupcake. It sparkled and had fondant ears and a horn. She hoped that meant the magical equivalent of edible glitter, not that it was going to make her levitate or turn her hair pink like some of the other party favors. It mostly tasted like sugar, and also the morning of the first day of summer, which was not off-putting enough to keep her from eating the rest.

"Nothing happened," Moira repeated encouragingly. "Let's talk about something else. Get your mind off it. Did you hear that Ms. Genevieve got caught by the booby trap Banderbridge had left on the library after hours to keep the students from getting into mischief?"

Vivian did not want to hear about people making fun of poor Ms. Genevieve. She needed to know about the things that were going to threaten her family, the things she didn't know to ask. She couldn't rely on being lucky like she'd been with the Fae. She suddenly remembered the thing she had been freaking out about before everyone had started freaking out. "Can you tell me how the Talent Show works?"

Moira looked a little disappointed not to get a hot gossip session, but she rallied. "Well, the kids draw lots, and then each of them goes up to show their talent. You're not allowed to help, of course, although I guess that's less of a concern for you. Once they're on the stage..." She trailed off. "Wait. Are you asking about the sequence of events, or about what the Talent Show is for?"

"It's for something?" Vivian asked. She blinked, trying to

focus even as the predicted adrenaline crash left her wanting to put her head down on a table. She'd heard a familiar name, and she'd assumed it was like the school talent show of her youth. A chance for the brave and the delusional to show off whatever they'd fooled themselves into thinking they could do well, plus an opportunity for the overly ambitious parents to force their kids to display the results of fancy lessons. There would be some unconvincing magic tricks, some endearingly terrible stand-up routines of mostly knock-knock jokes, and half a dozen kids butchering classics on violin or piano. And there would be that one kid who would shock everyone by turning out to be a virtuoso on the oboe or the hammer dulcimer or something. Not the kind of thing you needed a consultant for.

Moira was giving her a look. A pitying look. "It's the first of the Trials. You know. To see if they'll be allowed to continue to first grade?"

"You never told me Aria could only stay for one year!"

Vivian had not thought she was capable of yelling at someone with the steely grandeur of Mrs. Fairhair, but it seemed like motherhood was never finished teaching her things.

"I thought it common knowledge," Mrs. Fairhair said calmly, stirring her tea. "Do the mundane schools not have any kind of standards?" They sat in the front parlor of the pack's grand Victorian house. The furnishings had the kind of shabbiness Vivian had learned to associate with old-money WASPs and the kind of antique store in which you had better not touch anything. Carved wood, worn Persian carpets, rock-hard brocade cushions that were immaculately clean except for the occasional unavoidable dog hair. Mrs. Fairhair had offered Vivian a cup, which Vivian had been slightly dismayed to find contained a white tea so subtle it reminded her more of hot water than anything else. Then again, Aria's nose had become so sensitive of late that they'd had to stop cooking with garlic. Vivian had thought that was only vampires, but Aria whined every time they peeled a clove.

"Regardless," Mrs. Fairhair continued, "whether Aria continues at Grimoire Grammar School is entirely up to her. And you."

Vivian wanted very much to leap over the table and strangle the woman, but the small, scared mammal at the back of her brain helpfully informed her, yet again, that that would be certain death. And she did not mean that with any hyperbole.

Vivian had seen the woman in her wolf form exactly once, and she still had nightmares.

She had taken Aria hiking. Daniel hated hiking—getting dirty and covered in bugs so you could go in a big circle and then have blisters at the end was not his idea of a good time. He'd play catch or Go Fish as long as Aria wanted, and he laid out a mean tea party table, but he liked his environments controlled. Aria, on the other hand, had never met a rock she didn't want to scramble up. Vivian was usually up for a good rock scramble herself, and she loved Daniel enough not to make him go, so the two girls had headed out for the day on their own.

She'd done everything you were supposed to do. She had picked a trail that was enthusiastically recommended as perfect for adventurous small children, and checked all the reviews and walkthroughs to make sure it wasn't too difficult or confusing. She had downloaded and printed the trail map ahead of time in case she lost reception. She had told Daniel exactly where they were going and which trail they were taking and how long it should take them. She'd texted him when they left the car. She had a day pack with a first aid kit and rain gear and snacks and water and a whistle. They were wearing sunscreen and bug repellent, hats and sunglasses, long pants in case of ticks, and bright colors so they would stand out from the landscape. She'd sent Daniel a photo of them so search parties would know what they were wearing, on the off chance that they somehow got lost on the well-marked and well-traveled trail. She had drilled Aria in the car and on the trail about trail safety—how to look for blazes, what to do if you got lost, how to call 911 from Vivian's phone, what to do in the unlikely event they saw a cougar or a bear. She had looked up a checklist online the night before about how to safely hike with your preschooler and went right down the list. She had done absolutely everything right.

No one had put anything about what to do if a slavering wolf whose shoulders came up to your chest burst out of the woods and tore open your preschooler's throat.

There had been no warning at all. One moment, Aria was chattering on about Dracorex as she had been for the last ten minutes while Vivian tried in vain to point out interesting and educational mushrooms. Then, a wall of mangy fur slammed into Aria. There was blood on the ground, so much blood, everywhere. Vivian had frozen.

It could only have been a moment that she stood there in shock, before she had grabbed a giant stick and started to hopelessly flail at the monster crouched over her child. But that moment had lasted a lifetime. Every night for three months after, and then every few nights after that, she dreamt of that moment. How she had just stood there, staring. Why hadn't she heard him crashing through the underbrush? Why hadn't she thrown herself in his way as soon as she saw the motion in the corner of her eye? He had knocked Aria down, pinning her to the ground. She knew, rationally, that there had only been a split second before he had reached down and ripped into her neck, but it had felt like forever. She had always thought she would be the kind of mom who lifted the car to save the baby, who grabbed the kid right before they fell off the bridge. Instead, she had frozen at the point where she could have changed the story. Stood there locked in fear and panic. Watched a werewolf kill her child.

The stick had done almost nothing. The wolf ignored it, leaned in and bit deeper, shook Aria's little body like a doll. Aria's eyes had been glassy with shock, her mouth an open O. Blood drenched her favorite t-shirt, the one Daniel washed three times a week. Later, when the rawness of her throat made it hard to talk or cough, Vivian realized that she must have been screaming, but she heard nothing in the moment. So when the rest of the wolves bounded onto the path, it had been just another shock.

Vivian had already realized that she was going to die. She didn't want to live when she'd watched her daughter mauled, anyway. More wolves meant it would be quicker. But her hindbrain hadn't quite got the message, and she had whirled around, big useless stick at the ready.

The other wolves had ignored her. They leapt at the first wolf, knocking him off his prey. Vivian scrambled to Aria's side as the pack descended on Aria's attacker. Vivian hadn't looked. She had clutched Aria's mangled body to her chest, rocking, her eyes focused on Aria's perfect little hand lying on the dirt of the trail. Sound returned, the sound of baying and pain-filled howling, and cracking bones. Vivian had closed her eyes and curled over her daughter, waiting to be rent limb from limb.

Then silence descended. Near-silence, anyway. She could hear the panting of the wolf pack around her. Then footsteps that stopped a few feet in front of her.

"Let me see," said an imperious voice.

Vivian had opened her eyes to see a pair of bare human feet, well-manicured but with delicate skin spotted with age. She had looked up slowly, to a steely woman wearing a steel-gray robe, her hair already looped back in a bun.

The other wolves lay panting amongst the trees, muzzles liberally splashed with red. Torn bits of fur and a few grisly bones scattered about told the fate of the first wolf. None of the wolves were gnawing at the remains.

"I need to see her," the woman insisted again.

Vivian had stared uncomprehending, still clutching the body of her daughter.

One of the other wolves had paced over. And then shuddered, shaking like a wet dog. Only, as he shook out his fur, the fur had rippled. There was the sickening sound of cracking bones and then suddenly a naked man with thick white hair stood up from a crouch. He'd pulled the collar from his neck—all the wolves were wearing collars, she had suddenly realized—and shook it out with an odd gesture, and swirled the red bathrobe that rippled out from his hands around his shoulders, tying the front shut.

"You don't think he—" the male werewolf, because what else could she possibly be looking at, started to say.

"I don't think anything until I can see it," the steely woman replied. She turned back to Vivian. "Let. Me. See."

Vivian had found herself compelled to pull back for no reason she could identify. The woman crouched down. To her shock, Vivian had seen that the gaping wounds had already begun to close. Even as she had watched, the skin on Aria's neck began to knit itself back together.

"Well," the woman had said grimly. "It seems my son has given me grandchildren after all."

Now the alpha wolf sat across from her with all the primness of a Boston Brahmin, stirring a nearly scentless tea and looking as if she had no responsibility for the situation.

Vivian did her best to rein in her temper. Getting angry wouldn't help, and it wouldn't impress this woman. "I'm very grateful that you helped us get Aria into this school, but we were under the impression that it would be a long-term solution."

Mrs. Fairhair took a sip of her tea. "As long as it can be. Grimoire Grammar continues up through eighth grade, and the majority of its graduates go on to some of the most prestigious magical academies on the East Coast."

"But only if she passes some kind of ridiculous test every year!"

"Every three years. During kindergarten to move up to lower elementary, during third grade to move up to upper elementary, and during sixth grade to move up to middle school."

"She's only in kindergarten! What's she supposed to show, that she can tie her shoes?"

"No," Mrs. Fairhair said coldly, setting down her cup. "She's supposed to show that she is progressing in her control of her talents, and that she continues to display the level of potential expected of the students of such a high-achieving institution."

"I've heard of high-stakes testing, but this is ridiculous!" Vivian set down her teacup before the sloshing could betray her shaky hands.

Mrs. Fairhair's eyes narrowed. If she had been in wolf form, Vivian suspected the fur around her neck would have raised.

"If you think the Trials for the kindergartners are high stakes, perhaps you should remove her from the curriculum before she must face the high school or college admissions tests. Honors English, or whatever it is the mundane world tests its children on, is nothing. By the time Aria is an adolescent, she and her peers will be more than capable of killing grown men, and burning down towns, and any other number of things that your kinsfolk would consider a dangerous affront to reality."

Vivian swallowed. "But if she fails out of this school, where will we go?"

"There are a number of lesser schools, which I do not believe you will like as much," Mrs. Fairhair replied after a moment. "The Western schools that will take wolf shifters are less, shall we say, *refined* than Grimoire Grammar. Idaho will not be so welcoming to someone of her background. Or you could, of course, reconsider my initial offer."

"Aria belongs with her family." Vivian bit off the sentence.

"She belongs with her pack," Mrs. Fairhair retorted. "A werewolf's family is their pack."

"She's my daughter, not yours," Vivian countered.

"It's not right that she grow up not among her own kind," Mrs. Fairhair said.

"Well, whose fault is that?"

At that, the alpha wolf was silent. What had happened to Aria shouldn't have happened, Vivian had come to understand. For generations, werewolves had carefully kept the bite to within their own clans. But Mrs. Fairhair's son, the wolf who had attacked Aria that day, had been mentally ill to begin with and then gone off the deep end into some wolf-rights conspiracy theory no one wanted to fully explain. He'd refused his medication and run wild hunting for humans. Given another few seconds, he would have killed them both, and any other humans unfortunate enough to be on the mountain that day. His family had been tracking him, hoping to prevent tragedy, but been forced into the decision by his actions. Not fast enough for Aria, though. It was a deep shame, Vivian now understood, a blotch on the family name that the Fairhairs and the rest of the Connecticut pack wanted as little said about as possible. She was not sure how much of Mrs. Fairhair's sponsorship of Aria was shame and how much was guilt, but they could never have found the place or afforded it without her.

"I forced them to bend the rules as far as they would go to admit her," Mrs. Fairhair finally said stiffly. "You have no idea how many tests and applications you were spared. But that is as far as I can push. If you want Aria to remain with her family *of origin,* she will need to succeed at the Trials. All of them, starting with the Talent Show."

"She doesn't have any talents," Vivian admitted, feeling like she was betraying her daughter. She was fairly certain that drawing lopsided ponies and reciting dinosaur facts would not count here. "She can barely control her shape as it is. She's *five.*"

"And she has only been a shifter for a few months," Mrs. Fairhair unbent enough to admit.

They sat in silence. Somewhere deeper in the house, a door slammed open and the sound of a dozen sets of claws scrabbling on hardwood echoed down the hall. Vivian felt faintly cheered to know that her household was not the only one with that problem, and that for all Mrs. Fairhair's regal presence, the rest of the pack was perhaps not quite so refined.

"What do you do about the floors?" Vivian asked, suddenly curious and desperate to think about something else for a moment.

Mrs. Fairhair sighed. "We have them refinished once a year. I have a carpenter on retainer."

"Have you tried the booties?" Vivian had found a set that was intended for sled dogs. Aria hated them passionately.

"No one else will wear them," Mrs. Fairhair admitted with some reluctance.

Someone barked, and there was an audible scuffle followed by playful yips. Mrs. Fairhair gave the tiniest sigh, resigned and amused by her boisterous pack. Not for the first time, Vivian wondered if Aria would be better growing up here, where people would understand her and be able to help her far more than Vivian ever could. But the idea of leaving her daughter to grow up with strangers, of seeing her on the occasional weekend, of no longer being the person Aria thought of when she thought of "family"—Vivian couldn't. Maybe she was being selfish. But she couldn't bear to give up her daughter. She had to make this work.

"Perhaps one of her friends is performing a trick she could assist with," Mrs. Fairhair finally suggested.

Vivian couldn't help but feel insulted that that was the best the alpha wolf could think of, but she also couldn't help but be grateful for the suggestion. "Would that work?"

"I don't know," she answered candidly. "But the expectations for the kindergartners truly aren't that high, and the decision is cumulative over the Trials. If she can eke out a middling score, perhaps she can make up for it later in the year when she's had more time to adjust."

Every parent started off secretly thinking their child was brilliant, Vivian thought as she drove home. Aria had walked so early. She seemed so precocious as a preschooler, so imaginative. Vivian had tried to temper her expectations, tried not to leap straight to proclaiming her child's genius, but there had been part of her who had thought that surely her daughter would be at the top of her class. To find herself wondering if Aria would pass at all, if she would fail kindergarten, made Vivian's stomach clench.

Well. She would have to make sure that didn't happen. Somehow.

4

Oct 4 9:55AM

It's safety drill week! While all classes have been instructed in proper procedures, please be ready to reassure younger students, as our littlest friends are sometimes disturbed by the alarms and engage in less socially positive rampages. (Sorry about your begonias, Mrs. Lipinsky!) We will be practicing fire drills tomorrow and planar incursion drills on Thursday. After drills, we will calm down together with a soothing Tibetan meditation ritual.

"They're seriously going to kick us out over magical SATs they're running on kindergartners?" Daniel demanded when she told him later that night.

"Keep your voice down, you'll wake Aria," Vivian said from the floor next to the crate.

"A herd of elephants couldn't wake that kid once she's down," he countered in a lower voice. "We're going to need a new toy car, by the way."

The best thing about the new house was the unfurnished basement. Daniel had put in some soundproofing tiles on the walls and linoleum tile on the floor, and then they threw in a bunch of floor pillows they didn't mind being savaged. They'd figured out early that full moon nights went better if Aria had something to hunt, but setting a kindergartner with claws loose on an unsuspecting neighborhood was not a real option. So far, she seemed to be willing to chase the remote-controlled car around if Daddy sat on the top step and controlled it, as long as she got a raw rabbit at the end to make the game worthwhile. Vivian felt terrible about the crate, but the puppy training videos had suggested it would help with the anxiety, and Aria had agreed she slept better there when she was stuck in wolf form, as long as Mommy's scent was near. She only woke up howling with nightmares every couple of weeks these days. The floor cushions were leaking stuffing after too many bites, but they didn't make as bad a bed as Vivian had feared. She wished she could ask Daniel to take a turn, but she kept reminding herself that he had to be awake at work. Vivian always had painkillers and even more coffee to fall back on.

"I was going to call Moira and see if Cara was willing to work with Aria," Vivian ventured. She'd picked Cara up for Moira three times already—surely that was worth something? No, that kind of thinking was her mother talking. She picked Cara up because she and Moira were friends and friends helped each other.

"It's great that Moira is being such a good friend to you," Daniel said, rubbing the bridge of his nose. "But we can't keep running to her for help. Aria's going to have to learn how to handle this stuff on her own."

"But she can't, Daniel," Vivian said, her voice sharper than she'd meant for it to be. "She's five. All the other kids were born into this, and she's playing catch-up. She can't do this on her own."

"Look, you know how I feel about this school. About their mumbo jumbo and their batshit safety policies and especially their obsessive elitist crap." His voice had sharpened to meet hers. "I don't want to fight about this again, and I know if I point out, again, how ridiculous the entire system is, you'll end up defending them. Because that's what you do every time someone you want to please snaps their fingers. I've met your parents, I understand why, but it's not helping here. You can't fix everything yourself."

But it was her fault it was broken. "So what's your plan, then? She fails out of kindergarten and then what?"

"She hasn't failed out of kindergarten!" He threw up his hands. "Look, we can have the meds discussion again."

"I don't want to have the meds discussion. She's too young."

"ADHD meds have been tried as young as six. It's one more year."

"And it's a wild guess that they'd help. You know how much trouble I had." Vivian knew plenty of people who had had life-changing experiences with SSRIs. Her own experience involved escalating panic attacks, an ER trip from chest pains, then another two weeks of additional panic attacks before the drugs had completely left her system. And the less said about Wellbutrin, the better. It had taken them four tries to find the right combo of meds to help and not make things worse. She knew the ADHD meds were different, but she couldn't bear the thought of putting Aria through a series of drug trials this young, when the poor kid barely knew what her unmedicated brain ought to feel like.

"They make potions, you know," Daniel said. "Sasha told me about one that's supposed to slow down the change a bit, or something like that. The child drinks one every day, and it helps them with their control, at least until they're a little older."

"I don't know how I feel about Aria taking a potion every day," Vivian said. She'd seen the floating eyeballs in the apothecary in the Village.

"At least with Ritalin, we'd know it's been through a double-blind trial," he agreed reluctantly.

"I don't think either one is right for her right now," she said stubbornly. She'd been assured, repeatedly, by multiple parties that shifting wasn't a disease to be cured. So that meant she had to parent better.

"I don't know what you want me to tell you," he said. He sounded so lost that her sharpness drained out of her.

"Maybe she should be spending more time with the werewolves," she said.

"We're her family. We're not farming out raising our kid, I don't care how difficult it is." He'd fight for Aria, she knew. Unfortunately, there wasn't anyone convenient to fight.

"Not letting them raise her. But maybe we should take the pack up on their offer for her to spend an afternoon or two a week with them," she said, deflating a little. "I know how you felt about Japanese school—"

"No, you do not know how I felt about Japanese school," Daniel said through gritted teeth. "You have no idea what it's like to spend week after week with a bunch of kids whose parents are both Japanese, who speak Japanese at home, who celebrate Japanese holidays without having to look them up in the encyclopedia at the library. While your mom keeps telling you how important it is that you learn about your heritage and how you need to honor your dad, but she doesn't have the foggiest idea of how to be Japanese herself. You want to go send her to try to fit in somewhere she will never belong, where we can't help her."

For a moment, they stared at each other. Vivian gave up first. "I'm sorry."

"No, I'm sorry." He stepped forward and wrapped his arms around her. "We're both on edge."

"I have to find some way to make this work."

"I know you, and I know you'll jump through all the hoops they put out. But you don't have to. Either their hoops are fair, and this is right for her, and she'll get through fine. Or they're not fair, this school isn't helping, and they kick her out. And then maybe it's a sign that that's not where she belongs in the first place?"

"Where else will we go?"

"I don't know," he said. "But I'll look into it. Mrs. Fairhair said there were other packs. It's a bougie town, maybe this is the bougie pack. Maybe there are less elitist packs out there. That Idaho pack can't possibly be all about test scores and touchy-feely schools. They'll be farther away, but maybe I can transfer to Chicago or something. Or work out some kind of work-from-home thing, or fly to you guys on the weekends."

The Chicago office was a backwater with a small handful of people, she knew. And his work was trending towards a back-to-the-office mandate. His hours were already bad enough: she would barely see him. It sounded like hell.

He kissed her forehead. "I'm going to bed, Viv. I need to be up at five tomorrow to take the train into the city for work so we can afford the ungodly rent in this fancy-ass town, because maybe the pack felt bad enough to get us a break on the tuition but they certainly didn't help with the real estate issues. And in the event the school graciously deigns to allow our kid to

THE GRIMOIRE GRAMMAR SCHOOL PARENT TEACHER ASSOCIATION

continue paying for first grade, I want to make sure we've got enough stored up that we don't have to keep depending on that generosity."

She hated hearing him sound so defeated, when she knew it was all her fault. "I love you," she offered.

"I love you, too," he said with a sigh. "I'd suggest you get some sleep, too, but we both know you're going to be puttering all night no matter what I say."

She knew he was right about the sleep. But he was wrong about helping Aria. She gently stroked the floof of tail that stuck out of the crate. Aria's legs twitched as she hunted prey through her dreams, and under one paw she clutched a stuffed rabbit that had been ripped repeatedly limb from limb. Vivian had clumsily sewn it back together, hiding tooth marks as best she could, so many times it was scarcely possible to tell what the animal's shape had originally been. One of the ears had disappeared entirely, and Vivian had replaced it with something similar in shape made out of one of Daniel's old pairs of sweatpants. Aria didn't care how bad it looked, and went into hysterics whenever Daniel or Vivian suggested replacing it with something less savaged and more chew-toy shaped. So Vivian kept repairing it, occasionally adding in more chunks of random fabric when too much had been destroyed to get the ends to meet. Vivian had to do better. Aria deserved better. She sat down to start brainstorming a list of potential Talent Show acts to run past her daughter in the morning, wondering if the agility courses they had at dog shows would count.

"Is it that you have failed, or that you fear that you might fail?" her therapist asked.

Dr. Kumar had perfected the art of projecting warm non-judgment even through a laptop screen. Vivian still felt judged.

"I guess it's that I fear I already have failed, but nobody has told me yet." Vivian chewed at her lip.

Dr. Kumar was great, but there was only so much truth Vivian could tell her. And it made things awkward. She'd needed to explain some of the behaviors she was struggling with without making it sound like she needed antipsychotics instead of beta-blockers. So she'd grabbed at some near-truths. An attack by feral dogs that left them both traumatized. An ADHD diagnosis for impulsiveness and meltdowns. An unsupportive public school district. Fictional professional help for Aria, because she hadn't managed to find anyone qualified. When talking Vivian through her own trauma and stress, Dr. Kumar was the best. But she couldn't really help here.

Because how was she supposed to explain to a normal medical professional who lived in a rational world and had gone to regular-people medical school that she was constantly waiting for the other ruby slipper to drop?

"Well, let's look at results. How are you doing at the moment?" Dr. Kumar suggested.

"Aria's nightmares are less frequent. She does seem to be doing better here, even if I feel like I have no idea what I'm doing most of the time."

"I'll let you in on a secret." Dr. Kumar's lips quirked. "None of us feel like we know what we're doing most of the time. But I didn't ask about Aria, I asked about you. How are you doing?"

"My nightmares are less frequent, too, I guess." She'd started therapy to deal with the trauma of watching her daughter bleed out in her arms, and she really was handling that better. Really.

"That's excellent progress. And are you getting what you want out of the new town?"

"Yes." That, at least she felt sure of. "Aria has friends again. People don't stop and whisper when she goes by. I feel like maybe she'll fit in here."

If only Aria could stay here. If only Vivian wasn't about to fail her daughter again, by not asking the right questions in time.

"Vivian." Dr. Kumar leaned in and caught her eye. She raised her eyebrows meaningfully. "That's still not what I asked."

"I'm… sorry?" Vivian wasn't sure what she meant. She knew her fears were rational, but she couldn't figure out how to explain—about the tests, about the fact she was different from the other parents, about the endless potential for missteps that could be literally fatal. Maybe she'd need to do some more research on esoteric disorders a mundane human child might have to deal with, something rare enough to substitute. More research. Hooray.

"I asked about you. About Vivian. What do you want? For your child to be safe and happy, of course. Every good parent wants that. But what do you want for you?"

A dozen things flashed into her head, all of them impossible. Rest. Two weeks of absolute silence in which no one asked her for anything. To have time between work and chores and sleep to talk to Daniel about something other than logistics. For Aria to agree to wear the booties and stop scratching up the floor. A time machine. To be able to look at her husband and child without feeling crushing guilt that she'd allowed their lives to be destroyed. "I mean, I've got everything, right?"

"Do you?" Dr. Kumar gave her a look, the one that said that the psychiatrist had noticed the pause and realized it meant there had been a lot of answers discarded before Vivian had said something out loud. She'd come back to it, Vivian knew. It was like having a personal trainer, who Vivian paid large sums of money to make her very uncomfortable, only worse. But like exercise, she knew she had to do it. "It sounds like you feel very isolated."

"I guess I have been for a while. Daniel is working so hard, he doesn't have much time to help. I kind of lost touch with a lot of my friends when Aria was born. I thought I'd make some new ones through playgroups and so on…"

"Only things went badly and now you have to start over."

"Yes," she said. That was an understatement. It wasn't only Aria that people had rejected. As soon as Vivian had stopped being a source of playdates and started being the source of rumors, she'd found herself shunned. She'd gone from being the designated one to bring cut grapes to Mommy and Me classes to being asked to not volunteer at the Fun Fair even if Aria didn't come.

"Tell me about some of the other parents you've met."

She twisted her engagement ring back and forth next to the wedding ring. "There's a mom who's been really helpful with settling in, and a couple who seem nice enough. I think Daniel's closer to the dad, at least."

Dr. Kumar made a note on her pad. There would be follow-ups later. "But you like them?"

"I… I guess?"

"Vivian, why did you move to Connecticut?"

They'd covered this, repeatedly, which meant there was some other reason that she was asking. Vivian wasn't sure what she was getting at, though, so she had to state the obvious again. "So Aria could attend this school."

"Exactly. So Aria could attend the school. Not so you could do penance."

She opened her mouth and closed it again. That wasn't why she was doing this. Was it?

Dr. Kumar pressed gently. "This isn't a sentence, Vivian. It's your life. Yes, you should do your best for Aria but you get to have a life too. If you think these people you've met have the potential to be friends, and friends are a thing you want, then you should try to make friends. If you're only socializing with them for Aria's sake, that's fine, but you should see about putting down some roots for your sake too. You're allowed to want good things, Vivian. You're allowed to have good things."

That's only because Dr. Kumar thought the outcomes of the attack were some visible scars and some behavior issues. Not an effective change of species.

"I see you don't believe me, do you." Dr. Kumar smiled gently, sadly.

She was trying, she really was. Before she could think about it too hard, she blurted, "Just because I deserve good things doesn't mean anyone's obliged to give them to me."

Her therapist cocked her head. "Is 'obligation' the only reason someone might be friends with you? People can choose to be friends because they like each other, not in exchange for something."

She knew it wasn't particularly productive to tell your therapist that sounded fake, but OK. She fiddled some more with her rings instead.

"We can come back to this. We have only a minute or two left today," she noted. "And how's Aria's therapy?"

She'd snuck that one in right where Vivian had not expected it. Aria's therapy had ended when Aria had bitten the therapist. Mrs. Fairhair had said she'd dealt with it, but it had been the final trigger that impelled them to move to Connecticut.

"Fine," she lied.

As they ended the video conference, she wondered, not for the first time, if this all would have been more effective if she could have told Dr. Kumar the truth. Maybe there were therapists in the magical community. The idea of baring her soul to one of them, though? Maybe in a few years. She realized with a start that Dr. Kumar was one of the few mundane people she even spoke to anymore.

She sighed and stretched. Her shoulders always tensed up during therapy; part of her wanted to hide in a closet, knees against her chest, until she stopped feeling quite so exposed.

Her phone buzzed. It was the WhatsApp group.

Moira had warned her it was a hotbed of drama, but it hadn't seemed that bad so far. A little annoying, maybe, and terribly gossipy. She knew more about people's feelings on the new swim instructor at the municipal pool being a kelpie instead of the traditional mermaid than she wanted to know. But occasionally it was useful.

> **Henry Alfson**
> Has anyone finished the family tree assignment?

> **~K**
> lol no it's not the night before why would my child even look at the assignment

For once, Vivian felt like they were ahead of the game. Oh, she'd expected the assignment to be deeply awkward, and had been unjustifiably annoyed that Daniel got to skip dealing with it. She knew the names they needed to fill in on all the branches, but she'd expected Aria to ask why she had never met any of the people mentioned. But Aria had seemed to consider the matter of her grandparents' and great-grandparents' names to be on par with the various evolutions of Pokémon—mildly interesting trivia to be spouted rather than actual people. So she'd zoomed right on through, unbothered by the way the paper tree drew on its own roots and leaves in inky curlicues as they filled in the names, and then begged for screentime.

TomandLarryandKirrikpt
What are we supposed to do if your tree has more than two parent branches? We're not all Mom + Dad you know

Ginger CHI CONSULTANT
Super heteronormative

TomandLarryandKirrikpt
Some of us parent in groups, it's really speciesist!

Priya🐾
Some of us also didn't keep track of what our great-grandparents were up to, I don't even know how to fill in half this chart

Cecily Dragonsbane
I just went to the town library to fill in the last of the gaps

> **~K**
> Thanks Cecily that's super helpful for all of us whose ancestors EVER LEFT TOWN

> **Cecily Dragonsbane**
> I don't see why stability and tradition is a thing to ridicule

> **Kombucha4Eva**🖤🖤🖤
> blah blah blah your ancestors were here to listen to the damn Prophecy we know

Prophecy? Of course there was a prophecy, you could hardly call yourself a hidden magical town without a prophecy. Vivian bit her lip, trying to decide whether to be concerned with yet another thing to have to ask about.

> **Ginger CHI CONSULTANT**
> Hey be nice

> **Dr. Sasha**
> Just email Ms Immacolata, this can't be the first time any of these questions have come up

> **Wenjun Chan**
> I'm just glad we're not the only ones struggling. We're all in this together, right? :P

Elsewhere in the house, she heard the garage door open and the car drive in. She couldn't explain to someone how she could tell that Aria was despondent from the sound of her claws on the wood, but she knew the sound of her daughter's misery. For a moment, she closed her eyes, wanting very much to let this continue being Daniel's problem. But he'd taken the skirmedge game and was probably at the end of his own rope. She took a deep breath and rallied.

Aria pushed past her as she opened the door from the study. "How did the game go, sweetie?" she asked, trying to balance her tone into nonchalance without being unsympathetic. Aria had yelled at her before for assuming things were bad before being told they'd been bad. Never mind that the badness dripped so obviously from her child's posture that Vivian was surprised it didn't leave puddles on the floor. Maybe in Moira's house it did.

Aria gave her tail a half-hearted wag but didn't turn her head as she drooped her way up the stairs. Vivian heard the firm click of Aria's bedroom door as she nosed it shut behind her. She'd need a few minutes.

Daniel was in the kitchen, pulling a beer from the fridge.

"Rough game?" she asked. Most of the time, she was jealous that he got to play sports while she had to handle homework and take care of the class jackalope on their designated weekend. But today she may have gotten the better end of the bargain.

"How many of these do we have left?" he joked.

"Ah. That good."

He sighed and leaned against the counter. "Apparently tail-thumps count as fouls. And this week's ref was a lot more strict than last week's. She spent half the time in the penalty box."

"Oh, no. Poor Aria."

"I think she wouldn't have minded so much—there was

another kid in there with her, who kept getting sent back for making the grass entangle the opposing team, and they were both about as interested in the clover as the game. But there was an older kids' game going on the next field over, and their spiky-ball-thing went out of bounds, and Aria forgot herself and pounced on it, and everyone yelled at her."

"Consolation ice cream?"

"I offered, she didn't want it."

"…consolation raw filet?"

"Might go over better." He took another long pull on the beer. It was already more than half gone, which was very unlike him.

"What else happened?"

He offered her a rueful half smile.

"You want to talk about it?"

He stared off into the middle distance. She gave him a moment. He took another sip of beer, more judicious this time. "The other game, it was a travel team."

"Ugh. I almost hope she decides she hates this game. I do not want to deal with travel teams."

"Yeah, you and me both. Especially since there aren't that many skirmedge teams, apparently, so the travel involves, like, Mackinac Island up in Michigan and some random swamp near New Orleans." He made a face. "Anyway, the opposing team was from Idaho. Specifically, they were from the Idaho pack."

"Oh? Were you able to talk to any of the parents? What are their schools like?" She perked up.

"Oh, I tried. I understand better what Mrs. Fairhair meant by 'less refined.'" He tried to take another swallow of beer, then looked at the empty bottle, surprised.

"You want another?" she said, torn between wanting to

hear the bad news and wanting to put it off. Her pocket buzzed and her hand went to it, but at Daniel's look of annoyance, she forced herself to leave it be.

"After today? Definitely not." He grimaced. "Not a road I want to go down. Anyway, Steve pulled me back right before the coach literally tried to take my arm off. Turns out they're out in Idaho because they're the ones who don't want their kids integrated with other folks in the magical community, let alone the mundane one."

"The other werewolves are wolf supremacists?" she said, horrified.

"I dunno if the other folks around here would agree with that assessment, but it sounds a lot like it to me," he said grimly. "At least, that group. The ones who are willing to integrate all bought into this school network. Steve says they're not all quite as, well, aggressive as the Idaho group, but most packs are apparently super insular and try to deal with the mundane world as little as possible."

"And the ones who are willing all put their kids in the feeder schools for the fancy high schools."

"More or less."

"Crap."

"Exactly." He rubbed his hands over his face.

"So, if we want her socialized with other kids even kind of like her, it's not going to be better than here," she said slowly. She needed to make sure they were on the same page.

"Yeah," he said with a heavy sigh. "We're screwed."

It was like she'd thought, but at least now he wasn't fighting her. There was a certain relief in having the decision made for them. If this was going to be her life, then, well, she'd have to make a life of it.

She wanted to go watch cooking shows until it was time to go to bed, but she also didn't want to admit to Dr. Kumar that she'd done nothing, and shame was a powerful motivator. She picked up her phone and texted Moira.

Free tonight by any chance?

Problems with the family tree?

Had she only been reaching out if she needed something? She had, actually. No wonder no one thought she was friend material.

I thought we deserved a reward for
dealing with that worksheet. Drinks?

Hon, if you're buying, I'm in

She hadn't intended to, but hey, she was the one extending the invite. She could foot the bill. They settled on a time and place.

Daniel poked his head in. "For post-bedtime, are you feeling wacky cooking competition, or fantasy drama series that will end on a cliffhanger and Netflix will cancel rather than resolve?"

"Our lives are a fantasy drama series," she said. "But if you can wrangle bedtime, I've got plans."

"Wait, really?" Daniel's genuine confusion made her realize exactly how long it had been since she'd had any plans.

"With Moira," she clarified. Her phone buzzed.

Cecily's in too, but only if we switch
to the swanky place on Main

She hadn't intended to pay for Cecily's drinks, but what the hell. An overpriced cocktail or two was a low cost for entry into society. Sure, Cecily was probably only in it for the hope of gossip about the Fairhairs, but relationships had been built on less. "For drinks. With Cecily."

"If you say so," Daniel said, looking skeptical. Then he caught himself. "No, that's great. I got bedtime. You go have fun. Let me know if wizard drinks turn your hair purple or something."

If nothing else, she'd at least be able to report to Dr. Kumar that she'd tried.

5

Oct 27 12:01 PM

Please note that Halloween costumes are not allowed to be worn in the classroom next week, as some of our younger friends may find them upsetting. However, all are encouraged to participate in the parade at the Veilport Samhain Festival!

Oct 27 12:05 PM

A kind reminder after last year's incident that many of the off-the-shelf costumes sold in mundane stores are considered to be offensive stereotypes by the witch, shifter, undead, and other populations of our community. In an effort to help our children make thoughtful choices, we will be holding a mandatory Cultural Sensitivity workshop on Friday.

While there were no traces of the usual Halloween standards—a complete lack of black pointy hats or "I vant to suck your blood" cloaks—Vivian had to admit that Veilport knew how to throw a Halloween party.

The square looked like it had been decorated by the set-dressers for the Hallmark Channel. Sheaves of corn stalks and golden wheat had been tied around every wrought-iron lamp post. Swags of fake fall leaves in orange and red draped like bunting from one side of Main Street to the other. The little white gazebo had mounds of more kinds of decorative gourds than Vivian had ever seen before piled around its base. From inside, a small ensemble was playing "Danse Macabre," the haunting violin notes soaring over the crowd. An elderly couple waltzed in the middle of the street, which had been blocked off from traffic for the evening. She wore a crown of straw and chrysanthemums on her silver hair; they both wore half masks and wide smiles. Their movements were slow and careful, but the crowd around them smiled back. She wished Daniel could be here. Maybe he'd like the town more if he saw how charming it could be.

The shopkeepers treated pumpkins more like lumières. Lit jack-o'-lanterns lined the sidewalks, spaced at regular intervals. Faces, of course: smiling, leering, tongues bugged out. But also more fanciful carvings. Cats and owls and chupacabras (which Vivian could now recognize from the biweekly envelope from the chupacabra rescue people). Castles, pirate ships, octopuses clutching treasure chests, books with faces. And the pop culture references she still found so jarring here—a Death Star, Pokémon, horror movie characters.

Many were left alone but some were enchanted. In front of the toy store, the carved rocking horse somehow shifted back and forth, the kite's tail fluttered in the breeze, the teddy bear waved a paw. The jack-o'-lanterns by the ice cream shop grimaced and rolled their eyes. Glancing down the hidden alley, Vivian was shocked to see that the door had been left open, the trail of pumpkins leading off into the magical part of Main Street.

"What if someone sees?" she asked Moira.

"There isn't anyone here to see, today," Moira said. "For this one night, the town council puts up a redirection field on the roads into town. Anyone who isn't part of the community finds themselves with an urge to take I-95 instead of the local roads. Today's for us."

"No tourists at all?" Ahead of her, Aria swirled in a circle, admiring how her cape swished. She'd insisted on being Red Riding Hood for Halloween. Vivian half-suspected Daniel of having put her up to it, although Aria insisted it was her own idea. Vivian had to admit, Aria was absolutely adorable in the gingham dress and red cloak, her hair in pigtails. And the basket was very convenient for storing the treats the shopkeepers were handing out with abandon. She hoped it wouldn't be ironic.

"We don't usually get many; we try very hard to stay off Instagram and cutest-town lists. If people are looking for fall sightseeing in general, the spell gives them an urge to continue on to Old Saybrook or something." Moira laughed. When Aria had told Vivian that Cara was going to be Cinderella, Vivian had feared that she was going to show up in some literally magical costume of gold tissue or something. Cara's gorgeous blue dress probably cost fifty bucks, but it was also clearly made of polyester and had probably come from Amazon, the same as Aria's hood. It made Vivian feel like maybe she wasn't a bad mom for not hand-sewing or enchanting mice to construct a costume. Moira, on the other hand, was dressed as a Starbucks frappuccino, with tulle foam out of the top of her tan dress and a fascinator with a green straw sticking out. It put Vivian's "static cling" last-minute costume (which was just socks and dryer sheets safety pinned onto a black sweatshirt) to shame. "We did have trouble the first year Google Maps became popular—it kept sending people through here, but then people didn't want to be here, so we ended up with a traffic jam of about fifty cars stuck in an endless loop before someone figured out what was going on."

"Did someone have to hex Google for the next year?"

"Don't be ridiculous. We had one of the Google engineers who lives in town work their way into the Maps group and change the code. I think we've got at least three."

"Mommy, can I eat this?" Aria held up a candy bar.

"No, sweetie, that one goes in the trade-in pile," she said. She rummaged through Aria's basket and handed her a Starburst instead. She explained to Moira, "I have a bag of lollipops and Skittles at home. I told her I'd trade her one-for-one for anything she's allergic to."

"I'd just eat them myself." Moira snickered.

Vivian's pocket buzzed, and she pulled out her phone, half-expecting a message from Daniel. Instead, it was another parent on the class WhatsApp list, complaining under the guise of warning that the teenagers hanging around the gazebo were wearing "inappropriate" costumes.

"Did our parents gossip this much?" Vivian wondered, looking back at the last week's worth of messages complaining about the disappointing nature of the school lunch program, warnings about the local pediatrician being inadequately gentle with distemper shots, and a two-week argument about whether the children had insufficient herbology homework or too much herbology homework. Since herbology homework for kindergartners had been "collect three different leaves," Vivian had not summoned the energy to care.

"Hmm?" Moira glanced over her shoulder. "Oh, I mute those."

Vivian wanted to, rather badly. But she was afraid to miss something important. She was already so behind.

"Does everyone around here work mundane jobs?" Vivian came back to the original subject. She couldn't imagine why someone would. If she could make things appear with a wave of her hand, she certainly wouldn't opt to sit through another staff meeting.

"Not everyone," Moira said. "Cara Iona Craigie, I saw you eat that! That's the fourth Pixie Stick you've had in four minutes. Give it a rest or you're going to throw up on your pretty dress. What was I saying? Oh, right. There's a ton of generational wealth, of course. Some of them still work mundane jobs because they like them. A lot do research or play politics. But most of us need to work for a living, same as anyone. The Shadow Council frowns on anything that makes magic stick out too obviously."

"Shadow Council?" That sounded like the kind of ominous she'd been waiting for.

"Muckety-mucks in charge of the magical world, at least in this country. They're supposed to make sure that no Dark Mages start enslaving small towns and no one starts World War III. Mostly politicians and bureaucrats, but they've got an enforcement arm, too. We're not supposed to do stuff that will get the mundanes' attention, blah blah blah."

"Should… I be registering with them or something?"

"Your kid's enrolled in a mage academy. Trust me, they know who you are."

"Oh." Of course there was a mage government. Were there mage taxes? Maybe there was some kind of FDA for potions after all.

"Anyway, point is, no turning lead into gold, at least not

in large quantities. Fairy gold turns to leaves the next day. And Amazon only wants dollars. Some people do all right specializing in serving the community, like most of the shop owners here. But most families make money the old-fashioned way. Just, you know, with the occasional help from our gifts."

"Like?"

Moira shrugged. "Physical mages make great engineers. If you're a farmer, having some influence with the weather is a big help. There are a lot of performers whose charisma is not baseline human. And the entropy mages, well, you can usually tell which hedge funds have one on staff, if you know what I mean."

"If someone could give Daniel a hand, that would be great."

"That's so not my crowd, but they usually seem pretty worried about the insider trading stuff," said Moira. "Look at what happened to Martha Stewart."

"Martha Stewart is a mage?"

"You thought people started spontaneously yearning to hand-gild acorns?"

"And they let her get arrested?"

"Look, it's not like the Shadow Council exactly calls me up and tells me stuff, but the rumors were she'd gotten a little too flagrant, and it was meant as a warning to the rest of us. I'm sure she preferred a couple years in a minimum-security prison to getting turned into a tree or blood-eagled or something, like the old days. These days, it's quieter. People mess up, they're usually dealt with discreetly."

"Who else would I know?"

Moira bit her lip. "I probably shouldn't have even told you that much."

"Someone who's dead."

"Hmm, OK. How about this one? Lon Chaney only added

the Wolfman makeup after the dailies came back looking too real, if you know what I mean."

"Really?" Vivian reached out and redirected Aria from poking the moving pumpkin in the nose.

"Lovecraft's pretty much a textbook case of why summoning rituals that call on certain planes are banned until post-graduate studies—poor kid was apparently never the same," Moira continued. "Oh, and Mr. Rogers was a full-on projective empath."

"Well, that explains a lot." A thought occurred to her. "What do you guys do?"

"Me and Ewan, you mean?" Moira shrugged. "Ewan's a water mage. He runs a fishing fleet and some processing plants, so he spends about half the year up near Nova Scotia. It's how we met, you know—my father was so mad that I picked a fisherman, of all people. I told him it was traditional and besides, Ewan's less a fisherman and more an executive, but he was pissed because the commercial nets are so hard to avoid for the seals. But it's good money—like, *really good* when you own that many boats—and you do what you have to do, right?"

They turned down the alley into the heart of the magical community.

The costumes here bordered on the fantastic, making it all the more difficult to tell what was an accessory and what was part of someone's body. Diana the Huntress in a chiton and a moon headdress walked by, silver bow in one hand and a deer-headed Acteon holding the other, their dog trotting behind. Two eighteenth-century French courtiers complete with powdered wigs handed out candy apples. An astronaut with a bubble helmet bounded by as if in one-sixth gravity, leaving her dazzled by the idea of casting some kind of weightlessness charm for the sake of a costume. Two young women darted by, giggling, their gossamer butterfly wings fluttering as they ducked through the crowd. A teenage boy with swirling eye makeup had a miniature dragon perched on his shoulder that could have been a puppet, or an illusion, or a pet.

Cara and Aria *ooh*ed and *ahh*ed, but mostly made for the candy along with the other kids. Despite their parents' abilities to illusion them into nearly anything, most of the boys were dressed like movie superheroes and most of the girls had some variation of fairy-princess-ballerina. Still, a firebird darted overhead. A woman with a table set up in front of the wine shop handed Vivian a plastic cup of an amber liquid that shimmered with fine golden glitter.

"Sparkling wine," said Moira, clinking the rim of her own cup soundlessly against Vivian's. "Cheers!"

The wine tasted like honeyed apples and smoke and liquid sparks.

She tried to relax into the festivities swirling around her. Not everything had to have a catch, surely. She was allowed to enjoy things. In her purse, her phone buzzed again and her pulse spiked.

> 🌑 🪄 🔍 Sil 🎄 🚀
> Third grade meet-up over by the hay bales!

> **Gryphon (not Griffin)**
> The teenagers are still loitering around the gazebo

> **Priya**🧋
> What, they're not allowed to hang out anymore?

Gryphon (not Griffin)
Someone should keep an eye on them, is all I'm saying

Steve 🏌
Did anyone get the order list for the Talent Show yet?

~K
Just because you were a hooligan when you were their age doesn't mean all kids are hooligans, Gryphon

Wenjun Chan
I don't think they posted it yet

Ginger CHI CONSULTANT
I'm so nervous, why aren't the rest of you nervous

Gryphon (not Griffin)
It's BECAUSE I was a hooligan I'm concerned

Henry Alfson
Has anyone looked into one of those high school application consultants yet

The speed of the chat slowed. Two or three people started typing, but no words appeared.

> **Kombucha4Eva**🖤🖤🖤
> Whoa guys the teenagers just set fire to the gazebo

> **Kombucha4Eva**🖤🖤🖤
> Wait, it's out already

> **Kombucha4Eva**🖤🖤🖤
> Whose kid is the one with the Michael Myers mask?

> **Kombucha4Eva**🖤🖤🖤
> He turned himself into a bush to hide but I don't think he can turn himself back

> **Kombucha4Eva**🖤🖤🖤
> It's easy to tell which bush, it's the one with the Michael Myers mask on the branch

And then the chat proceeded into recriminations about teenagers, without anyone picking up the consultant question at all. She wondered if it was one of those things no one wanted to admit talking about. She'd heard of consultants for mundane college applications, of course. Now that she thought about it, she'd read the occasional *New York Times* article about fancy consultants for the Manhattan private schools. She'd never really thought about it as something that she might encounter, any more than she'd thought about the articles about dehydrating placentas or adult day camp or any of the other ridiculous "trends" reported in the Style section. But then again, she'd never thought she'd have to worry about flea collars, either.

"Hey, get out of the phone," Moira chided her with a smile. "All the interesting people are out here."

Vivian tried to see if there was anyone else besides Moira that she knew from school. She caught Madhuri's eye from across the road, and the mage waved but continued talking on her phone.

"What did I tell you." Moira snorted. "That woman lives to work."

"Mommy!" Aria slammed into Vivian like a knee-seeking missile, burying her face in the dryer sheet pinned to Vivian's thigh.

Vivian tried to detach her enough so that she could crouch down. "What's wrong, sweetheart?"

For a minute, Aria struggled with words, rubbing her fists into her eyes hard enough to give herself conjunctivitis. Only hiccups interrupted the steady keen of distress. Moira drifted away politely, giving them the fiction of privacy on the crowded street.

"I don't—*hic*—want—*hic*—to be Little Red Riding Hood anymore!" Aria finally managed to wail.

The part of Vivian that had tensed up for an actual disaster relaxed, while the part that tensed for a kid-level disaster winced. She was familiar with Halloween costume regret, but unlike some of the parents here, she couldn't wave a magic wand and send this one back to Target. "But you look so pretty, and you were having so much fun with the cape."

"But everyone else is a princess," Aria sobbed. Vivian tried to gently pull her fists out of her eyes and substitute a tissue.

"You can be a princess next year?" Vivian knew how

inadequate that suggestion was to a five-year-old. Next year was a century from now. "You have princess dress-ups at home, you could wear one all weekend."

"But I can't, I'm just a—a—a wolf!"

Vivian glared at the flock of sparkly tulle. Cara was happily twirling to show off her skirt; even if she hadn't been the instigator, she clearly wasn't willing to turn down Princess Club in defense of her friend. Vivian knew she shouldn't hate a bunch of little kids, even if they were being little jerks, but they were being little jerks to her kid and she would have happily thrown them all in the fountain. "Is that what they said?"

Aria nodded, tearfully. "They said I was dressed like a peasant girl and I couldn't be in their group and I said I had princess dresses and they said it didn't matter and I would always be a mangy wolf with no manners."

"Well." Vivian's heart was breaking for her, but none of the platitudes seemed very believable. She knew herself that "it doesn't matter what other people think" and "what matters is what's in your heart" and "ignore them and they'll leave you alone" were all untrue and not particularly helpful. What would make a bunch of snobby little girls want to like her daughter? Bribery? "Maybe we could buy everyone..." She looked around quickly. "Candy apples?"

Aria sniffled and looked doubtful as Vivian tried to calculate how much that many apples would cost and if she had enough cash on her. Maybe they'd turn out to be magic apples and the whole lot of them would go to sleep. She wasn't stupid; she knew that buying friends wasn't a good long-term solution. But here in the moment, she was willing to try almost anything.

Something else had caught Aria's attention. Over by the little stage set up at the far end of the street, Vivian spotted Sasha and

Steve with a couple of the other class parents. Their kids were jumping into a pile of hay bales.

"Mommy?" Aria sniffled. "Can I go play with Shuri instead?"

Shuri, Vivian was delighted to see, was not wearing a princess dress. She didn't look forward to picking hay splinters out of Aria's hair, and maybe fur, but it was definitely easier than trying to bribe a horde of princesses. "Go for it, pumpkin."

Aria trotted off, cape askew. She accelerated as she got closer, excitement at hay bales overcoming her woe. Vivian tried to relax again.

The twins were dressed as what Vivian guessed were superheroes of some kind, but didn't know enough to identify. Shuri seemed to have some kind of bee theme, black and yellow stripes with wings, her hair pulled into two puffs on either side of her head. Lucius jumped from a hay bale, metallic red wings streaming from his arms.

"On your left!" he shouted.

"I didn't even let him watch those movies," Steve sighed.

"I gave them perfectly good superhero names, and they decide they need to be totally different superheroes," Sasha replied.

"Lucius isn't from, uh." Vivian stuttered to a halt, realizing exactly how odd it would be to name a Black mage's kid after the racist villain in a series about child wizards.

"Lucius Fox was introduced in *Batman* #307 in 1979, thank you very much," Sasha said, laughing.

"And when my sweet comic book nerd here spent twenty-seven hours in labor, and then turned to me and declared we were naming the twins after her favorite characters instead of the nice traditional family names we'd picked out, I didn't have the heart to say no," Steve explained.

"It seemed like a good idea at the time, and I think they'd overdone the pain-blocking potion." Sasha shrugged.

"It was the only way I could convince you to remove the fingers you were digging into my bicep." Steve smiled at her fondly.

"What were some of the names you'd originally been thinking?" Naming Aria had turned out to be predictably fraught.

"Boring ones," Sasha said. "My family's been recycling the names of dead abolitionist mages since we arrived in Connecticut. At this point, it would have really been naming them for my grandparents instead of some long-ago white people, but I would have rather named them for the ancestors whose names we lost."

Vivian nodded, aware there wasn't anything she could say in this situation.

Sasha shrugged. "I probably should have tried to emotionally work that out some time before the multi-day labor and the pain-blocks, but I didn't, so superheroes it was. Anyway, Shuri and Lucius are way more epic than Elizabeth and Randolph, so no regrets."

Aria leapt in the air after Lucius but missed the bale she'd been aiming for. She twisted in midair and came down on four paws. The Red Riding Hood dress stayed more or less intact; Vivian made a mental note to see about getting her some more skirts. It looked like Grandma was not the only one being impersonated by a wolf today. The tail wagged from beneath the red cape.

"She's getting better at not destroying her clothes," she sighed, changing the topic. "Maybe that can be her talent."

Moira looked over at her, guiltily. "You still haven't figured out what to do for the Talent Show?"

Vivian had asked Moira weeks ago if Cara could use a sidekick, but had been turned down. (*She's got her heart set on a solo act.* Moira had shrugged apologetically. *Kids will be kids.*) She tried not to be bitter. It didn't help that Daniel had had a huge project at work, and he kept coming home so late and looking so beaten that she didn't want to bother him with brainstorming for something she knew he already resented. "Still working on it."

"Ladies and gentlemen, if I can have your attention." A pleasant-looking fellow with sandy hair that was starting to thread with silver waved for their attention from the stage. He had the kind of build that had once probably been intimidatingly muscular but was now starting to soften with age. He leaned on a silver-topped cane; one leg had been replaced from the knee down with an elegant silver prosthesis, ornately engraved with runes. It disappeared into a buckled shoe that matched the Pilgrim-like costume he wore.

Moira saw her staring. "It's the mayor, Giles Peregrine. His family's been here basically since the beginning."

"Welcome to the annual Samhain Festival!" the mayor continued. The street erupted in cheers. Vivian wondered exactly how much sparkling wine had been handed out. Madhuri drifted up next to her, dropping her phone into her purse and giving Vivian a little wave. "And with the close of another season, it's time to remember and be thankful once more for our little refuge here."

He raised his hands. Vivian wasn't sure what was happening, but the hairs on the back of her head stood up. The crowd was murmuring to itself, but paying attention, like they were at an outdoor concert. The kids settled down on the hay bales. Aria continued to romp, but then realized everyone else had stopped and sat, tail thumping.

"What's going on?" she whispered to Steve.

"It's the retelling of the town's founding," Steve said. "It's the same every year, but the effects are fun."

"Long ago," Mayor Peregrine began, "our peoples had great gifts."

Transparent images rose from the floor like ghosts. A woman wearing a pointed hat and a flowing gown rode on the back of a dragon. A man raised his hands and a tree burst into flames, searing the dragon and sending the rider tumbling from the sky. A girl ran through the woods, pulling a cloak of feathers around her and transforming into a swan that flew into the night. A man with sidelocks sculpted a person out of clay, writing letters on its head that made it come alive, tottering off into the crowd. People gave way as it passed. A teenager pushed another into its path, giggling, and the illusion walked through her as if she were not there.

"But we were arrogant, and we were greedy. Or sometimes we were unlucky, or just different. And the people feared us, and hated us, and hunted us."

Now, the image of a young woman came fleeing through the crowd towards the stage. An angry mob followed her, holding torches and crying out soundlessly. She paused at the back of the stage, her eyes wide with terror, and then fled through the backdrop followed by the crowd. Aria whimpered, ducking her head between her paws.

"But we heard of a new land," he proclaimed. "A land across the ocean, where we could be free."

Transparent waves swept down the street, an exhilarating rush. Vivian had the sense of standing on the prow of a ship, plowing through the ocean, winds billowing in the sails behind her. In front, the hint of land, growing with every second, until they reached the rocky shores crowned with towering trees.

"Here, we built a haven for everyone who needed it, mage and non-human alike," he boomed, triumphant.

"And the folks who already lived here?" Vivian muttered.

"Did about as well in the long run as the ones up in Plymouth," Steve whispered back. "He never really gets around to telling that part."

"And so, with the turning of the year, people of Veilport, I welcome you home!" He swept his hands up. In a couple of seconds, centuries of history flashed by—the building of small stone houses, then larger ones, the paving of roads, flickers of changing building styles, until the ghostly outlines resolved into the current buildings themselves.

The ghostly doors opened, and more ghosts poured out. They didn't really fit the present-day scene, though. The costumes were a bizarre mix of time periods: a woman with a colonial-era dress with mob cap chatted with a young man with flowing hair and bell bottom jeans; an elderly couple wearing Ralph Lauren and Laura Ashley pointedly snubbed a man in a tattered Union jacket, one sleeve pinned up from a missing arm; a Gibson girl and a girl in a poodle skirt twirled in their respective finery. The crowd of real people clapped politely and then began milling about, interweaving with the ghostly illusions.

"Is the show over?" Vivian whispered to Moira. "It seems a little rude to the illusionist to wander off, with all the ghost illusions still wandering around."

Moira's eyes grew round. "Oh, no, I'm sorry. I thought you knew. Those aren't illusions of ghosts. Those are actual ghosts."

Vivian felt her own eyes widen. "Actual… ghosts?"

"They're not *haunting*, of course," Steve said quickly.

"They're just visiting for the evening. It's Samhain, one of the most powerful ritual nights of the year. It's easy for the souls to cross over, if they want to. Any of the former residents of the town."

Madhuri looked up from her phone and smirked. "Given the number that are here compared to the number of people who have died over the years, most of them clearly have better things to do."

Steve shrugged. "But some like to check in on us, and some make it a yearly thing."

Madhuri continued for him. "Get the latest gossip, nag your descendants about how little they've lived up to the family potential, complain about Kids These Days and how the current green paint on the General Store is infinitely less tasteful than the green paint from 1918. I'm kind of looking forward to it myself someday, seems like fun. I was planning on making increasingly ludicrous claims about my own past each time and seeing if anyone calls me on it. Maybe hinting about buried treasure in the woods and giving the teenagers something to do out there besides sneak warm, shitty beer."

"It also means, on the average year, the majority of the town is here where people can keep an eye on them, rather than getting into trouble trying big spells of their own. It's the one night no one is too careful about carding over at the free wine table—means those teenagers have a reason to stay here where we can keep an eye on them." Steve rolled his eyes. He called over to his kids, who had gone back to pushing each other off the hay bale. "Not that my children are going to summon any Shoggoths in the woods, am I right?"

"Yes, Daddy," they chorused obediently and then went back to seeing if they could successfully ride Aria.

"Well, this is a new face," said someone over Vivian's shoulder. She turned and tried not to blanch too obviously. The sour-faced woman with a hatchet of a nose was dressed in clothes like a Thanksgiving pageant, only duller. Vivian could see right through her to the mayor chatting with a transparent man in a three-piece suit. "New to town?"

"Just moved." Vivian swallowed hard. "Ma'am."

"You don't smell like a witch and you don't look like a beastie," the woman said.

"Now, Mistress Widdershins," Steve broke in. "You know we don't call the cryptid community 'beasts' anymore."

"Bah, you don't say this, you don't say that. In my day, as long as they didn't call you to the stake, you didn't mind what they called you. And some of my best friends were beasties." She leaned into Vivian's face, and Vivian barely restrained herself from taking a step back. "What gives you right to be here?"

What indeed. "My daughter," Vivian's voice wavered.

The ghost sighed. "Well. Take out your fin, you'll be wanting to make a picture."

"My fin?"

"The little scrying slate you all carry in your pockets these days. The one with the talking spells. You'll want a picture with old Mistress Widdershins, you all do."

"My phone?" Vivian took her phone out hesitantly. "You know about phones?"

"I come back every Samhain, you've all had them for years," Mistress Widdershins snapped at her. "Did you expect me to think you're still all riding horses around and dying left and right of smallpox? We aren't stupid, you know. Having a little box to scry with isn't that hard a concept to grasp. Now, do you want your friends to make the picture, or do you want to do that awkward thing where you stretch your arm out and our faces get all distorted?"

Vivian handed her phone to Steve, who smiled encouragingly. She posed awkwardly, unsure of what to do with her hands. The ghost leaned forward a bit.

"Say cheese!" said Steve.

"Bah," said Mistress Widdershins.

Vivian glanced at the picture when Steve handed back the phone, wondering if the ghost would even be there, or if it would only show her leaning away from an empty place in the air. But no, there was Mistress Widdershins, her shoulder halfway embedded in Vivian's.

"They didn't show up on film, but digital captures them fine," Madhuri said. "Something about mirrors. Same thing with vampires. Don't try to use a DSLR, but a mirrorless camera works great."

"Go ahead and talk to some of the other ghosts," Moira encouraged. "It's a hoot."

Aria seemed to still be having a good time with the hay bales. It was a chance to catch up on the history everyone else knew. Maybe keep from getting caught by the next surprise. She wouldn't go far.

The first couple of ghosts she wandered up to, she lost her nerve. Instead, she hung back, watching them chat with other townsfolk, living and dead. When she finally did manage to introduce herself to a woman in a flapper dress to compliment her shoes, she got a pleasantly warm welcome and a short conversation about the importance of garters for flask storage.

It was with a bit more confidence that she approached an appropriately spooky ghost in a brocade coat with tattered sleeves. He lingered in the corner of the square, back turned and shoulders hunched, looking terribly lonely as the other ghosts ignored him. He was tall, with his head bent so she couldn't even catch the color of his hair. He carried something.

"Excuse me, sir," she said. "I'm new to town, and you look like you could use some company—"

"Wait," Moira called, suddenly noticing who she had approached.

"Don't—" Madhuri added, far too late.

The ghost turned.

"The time is upon us!" An aura of menace threaded through the crowd like a chill wind. Lace cascaded from his collar. She wasn't sure what kept the elaborate cravat from falling off, because the ghost had no neck. Instead, he carried his wailing head tucked under one arm. "The Reckoning is nigh! You celebrate now, but soon we shall all find our doom!"

Fear curdled in Vivian's stomach. She stumbled backwards. What had she done? It was like the Fae all over again, blundering into something dangerous because she hadn't known better. Only this time, it was entirely her fault.

"Wolf and shadow, thief and darkness, the Reckoning will roll over us like a storm," he continued.

Somehow, she'd known this was going to happen. It came with the territory, didn't it? Secret towns on the New England coast. Hints of witches having been burned, indigenous peoples destroyed, forces humanity was not meant to reckon with. Selfies with ghosts and birthday party unicorn rides were a distraction. The blood on the hiking path was the truth.

"What was done cannot be undone, and the echoes of our greatest mistakes shall engulf us all!" His voice rose to a wail, raising all the hairs on the back of Vivian's neck.

"Shut up, Henry," said half a dozen voices, Mistress Widdershins' among them.

"But, it's coming," he quavered, his voice losing steam. "The prophecy..."

"It's the same thing you said last year, and every year." Mayor Peregrine came up. "That's quite enough haunting for this time round."

Vivian tried to catch her breath, her heartbeat loud in her ears.

"But I know it's this year, I know it," the ghost said forlornly. Another ghost in disco pants which he had clearly continued to wear despite dying some time after the '70s, going by the belly hanging over the waistband, came up and took him firmly by the elbow. The Disco Ghost steered him towards one of the doors, even as Henry continued to mutter to himself.

"The Reckoning?" Vivian asked, uncertain. She looked around, feeling a bit foolish. Many of the revelers were ignoring Henry's doomsaying or rolling their eyes.

But there was a brittle air that hadn't been there before.

Steve shrugged. "Local legend. Gets trotted out now and again. Most of the time, I don't think anyone thinks about it. It's like, someday the Yellowstone supervolcano may blow, but no one in Wyoming loses sleep over it."

"Assuming it's even true. It's amazing what people will believe," added Moira. "But we're not a proper New England town without a good legend, right?"

That was... not as reassuring as they seemed to think it was. It was true that no one worried on a daily basis about the Yellowstone supervolcano someday blowing up half of the continent, but the fact that there was an undiscussed supernatural equivalent of a supervolcano that might or might not be under their feet was something she would have preferred to know sooner rather than later. And it was true that most of the crowd had gone back to their conversations, but that was only after the local authorities had swiftly ended the conversation. Wasn't that exactly what they might do if there really was some kind of danger and they didn't want panic?

She opened her mouth to ask for more details but Aria bounded over, back in human form, her sleeves only somewhat mangled. Suddenly she had more pressing worries, such as if her daughter still had her underwear or had left the shreds somewhere.

"Mommy, Lucius and Shuri want me to be part of their act for the Talent Show. Can I? Can I please?"

Oh, thank goodness. Vivian felt like she'd let out a breath she'd been holding for weeks. "Yes, of course, that sounds like a wonderful idea."

It was only after she'd agreed that she realized she hadn't asked what the act would consist of. The evening quickly devolved into negotiations of parents against kindergartners, who had an increasingly elaborate plan involving pyrotechnics and no safety measures. There was no time left to ask other adults about anything else. And after all, they still lived in the town despite knowing about this, right? And no one besides Henry the ghost seemed to think it was going to affect anyone in the near future. For now, like the fine citizens of Wyoming, she had more pressing concerns, such as getting Aria home without losing any more clothing, hopefully to eat something besides sugar adulterated only with artificial flavorings.

6

Nov 14 5:32 PM

*Don't forget to sign up for your child's slot at the Talent Show!
(Please remember school guidelines: no mortals may be
harmed as part of a Talent Show act. Even if they are put back
together again. Even if they are subsequently mindwiped.)*

"Now, I have complete confidence in the school, of course, but some of the parents in the class have expressed concerns that Ms. Immacolata's credentials have not been updated in over 50 years," Cecily was saying.

"For Merlin's sake," one of the other PTA members, some kind of dryad or nymph who had willow branches instead of hair, muttered. She fit well with the surroundings, better than Vivian felt she did. The faculty lounge where the Parent Advisory Council met followed the Ivy League faux-medieval European theme of the front of the building. The vaulted ceiling and leaded windows went well with the dark leather chairs. The battered Mr. Coffee machine and the slightly less battered Keurig were tucked in the corner of the counter where it was clear that it was hoped they would be overlooked.

"The woman worked with Maria Montessori herself; she *wrote* the credentials."

"This never happened when Ms. Genevieve was still vice-principal," someone else whispered back. "I wish Banderbridge had stayed around to help pick a proper successor. I still can't believe he just left after retiring, I thought he'd be here to manage the transition. I thought Veilport was his home!"

"Maybe that's why he left," the dryad replied. "To let poor Ms. Genevieve out from his shadow."

While she'd gotten an earful about Ms. Genevieve, who still seemed perfectly competent to her, Vivian had not heard anyone express concerns about Ms. Immacolata's credentials in her hearing. She had been rather concerned to discover that the kindergarten teacher was a vampire (What if she lost control and started biting children? What if Aria got too rambunctious at recess, knocked her parasol out of her hand, and turned her teacher into dust?), but she had been reassured on Bring Your Adult to Class day. Ms. Immacolata was a marvelous teacher—the kind Vivian wished she'd had herself. She ruled that classroom with an iron fist covered in a velvet glove, gently but firmly keeping her class of budding mages, nymphs, selkies, and other assorted cryptids happily engaged in their rounds of Works with only the occasional carefully sanctioned mischief. Aria came home every day telling of the latest amazing lesson Ms. Immacolata had to share, most of which Vivian herself had tried to introduce to a total lack of interest. She'd also been relieved to hear that Ms. Immacolata's cameo brooch was enchanted by one of the other teachers to protect her from accidental sun damage.

Of course, it seemed somewhat less likely that other parents would come to Vivian with their concerns. Other than a few of Aria's closest friends' parents, most of the other parents tended to politely ignore her. But Vivian wondered if maybe the "parents" in question were just Cecily herself.

She reminded herself again that she needed Cecily's goodwill. If only because she still hadn't managed to get the books from last year. She was going to get those files today, she promised herself. It was one thing she could do today that was at least under her control. Unlike everything else.

Ms. Genevieve smiled at them all, every hair in place but her smile somewhat less effortlessly serene than that of the teacher in question. She calmly reviewed the school requirements for faculty, which included rigorous professional development certifications, her voice betraying only a hint of strain. Vivian felt rather bad for her, and also impressed. She was pretty sure that she would have snapped and started weeping by now.

She tried to focus on the meeting, she really did. But anxiety gnawed at her stomach. They were going to break fifteen minutes early today so they could watch the Talent Show.

With every student in the school expected to take part, this first Trial started in the mid-morning. The middle schoolers would go first—apparently as a courtesy to the high school recruiters here to observe. The younger kids would start after lunch, kindergartners first and then working their way up through the age groups. The kids would watch the proceedings with their classes, which Vivian wasn't thrilled about. She was afraid Aria would see what the older kids were expected to do and get nervous. She was afraid she'd get nervous herself.

Not that Aria was nervous at all. She loved being Lucius and Shuri's minion. The twins had stuck to their specialties— Lucius was making things invisible and visible again, and

Shuri was conjuring fire. Aria added an exciting new element, apparently, running around in wolf form jumping over hurdles as they appeared and dodging away from flames like it was some kind of agility course. Whether the objects faded all the way or the candle-sized flames appeared on command was pretty hit or miss, but the idea of five-year-olds with any such powers was fairly terrifying. Daniel had liked it even less than Vivian did, but Steve assured them that the school staff had plenty of safety precaution spells to keep Aria from getting singed. And Daniel had not come up with any better ideas, so Vivian had found herself once again defending what she was herself not quite sure of. Aria herself was supposed to switch back to human halfway through, to show her growing control. Vivian was terribly afraid she'd get too excited and forget, or that the skirt and bloomer combo they'd chosen, with its discreet tail slit, would end up in shreds. But Aria was so delighted to have been included.

Her phone vibrated against her hip. She slid it out surreptitiously. It was Daniel.

How's it going so far?

She glanced up. Half the room seemed riveted as Ms. Genevieve continued her measured defense of the school's certification procedures. The other half stared into space or doodled arcane symbols that glowed as their fingertips traced the table or fiddled with their own phones.

We're still in the meeting. We just spent twenty-three minutes debating whether frogs count as acceptable familiars if the

school handbook only lists toads. I counted.
And that's after the debate over how much we
should collect for the teacher holiday gifts

You're a saint for doing this

One of us had to

You'd think magic would make things easier,
but these people use it to be even more nuts.
I would have flipped a table by now

That's why I'm the best wife

Always

The fact that he acknowledged it helped keep it bearable sometimes. She resisted the urge to ask what it was like out in normal grown-up land. He had his own stuff to deal with: he didn't need more whining from her.

Keep me updated, ok?
And try not to flip any tables

I don't know, what if I pin
Cecily under it?

Then I think Steve will give you a medal

She tried not to smile too much as Cecily made an enormous show of graciously conceding the point.

Then they had to have the report from the gala committee, which she could not manage to care less about. The party wasn't for months. She knew perfectly well that it did indeed take months to plan an event, and that the funds raised would benefit her child. She could not believe that whether they chose "Last Night in Atlantis" or "The Road to Fair Elfland" would actually have that much of an impact on whether people bid enough at the charity auction. But apparently there were passionate supporters of each side, with a number of odd glances cast her way.

Finally, she gathered enough courage to whisper to Madhuri next to her. "Why does everyone keep looking at me?"

"Because the last treasurer made us do "Fall of Camelot" three years running, and no one wants to wear armor again," Madhuri whispered back.

She tried to remember what she knew about the last treasurer. That she'd left unexpectedly, of course, and left the position open. But not much else—was she the person no one had wanted to name at the welcome picnic?

"Everything all right, Madhuri?" Cecily asked with honeyed concern.

Madhuri nodded. Vivian repressed the immature urge to whisper something catty about Cecily to Madhuri. *No*, she reminded herself, *Aria loves Elowen*. She needed to be charitable. Just because everything Cecily did annoyed her didn't mean that she had any right to be annoyed.

When a vote was finally called, Vivian hesitated long enough to have a sense of where the room was going before raising her hand in favor of Elfland. The togas for Atlantis would have been easier, but the barely pre-apocalyptic vibe seemed kind of tasteless. It didn't matter, though—mostly she didn't want people to think she was going to be difficult like her predecessor.

The meeting broke up into little cliques of moms. Vivian had hardly been delighted to find that the gender dynamics she remembered from her youth persisted regardless of generation or ability to cast fireballs. Of the room of thirty-odd parents, only two were dads.

In a few minutes, she'd deal with the Talent Show, but first she had a mission. She gritted her teeth and pasted on a smile. "Cecily? Do you have a moment?"

"Of course," Cecily said, smiling.

"I was supposed to get the accounting files the last treasurer left," Vivian said. "I'm a little behind, since we're already collecting for teacher gifts. Could you please share them with me?"

From what she understood, the files were supposed to have been turned over automatically as soon as Vivian had taken the treasurer position. A month ago. But she suspected Cecily had been waiting for her to have to ask her publicly. It seemed like the kind of little power game Cecily would like to play, to make sure everyone knew that she was officially Parent Advisory Council president now.

She wondered how much of it was to put her in her place after inadvertently saving the day at Elowen's birthday party. How much had she owed the Fae, and how much more would it have been if Vivian hadn't intervened? Cecily didn't strike her as the kind of person to enjoy being grateful.

"Oh, you still don't have access to those? Why didn't you say something?" Cecily continued smiling, and Vivian continued smiling, and no one stomped on anyone's toes no matter how much they might want to. Cecily fiddled with her phone and Vivian's phone vibrated in her hand. "There you go! Now, we'd better skedaddle if we want good seats!"

A part of her that had long been dormant wanted to dig

into the files right away. It wasn't like starting an audit, not really. There couldn't possibly be that much there: it was just one school. But she was surprised at how eager she was to have something to do that used her old skills.

Vivian let Cecily get a little ahead of her, and then made her way down to the auditorium, alone in a flow of people. More parents had already staked out seats. There, at least, were the dads, waving to their respective spouses. She wished again Daniel could be here, but he couldn't miss the full day of work. The bank had already been more generous with extending the family and medical leave further than she'd honestly expected. She would have to take the responsibility of scoping out what they faced in a few years by herself.

She was scanning the back for a seat suitably out of the way when she saw Moira and her husband Ewan. She caught Moira's eye, and the selkie waved her over. Moira smiled as Vivian approached, but the smile looked a little strained.

Oh right—her son was in middle school, wasn't he? "Is Rory ready for today?"

"As ready as he's going to be," Ewan said, his own smile looking forced.

"And Cara?"

"Oh, Cara will be fine," Moira said, waving a hand. "For the kindergartners, it's about showing that they're keeping up with expectations. But the high school recruiters are looking for something special."

Vivian swallowed. How was Aria going to keep up with expectations when she'd only had two months to adjust to a world the other kids had been immersed in since birth?

"What's Rory planning, if you don't mind my asking?" she said.

"Well, he takes after his mom more than his old man," Ewan said. Ewan was a water mage, she remembered. "So he's got some trained fish he's going to make do tricks in the big tub over there. But it would have been better if he'd spent a little more time on his watercrafting. The recruiters expect to see something from both sides of the dual heritage kids. It's a chance to show a little something extra, if he'd apply himself."

"He'll be fine," Moira said.

"Of course he'll be fine, you made sure he'd be fine," said his dad, with the air of a long-repeated argument. "Fine won't get him into Pendragon Prep. He has to do better than fine."

"He'll be *fine*," Moira repeated.

"Oh, what's that they're setting up over there?" Vivian said brightly. Moira and Ewan turned obediently, with what Vivian suspected was relief.

"Shielding," Moira said.

"The acts are that dangerous?" Vivian tried not to sound too alarmed.

"Not usually," Ewan said. "And the teachers are right there to keep anything from getting out of hand."

"This seat taken?" Steve waved from the aisle. When Vivian shook her head, he slid in. "What are you guys telling Vivian here that's making her look so worried?"

"She asked about the shielding," Moira said.

"Oh, that." Steve smiled. "Yeah, I guess it's a little alarming all by itself, isn't it? It's not to protect us, though, it's to keep us from interfering."

"What do you mean?"

Steve gestured at the rapidly filling auditorium. "Room full of ambitious magic-wielding parents plus probably a couple hired consultants lurking around? Big-ass scary test that'll determine your kid's future? You know as well as I do that if mundane parents could cast a spell on their standardized tests, every damn kid would have a perfect score even if they couldn't spell their own name."

"When you put it that way…" Vivian made a face. Parents were parents wherever you went. She thought about what hers would have done if they could cast, or buy, a spell that would have made her look better to their friends. They had never been willing to help her with anything she actually needed, but were more than happy to excoriate her for failing to meet their ever-changing expectations. That was what had finally convinced her to cut them off for good—no one would ever talk to Aria like that. Consultants had been less of a thing when she was a kid, but she could picture them pressuring her to hire one for Aria. Who here alone was a parent flying solo like her or Steve, and who had been paid? The woman in the black skirt suit with the raven perched on her shoulder? The sharply dressed man with silver streaks at his temples? The lady with the clipboard and the Afro and the neatly folded dragonfly wings? She changed the subject. "Is Sasha coming?"

Steve shook his head. "No, she's got surgery scheduled for today and couldn't get off. She'll be here for the Research Fair, though—I made her get the date cleared with the hospital as soon as we realized she was missing this one."

Of course, given that their kids were already being hailed as prodigies, they probably weren't nearly as worried. "So she does healing magic, then?"

"No," he said. "True healers are pretty rare. Sasha's a specialist in microscopic telekinesis. If she tries to levitate more than five pounds, she breaks into a cold sweat, but no one has finer control than she does. She can use her magic right out in the open and none of the mundanes even notice. She's the best prenatal surgeon in the country."

He looked so proud of her. Vivian felt a flash of jealousy. There had been a time when she'd had a career worth being proud of. Not that she regretted taking the time off for Aria— she knew herself and knew that she couldn't have handled busy season with a small child. But she'd always thought she would go back, and that seemed rather unlikely now. "Remind me what you do?"

"I, uh, I'm a writer," he said, looking a little abashed.

"Fantasy?" she guessed. He'd certainly have the source material.

Moira snickered.

"What?" she demanded.

Ewan grinned. "He writes romances."

"Seriously?" she asked.

"I like happy endings," Steve said, sounding a little defensive.

"So do I," she assured him. "It just seems like such an implausible career choice for someone who can do literal magic."

"I'm a combat mage," he said, looking away and fidgeting with the hem of his shirt. "I've done some… stuff. And I might have to again some day."

"Oh." She wasn't even sure what to picture there, but she was willing to bet his nightmares looked a lot like hers. Maybe worse. "So right now you like happy endings."

"Exactly."

"You said the next Trial is some kind of Research Fair?" she asked, changing the topic.

"That's right." He looked grateful. "The Talent Show lets the kids showcase their strongest talent. The Research Fair gives the more academically oriented kids a chance to shine. They all choose a long-term project—it can be a science fair kind of experiment, it can be digging into the history of something. Half of magic is preparation, anyway. Field Day puts everyone in the same conditions—races, obstacle courses, teamwork challenges. It's the physical day. Gives everyone a chance to shine."

"We should start thinking about research topics, then." Vivian's stomach plummeted. She wasn't ready to deal with another thing yet.

"Well, the Fair isn't until March, but it's not a bad idea to start thinking," Moira said.

Vivian's mouth twisted.

"You want to know my secret to getting through these things?" Moira opened her purse and pulled out a bottle of seltzer. "Take a swig, you look like you need it."

Vivian opened the cap and took a sip to be polite. Her eyebrows rose as the gin and tonic hit her tongue, but she managed not to splutter. "I feel like I'm in high school again." It was better than asking if her friend was a closet alcoholic, which was the first thought that came to mind. Moira might not wear a t-shirt with a wine pun in curly script, but she was leaning a little too hard into the Wine Mom thing for Vivian's comfort.

"Oh, may I?" Steve asked. Moira passed him the bottle. He shrugged when Vivian gave him a look. "It's a long afternoon. If you set up enough energy vampires in here with some transference mages, you could probably power the town for a week on the anxiety levels. Half the folks here either snuck something in or pre-gamed, I'd bet."

Vivian saw how Moira kept shifting in her seat, and how she and Ewan were carefully not touching each other, and thought Steve might be right about the anxiety.

Up front, the classes of kids filed in. Vivian craned her neck, trying to find Ms. Immacolata and her group. There she was. And behind her was Cara, and Elowen, and then Aria followed by the twins. The kids looked around, trying to find their parents. Vivian and the parents around her waved like mad, which probably didn't help. But Steve traced a heart in the air that briefly glowed pink. It caught Shuri's eye, and she bounced up and down, gesturing to her friends. Aria saw Vivian and her face lit up. Vivian blew her a kiss, and then it was time to sit down.

The lights in the house dimmed, and the audience quieted down. Ms. Genevieve walked out onto the stage. Since the end of the Parents Advisory Council meeting, she had changed from the sleek gray twinset and matching pumps she had been wearing to a velvet robe in a deep plum with trailing sleeves and a gold belt low on her hips. For once, someone genuinely looked the way Vivian had pictured when she'd heard the word "mage." She still had her dark hair swept up in her regular chignon, though. She looked a great deal more in control with the parents all on the other side of the protective barrier.

"Welcome, everyone, to the annual Talent Show. Thank you for coming out to support our students as they share their gifts with us all." Vivian shifted uncomfortably. Ms. Genevieve made it sound as if the kids had had an option. "We would like to especially welcome the guests who are visiting our community today—Headmaster Archibald Leicester of Highwater Academy, Professor Sophronia Eigelstein of the Geheime Künste School, Ms. Eugenia Kim from Miss Gulch's School for Witchcraft, Professor Chases-the-Moon from Taliesen Northwest, and Dr. Vivek Varadkar of Pendragon Preparatory Academy. Thank you for joining us."

There was a polite smattering of applause.

"And now our first student, eighth grader Gauri Chandekar, has graciously and bravely agreed to begin our program," Ms. Genevieve concluded.

A lovely girl with a waist-length braid and a face that left no question that Madhuri was her mother walked out onto the stage. She wore a gorgeous sari in peacock blue, heavily embroidered with copper thread. Vivian thought of the stretchy rainbow sweatshirt Aria had insisted on wearing for luck today with her skirt and bloomers, and winced. She hoped Aria wouldn't be the only kid who hadn't dressed up. Gauri reached the middle of the stage and stopped. She clapped her hands twice and then held them out in front of her, palms up. For a moment, nothing happened. Then twin banks of fog gathered over her palms, as if she were cradling steaming cups. The fog thickened into exquisite miniature clouds. It was too far away to make out details at first, but a tiny bolt of lightning crackled from one and Vivian realized that the clouds were each raining into the young mage's outstretched hands. The rain ran down her arms, dripping off her elbows to leave dark tracks down her skirt. Then as slowly as they had gathered, the clouds dissipated. Gauri lowered her hands, smoothing her sari. The water marks vanished as her hands passed over them.

The room burst into applause, and the girl broke out into a relieved grin. Vivian clapped, looking around to see if she could see Madhuri. There she was, over in the corner, next to a cheering man with a neatly trimmed beard. The two of them beamed at their daughter while other parents leaned over to congratulate them.

The next girl was yet another stunner, barely into puberty but already heartbreakingly beautiful. Vivian's heart broke pre-emptively for Aria. So many of the cryptid community seemed to include dazzling beauty as one of their natural gifts. It was early yet, Vivian knew, to tell how her roly-poly little tomboy was going to develop. But Vivian had enough self-awareness to know that great beauty didn't lie on either side of Aria's family, and the chances were her daughter was going to be outshone. She kept meaning to play her ancient copy of *Free to Be… You and Me* to Aria, but somehow she didn't think that was going to help offset growing up in a community full of wood nymphs and sirens and rusalkas.

This girl wore her hair loose, red tresses streaming nearly to her knees. Her skin was so pale that she looked like a china doll. She carried a brass cage containing a mouse in one hand and a bucket in the other. Setting both down, she scooped a few pale gray river rocks out of the bucket. She carefully arranged the stones in a circle around herself and the birdcage. The air around her trembled very slightly, like a heat shimmer. Then she took a deep breath and began to sing.

The wailing song was not in English. Given the hair, Vivian's first guess would have been Gaelic, but it wasn't like she could understand anything to identify it for sure. But somehow, she could tell that it was sad, incredibly, soul-rendingly sad. Tears rolled down her cheeks unbidden. Around her, she could hear quiet sobs, and uncomfortable shifting.

The mouse in the cage trembled. And then exploded.

"Oh my god!" Vivian gasped, her hands flying to her mouth. She started to spring to her feet, uncertain if she could make it to Aria before the effect could spread.

"Well, they'll dock her points for that one," Moira said, sounding completely unconcerned. Around them, the crowd muttered. Onstage, the girl looked mortified. Blood spattered her white skirt.

"Was that supposed to happen?" Vivian whispered, horrified. She'd known this was serious, but not killing-things-onstage serious.

"Banshee victims are supposed to die, yes, but not typically explode," Steve explained. He pulled a handkerchief and dabbed the tears off his cheeks, nonchalant. "Also, the shield she put up was leaking if we were having that much of an emotional effect."

"Wait, the shield was *leaking*?" But Aria was in the first few rows. "I thought you said the teachers had this under control!"

"They do," Steve assured her. "They only let the emotional wave through. No one's going to explode, I promise."

She leaned back in her seat reluctantly. The banshee picked up her stones more quickly than she'd laid them, hurrying off the stage with her shoulders slumped. The crowd murmured sympathetically, but Vivian could see the smug looks exchanged as well.

As the next few acts followed, Vivian tried to gauge from the crowd's reactions what was considered a good showing and what wasn't. There were clearly subtleties she wasn't getting. A boy with a Hispanic name and a green streak in his hair did something with a giant plinko board and little balls that sorted themselves into piles that she didn't see as particularly showy. Everyone *ooh*ed and *ahh*ed. She thought the girl who twirled a ball of fire around her head and body like a rhythmic gymnast was very impressive, but the applause was lukewarm. But when the paper crane a blond boy had folded and tossed up in the air to fly, whirring, around the room suddenly fell apart in a shower of feathers and he ran off the stage in tears, everyone surged to their feet in a standing ovation.

"It's about the degree of difficulty," Moira explained in the thundering applause. "Fireballs are easy to control, once you manifest them. Apparently they like being controlled: don't ask me, fire magic and I never got on. But transforming inanimate to animate takes real skill, and while he slid too far in suggesting to the paper that it was a bird, the fact it manifested feathers is a sign of potential."

"The recruiters like control, but at this age, they like ambition even more," Steve said.

"What did you do?" Moira asked, looking a little jealous.

"Long time ago, barely remember," Steve said, his eyes sliding away. "Shh, the next kid is up."

The next kid stomped onto stage in full goth-y rebellion, and Vivian felt downright normal. She hadn't been a goth kid in middle school; she hadn't dared. But she'd identified with the nihilism and pined a bit after dark red velvet and white pancake makeup. Goth's heyday had predated Vivian's adolescence, but as this kid proved, in every generation, someone wants to wear bird skull jewelry, too much eyeliner, and stompy boots. It was nice to see someone who felt normal in their rebellion.

"I'm gonna summon a demon," announced the girl.

OK, maybe not so normal.

There was muttering in the crowd that made Vivian realize that she was not the only one slightly alarmed by this announcement. That was not at all reassuring. She wanted her fellow parents to treat this with the same slightly condescending encouragement they'd applauded with for fireballs and exploding mice. Moira's eyes were darting back and forth. Steve didn't seem to be aware, but he'd leaned forward in his chair and braced his feet, ready to surge to a standing position.

The goth girl was drawing on the floor with a stick of chalk, her black hair with bright red highlights falling to the floor and threatening to smudge her marks. She straightened, clapped her hands together, and then dropped to one knee, planting both palms on the ground right outside the circle.

The circle surged with light.

Several teachers and parents around the room, including Steve, rocketed to their feet, hands up and fingers twisting.

The shield between the audience and the stage flared so bright Vivian couldn't see.

Something crashed and something rumbled. Vivian's body was already moving. She'd relived the moment in the woods so many times, willing her past self to move instead of freezing. Now in the face of another disaster, she resisted the urge to dive for the ground like the earthquake drills from her California childhood. Instead, she scrambled up onto the seat in front of her, ready to climb over as many rows as necessary to get to her child.

But arms around her waist yanked her back down.

"You've got no spells yet," Steve was shouting in her ear. "Stay clear so we don't have to rescue you, too."

For a moment, she twisted in his arms, trying to get free. She couldn't not do anything. But then she realized that every moment he was fighting her, he wasn't saving their kids. She let her feet hit the floor again and clutched the back of the chair. Steve went back to whatever spellcasting he'd been trying to do. She blinked back tears of helplessness.

The light from the shield had dimmed. In the front rows, the kids were screaming, but no one seemed hurt. Aria was in wolf form, standing on the seat, every hair on her standing straight out while she barked at the stage. Ms. Immacolata, and all the other teachers, were on their feet, holding some kind of artifacts in the air that cast a shimmering bubble over their charges. Nothing was falling. At least, not anymore. The goth girl on the stage, miraculously, seemed mostly OK. She had a cut on her arm that dripped blood and her hair was full of dust, but no worse than that. She was standing, back to the audience, staring up at the gaping hole where the fancy lighting rigs and the ceiling of the stage used to be.

Moira grabbed Vivian's arm. "You gotta stay put until they've cleared us. It's the only safe thing for the kids."

"Spirit check—clear!" someone shouted.

"Necro check—clear!" a deeper voice from the other side of the auditorium boomed.

"Forces check—clear!" Steve called out, startling Vivian.

She looked around as several others reported in—time, matter, trans-dim, psychic, structural, whatever those were. There was some kind of command structure, people with authority and a system in place that she had never had an opportunity to notice before. Like the National Guard, only with magic. She wondered again what exactly Steve had meant when he'd said he was a combat mage.

"Kassie, stay there," ordered Ms. Genevieve, as calmly as she might have broken up a food fight in the lunchroom. "Parents, remain where you are. Bringing down the shield wall now."

As soon as the shield came down, Kassie fled the stage into the arms of a well-rounded woman with a blond bob that screamed homeowner association member. No wonder the poor kid wanted stompy boots, Vivian thought, feeling a little shaky as the adrenaline pooled with nowhere to go. "I'm sorry, Mom!" Kassie cried. "I didn't mean to break the school!"

Ms. Genevieve was standing on the stage, staring up at the hole with calculation. She seemed calmer, less brittle, in the face of an actual emergency than she had in front of whining parents. "We'll need a full investigation, but I think I can say as a preliminary that you didn't, my dear. Professor Eigelstein?"

The diminutive woman with a Heidi braid wrapped around her head and a sharply cut suit slowly climbed the stairs from the orchestra pit to the stage. "Indeed, not. The portal was never completed; I can say with some assurance that nothing came through. Perhaps a previously unseen layering effect from the previous spells?"

"We'll conduct a full review, of course," Ms. Genevieve said decisively. "And I'll alert the Shadow Council, if one of the local reps hasn't already."

"Full team's already on the way," Steve spoke up, putting away his phone.

She nodded. "However, under the circumstances, I regret to say that the rest of this year's Talent Show will be canceled. We cannot afford any additional layers of magic until we've isolated the cause of the accident."

Angry shouting broke out across the auditorium. Several people were shouting the Reckoning, which Vivian made a mental note about. Now was not the time to be asking, though.

"But what about our kids?" she said.

Steve's eyes briefly focused. "Their teachers had class shields up, they'll be OK."

"What happens to the kids who didn't perform?" she asked Moira.

Moira tensed. "We're about to find out."

"Parents. Parents!" An Indian man with glasses like an architect and a black turtleneck held up his hands. "I understand your concerns. Your children have worked very hard for this day, and we all know the stakes. However, under the circumstances, Pendragon Preparatory Academy will waive the talent requirements for entrance for this year's rising freshmen from Grimoire Grammar. Archie?"

The balding man wearing a tweed jacket, arm-patches included, nodded. "Same for Highwater."

The other visiting recruiters nodded their assent.

"Thank you for your gracious offer," Ms. Genevieve said, her voice pitched to carry over the hubbub. "Now, I'm afraid I'll have to ask you all to leave the building. We'll bring the children around to be picked up in front of the school. I know you all want to be reunited as soon as possible; let's prevent any kind of crush or panic. I repeat, you may pick up your children at the *front* of the school. Thank you all for your cooperation."

As much as she hated it, she could see the wisdom of the arrangement. There was a little grumbling and a little yelling, but most of the other parents acquiesced as well.

They shuffled out, parents muttering and casting suspicious looks at each other, the smoking line that had been the shield wall, and the hole in the ceiling. In her pocket, Vivian's phone started to buzz like crazy. She took a quick glance—she already had thirty-eight WhatsApp messages and counting. She shoved it back in. Steve broke off and headed for the stage, along with the other parents who had checked in. Moira called after him. "Want us to get the twins?"

"Yes, thank you!" Steve shot them a relieved smile and then that look of focused concentration descended again.

"Thank goodness for the alternate pick-up form!" Moira chirped.

As they slowly shuffled their way out of the auditorium, she kept replaying the moment over in her head. She'd moved fast enough this time, really, she had. But there had been nothing she had been able to do. She hated this, the feeling of powerlessness. When she got home, she was going to start those spell exercises after all. Anything was better than feeling this helpless again.

"I'm sorry Rory didn't get a chance to go," Vivian offered. She was not at all sorry that Aria hadn't, although she was sure her daughter would be disappointed. Maybe they could have a playdate with the Cunninghams and she could run around while the twins pointed at things for her to dodge.

Moira nodded. She kept returning her face to a somber expression, but Vivian could see the relief in her eyes. She must have been even more worried about Rory than Vivian had thought. Vivian joined her in that relief—the more she thought about it, the better this seemed for Aria. "He'll just need an extra-great research project!"

Vivian nearly groaned out loud. This was a temporary reprieve at best. It seemed churlish to complain when they had all nearly been squashed by flying debris, but she had no idea what the appropriate equivalent of the trifold board would be for a wizard science fair. Somehow she didn't think baking soda volcanoes were going to cut it.

On her way out, she couldn't help but take one more glance through the hole in the roof and wonder about the wisdom of living on top of a supervolcano. No one had wanted to talk directly about whatever the Reckoning was. Steve and Madhuri had laughed it off. But you didn't bring up a running joke while the dust was still settling; some of these people were taking it seriously. What exactly had been in that prophecy?

7

"It doesn't look like the picture."

Cecily set down the half-finished snow globe and her
wand. She picked up a store-bought gingerbread man Vivian
had set in the middle of Cecily's reclaimed barnwood kitchen
table and bit the head off with brittle precision.

As frustrated as she was, Vivian also had to hide a thrill
of delight. After the parent leaders of the fourth-grade class
had casually announced that they had handcrafted a holiday
ornament for each child in the room to commemorate their
fourth-grade year, Cecily had declared that Mandrake Room
would be doing the same. Vivian knew perfectly well that she

had been included only for form's sake, and possibly to give Cecily an audience to show off for. No one expected her to contribute meaningfully to the effort.

But Moira had saved the day, as far as Vivian was concerned, by suggesting a combined playdate/crafting day. It was the first time they'd managed to get together again since the accident; the minutia of Thanksgiving had prevented much in the way of socializing. Daniel had taken a look at the craft instructions and opened his mouth to say something snarky about it, but she'd glared at him until he closed it again. She knew it was silly, but she needed this. The plan had been for the kids to play together while the adults assembled the class ornaments. Cecily would do the important bits, as everyone was sure to be aware. She was the one responsible for the delicate spells first to form the glass and then to animate it. Moira's water control was apparently critical to filling the ornament with the miniature weather pattern that would allow it to continue to snow real snow on the tiny glass snowman who waved from the bottom. Vivian had been entrusted with the difficult and important job of tying a ribbon around the bottom.

She had yet to tie any ribbons.

It seemed ridiculous to be failing at crafts. The school auditorium had gotten a new roof, courtesy of a number of the adult mages collaborating and far too many WhatsApp messages, but Vivian couldn't drive by without remembering the flash of light or the smell of debris floating in the air. What if it had happened later? What if it had happened when Aria was on stage?

What if it hadn't happened at all, and Aria had failed miserably at her Talent Show act?

And that was why she was sitting here. Because she needed

answers the other moms had. She just had to figure out the right questions to ask. But in the meantime, it was nice. To be invited to someone's house to hang out with friends. Well, a friend and another person who only liked her to suck up to her benefactress, but still, two people who were continuing to voluntarily spend time with her even if they were all completely failing the stated purpose of the evening. She merely needed to keep making herself indispensable. She looked forward to telling Dr. Kumar.

Cecily scrolled back up to the top of the instructions. "I did that part. And that part. And I followed this part exactly like in the video. So why doesn't it look anything like the picture?"

"Maybe it's one of those crafts where they cheated, and no one can actually get it to work?" Vivian ventured.

"No, Gillian Winklesmith posted a photo of her kids doing this exact craft last week. Her kids! And I commented that I'd make them for the class, and Elowen has her heart set on helping make these for everyone. I am not going to break her heart."

Vivian privately doubted Elowen much cared, given how quickly she'd abandoned the project and dragged the other two girls off to her room.

Whether Gillian Winklesmith had gotten this to work or not, it wasn't working for them. There was a series of misshapen lumps lined up on the table, each a potential *Nailed it!* meme. The one snowman Cecily had successfully animated was slowly melting. It waved cheerily, its features dripping down its face like the effects from a 1950s horror movie about the mutagenic properties of nuclear war.

Moira opened the bottle of merlot she'd asked Vivian to bring along with the cookies. "Let's take a break."

They abandoned the disaster in the kitchen and moved to the

living room. Vivian had expected something more fantastical, but the house mostly looked like a mundane house, albeit a really tasteful one. Instagram-worthy neutrals, with the occasional dramatic plant. Not an animate plant, just very healthy-looking monstera and succulents. Maybe that's where the magic went—keeping the houseplants alive.

But this, too, was nice. Wine and gossip.

"How is the bookkeeping going?" Cecily asked, clearly to be polite.

"Oh, it's a mess," Vivian admitted. "The records from last year are awful. I'm still trying to reconcile what I can find of the receipts. Honestly, I can't quite figure out how—what was her name again, the old treasurer?"

"Adelaide," Cecily supplied. "Adelaide Lee."

"Well, I cannot make heads or tails of Adelaide's system. It's certainly not GAAP-compliant, that's for sure." Vivian rolled her eyes. This is why you didn't leave things to amateurs. "I haven't managed to figure out how the numbers add up to what she had, which is making it a little tricky to get you the gala budget you asked for."

Cecily's eyes widened. "You don't think she was embezzling, do you?"

"Given that, at the moment, the revenues from last year's gala are higher than I can account for, hardly. My guess is that she forgot to add in the 50–50 or something like that when she wrote stuff down, and she just counted up the pile of money at the end of the night and wrote in the grand total instead of working through the math. I'm still combing through all the paperwork, though."

"Oh," Cecily said, leaning back. Her face was a perfect mix—relief as president that there was most likely no wrongdoing, disappointment as town gossip that there was no scandal. "Well, Banderbridge signed off on the whole thing, and he was there that night, so it's fine. You don't have to add up every raffle ticket and every candleholder."

But Vivian liked adding up all the numbers. Not having numbers add up made her itch. On the other hand, she'd spent the better part of the last week researching science fairs and unsuccessfully trying to light a candle with the very first spell in the primer. Aria had tried to give her pointers from Ms. Immacolata's lessons, which had made her inability to do something her kindergartner had mastered all the more humiliating. Daniel had been home late nearly every night, so she'd had to deal solo with both a clogged toilet and an owl who couldn't seem to remember that the previous owners of the house had moved and kept misdelivering messages. By the time Friday had rolled around, Daniel had tried to lure her into doing a puzzle with him and she'd had to turn him down to practice her ritual chants. He'd been annoyed, and finally made her hide in the basement to chant so he could at least watch a movie in peace. She had hardly made the progress she'd been hoping to on the receipts.

But that gave her the perfect opening. She was hoping that Cecily—thoroughly-in-everyone's-business Cecily—might have more answers to the questions that she never seemed to be able to keep up with. "What happened to the last treasurer, anyway? Adelaide, I mean. The bookkeeping stops the week before the school year ended."

"Both her kids failed out." Cecily took a long sip of her wine. She waved a hand, and the plate of cookies levitated in from the kitchen.

"What happened?" Vivian asked.

Cecily leaned in, delighted again, her eyes gleaming with the juiciest of gossip. "The eighth grader failed to get a bid anywhere good. Completely flamed out at Field Day, then failed her finals. But the third grader, she failed out the same year. That poor woman."

"What… what happened to them?"

Cecily shrugged. "What could they do? They had to move to the only place they could get the kids enrolled. I think somewhere out in Ohio or Oklahoma or something like that, one of the little rural communities out in the middle of nowhere. They couldn't get in anywhere respectable—I know the New Orleans locus and the Chesapeake coterie refused to have them for certain, and I'm sure if they could have gotten into any of the West Coast enclaves, they would have. Instead, they're cooling their heels in some Cincinnati suburb or something."

Cincinnati was hardly a rural community, but that was Cecily. Vivian would have happily moved to Cincinnati; maybe in Cincinnati, the eighth graders didn't blow holes in the school ceiling. But the Cincinnati school wouldn't take shifters at all, like most of the Midwest. She'd checked.

"They really kicked someone out of third grade?" Somehow, she still hadn't believed it could happen.

Moira nodded and took a big gulp of wine. "They really did. They will again. It's a big deal."

Given how nonchalant Moira tended to be about, well, everything, that gave her pause. "Is that why no one talks about her?"

The two other moms exchanged glances, reminding Vivian once again that they'd known each other for years, and she was an interloper.

"It seems a bit gauche," Cecily began.

"Everyone's a little afraid failure will rub off on them," Moira corrected bluntly. "But mostly no one liked her very much. It's bad manners to speak ill of the dead-to-us and all."

"How is Rory doing?" Cecily turned to Moira, her voice far too sweet and sympathetic.

"He's doing fine," Moira said. Her hand gripped the stem of her wineglass tightly.

"It was such a pity he didn't have a chance to exhibit at the Talent Show. Raidne said you hired a consultant?"

"Well," Moira said stiffly. "The high school admissions process can be very stressful for them to navigate. We wanted to do what's best for Rory."

Vivian turned to Moira in surprise.

"Maybe you should look into it for Aria," Cecily said, as if she'd just thought of it. Vivian did not believe she'd just thought of it. "To help her catch up a bit."

Vivian wanted to turn her down. Airily, maybe. Or haughtily. Or coldly.

"Oh, I hadn't thought of that," Moira said. "Do… do you want his number?"

That stopped Vivian cold. If Moira thought Aria needed it, maybe she did. But she didn't want to say so in front of Cecily.

"So, how 'bout that Reckoning?" she blurted and immediately regretted it. It wasn't that she didn't want to know—she did, desperately. But she hadn't been able to figure out a graceful way to bring it up. She'd typed it into a text three times since the accident and deleted it each time. Somehow, thinking about it made her feel nauseated, but seeing it written out made her feel silly. She'd told herself sternly to get an answer today. Good job. Texting would have been less awkward than this. But she was committed now, and she did need to know, so she plowed on. "Everyone said it wasn't a big deal at Samhain, but then it came up again at the Talent Show."

"Landfolk superstition." Moira waved her glass of wine, dismissing the idea. The merlot sloshed onto the white couch where it puddled and failed to sink in.

Cecily plucked the glass from her fingers, irritated, and shooed the puddle off the stainproof-bespelled couch and back into the glass with a gesture. "I'm a direct descendant of Minerva Vondelshank, I'll have you know."

She'd said it the way someone might claim to have been descended from George Washington. Vivian had no idea who that was. "Congratulations?" she offered.

"One of the town founders," Moira interpreted for her. "Lost her marbles, started raving."

"Minerva Vondelshank did *not* lose her marbles," Cecily said.

"I'm pretty sure that phrase is considered ableist—" Vivian started to say.

"Minerva Vondelshank," Cecily said more loudly, "was a respected seer even before she helped found our beloved home."

"What did she see?" Vivian asked.

"The rebounding of karma," Cecily said grimly.

"That's... bad?" Vivian wasn't sure what the expected reaction was supposed to be here.

"What you have to understand," Moira interrupted, reclaiming her wineglass, "is that the same plague that wiped out the indigenous folks around Plymouth a couple years before the Pilgrims got there took out the people who lived down here, too. Smallpox, bubonic plague, no one's sure, since the ones who survived didn't leave a whole lot of records. So awful. Anyway, when the Vondelshanks and the rest showed up, they didn't even have a Squanto to greet them, just some decaying villages with no people left. So they basically moved right in. Prime location, nice little harbor."

"Does this end with the dead Native Americans cursing the settlers?" Vivian asked, horrified.

"What? No," Moira scoffed. "Quinnipiac magic doesn't work like that. The whole 'sacred Indian burial ground' thing is a trope invented by lazy racist horror writers, it's kind of offensive, no offense."

"Oh. I'm sorry," she said, cheeks flaming.

"But traditional English ritual magic, on the other hand, does work on balance. And benefitting so heavily from others' misfortune unbalanced their fates." Cecily's voice had slid into a deeper tone along with the more formal language. Vivian wondered if she was reciting something she'd learned by heart.

Moira cut in again. "So stuff starts going wrong for the settlers. Crops fail, spells fail, people and livestock get weird diseases. The kind of stuff that elsewhere would get people burned as witches, only everyone there's already a witch."

"The colonists decided only a major Working could restore the balance," Cecily said, her cheek twitching as if she were trying hard not to grit her teeth.

"When most likely it's that they were blundering around on a new continent and didn't know what the hell they were doing," said Moira.

"The Working succeeded," Cecily continued as if Moira hadn't spoken. "The balance was restored, and the colony would go on to become the success we are today. But not without cost. Three of the colonists died in the process, including Minerva's husband. And Minerva insisted that the town's dark fate had not been averted, but merely postponed. At the foot of the town hall, she fell into a seer's fit, and revealed the prophecy that was recorded by Mistress Widdershins and has been handed down even unto today—"

"Despite never having shown a single sign of having come true." Moira rolled her eyes. "We're fine. We're all obviously fine. We made it through a bunch of wars. We were a bootlegger hub during Prohibition and never got so much as raided. We sailed through the Great Depression. Hell, we didn't even lose anyone in the city on 9/11. It's only a legend. A bit of local color. No one takes it seriously."

"Maybe outsiders like you might not take it seriously—"

"Oh come off it! I'm not even human, and Ewan's family moved here eighty years ago. I think you hang on to that stupid legend so you can be suspicious of anyone who hasn't been here for three generations."

"It's not a stupid legend!"

"You actually take the prophecy seriously?" Moira looked at Cecily's tense face and paused. "Wait, you do, don't you."

Cecily pulled herself up. "As I said, Minerva Vondelshank was a respected seer. It will hardly be the first prophecy to come to fruition generations later. Remember the Meyerschmidt tablet? Or the fall of the house of Wu?"

"Oh, for currents' sake, those were totally different things." Moira looked uncertain, though. "Weren't they?"

Vivian started to ask what those even were, but hesitated, too embarrassed. Something to do with other prophecies, she guessed. She wondered if there was a magical Wikipedia she could look up cultural references in.

"Are all the older families sitting there waiting for the other shoe to drop, then?" Moira was saying.

"I mean, not day to day," Cecily replied, settling down a little. "But it's wise to keep an eye out for the signs, don't you think?"

Vivian was not thrilled that Moira, who had started out so blasé, seemed to be taking Cecily seriously. She bit her lip, trying to decide how foolish she'd look if she asked for more details on these signs.

Moira looked thoughtful. "What would you do if you thought it was coming true?"

"Well, if signs were detected, I imagine some people might try to run," said Cecily. "But it says right in the prophecy what has to be done to prevent total disaster."

"And people would do it? No questions asked?"

"To avert the Reckoning? We'd be fools not to."

Vivian broke in. "But what are the—"

There was a crash and a wail, and all three moms jumped up. Moira's wine tipped onto the couch, but the white upholstery magically repelled the spill once more, this time ending up mostly on Vivian's shoe. Vivian lost a precious second getting turned around in the foyer, ending up behind the other two, and so was the last to arrive in the playroom in the basement. Aria was huddled in the corner, her ruff flared but already settling down, her tail creeping between her legs. A dollhouse lay face down on the carpet, the source of the crash. Vivian thought she recognized an unruly tail's work. Elowen stood with her hands planted on her hips, looking exasperated. Cara's arms were folded.

"She wolfed out again," Cara reported, rolling her eyes, all the attitude of a teenager trapped in a five-year-old's body.

Aria tucked her tail the rest of the way between her back legs and whimpered.

Vivian fought her annoyance. She had finally managed to have something approaching a normal mom gossip session, like a normal mom (normal for here, at least) with normal friends. And she had finally been starting to piece together some of what was going on in this ridiculous town. And Aria had to go and ruin it all, like always.

She stopped that train of thought immediately. She was not going to resent her daughter. She couldn't, Aria needed her not to, so she was simply not going to. She dropped to one knee, acutely aware of the other two moms and their girls watching. Their perfect girls who never seemed to misbehave. She kept her face neutral, but her ears were flaming.

"OK, honey," she said. "Think it's time to go home?"

Aria's ears went back and she bared her teeth a little, angry to be made to leave. But Elowen, unfazed by the snarling wolf next to her dollhouse, gave a long-suffering sigh. Aria stopped growling immediately, her head drooping.

"C'mon, babe, let's go get your coat." She looked around for whatever Aria had been wearing.

Cara handed her some tights. "Mrs. Aria's mom? I think you want these."

"I'm sorry I couldn't help more with the class gifts," Vivian said as Cecily escorted them out. Sorry for the mess. Sorry that her daughter couldn't get through one single playdate without a meltdown. She didn't say any of what she was really thinking.

"We'll have to do this some other time," Cecily said. Vivian knew there would not be another time. All the previous playdates had been outside or at Vivian's house; she'd been wondering if Moira would ever take a turn hosting. She realized now the answer was no.

Once they got to the car, she turned to Aria. "Sweetie, do

you think you can get back into people form? I've got your robe right here, and we can turn on the heat as soon as I get the car started. But you know you don't fit in your car seat with the tail."

Aria gave a little shake and a sigh, and turned back into a girl with the remains of her dress hanging from her neck. Vivian bundled her into the robe they kept in the car now, and then into her car seat. As she backed out of the driveway, she glanced at Aria in the rearview mirror. Her daughter was staring out the car window into the twilight.

"Do you want to tell me what happened?" she asked.

"Dunno," Aria muttered.

"Did something startle you? Did you guys argue?"

"Dunno," she said again.

"Something must have set it off," Vivian started. She'd been doing so well in making herself someone these people would want to be friends with. Surely Aria could see the value of doing the same? "Did you make sure to offer to share the toys you brought like we talked about?"

But Aria growled and looked like she might change right there in the seat and Vivian dropped it.

"You're back early," Daniel said as they walked in. "Did the little snowmen go all Sorcerer's Apprentice on you?"

"Disaster," Vivian said, bundling Aria off for a pre-bedtime bath. It usually helped calm her down a little. She didn't want to explain everything to Daniel; he didn't understand why she kept hanging out with Cecily and she didn't want to deal with his criticism masked as concern.

Her phone binged, and she winced, expecting another round of WhatsApp notifications. Instead it was a text from Cecily.

Here's the contact info for Moira's consultant, it read. And then a name and phone number.

Vivian shoved it back in her pocket and grabbed the scent-free bubble bath they'd had to switch to after Aria's nose had gotten more sensitive. Forcing cheer into her voice, she asked as if nothing were the matter, "OK, into the tub. No, back to human form, we only have enough shampoo for your human hair. And remember, we use towels, not shaking off, inside."

"So even the witches have weird urban legends. So what?" Daniel tugged at the molly bolt he'd installed in the wall. Satisfied that it could hold forty pounds or so of wolf cub, he grabbed the other end of the guy-wire he'd attached to the Christmas tree.

"Don't you think it's interesting?" It wasn't just interesting. It made her nervous. Cecily had been so intense. And she wasn't the only one muttering about the Reckoning. But every time Vivian brought up something about the school or the community these days, he seemed so dismissive. She knew how he'd react if she told him that she was convinced that some prophecy from the Pilgrim era that half the town didn't even believe in was going to affect them somehow.

It wasn't even that she was convinced it was going to affect them. She just needed to know what it was so she could stop worrying about it. It was easy enough for Moira to decide what was and wasn't a legend. A year ago, she'd thought everyone in this town was a legend. She didn't have a built-in bullshit detector anymore. She found herself in a weird balancing act, worrying and trying to look like she wasn't worrying, searching for information without looking too much like she was searching.

She missed being able to tell Daniel everything. But she didn't have the energy to deal with his frustration with the magical community anymore.

"I wish I knew what Cecily had been about to say." She'd intended it to come out lighter than it did. She tried to make it look like she was focusing on tying little red bows to the doggie treats next to the raspberry-flavored candy canes. At least the former were supposed to keep Aria's teeth clean.

Daniel made that exasperated noise he seemed to make all too regularly these days. "Hey, I understand why you might not want to ask Cecily anything; I don't want to ask Cecily anything. Cecily's a pain in the ass. Even Moira thought she was being superstitious."

He gave the tree a shake. Anchored in three points along with the giant cast-iron stand, it wasn't going anywhere. Which was more than they could say for the china hutch, which had met a sad fate right before Thanksgiving. They'd briefly looked into asking an entropy mage to run the crash backwards for them, but enough time had passed that it would have cost more than the plates were worth. Then he sat down next to her with a sigh and put an arm around her shoulders. "If Steve wasn't worried about it, I'm not all that worried about it. But you need a project. Aria's out of the house most days, and you're always happier when you're busy. You need something you're interested in spending time on." Besides failing to work the basic spells in the grimoire primer, he left unsaid. "If you want to go poking into local history, why not try the library?"

She hadn't thought of the town library, a little white clapboard building on the edge of the secret square. She'd gotten so used to looking up things on Wikipedia that she'd forgotten that libraries were still a thing. Of course this would be the kind of information no one would have digitized, or if they had, it was probably on some website she'd need to cast a spell to access.

It felt better, having a direction to go. She stayed up late practicing, even after Daniel sighed heavily and went to bed without her.

The next day, after dropping Aria off at school in her warmest PJs with her beat-up stuffed rabbit under her arm, she parked her car in the weird parking lot (this time, next to a miniature submarine with wheels sticking out the bottom). Then found herself standing next to the little alleyway, clutching a butter knife and looking around nervously to see if anyone was watching her.

It was a miserable day, cold and drizzling, and the street was empty of pedestrians. Thank goodness. She took a deep breath and let it out. The knife was supposed to go this way, and then that, and then twist. Nothing happened. She tucked the handle of her cheap umbrella under her chin and fumbled out her grimoire. Maybe she'd gotten the angle wrong? Maybe it was the knife that was a problem. Aria needed her athame at school, and Vivian had considered taking one of the knives from the butcher's block, but couldn't figure out how to wrap it in her purse so she wouldn't stab herself by mistake. Maybe she was constitutionally incapable of performing magic, and would have to resign herself to always standing ignorantly on the sidelines of her daughter's life.

No. She could do this. Moira had said the most basic spells could be mastered by anyone determined enough, and she was determined.

She studied the text carefully. There, the knife was supposed to flick up a tiny bit at the tip. And she needed to focus on the desired result, according to the book. She'd been focusing on her desire to get to the library, but that wasn't the purpose of the spell, was it? She tried again, slowly, focusing on her desire for the knife tip to catch on the fold of reality, remembering how it looked when Moira had lifted the air like a latch.

She was concentrating so hard on what it had looked like that when it looked like that, she didn't initially realize what she was seeing. But the knife that had sliced through the air with no resistance suddenly caught on something. And as she tugged it towards herself, the door swung open.

Vivian squeaked in surprise. She glanced around again nervously, but there was still no one in sight. She allowed herself a giant grin. She could do it! Something that everyone here mastered in preschool, of course, but it was something. She slipped in and closed the door behind her, triumphantly heading towards the small clapboard building on the far side of the hidden square.

The inside of the library felt no less chill than outside, although at least it was less damp. The librarian, a tiny Black lady with a shock of white hair and a pair of cat-eye spectacles on a beaded chain that must have been issued by a props department, eyed her suspiciously.

"Excuse me," Vivian said, reminding herself that she was as entitled to be here as any other resident. After all, she'd opened the door, hadn't she? "Do you have any materials on, uh," she wracked her brain for the name, "Minerva Vondel-uh-something, and the Reckoning prophecy?"

The librarian's eyes narrowed. Vivian winced, wishing she'd written down Cecily's prophet ancestor's name before she'd forgotten it. "May I see your library card?"

"I, uh, don't have one. We moved here recently," Vivian said, stumbling over her words. Was this restricted somehow? How could she prove she belonged? Was there a secret code word? She had her driver's license with her town address on it, maybe that would be enough. Why would someone want to know about this? "My daughter was thinking about doing her project for the Research Fair on it, you see, and well, I wanted to make sure there was something for her to look at before I brought her in."

"Oh, she's a student at Grimoire Grammar?" The librarian's face suddenly warmed. "What year is she?"

"She's only in kindergarten," Vivian said and then wondered immediately if she should have lied. Kindergarten sounded much too young to be doing projects on dark prophecies. But then again, the whole point was to stay here for years. She'd run into the librarian again, surely, and it would be terribly awkward. She fumbled for an excuse, and then remembered Halloween. "But she heard Henry the ghost at the festival, and now she wants to know all about it."

The librarian nodded sagely, used to the random obsessions of five-year-olds. She gestured and Vivian followed her through the stacks of mystery novels, pop history, and potion cookbooks. "Well, I imagine she'll need some help understanding the handwriting, but the protective spells should be able to prevent any damage to the manuscript as long as you're both careful."

"Here," she continued, as they reached a large glass case at the back of the room, with heavy wooden drawers beneath. Local town artifacts—a belt buckle, a cracked and blackened wand, several silvery fish hooks—were displayed behind the glass. She pulled the top drawer out to reveal several ancient books and a few piles of papers covered in spidery handwriting. She lifted one of the books. "This is Mistress Widdershins' diary. The relevant passage is marked with a ribbon: it's the one people always want to read first. I'd say it was heavy going for a kindergartner, but I had a six-year-old in yesterday who couldn't remember which direction the p goes but could still tell me everything there is to know about Pachycephalosaurus."

Vivian wished Aria would hang out with the Pachycephalosaurus kid instead of Elowen, but fought that impulse down as uncharitable. She took the book gingerly. "Do I need cotton gloves or anything?"

"As long as you don't cast near it, the protection spells will keep skin oil and moisture from damaging anything." The librarian gave her a sharp look. "I don't need to remind you not to dog-ear the pages or, heaven forbid, write on it?"

"Of course not!" Vivian was faintly insulted. She might not be a mage, but she at least knew how to treat a book with respect.

The librarian looked satisfied. "I'll be at the desk if you need anything."

She started to sit down and then remembered where she'd heard the name before. "Mistress Widdershins—is she the one who shows up on Hallo—I mean, Samhain?"

"Yep, that's her," confirmed the librarian.

"I don't suppose there's any way to talk to her now?"

The librarian shook her head. "I'm afraid not, unless you're an extremely good medium. She comes by when the walls between the worlds are thin, but from what I've heard, she doesn't take kindly to people disturbing her rest any other time of year. Legend says the last one who tried ended up in a coma for two weeks and had a full head of white hair for the rest of her life."

Vivian sat back down, resigned. The handwriting was indeed hard to make out, and Vivian quickly decided that this was not going to be the project she encouraged Aria to take on. She struggled through a description of the Working—a mix of archaic and technical terms that might as well have been in a foreign language for all she understood them. She also did not understand the description of why Mistress Widdershins knew the Working had worked, but she did seem very confident. Vivian had the mental image of a sharp-elbowed old lady with a gimlet glare that missed nothing.

The prophecy apparently happened two days later. Vivian got the impression Mistress Widdershins didn't think much of Minerva Vondelshank, but the description of Mistress Vondelshank's fit was suitably evocative. And there, inset like poetry, was her prophecy.

> Unbalanced, unpaid-for, unearned
> Our Claims on this Land shall be overturned
> With the Outsider comes Calamity
> An unnatural Shifting, unwanted Legacy
> Expectations dashed by the Work of Thieves
> Darting between the night-bound Trees
> Wolves howling the Echo of Forces awake'd
> Fate's thirst for vengeance finally slaked.
> A Gathering unroofed, a Shadow unbound
> A Storm unleashed on common Ground.
> One hope: then may come the wingèd Scholar
> Rising up from the Crowd and shredding the Storm
> Come, send him on and crown him with Laurel
> To restore the Balance and bestride the World.

Beneath it was the sketch of a symbol, a stylized eye in a stormcloud. Suitably ominous and inscrutable.

Well, that was overblown. And cryptic. But then, that was supposed to be part of prophecy, wasn't it? That kind of thing never made sense until after you already knew the answer, at least in stories. She rubbed her face, wondering once again how this had become her life. The idea that this shitty poetry could predict the future seemed ludicrous. Almost as ludicrous as her daughter growing fur on a regular basis.

But then, how much did it matter if she believed or not? Cecily and her friends did, and that was enough of a reason to try to understand how they might interpret this thing. It was hard enough to make small talk while waiting for Spell Scouts to be over if you weren't up on the right TV shows and the right town gossip. If she wanted to fit in, she needed to understand everyone's references.

Alright. If she had grown up here and completely bought into Vondelshank's legend, how would she be applying this thing to current circumstances? "Unroofed," if it was even a word, did sound a bit like what had happened in the auditorium—that must have been what set everybody off. If they'd grown up hearing this thing like a nursery rhyme, it was the kind of weird phrasing that would stick in one's mind. But the rest?

Unnatural shifting—well, as far as she was concerned, all shifting was unnatural. But it wouldn't resonate like that to people used to watching humans turn into seals or wolves or whatever on a regular basis. What would make it seem unnatural to them?

Her. She was unnatural, she suddenly realized. Or rather, she made Aria unnatural, at least from the reactions of everyone they met. A shifter child with mundane human parents.

No, she was being paranoid. The process, for lack of a better word, which had created Aria wasn't impossible, just disapproved of. It had happened before, and would surely happen again. She thought her daughter was special, the same as any parent, but not prophecy-special. That prophecy had been around for hundreds of years without being fulfilled, and might merely be the delusional ravings of a grieving woman who'd had too little sleep. Deciding it had anything to do with her and her daughter on the basis of one or two words was sheer hubris.

Then it kept going. Doom, doom, Chosen One, save the world. Of course the wolf was the bad guy. She rubbed her face. The big question was, how many people took this seriously?

She wasn't sure what the policy was on copies. Photocopiers could damage old manuscripts, she knew. And there were copyright issues with photos. But it wasn't like she was planning to publish it anywhere. She could type out the words, but didn't think she'd do a very good job drawing that stormcloud sigil. The librarian's back was to her, head bent, absorbed in a task. She slipped her phone out, made sure the sound was off, and snapped a quick picture of the page. She then sat for another five minutes, gently leafing through the diary, but didn't find anything else useful. She resisted the urge to check over her shoulder. There was no reason to think that reading this was enough on its own to summon a mob with pitchforks. No one else was even here. But she couldn't shake the unsettled feeling. She thanked the librarian politely on the way out.

"Coming back?" the woman asked.

For a second, she panicked, and then remembered the school project she'd claimed. "I might try to steer her towards something else, if I can," she said.

"We've got some children's books on the founding of the town, if you want to go broader," the librarian offered. "And if she wants something mundane, we can always get it on an interlibrary loan. But it can take up to two weeks, so don't leave it too long!"

As she left, she thought about texting the photos to Daniel. But would it make sense on its own? He hadn't seen the dust drifting down from the hole in the roof, or felt the hairs rise on the back of his neck as the ghost spoke, or heard the anxious whispers of the other parents. He was going to see the bad poetry and he was going to crack a joke, and that's not what she needed right now. This wasn't something to be done by text.

There was time still to run errands, finish up a last bit of Christmas shopping. She'd ordered most of Aria's requested gifts online, but the shipping on a lot of the potential stocking stuffers was outrageous. She'd texted Moira to ask where she got her kids' stocking stuffers but Moira hadn't answered, and Vivian had wondered too late if they even celebrated Christmas. She stood in the aisle of the town candy store for a long time, missing the days of easy gifts like chocolate Santas and scented bath bombs. There were hard candies that promised to make your skin glow as you ate them, which sounded kind of awesome, but when she checked the packaging, they contained phoenix egg. Phoenix egg had not been on the list of tests they'd done at the allergist, but it sounded close enough to chicken egg that she didn't want to take the risk. She knew canines couldn't have peppermint, either, which ruled out half the aisle. The internet said marshmallows were also bad for dogs, but mostly based on the fact they contained too much sugar and no nutritional value. Which seemed equally true for humans, and that never stopped anyone. She grabbed a package of marshmallows shaped like snowmen and called it good enough. She wrapped it in an extra bag, and hoped Aria wouldn't be able to scent out the sugar.

When Vivian picked Aria up after school, she seemed subdued. "What's wrong, pumpkin?"

"Nothing," Aria said, staring out the window. But she shoved her bunny deep under the coat next to her on the back seat.

Vivian wanted to ask if the other kids had picked on her because of the rabbit. Because she had one, or because it had so obviously been destroyed so many times. She didn't want to suggest that there was something wrong with either thing. But before she could come up with the right phrasing, Aria cleared her throat.

"Mommy, is it too late to send a letter to Santa?" she asked, still looking out the window.

Vivian's stomach dropped out. All the presents were already purchased and wrapped. They only had a few days left before Christmas. What if she asked for something impossible to get in time? Maybe Daniel could get it on the way home from work. Except then he'd be late and miss bedtime again, and she knew how much that bothered him. He wouldn't complain, but she couldn't ask it of him.

What if Aria wanted something to replace the poor rabbit?

"I'm not sure, sweetie," she said cautiously. "We can try, if you promise not to get too disappointed if it turns out he's already loaded up his sleigh?"

"OK," she said, meeting Vivian's eyes in the rearview mirror.

When Vivian tried to turn down their street, though, Aria kicked the back of the seat in front of her. "Mommy! You promised!"

"I what?" Vivian asked, startled. "Don't kick the seat."

"You said I could write a letter!"

"And we can do that as soon as we get home, we'll be there in a minute."

"But it will be too late," Aria said, near tears. "We have to get to the post office right now. What if Santa is already loading his sleigh?"

If Aria had been yelling, Vivian would have lectured her on manners and patience. But the heartbroken note in her daughter's voice made her stop. She drove past their house and swung around the block. "All right. We'll go to the post office."

When they got there, Vivian rustled around in her purse and managed to produce a notepad that had been sent by the chupacabra conservation people. She handed it to Aria with a pen whose cap had disappeared months ago. "Do you need help with spelling?"

"I need privacy, Mommy," Aria said firmly. She painstakingly scrawled something down while Vivian tried to figure out a way to smuggle the note into her purse where she could read it. But Aria folded it into a tight little rectangle with ragged edges which she labeled with "Santa Claus, North Pole" and then popped her seatbelt and opened the car door.

"I can give it to them," she said stubbornly when Vivian tried to take the letter from her.

"They're going to need a stamp," Vivian said hopelessly, following her child's march up to the desk.

"Excuse me," Aria asked, carefully enunciating the way she did around adults when she wanted to get it perfect. "How much to send a letter to the North Pole?"

"Here, sweetie, I'll help you," Vivian tried to interject.

"I can do it, Mommy," Aria told her with some impatience. "How much, please?"

"Oh, postage to the North Pole is free, sweetheart," said the

East Asian man with kind eyes working the desk. Vivian wished he were a tiny bit less kind.

"Then please send this letter to Santa, first class," Aria said. "That means fastest, right?"

"As fast as it can go," the nice postal worker assured her.

Vivian looked at the letter with longing, but there was no way to intercept it and find out the contents. She'd have to tell her it must have been too late when whatever it was failed to show up under the tree. Maybe she should go ahead and get a new rabbit, just in case? But what if she were completely off base?

The postal worker smiled at her, and then took Aria's letter with great gravity. He tucked it under the counter. When Aria turned away, he winked at Vivian and patted his pocket ostentatiously.

She wasn't sure what he'd meant by that until she stepped outside and shoved her hand into the coat pocket for her keys. Next to her keys, paper crackled. It was folded into a thick rectangle with ragged edges. Aria's letter had appeared in Vivian's coat as if by magic. Or rather, by magic.

Vivian mentally bestowed all blessings upon the thoughtful postal worker.

She managed to wait until Aria was safely in bed before retrieving the crumpled paper from her pocket.

Dear Santa, it read in nearly illegible handwriting rife with misspellings. *I have been tried to be verry gud this yeer. For Crismas, I don't wanna be a weerwolf anymor. U can keepe my other pressnts if you need too. Pleese n thank u. Love, Aria.*

8

Jan 3 2:15 PM

We hope everyone had a meaningful Winter Break in whatever way feels personal to you! Sign-ups go live tomorrow for parent-teacher conferences. Please note that slots are first-come, first-serve and tend to fill up quickly. A reminder that hexing other parents' phones to protect your preferred slot, no matter how minor the hex, is STRICTLY forbidden.

"**A**ria," Ms. Immacolata said carefully, "is a very special child."

Vivian didn't need to ask what "special" meant in this context. She wanted to glance at Daniel but resisted. She wasn't entirely sure whether she was afraid he'd confirm his own despair in front of Ms. Immacolata or afraid he'd be annoyed at her for revealing her own despair, but she could add it to the simmering dread that seemed to lurk in her belly most of the time.

Aria hadn't complained when she woke up on Christmas morning still a werewolf. She'd started off subdued, although she had perked up a bit after opening a few of her presents. Vivian and Daniel had buzzed around in a state of forced jollity. Vivian had been torn between confessing she'd read her note so she could comfort her directly or at least pretending to respect her privacy. She'd finally settled on asking whether Aria liked the stuffed rabbit dressed like a princess that "Santa" had left her.

"Oh, she's pretty," Aria had said. "It wasn't what I asked for, but I asked too late. It's OK. It's my fault. Don't feel bad, Mommy."

And Vivian's heart had broken again.

"She's doing very well in Practical Life," Ms. Immacolata continued. Ms. Genevieve nodded along. Having the head of school sit in was not helping quell Vivian's roiling stomach. "She particularly likes the food preparation works, and she is very thoughtful in sharing her apple slices with her classmates. Her writing is excellent and she is also progressing nicely in her reading skills. I've arranged with the lower elementary teachers to borrow some of their books so she can continue at her own pace."

"That's great!" Daniel said, a shade too heartily. His knees came up close to his chin as he perched on one of the child-sized toadstool seats they'd been offered. Vivian could already feel her back complaining. The classroom was incredibly welcoming for five-year-olds: themed like a forest floor, with thick moss for the circle-time carpet and trailing vines half hiding a cozy reading nook. Benches and tables came up to Vivian's shins, a perfect invitation for children to sit and adults to get kneecapped.

"She's still struggling a little with some of her spellcasting works. I'd like to ask you to spend a little more time at home on ritual dagger work; five minutes two or three times a week is age-appropriate, and would help greatly with catching up."

Vivian swallowed, her mouth dry. Aria had been increasingly

difficult to get out of the house in the morning. Maybe this was why. "I don't suppose you have any resources you can recommend? Or age-appropriate exercises we could use?"

Ms. Genevieve nodded minutely. That had clearly been the correct thing to say.

"Oh yes," the kindergarten teacher agreed, smiling. Her fangs were barely visible. "I'll send you some PDFs and a few suggested books."

Another thing to ask Moira where to buy. Another thing to buy. It was lovely how capitalism had permeated the magical community as thoroughly as the mundane. There was no parenting problem that couldn't be tackled by buying yet more stuff. But it wasn't as if Vivian herself had the slightest idea of how to practice ritual dagger work.

"Her math skills are also progressing with support, and she loves cultural works," Ms. Immacolata was saying.

Daniel's patience broke first. "And the 'but'? I know there's a 'but.'"

Ms. Genevieve inserted herself. She showed no trace of the brittleness Vivian had seen when facing down the Parent Advisory Council. Vivian and Daniel were no threat to her. Vivian bit her tongue. "There is no 'but' on children's development, only 'ands.' We are very proud of her growing skills."

Daniel inhaled sharply through his nose and blew it out. He put on a "I am being very reasonable" tone which fooled no one. "All right. What is the 'and'?"

Ms. Immacolata continued serenely. "Some of the areas that she is working on include, of course, finer control over her shapeshifting. In addition, she is working on not disrupting other students' work in the classroom, as well as managing her emotions."

By which she meant Aria was frequently losing her temper and wolfing out, and it was bothering the other kids and making a nuisance.

"I also have some concerns about her ability to respect classroom materials," Ms. Immacolata continued. Vivian wasn't sure what that meant—was she destroying things? She appreciated how the school was trying to be gentle and non-accusatory with their language, but she wished they would come out and say what they meant. "Since there are some friends she's having trouble working with productively, we're gently guiding her to choosing her work partners from a smaller pool of friends who collectively create a less volatile dynamic."

"Wait, who is she having problems with?" Daniel asked.

"I hope you'll understand that we need to respect the privacy of all our students," Ms. Genevieve said.

"Now how is that—"

Vivian put her foot on top of his and applied gentle pressure. He subsided but gave her an annoyed look.

"Is there anything we can do at home?" Vivian asked instead.

"Meditation has been proven to have some effects on children's abilities to self-regulate," the vampire replied. "If she continues to struggle, it may be worth having her evaluated for additional intervention."

"Like therapy? Medication?" Was this just part of the wolf thing, or additional developmental issues?

"Both could be options," Ms. Immacolata said. "The school counselor has a sanctuary space where she can calm down on stressful days, and class safety protocols ensure she cannot cause serious harm in class. But additional work with a specialist in shifting may be effective."

"How will this affect her ability to stay at the school?" Vivian asked. Maybe she could get special accommodations for the testing.

Vivian did not miss the tiny glance the vampire gave Ms. Genevieve before answering. "Early interventions could have a strong impact on her comfort level and her relationships with her peers. But it's only tangentially a factor in whether she can matriculate."

"So you mean getting her therapy can help keep you from kicking her out for upsetting the other students, but there are no accommodations for it in the high-stakes testing," Daniel said bluntly.

"I know how much anxiety this produces," Ms. Immacolata said gently. "Your daughter is a wonderful child and an important part of our community. I want to help her feel increasing confidence and mastery of her special abilities, and I do believe she can succeed. Unfortunately, though, the rules for testing are set at the Council level and we must work within those frameworks."

Vivian could feel Daniel nearly vibrating with rage next to her. She had to get them out of here before he said something regrettable. "Thank you so much for your feedback. Please do send me those resources."

"You have got to be kidding me!" Daniel exploded as soon as they stepped into the parking lot behind the school. The back was significantly less imposing than the front—a later extension tacked on in orange brick and concrete. They'd had to be buzzed in from a buzzer that used a scrying spell instead of a camera but otherwise reminded Vivian of every other institutional front desk she'd ever dealt with.

Apparently one needed either a luck spell or a time-pause spell to manage one of the appointments that wasn't in the middle of the workday. Daniel had managed to move a few meetings to be able to get to make 11:05. Vivian had hoped to see Aria in the school environment, but it seemed they'd scheduled the conferences for when the kids were out of the classroom at music or movement class. "The other kids are picking on her and we're supposed to shell out even more money for more of their useless lessons?"

"Where did you get the idea other kids were picking on her?"

"Volatile dynamic? She's getting in fights, Viv."

"Yeah, I got the fights part," she snapped back. "She's disrupting the classroom. And probably breaking parts of it."

"Probably because people are picking on her for being different."

"This isn't about your childhood, Daniel," she rounded on him. "She growled and snapped at the last playdate. Snapped! No wonder the other kids don't want to work with her."

"So you're saying this is all her fault?"

"No! She's five. She's a little kid. But we have to do something now, before it gets worse and before they kick her out of the school. And you heard Ms. Immacolata—she thinks Aria's going to fail the Trials."

"What's your plan then?"

Vivian took a breath. "I think we should talk to Moira's consultant."

"The kindergarten consultant? Are you joking?"

"Look, I agree it's ridiculous, OK? I hate this, too! But I'm running out of ideas!"

"Fine. You know what? Fine." Daniel pinched the bridge of his nose. "Fine. We'll talk to the consultant."

"Fine." Vivian pulled out her phone, but something flashed

in the corner of her eye. She turned. A blue light protruding from the ugly brick that she hadn't noticed before was silently blinking.

"Oh my god." For a second, she was rooted to the spot.

"I said fine, OK?" Daniel was turned towards the parking lot.

"Daniel! Is that an active shooter alarm?"

He turned and his eyes widened. "Jesus Christ. Aria!"

They dashed back towards the glass school door. When Vivian reached for the handle though, her hand hit a barrier. The air glittered in front of her, and her palm felt like she had shoved it into a pan of soda, all tiny fizzy bubbles.

Daniel scrabbled desperately at the door.

"It's warded!" she cried.

He ignored her, pounding on the ward with his flat palm. "Aria!" With each strike, the door shimmered.

Vivian fumbled in her purse for her butterknife. She tried the opening spell. Nothing happened. She wasn't sure if she hadn't done it right, or if it only worked on the secret alley in town.

Daniel was still pounding on the door. Inside, no one was visible in the hallway, not even at the now-empty front office. They must be locked down in the classrooms—that's what they did these days, wasn't it? Shelter in place? Vivian wished desperately she'd asked more about active shooter protocols. She'd thought that, at least, was something they had left behind in the mundane world. Why was she so naive?

Her left palm buzzed, totally unlike the sensation from the ward. She realized she was still holding her phone and glanced at it by reflex.

INCURSION ALERT
INCURSION ALERT

The school is currently experiencing an interdimensional incursion and is in lockdown. Authorities have been notified. We will continue to update you as the situation evolves.

"What the hell is an incursion?" Vivian demanded to her phone. It was vibrating constantly now as the WhatsApp group exploded.

Cecily Dragonsbane
What's going on?

💀🎣🔍🎪🚀 Sil
Is it demons again?

Henry Alfson
Relax, the 8th graders prob summoned an imp or something

TomandLarryandKirrikpt
Easy for you to say HENRY your kid's fucking indestructable

Dr. Vienetta Lickstottle-Pratt, Ph.D
This never used to happen when Banderbridge was in charge

Vienetta'sAPrat
Are you kidding? When my eldest was there, we had an OGRE

> **Priya**🦉
> Why isn't anyone scrying in?!?!?

> **MoiraTheSeaQueen**
> Wards are up, I keep getting a bounceback

> **Dr. Vienetta Lickstottle-Pratt, Ph.D**
> This is why we need armed Shadow
> Council Wardens on campus!

Daniel abandoned the door as hopeless and sprinted for a window whose blinds were closed. But it would be no better. It had the same faint sheen she now noticed on the warded door. Vivian fumbled at her phone, frantic.

We're at the school for conferences, she typed. *We're right outside the door but it's warded. What do we do?*

The answers came back thick and fast and useless.

> **TomandLarryandKirrikpt**
> Throw up a beacon, I'll bypass the
> secondaries

> **Captain Ewan** 🌊
> Minzler's interdimensional window
> 3rd class

> **Wenjun Chan**
> If you're physically touching the school
> wards, you can probably tap in with a
> basic scrying spell

~K

Ewan they're mundane humans
they're not casting fucking Minzlers

Her phone rang. It was Steve.

"Where are you?" His voice was tight.

"The main entrance," she said. Daniel jumped and managed to lever himself up on a windowsill. The window glittered where his hand struck it.

"OK, what can you see in the hall?"

"Nothing, I mean, I can see, but there's nothing there." It was eerie, seeing it so empty. The lockers were dark wood instead of the cheap metal she'd grown up with, but they had the same paper hearts, notes, and stickers taped to them any kid might use to personalize their space, if kids' drawings could dance and wave on their own. You weren't supposed to have paper hearts and potential bloodshed in the same place.

"That's good, they're all in lockdown. Stay calm, there's a team on the way. Just keep talking to me, OK?" He was doing his best 911 operator impression, but she could hear the worry leaking through. The twins were in there, too. "The staff know what they're doing. It's going to be OK."

The phone went silent, the expectant silence of a muted line. Then he was back. "Hey. The team's inside. Can you go to the front gate?"

"I'm not leaving until I see Aria," she said, knowing she was being stubborn, maybe even stupidly so. But she was here and he was not.

"OK, OK, let me know if anything changes. Do you hear anything?"

She shook her head. Then stopped. "Wait. Yes. Something—is that howling? Aria!"

"You can hear—fuck, which entrance?"

"What do you mean? The place you go in next to the parking lot, with the front desk and the visitor book!" But only as she said it did she remember the big ceremonial double door with the wrought iron and stained glass, facing the road from the pretty Gothic side of the building. She'd never seen anyone come in or out of it: there wasn't even a path; someone had told her the doors only even opened on ceremonial days. But no, of course, to someone who'd graduated from this school, that would be the entrance, this was the back door.

Steve was talking to someone, muffled as if he had his hand over the phone mic. "—they can't go that way," he was saying, "they're right in the path. No, don't let the wards down—"

Suddenly his voice was clear again. "Viv, I need you to run."

"What?" The shock in her voice caught Daniel's attention and he stopped scrabbling at the window.

"RUN!"

She looked up through the glass doors. The howling was growing louder. Suddenly, from around the corner, they charged. Sleek like greyhounds, but the size of Great Danes, the black dog-like creatures seemed made half of smoke. They tumbled over each other so she couldn't tell how many there were, snapping at their fellows with teeth the length of her fingers. Their eyes burned, literal flames embedded in their faces. Nightmares made half-flesh, they bayed as they ran.

"Run, Daniel!" she screamed, taking off.

He was right behind her, thank god. But so were the nightmare hounds. She fumbled for the keys to the car. Glanced behind her. They were squeezing through the front door, the wards vanishing to let them through and then reappearing behind them. Locking them out. With Vivian and Daniel.

They were never going to make it. They'd had to park on the far side of the lot. But there was a tree, a big one, in the median of the parking lot, and she had a sudden desperate idea.

"Give me a boost," she demanded as she reached the tree, gasping. The first branch was barely in reach, but the one after that was close above.

"You're kidding," Daniel said, but he glanced over his shoulder. The nightmare hounds had paused for a moment after being evicted from the school, but one was staring at them. It raised its head to the sky, bellowing out a cry more like a siren than a howl. The pack's heads swiveled to the Tanakas, frozen under the tree.

"Up you go," Daniel said, cupping his hands. She stepped into them and he heaved her up. She scrambled onto the branch and reached down for him.

The pack was already halfway across the parking lot. He grabbed her hands. One dog leapt up onto the hood of a car and bounded off, leaving gouges in the metal. Daniel's feet scrabbled at the trunk. The hounds closed in. One snapped at him, his pants tore and he cursed loudly. And then he was up.

They climbed higher, the pack milling around the tree, occasionally leaping up and snapping at them. Daniel's leg bled through the hole in his pants and he poked at the long scratch on his calf, wincing.

Her phone rang.

She tried to answer, her hands shaking. She fumbled and barely grabbed it before it slipped out of her reach. One of the hounds below growled.

"Vivian?" Steve sounded frantic. "Where are you? Is Daniel all right?"

"We're in the tree," she said. "In the parking lot. They're all around the bottom. What the hell are they?"

"Hellhounds," he said. It took her a second to realize he wasn't repeating the word back to her. "At least, they're pretty sure. They'll need a closer look to confirm."

Another hellhound made the leap, scrabbling at the bark of the tree before falling back down. She swallowed. "Can they climb?"

"No, you should be safe. Stay where you are. They're checking room by room to make sure all the kids are alright and that there aren't any more. You keep them focused on you, OK? Someone will be there in fifteen minutes or so."

"Fifteen *minutes*?" But he had already hung up.

Her phone continued to vibrate, the WhatsApp messages pouring in. People asking questions, giving more useless advice, demanding she track down their individual kids. A growing flame war between a few hysterical parents demanding that the entire administration be sacked and another group demanding that the first group go ahead and leave if they no longer wanted to be part of the community, with the occasional sardonic comment from one of the more blasé group members, which didn't help at all. A few people were bringing up the Reckoning again, trying to decide if hellhounds counted as *Wolves howling the Echo of Forces awake'd* or not. She muted the entire group. "I don't have time to deal with any of you right now," she told the phone.

"Are you fucking joking? We're not dealing with any of them, ever again," Daniel declared from his branch. "As soon as we get out of this tree, we're pulling Aria out of this school and putting the house on the market and getting out of this town as soon as physically possible."

"And then what?" She gestured too big and nearly fell, grabbing a branch barely in time.

"I don't know! Does it matter? Homeschooling or something."

"Easy for you to say," she countered.

"Easy? I just got bit by a hellhound!"

"Sure, but you're not the one who will have to do any of it."

"What do you mean, any of it? I'm her dad, I spent five *hours* last weekend throwing her a stick."

"Great, weekends. When she's not trying to do schooling. And what am I supposed to do about the whole wolf situation, hmm? Or the temper tantrums? You missed the one at the park on Tuesday, she tore a soccer ball to shreds. One of the other parents had to put her in a stasis field!"

"We do more of the meditation and the yoga. And the anger management book."

"You mean *I* do more of the meditation. I'm the one reading the stupid books, it's always me. You're not here!" One of the bigger hounds crouched and managed a majestic leap. It snapped an inch short of her shoe. "And you! Shut up!"

She dug through her purse, cursing, and pulled out the bag of Aria snacks. Granola bars rained down on unsuspecting hellhounds, to their confusion. Then she had a better idea, and pulled out the baggie of Ghirardelli squares she kept hidden for herself. "Smell that? Yeah? Go get it, you stupid dog."

Vivian flung the bag with all her might. It didn't go all that far; it was a baggie of chocolate squares, not a baseball. But a couple of the hellhounds scrambled after it and stopped jumping at the tree.

She glared at Daniel. "It's easy for you to say we'll try something else, when we both know I'm the one who will have to try it."

His shoulders slumped a little. "Viv…"

One of the hellhounds who had been scarfing up little chocolate squares shook its head uneasily, coughing. Then it turned and threw up all over the wheel of the neighboring car. The tire sagged and melted, steam rising from the puddle of rubber and vomit.

The new exciting smell got the pack's attention. Most left the tree to sniff at the vomit/rubber puddle. One started eating it.

Suddenly the pack all whipped their heads around, listening for something beyond human hearing. They howled and took off. A pinpoint of sparks whirled into a portal to somewhere that would have looked like a worst nightmare to someone a generation earlier. Vivian rather thought the scene needed a little more lava and a flying demon or two, then considered that CGI had spoiled her. The last hellhound dove through and the portal snapped shut, leaving a belch of brimstone in the thin winter air.

The ruined car sagged, paint blistered, puddle still steaming.

When a teacher had finally helped them down from the tree and escorted them back to the designated pick-up area, Daniel was still not speaking.

There were healers now, checking over classes as they stumbled into the parking lot. The younger kids all looked fine, if a little freaked out. Some of the middle schoolers looked more roughed up. Disheveled hair, some burns. One boy cradled his arm like it had been sprained or broken, and a healer hurried over towards him. She spotted Moira corralling Cara and Rory. Some of the other kids were giving high fives to Rory, who apparently had managed to fend off some of the hellhounds. Moira gave Vivian a tight nod and bundled her kids into the car.

Steve saw them from across the parking lot and gave them a wave, looking relieved. She managed a weak wave back. All she wanted right now was to get Aria, get her safely into bed, and then stare into the middle distance while clutching a tumbler of Scotch. Or maybe call Dr. Kumar for a refill on her Klonopin.

Aria, however, was anything but subdued. "Mommy, Mommy, Daddy, did you see the doggies? They were big and loud and stinky, and so so fast and I liked their eyes. Didn't you like their eyes? I want flamey eyes when I grow up!"

Vivian managed somehow to peel her arms from her daughter instead of clutching her to her chest for the rest of their lives like she wanted to. She got her buckled into her car seat while Aria told them every minute detail of the adventure, sufficiently jumbled up as to be completely incomprehensible. She talked about Ms. Immacolata and the Quiet Game they played in the storage closet and how Evander's hair smelled like the beach. She chattered all the way home, giving Vivian and Daniel an excellent reason not to speak.

"Let's get pizza, OK?" Daniel said. Vivian nodded, far too exhausted to even think about cooking. It was the third pizza night this week, but she didn't currently care.

"This is the best day *ever*," Aria declared.

Vivian and Daniel exchanged an incredulous glance. "Because of the pizza, honey?" she asked.

Aria looked at them like they were morons. "No," she said, her voice full of scorn. How could they miss something so obvious? "Because *this* time, when the monsters came, I got to be on the kids' side of the door."

Daniel looked almost as stricken as Vivian felt. His shoulders slumped again. "OK. We'll call the consultant."

9

"What you need," said Lemere, twirling an ebony wand between immaculately manicured fingers, "is the will to win."

"I'm sorry?" Vivian said, trying to be polite.

Silvius Lemere's Manhattan office gleamed like a postmodern work of art protected by dust-proofing spells. The doorman had not known who they were looking for until Vivian had produced the business card the consultant had overnighted to them. As soon as the doorman caught sight of it, his eyes glazed over and he mechanically pointed them to the second elevator bank that Vivian somehow had not noticed when they came in. The elevator had whisked them up with customary elevator efficiency, but the blond wood door had swung open before them without any sign of being touched, which was most certainly not customary in the offices Vivian had frequented before Aria's birth.

Being back in Manhattan was deeply strange. It had been so long since she'd been to any kind of professional meeting. Her shoes, which she used to be able to stand in for hours, pinched in a way that promised limping by the end of the train line.

Next to her, Daniel stiffened, but he kept his mouth shut.

"School admissions are a zero-sum game," Lemere said, leaning across the desk to tap the tip of his wand in front of them. She recognized his silver-streaked hair from the Talent Show and wondered exactly how many clients he had at Grimoire Grammar. Moira hadn't given her many details—it was clearly a sore topic, and Vivian didn't want to press too hard. "It's you versus the other parents. There are winners and there are losers. You want to be a winner."

"And the kids?" Vivian asked, her tone studiously neutral.

He leaned back again, shrugging. His silvery-gray suit had been tailored to a slim fit and moved with him. "Let's be honest, at this age, does it matter?"

Daniel snorted despite himself.

"Now," Lemere said. "You want to make sure your daughter matriculates to first grade. Fortunately, the standards are not, shall we say, as strict as they will be for high school and college admissions. It's about putting on an appearance of belonging and of potential. But mostly of belonging.

"For kindergartners, I offer two packages. With the basic package, I can coach your daughter on her Research Fair topic and drill her on Field Day techniques. On your side of the equation, I will help you structure your application essays."

"Application essays?" Vivian and Daniel exchanged a confused glance.

"Yes, I realize you've already done one round of these for kindergarten admissions, but the family does need to reapply at each level. The key, of course, is to preserve whatever spark caught the admissions officer's eye in the first place but to repackage it so it continues to stay fresh."

"We didn't do any essays," Daniel blurted.

"Really?" Lemere's eyebrows rose a fraction.

"Aria's a scholarship student," Vivian admitted.

"I see. But her patron isn't planning to help with the next step?" he guessed.

Vivian bit her lip. Mrs. Fairhair had said they were on their own.

"I see," he said again. "Well, in that case, you are more likely to be interested in the second package, which includes additional heavy coaching for the two of you. I can help create opportunities, shall we say, for you to interface with influential members of the board. Additional expenses will be your own, of course."

It took a moment for Vivian to process what he was saying. Bribes. He was demanding they pay him to set them up with a graceful way to bribe the school. He was convinced that the only way Aria had managed to be accepted in the first place was because Mrs. Fairhair had bribed someone, and the only way she could stay was for them to take up the bribery themselves. She felt a little dizzy. Even if she had wanted to bribe anyone, and as a former accountant the idea alone nearly gave her hives, she doubted they had anywhere near the amount of money it would take.

"I think the first package would be more appropriate," she said firmly. Lemere gave a tiny shrug. "When you say coaching on the Research Fair, what do you mean?"

"Well, we would study the list of topics that this year's judges have seen in the past, and how those topics rated. We would then choose one with a high chance of success that is appropriate to your child's background and the aptitudes she is expected to express. We would then guide her on completing the project in a satisfactory manner."

"You'd do the project for her, is what you're saying," Daniel said.

"That would, of course, be against school regulations," Lemere said, raising an elegant palm. "We merely provide guidance."

"I see," Daniel parroted back to him. "And how much would all this guidance cost?"

"This is a unique situation," Lemere said. "And it poses some special challenges."

He wrote something on a card and passed it over to them. Vivian managed to keep her face straight but Daniel made a little choking sound in the back of his throat. Even as she watched, the ink faded from view.

"We'll think about it," Vivian said. "Thank you for your time."

Lemere nodded. "Remember, the longer you leave this, the more effort it will take."

"I understand." She stood. Daniel followed her. They were silent all the way down the elevator and out onto the street.

She had expected Daniel to explode as soon as they exited the building, but he stayed quiet. She glanced at him in the corner of her eye as they walked. He opened his mouth and then closed it again.

"I don't think we should do it, either," she said.

"Oh thank god." Daniel's shoulders came down as he let out the breath. "We can't afford that. We just can't."

"And even if we could, I don't like it," she said. "If that's what it takes—you're right. If we have to pay that much to fake her belonging there, she doesn't belong there."

"I'm glad you finally agree."

His tone would have stopped her in her tracks, but her feet remembered city ways and only stumbled a bit. "What exactly is that supposed to mean?"

"What?" The slight condescension was still there. Like he was arguing with a teenager and glad they had finally accepted the logic that was there all along. "I said we agreed."

"You know what," she snapped. "'Finally'? Don't talk to me like I'm being unreasonable."

"I'm not talking to you like you're being unreasonable," he said in the painfully patient way one spoke to someone who was being unreasonable. "I just think maybe, being in town all the time, you need a little more perspective."

"A little more perspective?" Screw sidewalk rules. She stopped dead in the middle of foot traffic, invoking her right as a former New Yorker to, if she were going to block the sidewalk, at least provide street theater. She threw out her arms. "You get to keep your job, going into work in the city with all the normal adults, while I get marooned out in freaking Stepford with *your child,* and you're going to lecture me about perspective?"

"One of us has to keep bringing in money." His voice rose to match hers.

"Oh, because you were going to quit your job to deal with our special needs kid?"

"That's right, honey, you tell him!" called an older lady in a fabulous hat as she passed by.

Daniel flushed. He grabbed her arm, careful not to crush her elbow, but she could feel his hand shaking as he guided her back into the flow of foot traffic. "That's not fair. I offered to swap."

He had, after Aria's change. And she'd refused, saying it was because he made more than she would be able to if she went back. But mostly because it wasn't fair to ask him to clean up her messes, and here she was throwing that back in his face. She deflated. "I'm sorry."

"I'm sorry this was harder than we thought it would be." They walked half a block in silence. "What do you want to do now?"

"I think we should take the pack up on their offer for her to spend an afternoon or two a week with them," she said, swallowing.

"I am not sending my kid off to go fail at being something everyone else has been since birth," he bit off.

"But that's who she is now," Vivian said softly. "And we can't teach her how to be who she needs to be."

"She's only a little kid," Daniel said. And the despair and frustration in his eyes almost made her forgive him.

"What do you want to do?" she asked, trying to give him a window of his own.

"I think we should try the potions," he said.

"You're kidding, right?" She couldn't believe what she was

hearing. "Dose our kid with some random concoction of who knows what? And then what—how is she supposed to learn how to handle any of this if she's always got magic as a crutch? What if it's addictive? What if she isn't able to get it one day— it's not like you can get a refill at Walgreens—or there's some kind of weird side effect they haven't told us about?"

"I talked to Steve, and he sent me to Sasha," he pushed on. "She's a doctor *and* a mage."

"She's a surgeon. It's not the same as a psychiatrist."

"I know that," he said, rolling his eyes. Then he clearly realized what he'd done, and visibly forced himself into a calmer expression. "I know that. But she's at least aware of how magic and modern medicine interact. And she said that at this point, the pharmaceutical potion community has embraced very similar trial protocols as the mundane pharma folks, and that she could hook us up with a board-certified psychiatric mage. And the potions for this kind of thing are short-acting. If it goes badly, it'll be out of her system in a couple hours."

She closed her eyes. Focused on some of the exercises Dr. Kumar had recommended. Breathe in for four, breathe out for eight. Daniel could hear her doing it, which was its own kind of manipulation, showing this level of distress. She felt bad. But it was better than exploding at him. "OK. I'll make you a deal. We'll try them both. I'll set something up with the pack, and I'll talk to Sasha about her contact."

"Fine," he said with forced grace. "Enroll her in werewolf school. But if she comes home crying one single time, I'm pulling her out."

"Maybe it'll be less like lessons and more like a playdate," Vivian said, pulling out her phone to send Mrs. Fairhair a request for a meeting. The WhatsApp notification gleamed at her. Thirty-four messages. She let out a frustrated noise she hadn't meant to make, and Daniel looked over at her.

"What now?"

"It's the damn WhatsApp group," she said, flicking it open despite herself.

"What are they fussing about now? Did some parent decide some kid's unicorn hoodie was culturally offensive or something?" He forced humor into his tone.

She took it as the peace offering it was meant to be. "No, they're still debating over the hellhounds incident. Apparently the Shadow Council ruled that it was an unfortunate mishap with the eighth graders' summoning exercises, but some people now are demanding that the curriculum be changed, and others want armed Wardens in the school at all times, and someone suggested putting dimensional pocket doors in each classroom, only apparently that's very expensive. And there's a small group who are calling for Ms. Genevieve to resign, and one who called for her to be eaten, and I'm only about eighty percent sure that's a joke."

"All since last week?"

"No, this is since we got on the train," Vivian sighed. "It's been like this every day. Sometimes, when I hear the WhatsApp chime, I want to hurl my phone into the sun."

"You could, y'know, leave the chat." Grand Central was coming up. He would go back to work, in a place that made sense, and she would get on a train and go pick their daughter up and ask if the selkie sat with her at lunch today and if wand practice had gone any better. And ignore how the vampire across the street still yanked her window shades down whenever Vivian walked past her house, even at night. And deal with the latest incursion of the weird bat-like things, since somehow

178

Daniel never got home in time to change the traps, and they were starting to smell funny.

"I can't leave the chat," she said for the hundredth time. "Because it's the only way I know what's going on. And if something goes wrong, I need to be part of the community, not the outsider."

"We're never going to be part of the community," Daniel said. The look of pity in his eyes was even more infuriating than the frustration, because she couldn't say anything without feeling like a bitch. "I know you're trying really hard. Don't bash yourself bloody against their walls. They're not going to take them down, no matter how much time you spend reading beginner grimoires."

She hadn't told him about the lock spell. Now wasn't the time. "I need to go. I have to catch the train."

"Love you. I'll bring you some of those macarons you like, OK?"

She knew a bribe when she saw one. At least this was one they could afford.

10

Feb 3 9:43 AM
FYI: A case of fleas has been confirmed in Mandrake Room. All
students will be examined for fleas on Monday, and any student
showing symptoms WILL BE sent home. All fur must be flea-
free for three days before students may return to school.

"**D**o you feel that that has resolved the conflict?" Dr. Kumar asked in the friendly, mild tone that Vivian had learned always came before a question she didn't want to answer. "Or merely delayed it?"

"He thinks I'm too enmeshed in the whole parent association thing," she admitted. "I don't know, maybe he's right. The drama is completely insane. I mean, some of the issues are really, really serious, and some of them are completely trivial, but the level of conflict isn't that different."

"You were concerned that you and Daniel were fighting more often?"

"Ugh, I see the connection. Yes, we're fighting over stupid things because we're worried about the big things. But that doesn't help all that much. I can't tell people they need to stop arguing over whether the centerpieces at the gala should be floating candles or stationary candles." The floating bit had turned out to be in the air rather than in water, but the triviality stayed the same. "I need these people to like me."

"Need or want?"

"…both?" Vivian sighed. The degree to which her parents had instilled a pathological impulse towards people-pleasing was something they'd spent several sessions on. "I'm trying to make friends."

"Is perfection a requirement for friendship, do you think?"

For Cecily, certainly. Moira seemed to lean into the messiness. "I'm just… I'm trying so hard to build those roots. To fit in."

"Trying to build connections to a community is an admirable thing," Dr. Kumar said. "And so is trying to be a good mom. And to maintain connections to a heritage, and to take responsibilities you've taken on seriously. But I'm still hearing a lot of you doing the things you feel you have to do, and not a lot of doing things that you want to do. Or that bring you confidence. You are a very capable person—can you try to lean more into the things that make you feel capable? That bring you joy?"

It was something she was still mulling as she continued to plow through her endless to-do list over the course of the day. She sewed a patch where Aria had burned a hole through her skirt in potions work. She bought some apple cider vinegar because it was supposed to repel fleas and she never wanted to spend that much time with a flea comb again. She trimmed the rose bushes that had come with the house and kept trying to wrap around her arm and she didn't even like all that much, because the internet had said to do it in deep winter. She called the glamourist (because the traps weren't working on the bat-things and one of the other parents had suggested blocking the chimney with an illusion that it was bricked up) and arranged for him to come and quote. She picked up the flower arrangement she'd promised to bring in for Teacher Appreciation Day. She grabbed an extra pack of leggings for Cara when she got some for Aria at Costco, because Moira had said Cara liked Aria's and hinted that it would be nice if the girls could wear the same outfit on Thursday. No matter how much she did, there was always more to do, an endless fractal of work to make people think better of her, none of which particularly brought her joy.

What would make her feel competent? Aria being accepted into first grade, being accepted by her peers. But that wasn't her accomplishment, was it. She'd never meant to be one of those moms who lived entirely through their children. She still felt like the same person inside. But she could see how somehow, over the years, she'd stopped showing the Vivian part of herself to the world until only Mrs. Aria's Mommy was visible.

She'd been a good accountant once. Accountants weren't exactly superstars by nature, but she'd been good at it. Respected. She could at least get the Parent Advisory Council funds in order. She looked guiltily at the pile of receipts that had been sitting in a stack for months. There were always more urgent things. Not more important, merely more urgent. Was she avoiding it? Maybe. She didn't even want the damn rose bushes, despite their eagerness to be her friend.

She put on a pot of coffee, grabbed a couple of focus-infused sugar cubes she'd bought from the drugstore in the Village, and got to work.

Two hours later, she leaned back and drummed her fingers on her keyboard, lightly enough not to type, but enough to make the satisfying clicky noise. She'd gone through everything twice, and it still didn't add up. She'd found enough math errors to not think much of Adelaide, but she didn't think the math was the problem. There was too much money in the account. For a while. This time, she'd traced it all the way to the end of the year. And at the end of the year, the numbers were pretty close to what they should have been, with a difference she would not have professionally considered materially significant.

It was possible Adelaide had just been careless. Maybe she'd deposited a check that was meant for her personal account and then noticed a few months later. It would have been a big check, though. Jaw-dropping, to Vivian. And yet, it hid among the other big checks people seem to have deliberately contributed. Daniel made a lot of money, compared to a lot of the world, and they were nowhere near playing in the league they'd gotten drafted into. The idea of making a mistake this large was boggling. But she didn't know what was normal for Adelaide.

Maybe Ms. Genevieve would know. She wasn't headmistress at the time, but she'd worked for the school then. Vivian sent a request for a quick meeting. The reply was fast and friendly, an offer to chat after the next Parent Advisory Council meeting. That would have to do. Daniel had sent her some cute meme she didn't have time to look at, and she didn't have time to explain to him all the things she'd done and why that was why she couldn't look at the meme. For now, she was out of her precious personal time for the week, and it was time to pick Aria up and make another pathetic try at Spell Scouts.

Aria hadn't recovered her bounce when they pulled into the driveway of what Daniel had started calling Werewolf Manor.

"Do I have to go?" she whined. "I want to go home."

"We can't go home," Vivian said, trying for patience. "We told them we were coming."

Daniel glanced at her, clearly also wishing they could go home.

"Yes, we can." Aria stared out the window, a sullen expression on her face, making no move to unbuckle herself. "You could turn on the car and drive away. You just don't want to."

She did want to, very much. But that wouldn't be the right thing to do in the long run. "Sometimes we have to do things that are a little scary, sweetie." She paused. That wasn't the right approach. She tried again. "But I don't think this will be hard. I think you're going to have fun."

Daniel rallied. "Like getting a bunch of cousins. Some of your friends have cousins."

"Are there other kids?" Aria said, eyeing her suspiciously.

"Some older ones, I think?" Vivian wasn't actually sure.

"Then it's not going to be fun."

Was this so terrible an idea that everyone had to fight her on it? Maybe it was. Maybe she was the world's worst mom. A good mom never would have gotten into this situation. Anger at herself made her tone sharper than she'd meant it to be. "Young lady. Unbuckle that seatbelt and get out of the car."

Aria growled. But slowly started unbuckling the seatbelt.

"We'll get ice cream after," Daniel said. They'd gotten a lot of ice cream after skirmedge practices, and Vivian wondered exactly how bad the practices had been.

"You only have to try it once," Vivian said, doing her best to soften her voice. She already felt bad for snapping. But was it really so hard to get out of a damn car? "If you hate it, you don't have to do it again, I promise."

Aria glared at her. But released the seatbelt. And got out of the car. Steadily enough that Vivian couldn't accuse her of not obeying, but slowly enough it was completely clear it was under duress. Protest scuffing.

She kept that sullen expression all the way to the door. Frowned at the long-suffering butler who let them in and offered to take their coats. Scuffed her way down the parquet floor, which was scarred by claws. And continued to stare downward as they were led into a library full of werewolves.

Daniel laced his fingers with hers, trying to make it look casual. But she could bet his knuckles were white from how tightly he squeezed them. She wondered how badly they stank of anxiety.

For once, the Fairhairs were all in human form. Mrs. Fairhair sat properly, as did a dignified gentleman about her age. He had the look of an athlete succumbing to time—he still had the sinewy neck and muscles bunched beneath his sport coat, but his cheeks had begun to hollow out and age spotted his hands. The shock of thick white hair still looked like a pelt she could have run her hands through. She recognized him suddenly from the day on the trail. She'd met all of them before, technically. But for the life of her, all she could remember was Mrs. Fairhair.

The rest of the pack was a mix of well-toned middle-aged couples, young adults, and a few middle schoolers. The older members sat more comfortably on the worn chairs, their clothes the kind of worn classics that would have been composed of tweed a generation or two before. The younger generation sprawled across sofas or the floor, wearing more up-to-date fashions with a few sweatshirts from various prestigious colleges in the mix.

"Aria," Mrs. Fairhair said crisply but not unkindly, "I would like to introduce you to the pack."

Vivian noticed she and Daniel had not been addressed, but chose to stay by the door. If something went wrong, she would do her best to swoop in. Not that there would be much she could do. But she bit her lip, hoping that this would somehow go well.

Aria rubbed at the floor with her toe, not looking up. She looked very small in the giant library overfilled with people.

"This is Mr. Fairhair, my husband. This is my daughter Lillian and her husband Joshua; my daughter Lisbeth and her wife Astrid; and my son Fletcher and his wife Julieta."

The couples nodded, friendly. No one remarked on the fourth, missing son.

"Fiona and Jared are Lillian's children." The two looked like poster children for modern WASP-hood; athletic and open-faced, Jared with shining gold hair and Fiona with black, the spitting image of their grandparents.

"Lisbeth and Astrid's boys, Connor, Thomas, and Simon are over in the corner." That set reminded Vivian more of mismatched hunting dogs. Connor matched the Fairhair blond mold. Thomas, though, had fiery red hair and laughing eyes. Simon was Black, his curls cut close to his skull, his eyes a stunning green. None of them looked particularly like Astrid. They lay piled over each other like puppies, their limbs post-adolescent but not filled out to their adult weights yet.

"And finally, Rolando and Pilar belong to Fletcher and Julieta." These two she'd thought she'd seen at the middle school. Rolando grinned and Pilar gave a shy wave.

"That's a lot," Aria observed to the ground.

"I suppose it is," Mrs. Fairhair said seriously. "Most packs split off when the next generation have children. But the Fairhairs have always been a strong pack. We can trace our lineage back to King Harald, you know."

"And you're all werewolves like me?" Aria risked a glance up.

"All but Astrid," Mrs. Fairhair said. Vivian caught her breath. Another human? Maybe she could fit into this family along with Aria, somehow? "She's a Jöfurr, a boar-shifter—well, sow in her case. And Thomas is a fox, but they're cousins to wolves." Never mind.

Aria cocked her head. "You're all related, but you don't all look like each other."

Vivian flushed, mortified. "Aria—"

"No, it's all right," Mr. Fairhair said, holding up a hand. "Thomas and Simon are adopted; Lisbeth and Astrid took them in as cubs when they needed a home."

Aria sucked in a breath. "Thank you, I want to go home now."

"Aria, we just got here," Vivian protested. Aria marched past her, grabbing her hand and doing her best to haul her along.

"No, I want to go home."

"But—"

"If she wants to go…" Daniel hissed at her.

"Hey, Aria," piped up Simon from the floor. "Are you scared we're going to adopt you, too?"

Aria froze, facing the door. She mutely nodded.

Mrs. Fairhair walked around to face Aria and knelt. She said with surprising gentleness, "Not all packs are related. Sometimes lone wolves join a pack by themselves. We don't have anyone like that right now, but we could. Being a lone wolf is very lonely."

"I'm not lonely," Aria insisted, clinging to Vivian's and Daniel's hands. "I have Mommy. And Daddy."

"That's all right, dear. You'll still have Mommy and Daddy. You'll just have us, too."

Aria glared at her suspiciously. "Promise?"

The wolf pack matriarch nodded. "I promise."

"And you'll help me stop wolfing so much?"

"Young lady," Mrs. Fairhair said, very serious. "Your wolf form is not a thing to be ashamed of. It's part of you, and you are a wonderful young person in both your human and wolf forms. What we will teach you is how to choose which form you want to be in, and when. And how to be proud of your wolf gifts, not ashamed of them."

Vivian's eyes smarted. She hadn't meant to make Aria feel like she was a bad kid. She hadn't thought of it as a gift at all, rather as something standing in the way of her learning how to use her gifts. But that wasn't true, was it? Mrs. Fairhair's wolfishness wasn't a "but," it was an "and."

Next to her, Daniel sucked in a breath as he had a similar realization. They exchanged a glance, silently resolving to do better. He squeezed her hand, and she squeezed back.

"OK." Aria turned around. "But Mommy said that if I don't have fun, I don't have to come back."

"We'll have fun!" Thomas dug his way out from under his brothers. "Do you like skirmedge?"

Aria looked back at the floor. "I'm not very good at it."

"That's OK, Fiona and I are *great* at it. We'll teach you all the secrets."

Which is how Vivian ended up freezing in the camp chair Daniel kept in the trunk.

Across the field, the older wolves chased each other in a

complicated pattern: some kind of exercise or dance. Aria bounded after them, tail high, tripping over her own paws in enthusiasm. Vivian had no idea whether she was doing well or not.

She could have dropped Aria off, of course. Mrs. Fairhair had broadly hinted it would be a good idea to do so. Leave Aria, come back in an hour. Spend the time in a nice snug coffee shop with a book whose pages she would be able to turn because her fingers hadn't frozen into blocks of ice. But it felt like bad parenting. She was monitoring the situation. She was being supportive. Aria might need her. She wouldn't have dropped her off for Gymboree at this age. Would she? So much of parenting was surreptitiously watching the other parents around you and trying to decide whether you were being normal. And there wasn't anyone else to watch.

Daniel had hung around for a bit, trying to explain the rules to her, but she'd finally sent him off to do the grocery shopping. They didn't both need to be here. He'd escaped with some relief, after setting up the chair for her. He spent enough time watching people chasing a spiky ball in the bitter cold.

Mrs. Fairhair appeared at her elbow, startling her. No one should be able to move across a field that quietly, even in sensible leather shoes.

"You could come inside, at least," she said. "We're not going to kidnap her. The youngsters might play a little rough, but their parents all have plenty of experience raising cubs. She'll be fine."

"I'm all right," Vivian insisted, despite her toes' reports to the contrary. They watched the wolves—mostly gray, with bits of brown and black and one striking red fox darting between their paws. "Thank you."

"We would never leave a cub on her own," Mrs. Fairhair said, slightly affronted.

"I meant for promising not to take her," Vivian said quietly.

"Well," said Mrs. Fairhair. "I can't say that she wouldn't be better off. But she is your cub, even if your pack is not quite suited to her. Astrid does well enough, I suppose, and Thomas."

"She is my pack," Vivian said, her ears warming slightly. "Her and Daniel. That's it."

"That's it?" Mrs. Fairhair gave her a startled glance. "The three of you? What about—I apologize. It's not my business."

"Daniel's parents are dead," Vivian said. "His dad when he was a baby, his mom right after Aria was born. And mine—mine are unsuitable. For children of any kind."

"I see." The older woman paused. Vivian braced herself for the condescending lecture on the importance of family that always came whenever she confessed the estrangement. "Well, in that case, perhaps we ought to adopt all three of you."

Vivian threw her a startled glance. She was smiling wryly. Vivian tentatively smiled back. "I don't think Daniel would be too happy about that."

"Men don't always make the family decisions, my dear, but I suppose it's important to let them feel heard."

Vivian chuckled. "I'll admit, your pack isn't quite what I was expecting."

"I should think not," Mrs. Fairhair said soberly.

For a moment, they sat in silence, each remembering how they had met. The younger wolves played, so different from the ruthless seriousness of the hunting pack.

"That wasn't what I meant," Vivian finally said.

"I'm glad," said Mrs. Fairhair. And then with a deliberately lighter tone, she added, "I can only imagine what horrible notions you brought from the mundane world. Some of your researchers got the most ridiculous ideas about wolf packs from terrible science back in the 1960s, and now look."

"So neither you nor Mr. Fairhair are the alpha wolf?" she asked hesitantly.

"Moon's sake, child. For one thing, canid shifters are *not* actually wolves. It's like trying to predict human behavior based on monkeys. And for another, real wolf packs are mostly families. The couple in charge aren't leading because of some mysterious alpha-ness, it's because they're the *parents*."

"So they all follow you because…"

"Because I'm their *grandmother*." She sniffed.

"And because you're terrifying."

"Well, naturally." Her mouth stayed firm but her eyes glinted with humor. "The two are not mutually exclusive, and as far as I'm concerned, should go together."

"There are a lot of human books you really should not read," Vivian finally managed.

"Don't I know it," she sighed. "Pilar loves them. She likes to read me passages just to see my hackles rise. And I let them rise because she loves it so, and because if you aren't allowed to spoil your grandchildren a bit, what is the point? Still, I feel like I may have brought it on myself for laughing at the mages when those boy-wizard books came out."

Aria came bounding over. She shook herself like she was going to turn human right there in the frigid field with no clothes. Mrs. Fairhair gave her a Look. Aria's tail lowered. Vivian held up her robe, and she practically leapt into it, wrapping it around herself with newly human fingers. She ended up in Vivian's lap.

"OK, love." Vivian laughed. "I don't think the chair can hold the both of us for long. Did you have a good time?"

"Yes!" Aria leaned in, almost lapped at Vivian's face, and turned it into a kiss just in time. Mrs. Fairhair humphed. "Can we come back tomorrow?"

"Tomorrow we need to work on your Research Fair project. But we can come back on Tuesday."

"Oh!" Aria jumped up, knocking both of them over. She scrambled to her feet while Vivian struggled to disentangle herself from the chair. "I had an idea! Simon said that he knew I was scared because my smell changed. And when he said it, I realized that I can smell it too, and I didn't used to be able to. I want to do my project on werewolf and human noses! Then you and Daddy can do it with me. Can we? Please?"

It was a perfect project. Focused on her strengths, but still something Vivian could help with. She'd come up with it all by herself. Or rather, all by herself with some inspiration from the pack. For the first time in a long time, Vivian felt hopeful.

11

Mar 1 4:52 PM

A reminder that necromancy is not an acceptable topic for the Research Fair and is restricted by Shadow Council guidelines to high school or older. If your child has planned a necromantic project, please contact your child's teacher immediately for help finding an alternate topic.

"I love how we always end up with the homework," Daniel grumbled.

"I think she's done a reasonably good job of putting this together herself," Vivian said, trying to figure out if the twenty-five dollar trifold presentation board was really better than the eleven-ninety-nine one. She added the cheaper one to the cart. "I should have ordered this stuff earlier."

"You've been reminding her to figure out what materials she needed every night at dinner for two weeks. I still think if the teachers care that much, they ought to be giving the kids a little more in the way of hints."

"Yes, well, I don't know what you expect me to do about that." She didn't like the sound of her own voice, but she'd caught herself using that tone more and more lately.

"I need to go, I'll miss my train." He paused. "You want to watch our show tonight? I'll make the popcorn."

"I can't," she said, with some regret. "It's the only time I've got this week to practice."

He made a face, the same way he always did when she mentioned trying to do magic.

"I have to go," he repeated, and pecked her on the cheek.

When Aria had first been born, even when they were exhausted, the morning kiss goodbye had been a luxuriant thing, full of promise. Vivian wasn't quite sure when that had stopped. She missed feeling like she could tell him anything. Or even feeling like she had time to tell him anything. Their lives had become so different, it felt like everything required so much backstory that it was easier to keep the conversation on pizza toppings and then collapse into bed.

"Is that my board?" Aria peered over her shoulder, pulling her attention back to the cart. "Is it going to be here in time? Why didn't you order it earlier?"

For all that the rows of trifold boards and dioramas were organized into neat formations, the full Research Fair was overwhelming.

Aria dragged them by the hand through the first rows too quickly for Vivian to see much. She would have liked to linger, if only to have a better idea what she would be in for should they make it to later years. She caught bits as they passed. Five identical miniature cauldrons issued different colored smoke. A diorama in a microwave box featured Barbies posed as if undertaking the town's Great Working, as described by Mistress

Widdershins. The runes covering a trifold twisted even as her eyes tried to scan them. A clock stuck out of a potato.

"Someone's parents phoned it in," Daniel muttered in her ear, and she stifled a giggle. She'd been so afraid they'd end up being the parents with the papier-mâché volcano.

"So are there science fair judges or something?" he asked. A tiny ghostly figure beat on the walls of the smoked glass cube as they passed. The cube was next to a papier-mâché volcano. Vivian breathed a sigh of relief. Her kid hadn't imprisoned a spirit in a homemade cell, but at least someone else was Volcano Mom.

From across the room, she saw Lemere surveying the layout, looking self-satisfied. She wondered how big a payday this one room was for the consultant. He slipped out without ever meeting her eye, job accomplished for the moment. She debated making a snarky comment to Daniel, and then chose the better part of valor.

"It's not a science fair, it's anything the kids wanted to research," Vivian reminded him instead. Again. No, that wasn't fair. He was the one who'd had to figure out how to apply the payment for Aria's potions against their deductible and call the plumber after Aria accidentally invited a water elemental to live in the tub, all while commuting every day. It wasn't his fault he couldn't stay on top of the school stuff too. "I don't think there's a judging panel or anything, I think the teachers grade their own class."

"Pity, 'cause Aria's project is definitely better than the potato clock," he said.

"But Elowen apparently taught that stupid glass snowman to dance," she said. All Aria had talked about for a week was the snowman.

"Sure, after you said Cecily had animated it. How hard could it be to teach it the 'Macarena'?" Daniel said, making a face. "It's like the Pinewood Derby from Boy Scouts all over again. You could always tell which dad had a workshop in the basement."

"Look, Mommy, Daddy! Here I am!" Aria dragged them over to her poster board proudly. Never mind that they had been the experimental subjects. Or that they had helped her figure out how to lay out her board. Or that, when she'd gone to turn off the lights last night, Vivian had noticed that the glue stick they'd used had failed and so had spent an extra forty minutes carefully gluing all the photos that had fallen off back onto the board.

"It looks wonderful, sweetheart!" A major key to supportive parenthood turned out to be the ability to fake enthusiasm on command. Although Aria had done an amazing job. She had carefully chosen three different scents—peppermint, coffee, and roadkill. (She had insisted on the roadkill. Vivian had insisted on doing the experiment outside the house.) She had marked a spot on the back patio with a piece of tape, and each experimental subject had stood on the X with their eyes closed ("No peeking, Daddy!"). Then the other parent would slowly walk closer from the other side of the yard with the sample until the subject could smell which it was. Finally, they measured the distance. Daniel and Vivian had represented humanity. Aria did her tests in both human and wolf form.

In wolf form, she could smell the roadkill from two doors down.

Vivian thought it was an impressive experiment for a kindergartner. She could think of all kinds of confounding variables, and the population size was obviously a major problem, but it was definitely an interesting question that had some relationship to Aria's unique talents. She was so damn proud of her girl. She wished there was some way to let people know that Aria came up with it on her own—it hadn't been Vivian or Daniel or some stupid consultant, it really was her. There wasn't a way to say that without accusing all the other kids of cheating, though, and she didn't imagine that would go over particularly well.

They had apparently learned about bar graphs in class, so Aria had insisted that her display had to include graphs. That part Vivian had helped with—there was no way a five-year-old was going to figure out how to do multi-variable bar charts on her own. Unless that counted as cheating? Where was the line? She'd done her best to take Aria's direction whenever possible, and had made her daughter draw them all herself. But everyone probably told themselves that. They all wanted the best for their kids, that's all. And the line seemed so very blurry sometimes.

Now that she was looking at the other boards, though, she wondered if maybe she should have given Aria more help. Her daughter's handwriting was atrocious. Vivian had thought that would be normal. She'd only known how to write for a year or so: of course her handwriting would be barely legible. But Elowen's could be easily deciphered and she had even got most of the punctuation correct. Cara's wasn't handwritten at all— Moira had let her type it and print it out. Or maybe Moira or Ewan had typed it and printed it out. It wasn't like anyone could tell. (Or maybe the teachers had spells for that kind of thing? She hoped they did.) Evander's baby thesis on bird identification and messenger spells was gorgeous—every one of his letters was painstakingly rounded, the product of still-developing motor skills but infinite patience. Aria did not have infinite patience. Aria did not have patience, full stop.

A swoop of black velvet caught her eye, and she chased Ms. Immacolata down.

"The kids did such a great job," Vivian said brightly.

"Indeed they have," the vampire responded with the serene smile of someone who has dealt with anxious parents for centuries.

Now that she had the kindergarten teacher's attention, she wasn't sure how to ask what she was dying to know. "Aria had a wonderful time working on her project."

Daniel jumped in, too. "So much fun. What did you think?"

It was a little more blunt than Vivian was going to go for, but she was grateful for him bringing it up.

"I'm glad she enjoyed it," Ms. Immacolata said, not answering. "We encourage our students to find work that they find satisfying."

"We haven't been to one of these before, and we weren't sure what was expected," Vivian hinted.

"We expect each child's project to reflect their own nature."

"Did she do well enough to stay in the school?" Daniel blurted. He was fidgeting with the pull of his zipper, which he only ever did when he was particularly nervous.

"The committee takes into account the growth of each child over the full year," Ms. Immacolata said gently, and Vivian realized that the teacher wasn't allowed to tell them whether Aria had passed or failed. She tried not to look crestfallen but swallowed harder than she'd meant to. Ms. Immacolata took pity. "You should be very proud of your daughter."

"We are," Vivian assured her fervently. Aria was watching the whole exchange. "We really are."

The teacher nodded and glided away.

"That's good, right?" Daniel muttered to Vivian. Fidget, fidget, fidget. "She meant Aria did OK?"

"I think so?" Vivian tried not to read too much into it, but she couldn't help the swell of hope. She thought Aria's project was amazing. Maybe the school agreed, for once? They shared a nervous smile.

"I'm going to go take a look at the older kids' experiments," Vivian said. If they were going to stay, next year would be easier if they had a better idea of what to expect.

"I want to see if Elowen will let me play with the snowman," Aria declared.

"Let's not play with anyone's displays until after the fair, OK?" Vivian said. "You know you'd be very upset if yours got messed up before it was over."

"Oh," Aria said, and pulled back the hand that had already been inching towards the snowman. "Maybe I better go somewhere else so I'm not tempted."

"Not tempted?" Daniel muttered under his breath. "Where did she learn that? What are they teaching them here?"

"She learned it from you," Vivian said, exasperated. "When you told her to back away from the stove last night when you were frying bacon."

Daniel did seem to have the situation under control, temptation or not. Vivian drifted up the aisle, pausing to see the jump in penmanship a year or two older. The younger kids' projects were simple, even if some of them involved dissolving eggshells in vinegar and some of them involved negotiating with brownies to have their rooms cleaned. But by the time she'd gotten to the middle schoolers, she was seriously intimidated. One kid had raised a firebird from the egg. Another had mapped out the history of teleportation spells and had drawn a timeline in sepia ink that scrolled itself across the board. (Apparently teleportation spells beyond a few feet had still not been normalized; the timeline included a number of impressively gruesome line drawings. The kid had real art skills and a taste like Edward Gorey.) She passed one kid and realized she recognized the girl who had caved in the roof. Krissy? Kassie? Something like that. Vivian had no idea what Kassie's project was about; the entire board was in a different language. When she surreptitiously aimed her phone at it, Google Translate's best guess was Sanskrit. Kassie's mom fussed over her, trying to adjust her daughter's hair, or the black candle in front of the board, while Kassie endured her mom's anxiety.

"Do you think the auditorium ceiling was an accident, with that one?" one parent was muttering to another as Vivian pressed by.

Given that the Shadow Council representatives had officially ruled the Talent Show incident an accident from too many interfering spells being cast repeatedly, Vivian had thought the matter closed. But then, when people got nervous, they looked for scapegoats and conspiracies. It didn't make her feel better knowing that the mages did the same.

"So it's definitely not the—"

The other parent cut them off before the first could finish. "Of course not. There would be other signs."

Signs of what? The only signs she'd heard anyone worrying about was the Reckoning thing, and surely if there had been additional signs of that, Cecily would have said something. She saw Moira and Rory and hurried over.

"Hi, Rory," she said, feeling slightly awkward. She knew how to talk to adults and how to talk to kindergartners, but middle schoolers were an entirely different realm. She hoped she figured it out before Aria was that age, but rather feared she wouldn't. "What did you do your project on?"

"The Reckoning," Rory muttered.

That again. Vivian was suddenly grateful that her comment to the librarian had been a ruse and that Aria had come up with her own project that had nothing to do with the Reckoning. She wouldn't have wanted to go up against a middle schooler. Or to draw more attention from the other parents.

She'd expected Moira to say something—maybe congratulate Aria on getting over another hurdle. But Moira gave her a tight smile and continued her conversation with another parent. Vivian flushed. Just because Moira was one of Vivian's few friends didn't make the reverse true. She was being clingy; she needed not to be so weird that Moira freaked out and pushed her away.

She examined the board to be polite. It was densely filled with what looked more like a term paper than a middle school project. She looked closer and realized that the bottom included a multi-page printout with an entire essay, stapled to the board. It seemed odd to Vivian that Rory would have chosen a topic Moira didn't seem to believe much in, but maybe that was why he was so awkward about it. Or maybe the awkwardness was because he was in middle school.

"Mommy, Daddy wants to know if you're ready to go yet," Aria announced, having wriggled through the crowd. Vivian envied her ability to dart through other people's personal space in a way an adult couldn't manage, and wished heartily she'd taken a few minutes longer to find her. She wanted a closer look at the project.

"Hold on a minute, sweetie, I wanted to see Cara's brother's project." She flashed a smile at Moira. Just taking a friendly interest. Not trying to learn more about the town bogeyman Moira thought was stupid, or trying to get more info on Vivian's own personal bogeyman: the school council's expectations.

The text was terribly dense. Vivian tried to skim it silently.

—but the last line is among the most controversial. The most logical interpretation is that only the coming and appropriate honoring of a promised one will be able to end the growing calamity which was foreseen by our ancestors. The word unmoored in the previous stanza is particularly interested in its nautical connotations—

"Mommy," Aria said in a stage whisper more than loud enough to be heard by everyone passing by. "Something smells funny again."

"Shh." Vivian blushed. "It's probably just someone's experiment. Please let Mommy finish reading this, OK?"

Moira had turned away and was chatting with someone else. She looked uncomfortable; her hands were clutched too tightly around her purse. Vivian wondered how much the consultant had cost. Moira didn't seem very confident about the result.

"But it smells like last time," Aria whined. "With the roof."

A few people gave her a nervous glance, including Kassie, who turned even paler under her foundation. Vivian patted her, trying to be reassuring while still reading.

—because the wing motif may have been chosen to contrast with that of the wolves. Whether this referred to literal or figurative wolves has been of some debate, especially within the cryptid community, as accusations of speciesism have been leveled against scholars in the past—

No way had Rory written that. She wondered again if the consultant took the poor kid into account at all, or if he just sent them a paper to print out.

Aria growled. Vivian looked away from the board. Aria was backing up, growling, her hair doing its best to rise like hackles. Some of the other adults had noticed and were giving Vivian disapproving looks.

"Aria," Vivian hissed. "What's the matter with you?"

Aria responded by changing right there, in the middle of the Research Fair.

"Aria Akiko Tanaka, you come here right this minute!" Vivian demanded. People were definitely watching now.

There was something weird about the shadows around Aria, but Vivian didn't have time to figure it out. She lunged for her daughter, but Aria sprang away. And then leapt up onto the table, knocking over Rory's display.

Vivian grabbed her cub with both arms, hauling her off the table as Aria whined and snapped. Vivian's ears burned. People were muttering. At first, Vivian thought they were complaining about Aria, but she realized with unease that other people weren't looking at her, they were looking around uncomfortably. Aria stopped barking and shivered in her arms. The shadows were shrinking, she suddenly understood. Like the sun rising towards high noon, only they were inside and there weren't any moving light sources.

She looked around at the other adults, who were shifting nervously. She had been focused on dragging Aria out in disgrace, but something else was happening besides her child melting down in public. One of the parents near her raised a hand in a gesture, starting to form the words of a spell.

Suddenly, the shadows raced back, flaring up from her feet. She leapt back, crashing into the table behind her. But her shadow continued to stretch, wavering like a banner in the wind, crawling up the wall. A whirlpool of overlapping grays reeled in shadows from all over the room, gaining mass with terrifying speed. For a moment, it coalesced into a symbol that looked vaguely familiar, a stormcloud around an eye. She recognized, with a start, the symbol from the prophecy. Then the shadows lifted off the surface of the wall, no longer a two-dimensional projection, the shadow mass somehow coalescing into a tangible object—no, a creature, whose features swirled, trying to break free. A snout took form, jaws dropping open. Eyes burned from within the shifting, billowing smoke. Deep in her ears, Vivian could feel the vibrations of a sound made without disturbing the air, a long, drawn-out howl that reached into the tiny, terrified mammal in the back of her brain. She was hunted. She was prey.

No, she was not going to fail Aria again. She fumbled the dagger out of her purse, losing her grip on her wriggling daughter. Around her, people panicked. Some crashed through tables, scattering experiments. Some threw up candy-colored bubbles of force, trying to protect themselves and their children. Several flung fireballs at the enormous shadow wolf that passed through the smoke that seethed back into the gaps. Vivian lunged at Aria, who stood with all four legs braced, hackles up, growling at the giant wolf looming over them all. She grabbed her daughter around her midsection, getting a tail in the face for her efforts. Aria tried to shrug her off, snapping at the shadow wolf. Vivian muscled her daughter behind her, fighting her own instincts to mindlessly flee. She waved the dagger frantically, trying to remember the words to a shield spell she'd never successfully cast.

Her dagger glowed, and for a moment she thought that the adrenaline had unlocked some hidden ability.

Instead, the light sputtered out in a shower of sparks, pathetic little stars that fell to the ground and glowed for a moment before snuffing themselves out.

The wolf, fully formed now, reared back. And then suddenly lunged. The last thing Vivian saw was a giant mouth full of teeth large enough to swallow her whole rushing straight at her. She closed her eyes and curled her body around Aria. Bitter cold sliced through her bones and a rush of air tore her hair loose from its ponytail. A jarring chord echoed over the sound of rushing wind.

She was screaming, she realized. She, and what sounded like half the people in the room. But a sore throat was not the sensation she had expected to be most powerful after having been eaten by a giant magical shadow wolf.

Cautiously, she opened her eyes. Her face was buried in Aria's fur. The lights were on. The shadow on the floor seemed normal, if untrustworthy. She lifted her head. The Research Fair was thoroughly trashed. But not any more than might have been caused by panicked mages. Tables lay upended, their contents strewn across the floor. The cinderblock walls of the auditorium sported a number of new holes punched by fireballs and lightning bolts. The shadow wolf had shrugged them off; the building, not so much.

To one side, she saw Evander, Raidne's kid. He stood defiantly, clutching his Elmo guitar, the source of the tinny power chord. One of his bird friends hopped tentatively out from his hair.

Closer stood Rory, eyes wide, holding his hands flared out in front of him, fingers spread wide like feathers.

She straightened painfully, her muscles confused why she would want them to relax when clearly they were about to be eaten. Aria looked around, equally confused. Her tail gave a half-hearted wag. Around them, everyone else slowly stood back up. Some of the kids burst into noisy tears. Some of the adults burst into noisy tears. Several of the kids seemed to be fine with the "giant shadow wolf tries to eat everyone" until they saw what had become of their projects, and then burst into noisy tears.

Daniel nearly tackled her with the force of his hug as he clambered over the upset table. Aria jumped up to lick his face, surprisingly resilient. Vivian ushered her family out, even as more official-looking mages pushed their way in, calling the increasingly familiar series of checks. Everyone looked shell-shocked. But she couldn't help but feel, as they pushed through to the exits, that far too many of them were looking at her and Aria and Evander and Rory. And while she heard the whispers of "winged scholar" for the two boys, it was the "wolves" and "night" and "unnatural" that kept catching her ear when they looked at Aria and her.

12

Mar 7 3:31 PM
Show and tell next week! Remember to write your child's
name clearly on any objects brought in. No cursed or culturally
insensitive objects, please.

Mar 7 3:33 PM
Living creatures do not count as objects.

Mar 7 3:36 PM
Unliving creatures also do not count as objects.

"All I'm saying is that if the wards can't keep our kids safe, then we're going to need stronger measures." It was at least the third time something to that effect had been said, mostly by parents whom Vivian had never seen at a meeting before, but all of whom she was starting to heartily dislike.

The Parent Advisory Council meeting had started with a presentation on the new security measures the school was taking. Ms. Genevieve had not yet managed to finish her presentation, forty-five minutes later.

"We are following all the protocols recommended by the Shadow Council," Ms. Genevieve repeated once more, tucking a loose hair back behind her ear. She was visibly starting to flag, but kept a polite, even tone. Vivian wanted to scream, and she wasn't even the one they were focused on. Mostly.

"What I want to know is if this town had a genuine Doom laid on it, why was it not classified properly as a cursed zone?" Madhuri demanded. "Our realtor didn't say anything about any Reckoning."

"That's because it's a myth," the mom with the doe head whose name Vivian had never caught called from the other side of the room.

"That sigil and the ghost wolf didn't look too fucking mythical to me," said a dad with a Bluetooth earpiece on his feathered ears, who was one of the new attendees. Three or four people glanced over at Vivian and then looked away before she could make eye contact.

It had been like that since she walked in the room. Since they'd left the Research Fair. Daniel had asked about the weird symbol. She'd mumbled something, not wanting him to make fun of her for believing in the prophecy doggerel. But she couldn't help pulling up her phone and staring at the photo of the sigil she'd taken in the library and wondering. She'd even texted Moira with a plausibly deniable "guess I should have read Rory's posterboard more carefully!" request for reassurance disguised as a joke that Moira had treated with all the gravity it deserved and ignored. Still, Vivian hadn't fully understood until she'd started getting hostile looks from other parents that she wasn't the only one wondering if the prophecy was somehow connected to Aria, though. She hadn't told her daughter anything yet—maybe it would all blow over soon.

But what if it didn't?

Kassie's mom spoke up. "We did a full seance last night, and there were no traces of spectral energy."

"Just because it's an echo from the past doesn't mean it's a ghost," someone else argued.

"We need to find the Winged Scholar," the Bluetooth dad started to say. Two or three others shouted him down.

"I know a lot of parents have been asking me about whether Banderbridge will be coming out of retirement," Cecily spoke up. "Surely in a crisis, it would make sense to have the most experienced leadership possible? Not that anyone thinks Ms. Genevieve is doing anything less than her best."

Ms. Genevieve's cool gaze had turned downright icy. "Professor Banderbridge will not be coming out of retirement," she said. "I can assure you that the current administration has everything well under control."

The meeting, at least, was not under control, and continued to simmer until Ms. Genevieve kicked them all out, a solid half hour after the scheduled finish.

She was pretty sure it wasn't just her imposter syndrome. People were giving her a wide berth as they filed out. She tried not to look like she was taking it personally while she fiddled with the tablet in her lap. She was supposed to talk to Ms. Genevieve about the discrepancies in the PAC accounts after the meeting. But her blood pressure felt so high she could hear it in her ears, and she couldn't imagine Ms. Genevieve felt much better. Vivian wasn't sure which she found more stressful—the thought that she'd moved her family to a cursed town and ended up in the middle of some insane multi-century prophecy that half the town seemed to blame her for, or the other parents bickering over safety measures.

Maybe accounting would be a good distraction?

She was here. She'd been avoiding dealing with this. She took a deep breath, and then another, waiting for the room to clear. Then she headed for Ms. Genevieve's office.

The headmistress was slumped at her desk, head down, poking at her phone. Vivian cleared her throat discreetly. Ms. Genevieve's shoulders snapped back into place, and she had her mask of cool competence back on by the time she'd looked up.

"I'm afraid anything else today will require an appointment," Ms. Genevieve began.

"I, uh, we had one? To talk about the gala finances?" Vivian held up the tablet, as if Ms. Genevieve could somehow see the files with it in sleep mode.

"Oh. Yes. Right," Ms. Genevieve said. "Come in."

The furniture in the office did not at all match Ms. Genevieve's customary twinsets. The heavy carved wood seemed more fitting for the velvet robe hanging on the ornate brass hat rack. It would take several strong men or a spell to get the furnishings out of the room, though, if the desk and chairs and bookcases could even fit through the doors. The delicate art prints on the walls, x-ray cross-sections of flowers, fit her better. A second glance showed that the wall behind had a slightly darker rectangle where a different frame must have hung for decades. The shelves and cabinets were full to bursting with old ledgers and yellowed pages. The surface of the desk was mercilessly bare except for a MacBook Pro, a silver mirror with an Art Deco frame, and the iPhone with a YouTube tab open to an analysis of last week's episode of *The Real Housewives of R'lyeh*. Ms. Genevieve quickly flipped the phone facedown.

"So about last year's gala," Vivian said, pretending not to have seen.

"It will be different without Banderbridge, I realize, but I assure you, I have it well in hand," Ms. Genevieve said tightly.

"I…" Vivian fumbled. "I wasn't here last year."

"Oh. Right." Ms. Genevieve softened a little.

"You've been getting a lot of that lately," Vivian ventured. She gave the headmistress a sympathetic smile.

For a moment, it looked like Ms. Genevieve would unbend a little. But then she stiffened again. "You said you had found a problem?"

Vivian sat gingerly, and pulled up the files. She walked through her findings, gaining confidence as she spoke. She'd been good at this once, including presenting results to clients. It was nice to do something where she didn't feel out of her depth.

She hadn't been sure how Ms. Genevieve would take the information. Surely she couldn't take it too personally—this had all happened on Banderbridge's watch. But she'd want to get to the bottom of it. It was a lot of money to have appeared and disappeared, and it would have had to pass through school coffers on its way out. "I'd like to take a look at the corresponding school records, if that would be all right," Vivian concluded. "If I could track down the matching deposits, then we could probably clear this right up."

"That won't be necessary." Ms. Genevieve's voice was as firm as when she'd responded to the concerned parents, but her eyes were distant. "I think we can consider this year to be a clean slate."

"But…" Vivian blinked. "I'm hoping there's a reasonable explanation for the discrepancies, but if there isn't, this could be evidence of fraud. Like, people going to jail levels of fraud."

"That's *enough*, Mrs. Tanaka," Ms. Genevieve replied, her tone sharp enough to make Vivian jump. "I realize that, given your background, you may feel that you have some, what is the phrase, fiduciary duty here. I assure you, that is not the case. If there was a problem, which there is not, it would be handled within the community. Do not concern yourself with last year's numbers. All you need to do is manage the funds from this year's gala with the accuracy and diligence you've displayed."

"Surely you—"

"Let it go." Her eyes narrowed.

Who would she even report this to? The feds? She'd already been warned to use an alternate zip code when filing FSA-dependent claims, as the school and its associated summer program didn't exist as far as the IRS was concerned. Someone on the mysterious Shadow Council? She nodded, uncertain.

Ms. Genevieve stood and Vivian found herself gently pushed out of the office by a pillow of air.

She tried to justify it to herself on the way to the car. Ms. Genevieve knew what she was doing. Vivian herself hadn't practiced accounting in years, although she'd kept renewing her CPA just in case. Of course Ms. Genevieve wouldn't trust her with school financial records. And with all these big fancy mages running hedge funds and tech companies, how could anyone hope to get away with a little embezzlement? Someone would have noticed. She wasn't responsible for any of it.

It wasn't true, though. People were people, even if they could cast fireballs. She'd lived here long enough to know that. And if she knew people, which she did, and she knew accounting, which she did, something here was rotten. Alongside the exploding auditorium and shadow wolf and prophecies.

But she didn't have the foggiest idea what to do about it.

∽

A few weeks ago, the class playdate had seemed like a wonderful idea. Cecily had found the venue, of course. Vivian hadn't even known that the local cafe had a back room with a treehouse-themed playroom and a miniature indoor waterfall. Then again, maybe two weeks ago, they didn't. Vivian had organized the potluck and wisely stuck to oatmeal bars this time.

Daniel had offered to take this one, but she'd looked at the RSVP list and none of the parents he liked were coming. He'd stand in a corner with his phone anyway, and someone needed to be out there showing that their family was friendly and harmless. She still hadn't brought up what she'd learned about the prophecy. She hadn't told him that people were starting to think it applied to Aria. She didn't want to worry him. She didn't want him to laugh at her. She didn't like what that said about where their marriage was at the moment, and she didn't want to think about that too hard.

Aria was glued to her leg. "Go play, sweetheart."

"Are Cara and Elowen here yet?" Aria asked.

"Well, Elowen's mommy is here, so she must be around here somewhere. But look, there's lots of kids here—why don't you go play with someone else for a while?"

"Cara and Elowen are my best friends," Aria insisted.

Vivian sighed, and went back to struggling with the lid on the homemade lumpia someone had brought. She'd tried to drift into a couple of the conversations between the various parents hanging around the food. It wasn't that anyone had blatantly turned their back on her. It's just that somehow their body language shifted to leave her out of the circle. Or rather, to keep Aria out of the circle. Everyone had half an eye on her child, and she didn't think it was because they were sizing her up for a playdate.

One of the other parents sighed and reached over, tracing a sigil on the lid. The lid obediently popped open. The mage never made eye contact with her.

"Sorry we're late!" Moira bustled over, dropping a bakery box with the other offerings. Vivian almost burst into tears of relief that someone would talk to her. Moira wasn't ignoring her texts because Aria had knocked over Rory's project, she was just busy. She still liked Vivian. Aria scampered after Cara. Maybe this wasn't going to be such a disaster after all.

Two minutes later, Aria was stomping off in a huff because she hadn't gotten her way. Vivian managed to derail the incipient tantrum before she could get wolf-y and got her turned back around. Rattled, she came back to Moira.

Moira took a good look at her. "You need some wine."

She poured them each a little plastic cup and steered them over to one of the conversation circles. Shoulders shifted to discourage Vivian from joining, and she almost backed out. Moira cheerfully barreled right in, asking direct questions and then relaying the conversation over to Vivian so the other parents had little choice but to include her. Even when she had to step out three times to help Aria remember to use her indoor voice, and her words, and not to throw blocks. And that was without any spectral disturbances.

Cecily stopped by as she made her social rounds. "Do you think we have enough forks?"

"They're in the white bag over by the bench." Cecily nodded and flashed her a smile, bustling off to keep the party running. But with the approval of the Queen Bee and the Party Girl bestowed upon her, the other parents noticeably thawed. When Moira moved on for a refill, no one shut Vivian out again. She breathed a sigh of relief, and gratitude.

She was almost starting to have a good time when she saw Aria off by herself, kicking at a fake root. She detangled herself from the conversation and went over to crouch down. "What's wrong, sunshine?"

Aria shook her head.

"Where are Cara and Elowen?"

Aria pointed mutely up at the little house half hidden in the branches of the fake tree near the back of the playroom.

"Why aren't you playing with them?"

"They said it's a mage game," Aria told the fake root.

"Ah." How was she supposed to handle this? On one hand, she wanted to stomp over there and demand that they choose something everyone could play. On the other, was it fair to demand that they never get to play the games they wanted to because Aria couldn't? And, as much as she loved her daughter, Aria was exhausting. Maybe the kids wanted some playtime that was a little less rough and tumble. Which was the lesson she was supposed to teach here? Self-assertion or resilience? How could Aria solve this problem on her own? "There are lots of other kids playing other games. Why don't you go play with some of them?"

"But Cara and Elowen are my *best* friends," Aria pleaded.

Privately, Vivian wasn't sure how good a friend either one was, if they kept leaving Aria out. But then again, their respective moms were the only ones standing between Vivian herself and total pariah-hood. Maybe Aria felt the same. She hadn't seen a parent actively drag their child away from Aria yet, but she couldn't help but notice that every time Aria got near someone else's kid, that parent started paying a lot more attention. Was Aria picking up on that?

"Maybe you can let them play that game for a few more

minutes, and then ask to play something else?" Vivian suggested helplessly.

Aria nodded, looking a little teary. But she didn't start to cry or sprout fur. Vivian went reluctantly back towards the grown-ups.

"Everything all right?" Moira asked.

"Cara and Elowen are playing some mage game and Aria feels left out," Vivian reported, half-hoping that Moira would swoop in and demand her daughter include Aria. She couldn't ask her for that, could she? There was only so much you could criticize someone else's parenting.

"Oof," Moira said sympathetically. "They'll work it out. Kids will be kids. Here, have another glass of wine."

She didn't want another glass of wine; she wanted Aria to play quietly with the other kids and the parents to be willing to let her. She'd been through this before: this place was supposed to be different. She wanted the knots in her shoulders that never seemed to dissipate to go away. She took the glass of wine, because that was what was on offer. Moira was trying to be nice. Vivian was already the town disaster—she might as well go full Wine Mom. Except she couldn't even drink this one, she had to drive Aria home later.

She drifted through, picking up snatches of conversation.

"...training for Field Day, but Carter hates running, he always ends up picking at the dandelions..."

"You know that skirt was enchanted, no one's butt does that naturally..."

"...two eggs, not one, but the real secret is pixie dust, it's got no carbs at all..."

"...part of the prophecy. Sure, she may have summoned the Reckoning, but that means the balance must be true, too, right? So we need to find the one who must be crowned."

The mention of the prophecy caught her attention, and she listened more closely.

"A Chosen One to rise in opposition is all well and good, but how are you supposed to recognize and crown them? It's not like there's a standardized test for that, they've tried."

"Look, we've got two professors and at least a handful of researchers in town. Any of them could be the scholar. But my money's on one of the kids. These kinds of things almost always turn out to be someone unproven."

"I think it's the siren's kid, what's his name, Evander? It's not just any scholar, it's the Winged Scholar. Kid has birds hanging off him half the time. And the family's so standoffish, they're almost never at these kinds of things. Who better to be a Chosen One than the kid of two immortals?"

"I dunno. Did you see the wing signs Moira's eldest did with his hands? I think it's way more likely that's what drove the shadow wolf off, not some toy guitar."

Vivian tried to pause unobtrusively, but the slightly pointed ears of the speaker must have caught her. Both parents glanced her way, and then pointedly turned their backs. Their heads bent towards each other, whispering, glancing at her. In fear?

Her ears burned hot. She'd read her share of fantasy novels. Like most kids, she'd pictured herself in the role of the Chosen One plenty of times. She hadn't given much thought to what it might be like to realize your kid wasn't the Chosen One. Worse, was the Unchosen One, the bad guy in the prophecy. Aria was special to her, of course, but Vivian knew she was just some kid, really. She got skinned knees and demanded to eat nothing but egg salad for a week and had trouble sleeping if Vivian didn't sing her the going-to-bed song. She wasn't some kind of mystical sign of the apocalypse. She wasn't a danger. Was she?

When Vivian had failed her daughter, had the stakes been even higher than she'd realized? She opened her mouth, uncertain what exactly she'd say—an apology? A plea for forgiveness, or for help? She never got the chance.

A familiar wail rose up from the other side of the room. Vivian dropped her cup and sprinted towards the sounds of Aria's distress as it shifted into a howl, first human-howl and then spiraling into wolf-howl. As she'd expected, Aria was sitting in a puddle of her own clothing, snout pointed to the ceiling. But instead of her usual bottlebrush of a tail, she sported the whippy spotted tail of a dog—a Dalmation or something. The spots went all the way up her short-haired haunches, with her fur only transitioning back to its normal thick pelt near her shoulders.

Two giggling heads peered through the doorway of the treehouse, and then slammed the door.

She wanted to yank open that door and demand to know what exactly those two little brats had done to her child, but she knelt down next to Aria instead. "It's all right, love. Your dress is fine; turn back for me, OK? Take a couple deep breaths like you've been practicing with Mrs. Fairhair."

Aria whined and buried her snout in Vivian's chest. But Vivian could hear her bringing her breathing back under control. At the tenth deep breath, Aria shivered in her arms, her skin rippling. Silently, Vivian blessed the invention of elastic. Smocking was wonderful for shapeshifters, it turned out, and so were skirts. She grabbed the scraps of bike shorts from the floor and shoved them into her purse. As long as Aria didn't turn any cartwheels, no problem.

Except there was a problem. Because as she looked up from the floor, she realized why Aria was so distressed in the first place. Sticking out from beneath the skirt was still a tail. Not Aria's proper wolf tail. A spotted, whippy, puppy dog tail.

"I want to go home," Aria whispered. The tail drooped between her legs, which were covered in short, spotted fur.

"What did they do?" Her head snapped towards the treehouse. Those little—her brain supplied several words which absolutely should not be applied to kindergartners, and yet.

She couldn't yell at them. It broke the parenting code. Which was stupid; she knew a generation or two ago people would have had no problem in disciplining someone else's child, but it was absolutely verboten now. She looked around frantically. Other people had noticed, and were whispering, but no one was screaming or anything. They looked mildly disapproving, not shocked. Was this normal? What was normal in this godforsaken community?

Someone muttered about "unnatural shifters" and the emotional temperature of the room plummeted fifty degrees.

What was she supposed to do? Yell at them that it was not her kid's fault, that she'd never even heard of the prophecy before moving here? Could she even be sure it was not their fault? Not in the sense that they'd done something deliberately, but that maybe somehow her half-wolf, half-dog mundane-born child had kicked off something merely by existing?

It was all too much. She had to stay focused on what she could do something about. There. Cecily and Moira were over near the dessert table. She marched over, clutching Aria's hand, frantically trying to decide how to play this. Righteous? Casual? She was angry enough to spit nails, but at the same time, the part of her head that sounded far too much like her mother's voice reminded her not to make a scene, that she needed these people.

"Cara and Elowen seem to have had a mishap," she said, choosing a neutral tone and hating herself for it.

"Oh, has Elowen been playing with transformation spells again?" Cecily seemed unconcerned.

Another dad, who Vivian vaguely recognized but couldn't name, glanced at the spotted tail sticking out from behind Vivian's legs, where Aria was huddled. "It'll dissipate on its own in an hour, maybe sooner."

"But—" Vivian started.

"You know kids," Moira said, and waggled a wine bottle invitingly.

She was going to punch her. No, she couldn't punch Moira, Moira was her only real friend here. Moira's kid was a brat. Who Aria loved, for some reason. But they'd hurt her child. Except no one seemed to think Aria had actually been hurt, this was normal. Normal or not, they had humiliated her child. But Vivian was trying to model keeping your temper, which Aria very much needed to learn. But you were also supposed to stick up for yourself. Only sticking up for Aria here would alienate everyone, and they needed these people to like them, because there was nowhere else for them to go. It didn't matter what she did, everyone was going to blame Aria anyway and then give Evander or Rory a crown or something. Vivian wavered, frozen with conflicting emotions.

There was another shriek, this one purely human.

Cara pushed past Vivian to bury her face in Moira's knees. "She tried to *bite* me!"

Vivian whirled, expecting to see Aria in wolf form once more, but she was entirely human save the doggy tail.

"She tried to pull my tail," Aria muttered.

"I think it's time to go home," Vivian said.

"That might be best," Cecily agreed, a bit frosty.

Other parents pulled their kids back as Vivian escorted Aria out the door.

Buckling Aria into her car seat in wolf form had given them both enough practice with dealing with tails that they could pretend nothing else was wrong. They drove home in silence. It gave her plenty of time to berate herself. She was a coward. She should have said something. Should have demanded that Cecily at least reverse the spell. That they make their kids behave. *You know kids?* Really? The tradeoff to helicopter-don't-mess-with-my-kids was supposed to be that the parents step in and stop the bullying. Wasn't it? Was she supposed to let a kindergartner transmogrify her child into a half-dog? Daniel was right, she was too much of a people-pleaser. She was a pushover. She was a terrible mother.

But what was she supposed to do? Forbid Aria to play with the kids she thought were her best friends? Blow up at the only other people who would give her the time of day, who didn't seem to think that she was personally responsible for triggering a calamity they all allegedly brought on themselves anyway?

People were supposed to be more understanding here. Only it turned out that the people here were still people, and people were shit.

Daniel did not help. He'd taken one look at Aria's pathetic little tail as she scuttled by to her room and rounded on Vivian. "What. The. Hell."

She'd needed a hug, and someone to tell her she wasn't the world's worst mom. All she was going to get was what the worst of the voices in her head had been telling her. Enough. "It'll wear off."

His jaw dropped. "Our daughter has a tail and all you're going to tell me is that it'll wear off?"

"She has a tail half the time, she's used to it."

"It's the wrong tail!" He rubbed his hand over his face. "Jesus. Listen to me."

"Look, things got out of hand with Cara and Elowen," she started.

"I don't want her around those two anymore," he snapped.

As if she hadn't already thought about that. "Oh, really? And who exactly do you expect her to play with then?"

"I don't know, any of the other kids there?"

"You don't understand," she said. He'd forgotten all about the prophecy, she knew; he hadn't seen how the other parents looked at Aria now. She opened her mouth to try to explain.

"I understand that you're too scared of not being liked to stand up to a bunch of bullies."

She sucked in a breath like she'd been punched. He immediately looked like he wanted to take it back.

"Look, Viv," he said, reaching for her.

She snapped. "Don't touch me." Her hand slashed out, almost of its own accord, forming the sign from the grimoire that she'd tried over and over without success.

His hand hit a sparkling barrier in the air.

"What the—" He froze in shock.

She covered her own shock with haughtiness, reveling in the feeling of being able to do something that he couldn't, of having the upper hand, for the first time in a very long time.

"What did you do?" he asked, taking a step back, and then another.

"I'm fitting in," she said.

His mouth tightened. "I don't recognize you anymore."

"Then keep up." She turned her back on him and went after Aria.

13

Apr 5 9:58AM
Don't forget to buy tickets to the Spring Gala. (We're still accepting donations for the Silent Auction, hint hint!) This year's proceeds will go to upgrading our interdimensional security systems, while 10% will be donated to the Chupacabra Conservation Society. Musical guests include Dio and the Bassarids, and refreshments will be provided by Fig & Walnut, Jenny's Falafel, the Red Cross, and Cupcakery! Tickets go on sale Monday.

She was as good as anyone here. She might have started out behind, but she was going to catch up. Vivian repeated it to herself, hoping she might eventually believe it. Fake it until you make it. It didn't matter what Daniel thought. Whatever it took to get through the school pick-up line.

As she neared the door, she took a breath. Catching Aria's eye, she waved her hand, praying the cantrip she'd been practicing would go off correctly. A purple wolf head burst in fireworks above her. It was small, no bigger than her fist, and kind of lopsided. But it was there.

Aria's eyes grew huge. "Mommy? Mommy, you did it!"

She dashed across the pavement and leapt into Vivian's arms. Vivian swung her around, bursting with pride. She had. She'd done it. It was a tiny thing, but she had done it.

Then she looked around at the shocked and appalled faces of the other parents and realized that maybe a wolf sigil had not been the best choice after the incident at the Research Fair. Her ears burned.

Aria hadn't noticed, though. "Mommy, Mommy, today was the best! We were practicing for Field Day, and guess what! There's going to be a skirmedge game! And guess what? The move the pack was teaching me really, really worked!"

"That's wonderful, sweetie!" Two victories, count them, two. She'd managed a piece of magic in front of the entire pick-up line and proved she wasn't a total outsider. Ignore the misstep, that was the key. And Aria was going to kick butt at Field Day. Who cared about her performance in the classroom? She would have good marks on at least two of the tests. Everything was going to be fine. Vivian and Daniel were barely speaking these days, but everything was going to be fine.

Aria had already moved on. She'd seen Cara across the parking lot. "Bye, Cara! Do you want to do a playdate?"

But Cara pointedly turned her back and climbed into the car without waving back.

"Oh." Aria shrank in on herself.

She had things she would rather do than try to make sense of some other kid's inexplicable impulses when she could barely understand those of her own, but she made the effort. "Sweetie, did something happen that upset Cara today?"

"She wasn't very good at skirmedge," Aria said slowly. "And she didn't like it."

Internally, Vivian winced, remembering how worried Moira had been before the Talent Show about Rory's performance. She couldn't imagine how stressful it must be to have two kids you had to worry about failing. "Well, sometimes when you're frustrated, you don't want to talk to anyone, either. But I'm sure it'll be OK, she still has time to practice."

Vivian had no idea if it was going to be OK, but she had become accustomed to how much of parenthood was pretending confidence.

It was only on the way out that she noticed the mark on the school lawn. Vivian recognized it from the book in the library. The eye in the stormcloud had been burned into the turf. She didn't remember it from yesterday—it had to have happened overnight. The groundskeeper had a bag of grass seed and a growth spell, and had managed to dig up a chunk of the lower corner, but the symbol was still easy to make out. She winced, thinking of the wolf sigil. How was she supposed to have known?

When she got to the car, a paper was tucked under the windshield wiper. She pulled it out and it stiffened in her hand. She dropped it but it flapped towards her face like a moth to a porch light. *GO HOME*, it read in big block letters. She batted it away and it disintegrated into ash.

"What was that, Mommy?" Aria asked, looking concerned.

"Just an ad," Vivian said. *Go home?* Veilport didn't feel much like a home, but neither did anywhere else. There was no home to go back to. She looked around, feeling paranoid, but all she saw were the same people she saw at pick-up every day, which made it all the worse.

Another hour and a half of running around with the pack and a skirmedge ball distracted Aria. Vivian was surprised to find Daniel's keys in the dish when they came in. He'd been working longer and longer hours. She was afraid it was to avoid her.

"I picked up Aria's potions," Daniel said before she could say anything about the note, setting out a wire rack with a month's worth of small glass vials. Vivian hadn't realized he even knew where the town pharmacy was.

"Oh!" Aria perked up. "Does this mean I won't turn into a wolf anymore?"

"Not entirely, pumpkin." Daniel ruffled her hair. "Just that you won't turn into one by accident quite as much."

"We hope," Vivian added. She didn't want Aria to get her hopes up too much. Or think it was her fault if it didn't work. She'd had enough trouble with that herself, with her own meds. "Sometimes it takes a little while to figure out the dosage, because everyone—"

"—is different," Aria finished with her, in a world-weary tone that promised extreme sass once she hit her teens.

"What did the pharma-mage say about side effects?"

"If she throws up or turns pale blue the first time, it should wear off in about twenty minutes. But if it happens the second, we should discontinue," he said, sharing a grimace with Vivian.

"I could turn blue?" Aria seemed delighted at the prospect.

"Not for long, sweetheart," Vivian told her. Aria pouted.

"And to watch for a loss of sleep or appetite, or an increase in irritability," Daniel continued.

"Is it going to taste bad?" Aria wrinkled her nose.

Daniel crouched down and wrinkled his nose back at her. "I don't know, I've never had a magic potion before. What do you think it will taste like? Pancakes? Old sour milk? Boogers?"

"Ewww! Not boogers!" Aria squealed.

"Well, let's find out," he said. "And as an incentive, I have a special surprise for a brave girl trying her first potion."

He produced a lollipop, but held it out of reach. "Uh uh, not until you've taken your potion. You have to drink the whole thing, remember. But if it's bad, you can have the lollipop right after."

Aria paused with the vial, looking at him suspiciously. "And if it's good?"

"You'll have the lollipop anyway." He winked.

Aria took a deep breath and then very dramatically sipped the world's tiniest sip of potion. Vivian and Daniel held their breaths. "It doesn't taste like anything," she complained.

"I guess potion technology has improved since the days of eyes of newt," Daniel murmured, and for a moment Vivian felt like they were back on the same team. She didn't have the heart to tell him that eye of newt was just a fancy term for mustard seeds. He said, louder, "Now finish the whole thing and you'll get your lollipop."

She did with a gulp. They all waited for a minute, silent. There was a remarkable lack of vomit or blue skin. Aria sighed, visibly disappointed.

"Why don't you go get your coloring book and come work here at the table where we can keep an eye on you?" Vivian suggested. Aria scampered off to her room.

"I'm going to turn blue as a blueberry," Vivian could hear her daughter announcing to her stuffed animals. She tried not to sigh.

"Oh, I forgot," she said to herself, texting Cecily.

"Forgot what?" Daniel asked.

"The decorating committee was going to put together centerpieces for the gala tomorrow night, but I don't know what time," she said. She could sense his disapproval, and the words kept coming out. "I know, I don't know how much I can help, it's not like I can enchant candles or anything, but I can bring some cookies and moral support."

"You know I wasn't going to criticize your lack of magic skills," he said dourly.

They'd argued twice in the last week about the misfires from her practice with the grimoire. She was getting results more often, although they often were not the results she was looking for. One of the misfires was a literal fire that had eaten half the kitchen curtains before she'd fumbled her way through the instructions on the fire extinguisher. He was convinced it was one of her spells that had summoned the flock of birds the previous week who had completely covered the car in bird shit. After the note under the wiper, she was starting to wonder if maybe someone else had hexed the car.

She lowered her voice. "Look, I'm not happy with Elowen either, but Aria loves her. Are you going to be the one to tell her she can't play with her best friend? Besides, Cecily's the only one still talking to me these days."

Her phone buzzed in her hand. She checked the message and sighed. "Apparently they had to reschedule and haven't set a new date. Although I don't know when they're going to fit it in, the gala's on Friday."

"Is this a semi-formal kind of thing? Black tie?"

"Umm…" She'd gone to all the trouble to order things, and suddenly realized she'd never brought him up to speed. Every time she tried to talk about stuff from the school, they ended up fighting. But when was the last time they'd talked about anything other than the school? "It's kind of a costume party."

His eyebrows went up. But before he could say anything, Aria jumped up, excited. "Mommy, Daddy, look! I'm blue!"

∽

"But you'll let me know if anything changes?" Vivian tried to brace the phone between her shoulder and her ear as she ironed. Cecily probably spelled the damn thing to stay in place. Or maybe Cecily simply didn't keep losing her earbuds. But she needed to get the wrinkles out so they didn't look like they'd thrown the costumes on right out of the package. Bad enough the costumes came from a package, instead of a trade with a local household spirit or however Cecily got hers.

"Of course." Ms. Immacolata's voice was soothing even over the phone. "So far, Aria's control over her changes appears to be consistent with earlier parts of the year."

Which meant not very good. "Is she still engaging in disruptive behavior?" Somehow she found herself sliding into the same euphemisms the school used. She wanted to tell herself that it was because she was trying to keep a consistent terminology, but she hated the way that Ms. Immacolata would correct her like a kindergartner who had drawn on the desk.

"I believe this particular potion has a known side effect of somewhat increased irritability?" Ms. Immacolata hinted.

Aria had not turned blue again after the first night. But she also hadn't slept much that night or the following. Just as well that the gala prep had been canceled: she and Daniel were losing their minds. And for no change, it seemed.

"All right. Thanks. We'll finish out the week and then talk to the pharma-mage about adjusting the dosage." She tried not to feel defeated. Or triumphant. She hadn't wanted to be right about this.

"Please keep me up to date," Ms. Immacolata said. She added,

"I saw them carrying the centerpieces over to the gym this morning. They came out wonderfully."

"The centerpieces?" For a moment, she was confused.

"You were on that committee, weren't you? Beautiful work," Ms. Immacolata offered, in what was surely intended as a sop to her ego.

She wasn't sure what exactly had happened, but she wasn't going to admit that to every-hair-in-its-place Ms. Immacolata. "Oh, I wasn't able to help with this round, but I'm glad they came out well!"

She thought she did a good job of keeping her voice light as they made an appointment for a follow-up call in two weeks and said their goodbyes. Then she hung up the phone and put down the iron and stared at them both.

The phone buzzed. And then buzzed again. And again. It was a pattern that she'd become used to: a storm of WhatsApp notifications. She could feel her blood pressure rising. She opened the app to the flood of cheerful pictures she'd halfway expected. The moms having a good time, putting the centerpieces together. Wineglasses and smiles galore. Cecily and Moira in the center of it all, Moira's arm outstretched to capture the group selfie. Other moms chimed in with comments and heart-eyes and their own photos.

Such a great time!

We should totally do this again

Anyone up for some potion brewing next week?

Thanks again for organizing, Cecily and Moira!

Moira wasn't even on the Parent Advisory Council. And yet there she was, getting all the credit. It would have been easy enough to create a new group, one that didn't have her in it. For all she knew, there was a new group that didn't have her in it. One where they could say the things they were whispering behind her back. But they'd chosen to post the photos here, where she could see them.

For a moment, she crumpled silently around her phone, throat tight and stomach roiling. She'd tried so hard. Aria was trying so hard. But it was never going to be enough. Her face hurt with the effort of holding back the tears, but she couldn't cry. Not in the open, where her family could hear. Where she would have to find some way to explain to Aria that she was sorry, so sorry, that the birthday party invitations were going to stop again. Where she would have to listen to Daniel tell her again that these people, the only people left willing to talk to her, weren't worth her time. He'd mean to be supportive, without ever realizing how condescending he sounded. Or maybe he wouldn't try to comfort her, maybe he'd merely give her that look of condemnation that had become his default. Because it was her fault. She'd ruined their lives, all three of them, and now they were trapped in this funhouse mirror of a world, which was going to be eaten by a centuries-old shadow wolf any day now.

Something crashed in the front of the house, a musical crunch of breaking glass. She ran to the living room. The first thing she noticed was the cold wind. The curtain billowed. Glass shards covered the carpet. A rock lay in the middle of the floor.

There was a note wrapped around it. She tiptoed through the glass, worried about stabbing a shard through the sole of her shoe or setting off some kind of hex. There was a note tied around it. She swallowed and picked it up.

The writing was conveniently face-out, the assailant thoughtful enough to ensure she did not have to untie it to read it. *Unnatural. Unwanted.*

"*With the Outsider comes Calamity,*" she repeated. "*An unnatural Shifting, unwanted Legacy.* I think that settles whether we're getting any more playdate invites."

She took a deep breath. Palmed the tears she hadn't noticed until then from her cheeks and dried her palms on her jeans. What other choice did she have? She swept up the glass and vacuumed three times. Called the glamourist for an emergency illusion patch. Called the contractor for a quote. Then she headed upstairs to dress for the party.

Vivian had been to her high school prom, on the arm of a boy from her parents' country club to whom she had spoken few words before or since. The theme was "A Magical Night" and it had not been in the least bit magical. All the carnations and votive candles in the world didn't change the fact it was the same people whose approval she could never win.

She couldn't win the approval of this room, either. But neither could she argue that the night was anything less than magical.

She'd been surprised when told the gala would be held in the school gymnasium; surely such a well-heeled group would prefer an upscale restaurant, or vineyard, or maybe a portal to another dimension? But now she saw that the gym was only the framework on which to hang a series of illusions built with the genteel viciousness of an extremely competitive bake sale. Different classes' parents had been assigned the floor, the walls, the bandstand. Each had done their best to outdo each other.

When they stepped through the doors, left ostentatiously alone down to the flecks of chipped paint along the edges, they stepped not onto the polished wood of the basketball court but soft, springy moss with slabs of river-smoothed granite set in strategic locations for dancing. Above, the rafters had disappeared, concealed by a velvety blackness spangled with stars the likes of which had not been seen since the invention of electric lights. Elaborate wrought lanterns hung in midair from nothing, casting a flattering light that faded out beyond the ring of sequoia-sized trees that surely must be disguising the walls and risers. There was no band onstage yet, but soft music floated from what sounded like the next glen over. Even the air was perfumed with the scent of ferns and night-blooming flowers.

For a moment, she let it carry her. She forgot about prophecies and shape changing and Trials, and let the wonder wash over her. A faun—real? Another illusion?—pranced by, stopping to offer them flutes of champagne from a silver tray. The glasses, at least, were real. They each took one, and when she sipped from hers, the bubbles changed color, shimmering in a rainbow as they spiraled up through the golden liquid. A laugh, half-incredulous, half-delighted, threatened to burble up.

And then one of the other parents from Aria's class, dressed as a fairy complete with shimmering wings despite being a metal magician who worked for some car manufacturer in real life, caught sight of her. And made some kind of symbol with his hands that reminded her of some old-country grandmother averting the evil eye, then pointedly turned his back.

She felt her face stiffen. She'd expected to feel awkward about their knockoff Lord of the Rings costumes from Party City's online store. But now that they were here, it didn't matter. She could have dressed like a centaur, and it wouldn't have offset the fact that people blamed her for threatening their perfect little town.

"What was that about?" Daniel whispered, shocked.

Her ears flamed beneath the cheap latex. This was not the place to have this discussion, but then that was her own damn fault, wasn't it? She hadn't made him take the prophecy, or at least the town's reaction to the prophecy, seriously when she'd first learned about it. It kept not being the right time, even as things escalated. He'd gotten home tonight well after the glamourist had come and gone, with so little time to spare before the gala that she hadn't even had a chance to show him the rock. If she told him right now, he'd make a scene. And he'd be right to do so. She was the coward he'd accused her of being. She just had to get through tonight. She'd tell him everything in the car on the way home, when they could do their inevitable yelling in private.

"I'll tell you later." She shouldn't have come. But she couldn't leave now. She raised her chin and walked on, her polyester train dragging behind her.

They drifted, not talking to anyone, not talking to each other. She could feel Daniel's discomfort at her elbow. A stab of longing shot through her. They'd been to fancy parties before Aria, work events where they'd needed to put on a good show despite having no interest in bidding on a three-night stay at a five-star resort or the services of a personal chef. They'd spent those evenings quietly muttering to each other, daring the other not to laugh. Daniel would say something scathing about the age gap between the grandfatherly man whose codpiece and hose were doing him no favors and the twenty-something on his arm; she would let him know that she was actually his fourth wife and speculate if whatever potions the perky young thing was giving him had as much heart-attack risk as Viagra. The table displaying auction items should have been worth at least twenty minutes of entertainment but she couldn't even identify half the items. (She'd had to discreetly check what a bezoar was on her phone; it was exactly as disgusting as it looked. She was sure the donor of the gorgeously embroidered invisibility cloak next to it was livid at the placement.) But every time she went to open her mouth, she imagined how he might react. Dismissive. Horrified. She wasn't sure, but she wasn't willing to find out anymore. He shifted his weight impatiently, his eyes flicking over the wings and horns and tails on display, unable to tell which was real or fake and unwilling to rest anywhere, including on her.

They'd made a circuit of the room three times without managing to speak to anyone. She'd hoped Steve and his wife would be here, so at least Daniel would have someone to talk to. They wouldn't shun her. She hoped. But she didn't see them. She saw Cecily and Moira across the room, and turned away. Daniel had done the same without speaking; at least they were on the same page about one thing tonight. She'd grabbed another glass of champagne and was already regretting it. Finally, Daniel's gaze did rest somewhere longer than a few seconds and she realized with sudden relief how much his restlessness had been bothering her. She followed his eyes to Raidne.

Raidne looked perfect, as always. Her glossy black hair was piled high and threaded with ivy, and if her flowing chiton was not exactly on theme, it wasn't *not* on theme either. Either she'd done something to enhance her skin's natural shimmer or she'd stopped doing something to repress it, because she glowed opalescent under the lantern light. Her wife wore a similar chiton, mercifully free of kittens.

"Raidne," Daniel said with some relief. He smiled warmly.

Vivian stiffened and then forced herself to relax. At this point, being associated with the town MLM addict might be a step up for her social standing. "And this is Orphne?"

Orphne smiled shyly, ducking her head.

Vivian tried not to resent the ease with which Daniel and Raidne chatted. They were comparing notes on the new raw bar in Grand Central. Daniel faced the siren, his body language as open to her as it was closed off to Vivian herself. Raidne smiled, the first time Vivian had ever seen that expression on the haughty woman's face. Of course she was relaxed. Her kid was one of the leading contenders to be town hero, instead of the one who doomed them.

She glanced again at Orphne, trying to evaluate what she thought of the whole prophecy thing. The ancient Greeks had been big on prophecies. Was she thrilled or dismayed?

The other woman smiled tentatively. "I like your glamour."

"I'm sorry?" Vivian had gotten as far as minor firestarting. She was nowhere near casting a glamour, and had begun to suspect she never would be.

"The elf ears," Orphne said, brushing her own ears. They came to the faintest hint of a point. The undertones of her skin were blue, darkening so that they stopped being undertones and started being tones at the base of her throat.

"Oh." Vivian laughed nervously. "It's not a glamour—they're Spock ears."

"Spock? Like the TV show?"

"Yeah," she said, touching the latex nervously. "I mean, there were elf versions on Etsy, too, but the Vulcan ones were the first I found with free shipping."

"You bought them?" Orphne looked impressed. She reached out and then hesitated. "May I?"

Daniel laughed at something she'd missed, and Raidne touched his elbow. Vivian didn't want to let her daughter's rival's mom touch her ears, but she also didn't want a scene. Not here, not when people were watching her out of the corner of their eyes. She nodded, trying to keep a pleasant smile on her face, fearing it would twist into a grimace.

Orphne touched the edge with one finger and let it spring back. "Oh! How clever humans have gotten. I never would have even guessed!"

"Have you and Raidne been together a while?" Vivian groped for a topic other than Chosen Ones.

"A few decades, this round." Orphne waved a hand. "It's been an on-again, off-again thing for a couple centuries now. We went most of the Middle Ages without speaking, I don't even remember about what."

That didn't make Vivian feel better.

"But Evander changed everything," she continued. "Raising a child together changes the whole dynamic, don't you think?"

Now that was a truth.

"Oh, it's nice to make a new friend," Orphne said suddenly, her eyes shining. She gestured a little too broadly and her wine splashed onto the floor and a bit of Vivian's shoes. Given the damage Aria had done last time she'd spoken to Raidne, it only seemed fair. Vivian suddenly realized the other woman was not on her first round. "I've never been very good at making live mortal friends. Most of the other chthonic nymphs tend to stick to the dead. I know, I'm having a party in a couple weeks. You should come!"

Exactly what Moira had warned her about. The last thing in the world Vivian wanted to do was go to Raidne's house and be sold Tupperware. Although it was likely the only invitation she was going to receive at this rate. "I need to check my schedule," she temporized.

"Oh, it will be so much fun!" Orphne continued. "No kids, plenty of wine. April twenty-third?"

And maybe Vivian could replace Moira with a tackier drunk. They could gossip about who the Thief in the Night from the prophecy was, maybe make Aria a little do-it-yourself pillory so she could be displayed in the town square while people crowned Evander with laurels or whatever.

"I think Aria has Spell Scouts that night," Vivian stammered, knowing full well that Spell Scouts was Wednesdays and the twenty-third was a Sunday.

Orphne looked crestfallen. "Oh. Another time?"

"That would be so nice," Vivian said. She couldn't keep this up. She tossed back the last of her drink. "I'm going to hunt down one of those waiters."

She stumbled away, leaving Daniel with them, where he seemed happy. But she couldn't keep standing there, cheerfully making small talk.

Someone bumped her elbow, and she apologized reflexively.

"You should be sorry," the cloaked man snarled at her. She didn't even recognize him. "You shouldn't even be here. Take your unnatural brat back where you came from before you wreck everything."

Vivian was too shocked to respond immediately. His companion, a woman with silvery scales down her neck, murmured something to him and drew him away. He glared over her shoulder at Vivian.

She grabbed another flute of champagne blindly and downed

it. There was a roaring in her ears, and she thought she might pass out. She shouldn't have drunk more. She shouldn't have come here.

She managed to get a glass of water from the bartender, who at least did not care who she was or how she'd failed. She stood in the shadow of one of the great illusory trees, waiting for her vision to clear.

The band started up, and people were milling around near the siren. Raidne shook her head, smiling. Her smile transformed her face from coldly lovely to radiant. Vivian had never been particularly attracted to women, but she knew she would be willing to do unsavory things to see that smile directed at her. Some of the other parents pleaded with her playfully. The siren sighed, and handed her champagne flute off to Orphne as she headed towards the stage.

It took Vivian a moment to understand, and then she felt even more like a fool. She looked around wildly. Odysseus had plugged his ears with wax; could she steal some from one of the candle centerpieces? It was too late. Raidne nodded graciously to the audience, then to the band leader, opened her mouth, and began to sing.

Vivian braced herself against the table, her knuckles white. The song started off softly, the words in a language that sounded almost, but not quite, familiar, the melody curling through the air like a beckoning finger. Couples took the floor, their steps languorous and sensual. The music felt like it was winding its way around her brainstem. A few of the more daring, or show-offy, couples took a few steps up, twirling until they danced in midair. The women's skirts floated, trailing their movements gracefully in ways she'd seen in Disney movie ballrooms but never in real life.

People without a partner in their arms trailed towards the stage.

She felt the tug herself, the urge to do whatever Raidne might ask. She grabbed a canapé, stabbing herself in the hand with a toothpick so hard that she drew blood. Daniel did not grab a canapé. Daniel drifted towards Raidne to stand at the foot of the stage, eyes gazing upwards.

No wonder he liked her. Raidne was everything she was not; polished, certain of herself. Professional like Vivian had once been, only better at it than she'd ever managed. Perfect hair, perfect skin, perfect clothes. Vivian wanted to be bitter at what she'd given up when she'd become a mother, and then when she'd become a mother of a werewolf. But she couldn't have competed with Raidne on her best day, even before she'd ruined herself. Gained weight despite the yoga, switched to stretchier pants, started dabbling in the dark arts. Stopped talking to her husband. Now he would rather talk to Raidne than her, and how could she blame him? Raidne could take everything she wanted from her with a few notes.

Or maybe she already had.

How else could the rumors have spread so fast? She pictured Raidne bringing up the prophecy, and Evander's birds, then humming a little siren-y melody. How easy it would be for people to put one and one together and get three? Orphne was having trouble making friends? Everyone would want to be friends with the Chosen One's parents. She'd never liked Vivian anyway. Whatever it was that had kicked off the Reckoning, whether it was Aria's fault or not, Raidne was certainly taking advantage of it. And Daniel was cozying up to her.

Raidne ended the song with a flourish, a crystalline high note held impossibly long. Then she smiled gracefully as the dancers descended to earth and the room burst into applause.

Daniel found Vivian a few songs later, standing in the shadows with her fourth glass of champagne.

"What is with you tonight?" he hissed. "I thought you wanted to impress these people, not make me fend them all off myself."

"I'm terribly sorry I'm not impressive enough," she countered, champagne loosening her tongue. "Maybe you would have been better off staying with Raidne. She's certainly cast a spell on enough people here."

"What are you talking about? We're friends from the train. I thought you wanted me to make friends. At least Raidne's better than Moira and Cecily."

She laughed bitterly. "You only like her because she's done her siren thing to you. The same as she has to everyone here, riding the coattails of that goddamn prophecy."

"Wait, what?" He paused, genuinely confused. "Prophecy? Viv, what are you even talking about? How much have you had to drink?"

"Too much, but just because I'm drunk doesn't mean I'm blind. Have you honestly not noticed how everyone is avoiding us like we're lepers?"

"I don't know, is it because their little brats keep casting spells on our kid?"

"No, Daniel. It's because the whole town is convinced that the Reckoning is bringing their doom, and that our daughter is the reason it happened, and that her son is some kind of Chosen One who's going to save them all. Which you'd know if you were ever here!" She was being mean, she could tell even as the words left her mouth, but she couldn't seem to help it.

"What—when—" he sputtered. "OK, hold up a second. You're telling me you actually believe that Reckoning nonsense?"

Their voices were rising. She brought hers back down. The

last thing she wanted was even more attention. "I don't even know, but it doesn't matter, because the rest of them believe it. And as long as they believe it, and your best friend Raidne keeps using her mind control powers to keep them roiled up, they're going to keep attacking Aria."

His eyes narrowed. "What do you mean, attacking?"

"What, you think the living room window broke itself?" She knew this wasn't the time or place to have this argument, but all the hurt and anxiety and alcohol swirled in her head.

He stared at her. "Someone broke our window to hurt Aria and you're only telling me this now?"

"There's never any time! And you never want to hear it! You roll your eyes whenever I try to tell you anything!" She blinked back tears. "I thought you were uncomfortable with magic, but you're perfectly happy to make friends with a siren who's bedazzling everyone."

"And you're perfectly happy to make friends with some jerks whose kids keep bullying our daughter!" he exploded. "And Raidne? Yes, she's been cozying up to me, like you said. She wants me to be her frigging personal financial adviser!"

That was not at all what she had expected to hear.

"She's an immortal, she needs someone to take care of her investments who isn't going to ask inconvenient questions about exactly how long she's owned certain stocks. Do you have any idea how big an account she could be? Like, instant partner offer for me. I didn't know commissions came that large. Aria would never have to worry about money again in her life. It's huge, Vivian—life-changingly huge."

"I... I didn't... you didn't say anything..." she stuttered.

"Well, you never want to hear about my work anymore," he said. "It's all 'parent council this' and 'grimoire that' and 'oh, what will Cecily say.' You're drifting off into some other world, and you have no interest in me or what world I live in anymore. And you don't even want me with you. And now this? Honestly, Vivian, I don't know why I've been trying so hard."

"Daniel—"

"Don't 'Daniel' at me. You don't have any right to criticize me for keeping things from you. Not when you've been sitting on something like this. Aria's in actual danger, and you're shutting me out? And then to go accuse Raidne, one of the few people who actually tells me anything, of brainwashing people into, what? Declaring her kid to be something from a prophecy? What does that get her? Do you have any proof at all?"

His voice had risen again. A few people glanced at their little nook in the trees and quickly looked away. She looked over her shoulder.

Raidne was a few steps away. She looked stricken. It was the most human expression Vivian had ever seen on her face.

The siren took a few steps forward. "Evander cannot possibly be the Winged Scholar from the prophecy," she said clearly, loudly enough to be heard by everyone in the immediate vicinity. "We had the Fates examine his thread at birth. He is subject to no prophecies at all."

There was a murmuring as the gossip raced through the hall.

"And as for a siren's song," she continued more quietly, "the effect only lasts as long as the song itself. I cannot change anyone's mind for more than a few moments. My condolences are with you—being mother to a fated one is a terrible burden. But I swear, I have played no role in your misfortune."

"I'm sorry," Vivian started, but the siren had already turned her back, shoulders bowed. Orphne hurried after her, looking concerned.

"Happy? She embarrassed you over some brownies, you've humiliated her in front of the entire school," Daniel said bitterly. "And none of it protects our daughter."

"I'm sorry," she said, her heart in her throat. How could she have messed this up so badly?

"Well, so am I," he said bitterly. He set down his glass.

"Where are you going?" she asked, alarmed.

"Home, to watch over our kid," he said. "No, you stay. You're supposed to be treasuring, go be treasurer. We both know you can't walk away and disappoint a bunch of strangers."

"I—" She raised a hand, but he'd already turned his back, pushing his way through the costumed revelers.

"There you are," said Cecily. "I need you to tally up the totals from the auction, it's about to begin."

All through the auction of rare manuscripts that looked like they'd been fished out of someone's attic and potions clumsily assembled by the middle school classes, Vivian kept notes mechanically. She recorded the bids, scribbling them by quill pen into a parchment that somehow turned the bids into binding debts. She checked each one twice, and then the number promptly left her head, driven out by the spiral of anxiety and remorse. All her excuses now seemed foolish and vain. It hadn't been the right time to tell him? She should have made time. She was afraid he wouldn't listen? She should have begged him to listen. She was slowly sobering up and realizing exactly how terribly she'd handled this. Again. Poor Raidne. Poor Aria, when everyone's parents came home gossiping. Poor Daniel.

He'd left. She'd driven him away and he'd left.

At least that meant he wasn't there when the windows exploded.

She was closing the book when suddenly there was a deafening crash, all around her. It turned out that actual glass from actual windows cut through illusory trees quite nicely. She ducked under the table, far too late to protect herself, but it wasn't necessary as most of the glass crashed straight to the floor in defiance of physics. Some of the bits shattered and tiny shards ricocheted into the crowd at ankle height. People shrieked and jumped towards the center of the room. The howling wind swept the glass up into a stormcloud taking form in the center of the room, in the shape of the eye she was becoming far too familiar with.

There was the screaming and the running that was also far too familiar. Tipsy parents slid on glass shards and dropped canapés. Several crashed into each other, and the stampede turned into a shoving match at the doors. Some of the parents ran towards the roiling cloud of broken glass, shouting. A shimmering shield wall shot up as Ms. Genevieve waved her arms. Vivian backed up through a melting illusion until her back hit the wall of the gym. Kassie's mom stood on the other side of the dance floor, chanting something Vivian couldn't hear. The usual crew of emergency response parents called instructions to each other, throwing lines of power over the stormcloud and wrestling it to the ground. The cloud collapsed suddenly, the glass tinkling as it hit the floor, the defenders wiping off sweat and blood from tiny cuts on their faces. They looked around cautiously, waiting for a second strike, but only the night wind came through the shattered windows.

She ended up in the parking lot with everyone else, with half a dozen small cuts that stung as they oozed blood. The dress was ruined, but it wasn't as if she'd ever intended to wear it again. It seemed that there were no major injuries; a lot of minor lacerations on lower legs and even more ruined shoes. A couple of people had sprained ankles or bad bruises from falling. The healers that showed up had little to do beyond applying healing poultices and Band-Aids, and handing out sobering-up potions. The emergency healer who looked Vivian over slapped a few ready-made poultices on the worst of her cuts. They burned intensely for a few moments and then settled down to a glowing warmth. The healer warned her to leave them until they cooled and promised there would be no scars.

Swimming in adrenaline and reluctant to go home, the majority of the crowd ended up milling around as the Shadow Council reps went over the wreckage again. The only good thing was that Aria wasn't here this time.

When she tried to join one of the circles of parents exchanging horrified gossip, she found herself facing stony looks and more of the evil-eye warding gestures. She slowly backed away, hands up.

The explosions hadn't been her fault. Unlike the rest of the disasters that evening.

At least the auction had already wrapped up.

She drank her sobering-up potion, which tasted of dried moss and battery acid, and cringed as the last haze of alcohol left her brain feeling bare. Daniel had taken the car; when the rideshare dropped her off, he wasn't waiting for her. His shoes were by the door, and he wouldn't have sent the sitter home if he wasn't in the house, but she couldn't find him. She didn't want to yell for fear of waking Aria. She went room-by-room. She finally found the note on her pillow.

I'm sleeping in Aria's room tonight. No, I don't want to talk.

Her phone buzzed and she nearly dropped it in her haste. It wasn't from him. It was from Cecily.

Well, that was an adventure! Never a
dull moment!

BTW we saw the final tally of the gala
proceeds. Doesn't it look a little… low?

I mean, no one's accusing you of
anything or anything

Just, it's much lower than last year's?
By a lot? But apparently it was the same
number of people and the auction went
even better? Other than the explosions and
all, but that was after so it doesn't count

Maybe you could check that math again

And send it to the council in the morning.
I know I had one too many champagnes,
and then a little more excitement than the
entertainment committee had bargained for!

Good night!

Vivian slid down the wall she hadn't realized she'd been leaning on. She texted back, for once uncaring of what Cecily thought.

How exactly is that not an accusation?

She tugged at the sliver of glass that had embedded itself

247

in the heel of her shoe. Then she took them off and dropped them both straight into the trash can. For a minute, she thought Cecily had turned her phone to silent for the night. But then the little three dots started to blink.

> I mean, I would never say something
> like that

> It's just some of the other parents,
> who were here for previous years,
> have expressed concerns

It was too much. It was all too much in one night, and her head was spinning even now she was sober and Daniel wasn't here to talk her down. He didn't want to talk to her at all.

> Who, Cecily?

Again, the silence. More than enough time for her to rethink everything that had happened, and remind herself exactly how terrible a person she was. She'd thought she was so alone, but she hadn't been. She'd always had Daniel, but she'd pushed him away, and now he wanted nothing to do with her.

Her phone buzzed.

> If you really must know, Moira
> has concerns

Her heart stuttered. How long? Had Moira never liked her, had it always been a front? Or was it that she poisoned every relationship she was in?

248

Cecily continued.

I'm not the kind of person to stir
up drama

But some people have noticed that
the timing is well

It lines up awfully well with the
prophecy

The bit about expectations and
trees and the night

And then there was the whole
explosions thing

She tried to remember and had to pull it up on her phone. Thieves. Thieves in the trees and the night. It wasn't enough for Aria to be town pariah, she had to be too. She started to type, stopped, and then threw the phone against the wall. It ricocheted and then skittered down the hallway, the face a spiderweb of cracks.

"Mommy?" Aria emerged, blinking.

"Mommy dropped her phone, sweetie," Vivian choked out. "Go back to bed."

Daniel stumbled up behind Aria, blinking bloodshot eyes. He looked down at Vivian sitting on the floor, his face unreadable. She opened her mouth, wanting to apologize. Wanting to explain. No words came out. What could she possibly say, especially with Aria standing right there? He snorted, as if she'd confirmed something, and shuffled back into the dark room, leaving her with the knowledge that she'd failed again.

"But you can fix it, right?" Aria looked up at her, trusting. It took Vivian a moment to realize Aria was still talking about the phone. "There's probably a spell in your book."

Were there spells for that? For fixing broken hearts? What if the wound was self-inflicted? She got Aria a glass of water and sent her back to bed, afraid to disturb Daniel further. The least she could do was let him sleep, since she couldn't seem to do anything else. Certainly not find a spell to repair what she'd broken. She couldn't even manage to toast bread without a fire extinguisher. Whether or not magic could fix this mess, she had to face the truth. She was no mage. All she had cast were aspersions, and look at where that had got her.

14

Apr 20 10:52 AM

Do you have a school t-shirt yet? How about a cape, flagon, virgin beeswax candle, or golf umbrella in Grimoire Grammar School colors? Stop by the School Spirit Shop this afternoon, where our eighth graders will be selling merchandise to support their end-of-year trip to Transylvania! (Please note that the "Spirit" in "School Spirit Shop" refers to school pride and that no captured spirits have been imprisoned in school merchandise.)

"We only talk about logistics," Vivian finished. "He picks Aria up and does bedtime, then leaves and goes who-knows-where for hours, and then goes to sleep in Aria's room."

She knew she was babbling, but it was easier to talk about timetables than about the fact that her husband hadn't started a conversation with her in nearly three weeks and she was too much of a coward to ask him anything more sensitive than whether he wanted fish or chicken for dinner. She wished she knew where he was even going in the evenings after tucking

Aria in. Somewhere far from anything magic, and far from her. Moira would have suggested a tracking spell on his car. She knew she shouldn't miss Moira, but she did. Or at least, having someone to text.

"And I've turned over all the paperwork matching up every single ticket sale and auction pledge, and it's all very clear where this year's money came from, but I never did get the numbers from last year to add up, and everyone agrees out loud that clearly I didn't do anything wrong, but they all blame me. And Cecily won't return my calls, and Moira blocked me, and Aria stopped asking why Daddy always sleeps with her now or when she can have a playdate with Cara and Elowen, and I just—" She looked up, tightening her nostrils and willing herself not to cry.

"You sound overwhelmed," Dr. Kumar said, not unkindly.

"I'm just… alone," Vivian confessed. One tear escaped, and she scrubbed it away angrily. "And it's my own fault, and I deserve it, and—"

"Let's unpack that a little," Dr. Kumar interjected.

"What, that I deserve it?" She'd told her therapist that she and Daniel had fought over how she was handling school bullying and who she was friends with, but it couldn't convey the magnitude of the betrayal. She liked Dr. Kumar, but she wasn't sure how she could possibly move forward when all she could do was lie to her. "This isn't like the hike, where I couldn't have known what was going to happen. I did this, I did it all by myself. You can't wave a hand and take that from me."

"No one is trying to take anything from you," Dr. Kumar said gently. She gave Vivian that gentle half smile that always seemed to say that she saw Vivian's brokenness but accepted her anyway. Vivian could never decide if she liked the smile or hated it. But it was why she kept coming back, even knowing she was sabotaging herself by not telling the truth the therapist couldn't understand. "I meant earlier. When you said you were alone."

"I have Aria, obviously. But that's not what I meant."

"That's not what I meant, either. Are Moira and Cecily the only people you know in your town?"

"I mean, no," she said. "But they're the gatekeepers."

"Perhaps. Or perhaps they're the queen bees, which is a very different thing. Is it possible you've done the other parents a disservice in thinking of them as a monolithic entity?"

"They certainly act like it," she said, thinking of the stares and whispers. And the notes and the rock. But as she thought about it more, were they?

"You've mentioned other names before. There were the parents of the twins, right?"

"Steve and Sasha? I suppose. They're always so busy, though."

"I've found that many busy people have an ability to make room for what's important."

"So, what, I'm supposed to call them up for a playdate?"

"It's a start."

"It will take more than a start."

"What would you rather do?"

She had trouble meeting Dr. Kumar's eyes, even with a screen between them. "Apologize," she whispered.

"To Daniel?"

Vivian nodded. "I don't… I don't know how." Her vision swam and she blinked hard. She opened her mouth to try to say something to him every day, but the words got stuck. And there were so few opportunities. They were never alone together anymore; Daniel saw to that.

"Is he the only one?"

"Raidne, too." The words were hard to get out. "I was horrible to her, when she hadn't even done anything wrong."

Dr. Kumar nodded. "I know you feel remorse. But remorse doesn't change things. Only actions can change things. Right now, you're telling yourself a story about how terrible things happen to you, and how it is your fault. And I wonder if this connects to some of the work we've done around your upbringing."

Vivian chewed at a loose bit of skin on her lip, puzzled. And then she picked up on what Dr. Kumar was suggesting. "You think I'm avoiding connections because I think I don't deserve them."

"Are you?"

"Maybe." Moira had given her a lot of reasons to avoid people, now that she thought of it. How many of them were justified? She flushed. "I was as much of a snob as my mother, wasn't I? And now I've embarrassed myself, but I'm still too proud to admit it."

"That wasn't quite where I was going, but pride and shame are very closely connected," said Dr. Kumar. "I do think you do not need to be as alone as you are keeping yourself. So that's what I want you to focus on for next week. Forgive yourself so that you can open yourself to allowing others to forgive you. And find a connection you have been ignoring and strengthen it."

Vivian nodded tearily, out of time to respond. She gave an awkward little wave goodbye and closed down the connection, leaning back.

She wanted to say it was impossible. That there was no one left who would be willing to accept her now. She was too deep into the magic world for Daniel to accept her, not deep enough for anyone else.

But that didn't mean she didn't owe people better.

She called the babysitter to see if she was available on Sunday.

"You made it!" Orphne looked genuinely happy to see her at the door.

Vivian swallowed. "I brought banana bread?" It seemed a paltry offering, but she didn't know what else you brought an immortal as an apology. All the Greek myths she knew in which a mortal offended an immortal involved the mortal getting turned into a plant or something.

But Orphne seemed delighted with the banana bread and showed her into a schizophrenic living room. The furnishings were mid-century modern, arranged around a pool that started indoors and then, if you ducked under a glass wall, continued outside. The decor, on the other hand, mixed several decades' worth of cheesy schlock, from Hummel figurines to Thomas Kincade prints to a *Bless This Mess* sign in curlicue letters on barn wood. There was no mess.

"I know." Orphne laughed. "We had to compromise. But that's marriage, right?"

"The pool and the furniture are Raidne?" Vivian said hesitantly, and Orphne nodded, smiling. Vivian wasn't sure what to say about the kitten poster. "I hope you'll forgive me, I don't know very much about... chthonic nymphs?"

Orphne laughed again. "Oh, just because I'm from the underworld doesn't mean I have to be a gloomy Gus! Now, make sure to look at the snack table. I made a Jell-O mold! It's so colorful, what will humans think of next?"

Vivian vaguely recognized a few of the other parents from school events. She'd seen Madhuri's red motorcycle out front, but wasn't sure where she stood with the other parent council members these days. There were some raised eyebrows and muttering, but no one made a move to throw her out or burn her at the stake, so she smiled weakly and went to look at the snacks. There was, in fact, a blue Jell-O mold with a whole fish suspended in it. She opted for a glass of the punch instead.

"It's watered ambrosia."

Vivian put the ladle back as she turned to face Raidne. "I'm sorry—I didn't mean to take something I shouldn't have."

"Oh, you're allowed to have it," Raidne said. "At that concentration, it won't make you immortal, and it might be good for your skin. It's only that most humans find it unbearably sweet. Orphne always forgets."

Vivian straightened her spine. "Raidne, may I speak to you? Privately?"

The siren weighed her with unreadable eyes. "Come join me in the kitchen."

Vivian had trouble not pausing in the doorway to gawk. This was the kind of room she'd originally expected to find in Cecily's house. Unlike the living room, this was all Raidne, and it was clear that no activity that remotely resembled her idea of cooking happened here. The floor was done in blue tile, but clearly enchanted, as the hues shifted like sunlight through ocean. There was no stove as Vivian would recognize it. In its place, she saw an enormous sink in the shape of a cresting wave, a wall of aquarium tanks full of lobsters, cockles, and small sea bass, and a butcher block table she was pretty sure came from IKEA.

She tried to bring her mind back to her goal, when she wanted very much to ask if Evander brought live lobsters to school in his lunchbox and if he ate Goldfish crackers. Her mouth was dry. "Raidne, I need to apologize. Aria's being accused because of who she is, not because of anything she can help, and I've been so angry and afraid, and then I turned around and did the same to you. Accusing you of using your powers to lie was a horrible thing to do, and I'm so, so sorry."

"Well." Raidne swirled her glass thoughtfully. "I'll admit, the usual is for other women to accuse me of seducing their husbands, so you have the advantage of novelty."

Vivian flushed, but made herself continue. "And doing so in a public place, where it could damage your reputation, was all the worse."

"Mmm." The siren looked thoughtful. "In that, you may have done me a favor. I had not realized the degree to which Evander had been pulled into the rumor mill. Having a chance to remove him from speculation has been a boon. I only wish I could do the same for your daughter. She seems like a sweet child, if a bit unruly."

"Thanks." That was more magnanimous than Vivian felt she deserved. "What—if you don't mind me asking—are you hearing?"

"Probably most of what you're fearing," Raidne said. Vivian didn't think her bluntness was meant to be unkind. In fact, she had the odd feeling that the siren meant the unvarnished truth to be a sign of respect, from someone who spun the truth by nature and profession. "A new flush of excitement that people have identified the thief in the prophecy, and all the delight a juicy scandal generates. A hope that if you and your daughter could be driven from town, there might be still time to avert the Fate, which is nonsense, of course. One cannot avert a Fate. Oh, and a lot of pity for Daniel, I'm afraid."

Vivian bit her lip. "What has he said to you about all this?"

Raidne raised one eyebrow. "If there's one thing I've learned in millennia, it's never to insert oneself into someone else's marriage." But at Vivian's crestfallen look, she relented. "He has always spoken highly of you, you know. Your wit, your determination, your insistence on taking on the weight of everything yourself. His dismay that you won't let him carry part of the load. A marriage isn't a fate—disaster can be averted, not merely borne. You need to talk to him."

"He doesn't want to talk to me," she said miserably.

"He did not tell me you were a coward."

Stung, Vivian opened her mouth to defend herself. And then closed it.

"Find a way," Raidne said. It was easy for her: she made people listen to her by nature. "And when you have patched things up, come over. I should have had you both over to dinner months ago, but the Nike account was in jeopardy and then Evander got the flu. It's always something. Anyway, Evander likes Aria, and he could use a friend who isn't a bird and can talk at least part of the time."

She blinked. Maybe sometimes things could be that easy.

"Thanks for coming, by the way," Raidne said. "Orphne has always had trouble making human friends, and she's never fit in very well with her cousins."

An underworld nymph who had gone to the surface for love but would never pass as a member of the wider community. Too familiar. "I could use some friends myself," Vivian made herself confess.

Raidne smiled. It wasn't a broad smile; Vivian didn't deserve one. But it was enough.

She drifted back out into the living room. The group here was less... polished than the one usually gathered at Cecily's behest. The humans, or human-seeming, tended towards ponytails instead of blowouts. But there was also a much higher percentage of people who couldn't pass for human. The willow-headed dryad from the Parent Advisory Council chatted with Madhuri while the doe-headed lady in yet another Lilly Pulitzer dress handed a cupcake to a very large badger in overalls.

"I didn't expect one of Cecily's set to be here, of all places." Madhuri made room for her, sounding less critical than surprised.

"I'm not one of Cecily's set," Vivian said, feeling awkward.

Madhuri grimaced sympathetically. "Oof, she finally turned on you?"

Vivian tried not to bite her lip. There be landmines here, surely.

"Oh no, is Cecily picking on her?" Orphne turned wide eyes towards her.

"Oh, she'd never pick on anyone. She hates drama, you know," Madhuri said, rolling her own eyes.

Some of the others started throwing their own Cecily-isms. Someone handed her a cup of tea.

It was gradually dawning on Vivian that, if Cecily was the Queen Bee of the Mean Girls, then naturally that must mean that there were an awful lot of whatever the parent equivalent of the band kids hiding off in the corners. And maybe Cecily wasn't quite the gatekeeper she thought she was.

"And then she basically accused me of stealing gala funds because it wasn't as much as last year," Vivian found herself saying at the end of her tale of woe, two glasses of ambrosia having gone straight to her head.

Madhuri got an odd look on her face. "She brought up last year's gala?"

"Yes, and how am I supposed to even answer questions about that?" Vivian handed her empty glass to the wall sconce that reached out and took it, and she'd had enough wine not to be surprised by that anymore. "I mean, I'd tried to tell Ms. Genevieve that the numbers from last year didn't add up, and she's stonewalling me. I wasn't even here last year!"

"You need to talk to Steve," Raidne said slowly. "There was something about the gala last year that turned into Shadow Council business. He said he'd be here soon, something about the sitter getting stuck in a salt circle again."

"Then mysteriously Banderbridge had to retire and Ms. Genevieve had to step in," Madhuri added, eyebrows raised significantly.

"You heard something?" Raidne cocked her head.

"A deeply beloved pillar of the community abruptly retires and then completely disappears? I've always thought the whole thing was suspicious," Madhuri said, crossing her arms. "Someone wants something forgotten."

"Did someone say forgetting?" Orphne jumped into the conversation, beaming nervously. "Because that's the perfect segue! I brought you all here today because I recently started using an amazing new health product, and I wanted to share my experience with all my friends! Have you ever had trouble falling asleep because you couldn't forget the day's worries? Soothing Lethe drops are the perfect thing to erase repetitive thoughts! You'll literally forget what you were worried about. And we all want a good night's sleep, right, ladies?"

It might have been slightly more compelling if she hadn't been hiding an index card in her hand that she'd checked halfway through.

Orphne started herding people into the chairs she'd placed

around the room. On the coffee table, a set of silvery vials shimmered, along with several glossy catalogs. Vivian had a sinking feeling of recognition. She whispered, "Madhuri, does the magical world know about LuLaRoe?"

"I know, I know," Raidne said softly, and Vivian started guiltily. She hadn't meant for her to overhear that. "But she wanted to contribute to the household after Evander started school. Not that we need the money, but she was so lonely, and her skin is too blue to get a job with the humans, and one of her cousins back in the underworld recruited her and now the basement is full of boxes. I promise I won't let her recruit anyone to be her downline in the pyramid scheme, but if you could..."

She trailed off without specifying whether she wanted Vivian to buy a scented candle or merely be kind. Instead, the polished siren gave her a pleading look. She could have used her song, Vivian realized, but then, that would completely undermine Orphne's determination to contribute on her own. On impulse, Vivian grabbed the siren's hand and gave it a squeeze. "Of course."

"Have you tried sneaking into the school?" Madhuri suggested in a low voice as Orphne opened up a box to pass around samples.

"No!" Vivian said, scandalized. She accepted the sampler and took a whiff. Stars burst in front of her eyes, tiny periwinkle blue stars that trailed sparks across her vision. For a moment, she completely forgot what she was doing. She muffled a cough and passed the sample along to the owl lady.

"Now, Lethe drops are best for stress relief, but if what you're looking for is a mood boost, it's all about essential oils from Elysium!" Orphne opened up the next bottle.

"Next PAC meeting," Madhuri continued, sotto voce. "Surely there are records in the headmistress's office?"

"I'm not breaking into anything!" Vivian protested.

"You're a bad influence," murmured Raidne.

"Oh!" Orphne said, perking up. "I don't have Hades' cap of invisibility, but a spritz or two of essential oil of Acheron is very distracting!"

Vivian wasn't sure whether there was any factual magical basis in any of these pronouncements, or if this was like New Age hippies declaring tiger's eye was good for motivation and citrine for creativity. Unless maybe they were? She should ask someone later.

"I bet you'll find all the evidence in the desk, and I have just the thing," Madhuri said, fishing in her purse. "Genevieve was the worst at lock spells when we were in boarding school."

"No one's breaking into anything," Raidne said firmly. "If there was evidence, I'm sure the Shadow Council would have taken it whenever they did whatever they did. I think we should wait for Steve and see what he has to say."

Madhuri wrinkled her nose. "You're no fun."

"Why are you helping me?" Vivian said, baffled. "Or do you not think Aria's part of the whole prophecy thing?"

A few of the other women looked at each other, some making the warding gesture.

"Hey, my ancestors had nothing to do with that shit," said Madhuri. "We were dealing with the Portuguese at the time, thank you very much. As for why, no one invites me on wacky hijinks anymore now that I'm a mom, and I'm bored and quarterly reports have very limited entertainment value. Also, I cannot stand Cecily. She's been a bitch since we moved here."

Vivian found that difficult to argue with.

Raidne pursed her lips. "If the prophecy is tied to the town rather than to the inhabitants at the time, it wouldn't necessarily matter. We're all here now, so we would all be considered culpable."

Orphne sighed and put down the bottle she was holding with such a look of disappointment that Raidne winced and mouthed *sorry* at her wife. But Orphne turned to Vivian.

"Everyone knows you cannot outrun the Fates," Orphne said firmly. Vivian was suddenly reminded that regardless of the frivolity, this woman was thousands of years old. "If it's time for a prophecy to rebound, then it's hardly your fault. What was predicted was going to happen, silly goose. Nothing you could have done. But what you *can* do something about," and she brightened again, fumbling with another notecard, "is sun damage to your skin, which you can erase with our newest addition to the line, Asphodel tincture!"

Steve stepped in, Sasha right behind. He found most of the room looking at him. "Umm. Hi? What did I miss?"

A clamor of voices met him.

"Does the Shadow Council think the prophecy is true?" Madhuri demanded.

"What happened to last year's gala funds?" The willow dryad's branches swished as she turned.

"Would you like to try a dab of pomegranate essential oil on your wrists?" Orphne asked hopefully.

"Uh," he said, blinking. "The Council hasn't made a declaration one way or another, I thought the gala funds were for repainting the cafeteria, and what does that have to do with pomegranates?"

"Half the Parent Advisory Council thinks I'm the thief in the prophecy because this year's gala raised so much less than last year's. And we were wondering if the Shadow Council thinks the gala and Banderbridge's sudden retirement have something to do with each other," Vivian explained. "But I don't know what pomegranate tincture is supposed to do."

"Reduces seasonal depression!" Orphne chirped. "And as a special bonus, I can throw in the seeds, too."

"Which is for what, bringing your lover back?" Madhuri asked.

"No, but they're a great source of fiber," Orphne said cheerfully.

"I'm good, thanks." Steve made a scooping motion with his hand, and from across the room, a cup filled itself with ambrosia and levitated over to him. "Umm. So here's the deal. Now, y'all know I can't talk about what I know about official Shadow Council business."

People leaned in. He was totally about to talk about official Shadow Council business, and that was far more interesting than poor Orphne's terrible sales pitch. Raidne made a questioning face and Orphne shook her head. The siren moved around the table to slip a consoling arm around her wife's waist and they both turned their attention to Steve.

"Steve," Vivian said slowly. "Remind me again what your relationship is to the Shadow Council?"

All along, she had been picturing ancient white men with flowing beards and dark robes, maybe a wizened vampire or two. Not a cheerful Black man in his thirties, father of two and writer of romance novels.

"Let's say I'm a special consultant," he said, and she knew that it was both something more complicated than that, and that she was not going to hear about it.

"So what can you tell them?" Sasha prompted, raising an eyebrow at her husband.

"Well, fortunately," he broke out his dazzling smile, "this

one wasn't under my jurisdiction and I don't officially know anything at all, so what I can do is point out a few very pertinent facts and you ladies are free to speculate to your hearts' desires. Fact one—it sounds like this year's gala take was apparently substantially less than previous years' takes. Right?"

Vivian nodded.

"OK, fact two—from what Daniel's told me, our current Parent Advisory Council treasurer is a kickass accountant," he continued, as Vivian blinked rapidly to keep from tearing up unexpectedly. Daniel had still been describing her that way? "He mentioned a couple of weeks ago at skirmedge practice that you've been trying for months to bring attention to some discrepancies in last year's accounting, and you had a meeting with the administration. How did that go?"

"She didn't seem particularly interested," Vivian said cautiously.

"Shocking," he said, sounding not at all shocked. "Fact three, the current administration consists of one Ms. Genevieve, who until the end of last spring had been merely the deputy administrator with no stated goal of moving up. But then shortly after the conclusion of the annual Trials, fact four, the universally beloved headmaster very abruptly took a leave of absence and then retired without fanfare, no announcement or party or anything."

"Fact five, you said this one wasn't under your jurisdiction, which means that there was a thing here to be under someone else's jurisdiction in the first place," Madhuri jumped in. He tipped an imaginary hat in her direction.

"There was a scandal," Vivian breathed. "Something related to the gala last year."

"Something someone, or multiple someones, didn't want

to be public knowledge," Raidne said. "But I would be willing to believe that Ms. Genevieve knows exactly what happened, which is why she wasn't interested in whatever it was you found in the accounting records."

"But why couldn't she let me know? Why is she letting everyone pin this on me when she knows it's not my fault?" Vivian tried to make it come out calmly, but her voice cracked a little at the end.

"If the Council approved a cover-up, she'll have been under an Interdiction. She probably can't talk about it if she wanted to." Raidne tapped her fingernail on the table, thinking. "You must speak with Banderbridge himself, perhaps."

"No one's seen him since last spring," Madhuri pointed out. "Do you know where he is?"

"No idea," Steve admitted.

"This is too juicy. Sorry to get all in your business, Vivian, but now I want to know, too." Madhuri rubbed her hands together gleefully, setting her bangles jingling. "Scrying time! Orphne, can I borrow a basin?"

Orphne looked sadly at the carefully arranged boxes that no one seemed interested in, and then she swept them off the side. From a cabinet, she produced what looked like a large salad bowl with an uneven rim. For a moment, Vivian thought it was made out of wood; with a shiver, she realized it was bone. The shape could only have been the top of a skull, but she had no idea what could possibly have possessed a skull that large. The skull basin contrasted jarringly with Orphne's cheerful bunny print cardigan. The dissonance made her teeth hurt; she had the sudden flash that Orphne had been made for skulls and shadows and layered her cutesiness over the top in defiance.

Everyone gathered around. Raidne handed her wife a pitcher of water, which Orphne held above her head and poured with the precision of a practiced ritual. Not a drop dared splash outside the basin.

Madhuri made a few passes of her hands over the surface, then sprinkled dried yellow flower petals she'd produced from her purse. They vanished as soon as they hit the surface of the water, which suddenly flattened to an unreflective black. Madhuri held her hands steady over the surface of the water and hummed, her alto voice resonating warmly. Tiny wisps of cloud formed, curling over her hands.

The blackness flickered, and her forehead creased. There was a pressure in the room that Vivian could feel, as if the surface of the water was pushing back at them. Deep inside her ear, she could feel the bones vibrating, a buzzing so low as to be barely noticeable on a conscious level.

"That's some impressive interference," the doe lady commented. Vivian wished she'd asked her name months ago but felt too awkward to do it now.

"He's no slouch with his wards," Madhuri gritted out. "Someone give me a hand?"

"Sorry, can't," said Steve, backing up.

But Orphne stepped in, putting her hands on top of Madhuri's. "It's not my specialty, but maybe I can give you a boost."

"I hope for your sake she's not that helpful," Sasha murmured to Vivian.

"Because she's not good at scrying?" Vivian whispered.

"Because she's very good at scrying, if the people you're looking for happen to be in the underworld," she said, barely moving her lips. "In which case, you may need a new plan."

"I've got something!" Madhuri said. The black surface shivered and suddenly an image appeared, of a rocky beach with a knotted pine tree.

"We did it!" Orphne clapped. "But where is it?"

"I don't—it's stuck," Madhuri said, beads of sweat starting to form on her brow.

The other party attendees gathered around, offering suggestions and trying to expand or shift the image without much result. After a few minutes, some of the less gifted at scrying wandered off to raid the snack table.

Vivian bit her lip. She felt so helpless. Scrying was advanced-level magic, far beyond anything she could manage, and the theories being tossed around about how Banderbridge was blocking them from getting a fix on him or the beach's location went right over her head. She had a thought, but didn't want to share it. It seemed too stupid as the mages argued over apertures and resonances. She snuck her phone under Madhuri's elbow and snapped a quick picture.

After a few more minutes of searching while the others argued, Vivian finally spoke up. "I think maybe I found him?"

"What did you use, al-Jazari's tracker?" Madhuri asked.

"I told you we should have used al-Jazari's," someone muttered ungraciously.

"Ah, no," Vivian admitted. She had no idea who al-Jazari was. "Google reverse image search. He's got an Instagram."

"No!" Madhuri grabbed the phone. "Oh my stars, he does. Oh, no, my dude, if you're going to do feet-in-the-sand pictures, you've got to do something about those scraggly toenails."

"He left the location off," Raidne pointed out.

"But if you then do a search on this other picture on the feed of the island from the water, you get this other guy's kayak trip from last week," Vivian explained. "Which does have the GPS coordinates attached."

"No island there on Google Maps," Steve noted. "But that doesn't mean anything. Other than the fact that you'd have to rent a boat to get there."

"Oh, I think I can do something about that." Madhuri grinned. "I haven't done something like this since high school."

"You were trouble, weren't you," Steve said, sighing.

"*Such* trouble," Madhuri replied, looking smug.

"I doubt those wards are his only defenses," the willow dryad cautioned. "He's not going to want to let you in."

"Raidne will help," Orphne said firmly. Raidne's eyebrows rose, and Orphne gave her a look. The siren's surprise changed to a thoughtful look, and then she nodded.

"You… none of you have to do this," Vivian faltered.

"What are you talking about?" Orphne said. "You came to my party, you're my friend! Also, Evander talks about Aria all the time. She can come over for a playdate next weekend and we'll take a run over while the fairy god-nanny watches them."

Tears welled up and Vivian had to blink them away. "You said one of the oil things was good for depression?"

"Yes?" Orphne said, confused by the non sequitur. "Oh. Yes!"

"I'll take it." She added recklessly, "I'll take one of each."

"Really?" The chthonic nymph's eyes widened. "Oh! Oh, let me pack those up for you. I can even throw in a Styx-mud face mask!"

With Vivian having gotten things rolling, others started to place their own orders (although Vivian noted no one else bought more than one item). On the way out, she managed to time her exit to coincide with Steve and Sasha. When the door had closed behind them, she screwed up her courage.

"I know Sasha gave Daniel a recommendation on the pharma-mage for Aria. And I was wondering…" She swallowed. It was so hard to say this out loud to someone, especially someone she had wanted to respect her. "I was wondering if she might know someone in the community who does marriage counseling?"

They exchange a glance. They didn't look at her with the disgust she felt she deserved, but she didn't love the looks of pity they chose instead.

Sasha said gently, "You guys are having a tough time, huh?"

"Did he say anything to you?"

"I mean, he's spending almost every evening at our house, it's not hard to tell," Steve said. His eyes widened a little. "Oh. You didn't know that, did you."

She shook her head, a little shocked. She'd assumed he'd wanted to get as far away from the magic community as he could without abandoning Aria.

"Well, anyway, I should have a name for you both tonight, since Daniel asked me for the exact same thing," Sasha said as Vivian stared at her in shock.

Steve patted her shoulder gently. "I'm glad you're looking for help and all. But it also sounds to me like maybe you need to do a little less talking to us and a little more talking to each other?"

"I thought you were hanging out in Stamford," she admitted, twirling a sprig of mint in between her fingers. "Or at least at some bar near the Interstate. I thought you hated it here."

"I don't—Viv, I never hated it here." Daniel had been leaning against a boulder, but pushed himself upright to pace.

Sasha's hobby had turned out to be gardening. Medicinal herbs, of course, not that Vivian could identify anything in the greenhouse. Having a husband who could manipulate temperature and light had some benefits, though—the microclimates inside the garden were incredible. She suspected Steve enjoyed this more than throwing fireballs, and he'd clearly poured love into the precision required. Instead of neat rows or planter boxes, plants spilled down a waist-height hill, irrigated by a tiny artificial stream. The whole thing was half the size of Vivian's dining room, but as they walked through, the temperature shifted noticeably into different growing zones.

Steve had offered them somewhere to talk that was neutral and private. He'd apparently had a word with the pack, too; some of the young adult members had shown up on the Tanakas' doorstep with a bucket of takeout ribs and shooed them out the door, promising to babysit all night, if need be. When they'd reluctantly left, Aria was bouncing with glee at the promise of a rousing game of Guess the Smell.

"You aren't comfortable with magic. You complain about the other parents all the time," she said. She had desperately wanted to talk to him for days, and now that he was here, she could barely bring herself to look at him. She dipped her fingers in the little waterfall spilling down between something with frilly leaves and something else with purple flowers.

"I complain about Cecily and Moira because they're horrible," he said, and she flushed because he was right. "I've never been comfortable, but you've also never let me get comfortable. Ever since the accident, it's like you've been punishing yourself. Like you're the reason this happened and so you have to fix it. I don't know what you want out of me here, but I'm tired of being pushed out of my own family and then blamed for it."

"I didn't—" she started to say reflexively. And then thought about it. About the pack meetings she hadn't invited him to stay for because he'd been so uncomfortable with the idea to begin with, about the school gossip she hadn't told him because he didn't know the backstory, about all the times she'd turned down his invitations to cuddle on the couch so she could practice her remedial spellwork. "I'm sorry."

"I'm sorry, too," he said.

"For what?"

"I don't even know." He ran his hands through his hair. "For making fun of stuff too much? I wanted to do what was best for Aria, and I'm skeptical about how much a lot of this was good for her. And I don't feel like I was wrong about a bunch of it. I mean, the Mean Girls and their Mini-Mes were bad enough. Now it turns out that it's not just the other kids, but the grown-ups threatening her, too, and you didn't tell me. You didn't trust me enough to help."

"I know, I—"

"Just—just let me say this all. At the same time, you were right that she does feel like she fits in better here, even with the bullies. And while I was thinking about what Aria needed, I think I lost track of what you needed, too. And I feel like maybe I was rejecting stuff you felt like you had to buy into, so then you felt like you had to fight me? Or something? But geez, Viv, I thought you were supposed to be on my team, not theirs."

"But if it's us versus them, then which team is Aria supposed to choose?"

He paused. "I don't want her to have to choose."

"She wouldn't pick us. Not in the end. She couldn't."

"Yeah. Maybe. But that didn't mean you had to drink quite so much of the Kool-Aid."

It was her turn to be silent. The water burbled down to the rocks. She couldn't tell if the pool at the end of the little stream was recycled by magic or a pump. Finally, she offered, "They're not all horrible."

"Yeah, I know. Raidne's kind of cold and prickly, but she grows on you. The Cunninghams are cool." He sighed. "And you were right about the wolf pack."

"I'm so, so sorry I didn't tell you about how bad the prophecy thing was getting," she burst out.

"I should hope so." He looked straight at her for the first time. It took all her willpower to meet his eyes, but she forced herself to do it. She was good at penance, she really was. Maybe too good. But this one was necessary. "That sucked, Vivian. I'm supposed to be her father. I couldn't protect her from what happened the first time—"

"I'm sorry, I know, it's my fault—"

"I don't blame you for Aria getting bitten, Viv! I never have! You didn't do anything wrong and I never held you responsible for it. That's all you, it's always been you!" His fists clenched by his sides. "But I do blame you for keeping me from protecting you both now!"

"But you haven't wanted to hear anything about magic," she protested. "You hate that I've been trying to learn."

"Yeah, because I thought you were learning because people were being snobs. I hated the idea that you thought there was something wrong with you, like they were shunning you because you had the wrong purse or something. I didn't know you were learning so you could protect our kid, because you didn't tell me she was in danger!" He threw up his hands. "Why do you think I've been getting these stupid magic lessons from Steve for the last week?"

"You've been trying to learn magic?"

"Yeah, after doing a full day of work and then coming home

to be Daddy and then going out again, and then sleeping on the floor." His shoulders dropped and he rubbed his face. "I thought Steve told you."

She felt a little like the wind had been knocked out of her. He was trying to learn magic? Had he not told her to get back at her? Or worse—had she broken things enough he didn't care what she thought anymore? "Why are you sleeping on the floor?"

He offered a tired laugh. "Have you seen how many stuffed animals our daughter owns?"

She gave a half-hearted snort and then lapsed into silence. The thought that he had been trying to engage with the magical world—with Steve, with Raidne—and she hadn't known hurt. He'd had a whole other life in parallel with hers, when they could have been together. How much had been because they each hadn't been willing to share? Or see? "I didn't mean to push you away. I swear."

"I realize you didn't do it on purpose. And I should have been listening more. And then maybe you would have trusted me better. Or at least said something in private instead of telling the whole town you think I'm a bad father."

"I'm so, so sorry." She didn't know what else to say. It seemed so inadequate.

He looked away. "And the worst of it is—"

She braced herself.

His voice broke a little. "I'm so incredibly angry at you, and at the same time, I miss you. I miss you so much. For the last year, you've been sliding farther and farther out of my grasp, and you won't let me follow. I don't know what I'm supposed to do here. Do I need to learn some spell or something to count? Do I need to find some punishment that makes you feel like you've atoned enough? I want my wife and kid back."

"I don't—we're right here," she choked.

"Are you? Because it's awfully lonely where I'm standing. Some days it feels like you don't think you're good enough, and some days it feels like you don't think I'm good enough. But whatever it is, it's never enough. And I'm tired of trying to be enough."

"It's my fault," she said. Tears spilled down her cheeks. "It's all my fault, I broke our child, she was perfect and I broke her, and I destroyed our lives, and then I broke our marriage, and I don't understand why you don't hate me."

"I don't hate you," he protested.

"You should," she said, turning away and wrapping her arms around herself. "I hate me."

She couldn't open her eyes. She didn't want to see whatever was on his face. Everything she'd locked away—all the panic and remorse and guilt—clawed at the inside of her chest until she felt like her heart would burst.

Strong arms slid along hers, pulling her back against his chest. "I don't hate you, Viv," he whispered into her hair. "And Aria's not broken. Nothing's broken that can't be mended."

The tension that rose up from her chest finally exploded. Somehow, he turned her around in his arms, whispering quiet nonsense into her ear as she shook with sobs. Time ceased as she cried out the shame and loneliness and terror.

She came back to herself gradually.

"Back now?" Daniel asked.

She nodded, her breath hiccuping. She rubbed the back of her hand against a swollen eye. "I'm sorry. I hurt you and instead of apologizing, I turned it into you having to comfort me."

He took a big breath and let it out slowly. "Yeah, not sure that was great. But maybe it wouldn't have happened in the first place if you'd let me comfort you to begin with."

"I suck."

"Yeah, a little. Me too," he said. "It's because we're made of people. Humans are a terrible building material."

"I don't know, is werewolf better?" She immediately regretted the weak joke.

But he smiled, a little unsteadily. His eyes were suspiciously damp and she wondered if he'd also been crying while she'd been wailing all over him. "I don't know. Let's ask Aria when she's an adult."

"If she's talking to us at all."

"That might have happened whether she was a werewolf or not." He tilted her chin up to look at him. "Hey. You didn't ruin our lives. What happened, the werewolf thing, it was an accident. And even if our lives don't look the way we thought they would, no one's life ever looks the way they thought it would."

She swallowed. "But did I ruin our marriage?" she asked in a small voice.

He sighed and tucked her under his chin. "I'm still pretty pissed off, but not as much as I was last week. What about me? Did I ruin our marriage?"

"This is my—"

"Viv." He lifted her chin gently with a finger. "A moment ago, you were really mad at me, and you had a right to be. And I'm not exactly proud of how I handled stuff, including the last week or so. Stop rewriting history so that everything is your fault, OK?"

She nodded, although it somehow felt easier if it were all her fault. At least then she could control something.

He gave her a half smile, the one she had first fallen for. "And we should talk to that therapist Sasha found."

"It's hard talking about stuff when you can't tell them the

most important bits," she admitted. "It's not like the regular human therapists are in network anyway."

He rolled his eyes. "One thing everyone can agree on, insurance sucks."

"Are we OK?"

"Right now, probably not," he said. "But we could be."

She nodded.

"Ready to go home?" he asked. "We can order a pizza, watch something stupid on TV. I kind of watched the next three episodes of our show out of spite, but now I don't mind watching them again with you."

"Umm. Soon? Because first, I kind of have to get ready to break into an ancient wizard's lair?"

"…do I even want to know?"

"Probably not," she admitted. "But that's probably why I should tell you. Can I fill you in on the drive home? Mrs. Fairhair's going to want to know what happened to her grandkids, and the grandkids probably ate everything in the freezer."

"Yeah," he said, his lips quirking. "I'd like that."

15

Apr 29 10:13AM
The next Parent Advisory Council meeting will be taking place
in the school cafeteria instead of the teachers' lounge.

Apr 29 10:15AM
Apologies for the change—the next Parent Advisory Council
meeting will be taking place on Zoom instead of the school
cafeteria. Link attached!

Apr 29 10:21AM
Another slight change! The PAC meeting will be on Google
Meet instead of Zoom. Please delete the previous link.

Apr 29 10:32AM
Last one, we promise! The PAC meeting will be taking place
in an interdimensional vortex. You'll receive an embossed
invitation 38 minutes before the beginning of the meeting. Don't
forget to bring a blood offering for Xrithgar the Restless!

T he waves rolled the pebbles on the shore back and forth. The sound was exactly like a soothing track on a YouTube meditation channel.

Vivian was not soothed.

"When does the boat get here?" she asked, shifting uncomfortably. She'd worn the wrong shoes; her sneakers had only kept the dampness out for a few minutes, and the little multicolored pebbles did not support her weight the way damp sand would have. She kept having to move a few inches over as she sank into the pebbles. One had already worked its way into her left shoe, and another was trapped between the side and her outside right ankle bone.

"Where we're going, we don't need boats," Raidne said. Vivian must have been getting used to her. She'd looked cool when she said it, but she gave Vivian the quickest sideways glance to see if the reference had been noticed, or perhaps if it had been correct.

Steve snorted, because the Dad Code required him to laugh at Dad Jokes, even if the person making them was an immortal lesbian. Who might have literally lived on Lesbos at some point, for all Vivian knew.

"Please come," Vivian begged him.

"I don't think it's a good idea," he repeated. "If he's twitchy about whatever the Council decreed, he's not going to be happy to see someone who sometimes works for the Council, even if I'm not on official business."

"But it could go the other way," she pressed. "He doesn't have any reason to speak to a random mundane mom, but maybe you could. You know."

"Imply this is somehow official business?" He raised an eyebrow. "Look at you, you'll be smoking up behind the bleachers in no time if you keep up this scofflaw business."

"It may also be more compelling coming from a mage," Raidne said, unexpectedly backing Vivian up. "Or another male. I didn't interact with the headmaster, but I have the impression he may have been a bit of a… traditionalist."

"If he's a traditionalist, I'm not sure how much this particular male mage is going to help you," Steve pointed out, raising a Black hand.

"I don't know anyone else," Vivian said, desperately. "I can't help with this Reckoning thing, I can't help Aria pass her tests, I need to solve one goddamn problem and get the stupid Parent Advisory Council off my back about the gala funds so I can deal with the rest of this shit!"

She only realized she was yelling when the stones crunched as Steve and Raidne shifted back. A man who could throw fireballs and a woman who could ensorcel people with a song, leaning away from her anger. "Sorry."

"Soooo maybe it's time to get on the raft," Madhuri suggested from the water's edge.

Vivian turned with some relief, which immediately dissipated when she saw what Madhuri had built. She'd pulled down what looked like a stormcloud, dark gray and roiling. It bobbed and skittered as the waves washed underneath it and pushed it gently against the beach. Vivian had flown through plenty of clouds; she knew perfectly well they were nothing but mist. Somehow, though, Madhuri was standing on top of it, scraps of cloud curling over her hiking boots. One edge curled up into a backsplash.

"Come on, let's do this thing," Madhuri prompted again. "Cloud's going to get impatient if we don't get moving."

Vivian swallowed hard and stepped onto the raft. It gave a little, but was solid underneath, like walking on a mattress.

Raidne stepped on and settled herself on the backsplash, as routinely as taking a seat in a chauffeured car. Steve heaved a sigh and jumped on as well.

Madhuri sat next to Raidne and patted the side of the cloud, which skimmed out over the waves. Vivian looked at the mist at her feet, expecting to plummet through at any moment.

"Couldn't we rent a boat?" she asked weakly.

"This is less likely to trigger the wards. Besides, this one owed me a favor, and boat rentals are expensive," Madhuri said casually. "Thanks for letting me tag along. I don't think I've gone on a quest since my history teacher got cursed by that mummy back in high school."

"Wait, you were part of the whole thing with Thoth and the ruby?" Steve said it like he was referring to a particularly well-known football game from his youth.

"Such a pain in the ass," Madhuri said. "Those were the days."

The ride was not smooth. The raft was mostly flat underneath as well as on top, so it didn't so much cut through the waves as bounce along on top of them. Vivian tried to perch on the backsplash like Raidne, but she nearly tumbled overboard on the first big swell and Raidne had to haul her back. She settled for huddling on the flat, back braced against the cloud, trying not to lose her breakfast. A gull kept pace with them, eyeing her speculatively.

"You OK?" Steve asked. "You look a little green."

"I don't suppose you have any spells for seasickness?" she croaked.

"Sorry," he said with far too much pity. "I've got some Dramamine in the backpack, though."

The raft crashed through another wave and Vivian was

pretty sure her stomach had been left behind. Flailing for a topic to distract herself, she found herself wondering exactly how selfish she'd been. "Is he going to give you trouble? I mean, because…"

"Because I'm Black?" Steve gave her a look. "Probably not overtly, at least. Might depend on how obligated he feels to toe the party line these days."

She hadn't thought enough about this, or what it might mean for Aria. She'd been so focused on how different species were treated in the magical community, she hadn't given a whole lot of thought to race. Which was a privileged mistake that could also bite her family in the butt. "But they seem so… so…"

"Hippy dippy?" Madhuri said. "With all the multicultural emails and shit? Veilport likes to think of itself as all progressive."

"But they're not."

Steve gave a half-shrug. "They try, a lot of them. Most of the time. It's better than many places. Doesn't mean there isn't a lot of room to keep trying."

She blushed. "I'm sorry. I shouldn't have pushed."

"Don't worry about this one. You do need the help, and I've faced a lot worse than one cranky old dude."

She hadn't wanted to push, but he seemed to be open. "You're sort of a cop? Retired cop?"

"Hmmm, more like… I dunno, a reservist. The Shadow Council needs to enforce things, sometimes. I put in my time, and then I stepped back from the active role when the twins were born."

"How did you get into that in the first place?"

He gave a laugh without a lot of humor in it. "When you're a Black teenage boy whose strongest talent is slinging fireballs, being on the inside of authority instead of the outside goes a long way towards keeping people's looks on the respectful instead of on the suspicious side of things, if you know what I mean."

"Oh." That was… not great, but pretty understandable.

"And then as I got older, it seemed to me that if I wanted my hypothetical kids to have more options someday, I should make sure people who looked like them were making some of the decisions. And then the kids weren't hypothetical, and they needed their daddy specifically. When they get older, well, we'll see then. Gotta get them there first."

Madhuri nodded. "A lot of the folks in power are trying, but they've got blind spots you could fly a dragon through. But we change things by being there, doing our thing instead of what was expected of us." She grinned wickedly. "And if that means harassing some asshole traditionalist, I'm all for it."

"Of course, this is all still about voluntary donations to a pricey elite private school," Vivian couldn't help but point out.

"No ethical consumption under capitalism and all." Madhuri waved a hand. "Not gonna fix any of this overnight, and meanwhile we've also got lives to lead. By the way, time to wrap up the navel-gazing, because we're almost here."

"But how do you decide—oh my god, what's that?"

A spire of rock suddenly erupted out of the water in front of them. Madhuri yelped and swirled her hands, and the cloud swerved, skidding against the barnacle-encrusted stone. Another shot up, and another, and another, bracketing the raft. Madhuri cursed.

Vivian turned back towards the shore of the little island they had been approaching. She couldn't see anyone, but there was a little house she could barely make out, nestled into the base of the rocks.

"Steven, I don't suppose…?" Raidne murmured.

"I've got this," Steve said grimly, pushing up his sleeves. He did something with his hands, folding his fingers in impossible angles while muttering under his breath, then aimed them palms-out at the nearest spire. Vivian expected a fireball, but instead the air rippled in front of him. There was a great crack that drove her hands to her ears, and then the stone crumbled into the sea. He repeated it twice more, clearing them a path through the rocks.

Madhuri was already kneeling on the edge of the raft, whispering to the cloud. The whole raft surged up, lifted over the remains of the spires. Vivian fell to her knees, trying to cling to an insubstantial surface. There were no sides, no safety belts, nothing. How high could they go? Cloud height? She hadn't been afraid of heights before, but it seemed an excellent time to develop a phobia. She focused on staying put and not hyperventilating.

Something above them screamed. Vivian looked up, blinking into the sun.

"Get down, protect your eyes!" Steve grabbed her and pulled her to the deck.

Something scraped the back of her neck, hard enough to draw blood. Madhuri hissed as another gull dive-bombed her, snapping its beak. They cowered on the deck of the raft as a flock of angry birds converged on them, diving and stabbing.

Raidne alone stood. She threw back her head, filling her lungs. Vivian clapped her hands back over her ears, for all the good it would do. The sound that came out of Raidne's mouth spiraled up into a painfully high range and then disappeared altogether. The birds, however, turned from an angry mob into a spiral, circling up and away from them all.

The spiral was reflected in the water beneath them. Slowly, and then faster, a waterspout began to form and rise up towards them. Madhuri spoke urgently to the cloud in a language Vivian didn't speak, arguing and pleading. The cloud rose a little farther, shuddering. But despite the utter lack of any kind of features, Vivian could feel the little cloud straining to bear them high enough to escape. A wisp of the waterspout lashed the bottom of the cloud, and the raft began to tilt precariously. Vivian grabbed at the edge, failing to find a finger hold as she struggled not to slide down the incline of the deck.

"Can you counter the rotation?" Raidne demanded, strain in her voice for the first time Vivian had heard.

"I'm trying," said Steve, one hand on the raft edge and one in the air. "But I'd guess he's been manipulating laminar boundary-layer flows since before I was born!"

A figure rose up beyond the waterspout, roughly the shape of a man but made of the seawater itself. The face had the uncanny valley look of something Aria might have sculpted out of clay and lovingly gifted to her parents to keep on their bedroom end table and give them nightmares for the rest of their lives.

"A weather mage to defeat my protections and a siren to beguile my mind," the figure said in a voice that hissed like waves over sand. The water beneath them churned and Vivian wondered what would happen if one of those stone spires shot up right through the cloud. "All for one old man. Were you afraid your fireballs alone would fail, Council puppet?"

Steve and Raidne opened their mouths, but Vivian had been preparing for this. She took a big breath and put on her biggest client-facing smile, and hoped he couldn't see how hard her hands were shaking. "Actually, they're helping me out. I'm a huge fan of your work, BeachMagic62. But since you don't seem to do any meet-and-greets, I was hoping maybe you'd be willing to indulge a fan?"

The water statue paused, mouth open. It blinked a few times, and then narrowed its eyes. "That's a new one, I'll admit. Good try. But it takes more than thirty seconds on social media to fool me. Now kindly die."

"Wait! Please!" She was not going to die out here in the middle of the ocean for a vain old man. "I was hoping to get your bouillabaisse recipe? The one you posted on April fifth?"

He paused again. She could feel Steve next to her, surreptitiously doing something with his fingers behind her back. Raidne was slowly inhaling, filling her lungs without seeming to take a big breath. "All right. That's a novel enough approach. I'll give you fifteen minutes. Come ashore. But one wrong twitch from that Council enforcer and you'll be back in the water before you can blink."

The waterspout collapsed with a splash. The cloud settled back down to the surface with a breezy sigh. One remaining wave behind gave their raft a tap that sent it skimming towards the shore.

Former Headmaster Banderbridge reminded Vivian of an academically minded Santa Claus. He had the flowing white beard. He had the tiny rectangular reading glasses perched on the end of his nose. He had the twinkle, clearly having decided to bring out the charm on the chance that she was a genuine fan. She could see why poor Ms. Genevieve was having trouble living up to the role.

The house, which he invited Vivian into with guarded enthusiasm and the other three with visible suspicion, turned out to be a great deal larger on the inside than the outside's weatherbeaten clapboard would suggest. This was what Vivian had expected from a proper wizard's home. The interior was all golden oak, with giant bay windows looking out onto the ocean. An enormous telescope was aimed at the window, an orrery next to it to suggest it was as much for stars as searching for unwanted visitors. The open floor plan gave her a view from the piles of alembics and beakers overflowing a wide scarred table, past a cozy sofa that looked like the scene of many naps, to the floor-to-ceiling bookshelves that lined most of the back walls. A kitchen nook included a full open fireplace, complete with a bubbling cauldron merrily stirring itself. Kites, articulated bird skeletons, and bunches of dried herbs hung from the rafters. A wrought-iron spiral staircase curled its way to a second floor. Near the door, an elderly fox snoozed in a basket.

It was easy enough to ignore the iPad abandoned on the couch, and the Roomba neatly docked next to the coat rack.

Banderbridge bustled her on to the back of the room, twinkling at her all the while. He fixed her a mug of tea and pulled out his recipe book (tucked among all the grimoires) and asked for her Instagram handle. They pored over the cookbook together, as he gave her all his suggested substitutions and waxed rhapsodic on the importance of including enough bay leaves. The others drifted tactfully away—Steve to examine the bookshelves, Raidne to peer through the telescope, Madhuri to try to cuddle the fox. She wasn't quite sure whether to be grateful they were giving her space or annoyed they'd left her alone to face the twinkle. She struggled a bit not to cave under the weight of his charm, glad he was not trying to convince her to endow a scholarship or donate a basketball court. Even though she had nowhere near that level of money, she suspected she would have been tempted.

Finally, after they had thoroughly exhausted the topic of

haddock, he sighed and pushed his mug away. "Well. It was kind, or at least clever, of you to indulge an old man. But I am not so much a fool as to think you came all the way out here for fish. I commend you on the flattering ruse, though. What does the Shadow Council want with me now?"

"Well to be clear, I'm not on the Shadow Council," Vivian said. He snorted at the obvious. "I'm on the Parent Advisory Council."

That earned her raised eyebrows. "Surely the rumors deterred you?"

"If there are rumors, no one's been sharing them with me," Vivian said. "And that's exactly the problem."

She'd given this a lot of thought over the last few days. What would convince him to open up to her? She'd considered trying to take the innocent and ignorant approach, which would have been basically true. But now that she'd met him, with his calculated twinkle, she didn't think he'd tell an innocent anything. What persona should she try to adopt? Concerned parent? Intimidating auditor? "I'm sure it will not surprise you," she said, going for flattery as fishing bait, "that this year's revenue picture looks different than last year's."

"Hmm," was all she got in return.

Banderbridge kept glancing at her friends drifting around the room. After a few such glances, Raidne caught her eye significantly and tilted her head towards the door. Vivian nodded; it didn't seem like the older wizard meant her harm, but he might speak more freely alone.

"I need some fresh air," Raidne announced.

Madhuri glared at her, clearly annoyed to be pulled away as soon as they got to the good part.

"Yep, fresh air," Steve said, catching on. He peered out the door. "Madhuri, I think your cloud is trying to run away."

"Oh, all right! I need to check my email anyway, and there's no reception in here." Madhuri gave the fox one last pet and stood. She paused by the door and waggled her phone significantly, clearly an invitation for Vivian to call her if she needed her.

Banderbridge heaved a sigh. "Your friends are kind."

"They are." Her eyes stung for a moment and she blinked quickly.

"Most people abandon you at a hint of scandal," he said bitterly, all twinkle extinguished. "Decades of service, gone in an instant."

"That sounds terrible," she said cautiously. On one hand, she could easily sympathize with how fast public opinion could turn on you. On the other, for all she knew, he was responsible for accidentally getting a student eaten by a dragon or a giant snake or something. She glanced at him sideways. He wasn't looking at her at all; he was fidgeting with a signet ring that bore the school crest, his gaze far away. She didn't need to be anyone, she suddenly realized. Just a sympathetic ear. "So unfair."

"I only ever wanted the best for the children, you know."

"Of course." She hoped she wouldn't regret nodding along. What if it wasn't an accident? What if she had agreed that he'd been justified in... in... poaching magical creatures? Or selling people's souls? What counted as a fireable offense?

"I've always thought the high-stakes testing left too many promising students behind."

That hadn't been where she had expected this to go, but she was hardly going to disagree. "It's not fair. They're kids—how are they supposed to live up to that kind of pressure?"

"Exactly." The twinkle was back. "Watching some of those students, students from the very best families, fail to get into the schools they had their hearts set on, well—it was enough to break your heart."

She kept smiling but wondered what exactly counted as "best families" in this context.

He sighed, stirring at the dregs of his tea. "So over time, it was only natural that a certain, shall we say, understanding evolved between our school and some of the better high schools. Nothing formal, mind you. A way for the parents of children who were struggling with standardized tests to express their children's merits in an alternate form."

Vivian blinked. "A way to recommend them to the heads of the high schools?" she guessed, feeling weirdly let down. She'd been working her way up to expecting a ritual murder cult. This was all just an admissions scandal?

"Oh, not the school heads," he said bitterly. "They preferred to keep their hands clean, of course. The high schools have far more staff than a little primary school possibly could, no matter how respected. But many of the departments are allowed to put in their own petitions on behalf of students showing particular talent. The sports coaches get a certain number of recruits, for example, or the summoners may want a few alternates to make sure they can assemble a full circle."

"And then if the child in question gets to the school and decides they're no longer interested in that particular activity…" she guessed shrewdly.

He shrugged. "Children change their minds all the time. Middle schoolers who show promise hit a growth spurt and lose some of their dexterity. Late bloomers bloom and take the place of earlier stars who fade out. Choosing a high school class is always a gamble; no one is surprised when there's some shuffling that first year."

"You know, I'm the Parent Advisory Council treasurer this year," she said, thinking fast. "So I can see how at, say, the gala, it's natural for parents to express their appreciation of the school and all its efforts. And while some of the funds are used to improve school facilities, it's also important to maintain all those relationships with the high schools? As well as recompensing everyone involved for all their hard efforts?"

He beamed at her. "I'm glad you understand. But then, I suppose that's why they made you treasurer."

That was most assuredly not why they made her treasurer. Every instinct instilled by a decade of auditing made her want to cringe back from the story of rampant bribery and fraud. But she forced a sympathetic smile instead. "I take it that the Shadow Council did not understand the subtleties of balancing the needs of the community?"

His mouth thinned. "Hardly. And I suppose I'm not surprised. But I would have thought that other school professionals would at least be sympathetic to parents' needs."

She took a stab in the dark. "Many of the parents are not happy with Ms. Genevieve."

"I should think not," he said with bitter satisfaction, confirming her guess.

"How unfortunate that this year's gala funds were so much less than last year's…"

"Well, if Genevieve hasn't been doing the necessary fundraising, I should hardly be surprised when funds are short," he said, as prissily as any aggrieved middle schooler.

Why couldn't he have been secretly building an army of golems in the basement? There was something so disappointingly sordid about finding out that the magical world was exactly as prone to stupid corruption as the mundane one. Not to mention the fact that the "best" families were stooping to massive bribery to place their kids meant that maybe she should have shelled out for that stupid consultant after all.

"I suppose the Trials must be even more desperate than usual this year, without that safety valve," he said.

"Well, it's pretty bad," she said. "But I think a lot of it's being overshadowed by the whole Reckoning thing."

"What?" He dropped the mug he was toying with. It rolled off the table and smashed into smithereens. He absently sketched a shape into the air and the pieces rebounded up to the table and re-formed back into the mug. If only everything broken could be fixed so easily. "But I haven't seen any of the signs."

"Well, the symbol, you know, the stormcloud thing? It's been burned into the school lawn, and appeared in the smoke tornado when the windows shattered at the gala. And there was the explosion at the Talent Show, and the hellhounds loose in the school, and a shadow wolf at the Research Fair. People are pretty spooked."

He looked more and more appalled as she spoke. "But none of my warning spells have triggered. I never took them down—they should have alerted me if it were actually the Reckoning. What else has happened in the town?"

"Oh. Uh." She wracked her brain. She was even less plugged into the town gossip network than the school one. Although surely if there were more disasters, people would have been accusing her of them? "I don't think anything has happened?"

"See, now that doesn't even make sense," he said. "There's no good reason why the Reckoning would center on the school rather than, I don't know, Town Hall or the harbor or some of the artifacts in the library. Mistress Widdershins didn't even establish the place until after the prophecy."

"Mistress Widdershins founded Grimoire Grammar?"

"Oh, yes, didn't you see the plaque? Not in its current form or anything, but she started the teaching circle that eventually became the school. What has she had to say about all this?"

"Mistress Widdershins?" So casually asking after the opinion of someone dead for a couple of centuries threw her. She struggled to remember what she had heard. "I thought she put the last medium who tried to disturb her into a coma?"

"Well, for most people, of course. But the headmaster of Grimoire Grammar has a special relationship," he dropped casually. He was enjoying this, she could tell. "But I suppose Genevieve never got that far in the notes. It's a pity they left the school in such inexperienced hands."

"I don't suppose you could…" she said, with rising hope.

"Oh, my dear, I couldn't possibly interfere now," he said, patting her hand condescendingly. "I'm sure the Shadow Council would never approve. Of course, if they were to ask me themselves…"

She could see him building his triumphant return in his mind, the smug bastard. "They would hardly listen to me."

"Ah, perhaps not you, my dear," he said, with even more condescension. He'd picked up on her lack of magical skills by now, she was sure. She had no idea how powerful mages recognized each other, but it was probably something like rich people recognizing each other's watches. That was all right, she didn't want to belong to a club with this embezzling, extorting jerk. "But that fine fireball-throwing fellow you came with most certainly can pass the message on. I'm happy to help, they always know where to find me."

"Thank you so much for your advice," she said, with the

biggest smile she could re-summon from her client-dealing days. "You have no idea how much help you've been."

He ushered her out the door with promises of additional fish recipes on his Instagram.

"So?" Steve asked, once the raft was well out of earshot, and he'd thrown up some kind of ward for good measure.

"He was running a bribery scheme where parents 'donated' to the gala, and then he funneled the bribes to coaches and teachers at the high schools to make underqualified kids into special recruits while skimming a bunch off the top," she said sourly. "Ms. Genevieve must have tipped off the Shadow Council. I'm guessing they decided to hush it all up rather than cast doubts on the system as a whole, or perhaps because a lot of important people would have been wrapped up in the scandal."

"Oh, geez." Steve exchanged a glance with Raidne. "That… explains some things."

"Did you get what you needed?" Raidne asked.

"I don't know," she said slowly. "I don't have any proof, and I don't think he would have provided any. But maybe it's enough to pressure Ms. Genevieve into getting the board off my back. Although, he said something else that was very interesting."

"Oh?"

"Well apparently, he had wards up about the Reckoning, and none of them have gone off."

"This much water between him and the wards may have affected something," Steve said doubtfully.

"I'll take your word for it," she said. "But the other interesting thing he said is that the headmaster of Grimoire Grammar has a special relationship with Mistress Widdershins."

"Genevieve, Genevieve, Genevieve," Madhuri mused. "Have you been holding out on us or did you get too focused on the obvious problem to do the background research? It's like the newt incident all over again."

"Raidne, is Orphne's, uh, chthonic-ness limited to Hades' realm, or is it afterlives in general?" Vivian asked. "I need to make an appointment with Ms. Genevieve anyway, and I wonder if Orphne might be willing to do me a favor."

16

May 3 8:03 AM
While we are aware that "goat-sucker" is the literal translation of "chupacabra," it is considered offensive by the Chupacabra Conservation Society and is banned from usage in the classroom. We will be holding a mandatory Cultural Sensitivity workshop on Wednesday.

"I'm always happy to talk to parents, but we'll have to keep this short today. I'm afraid the preparations for tomorrow's Field Day can't wait." Ms. Genevieve gave Vivian and Orphne a practiced, polished smile. Her phone was already facedown so Vivian only heard the theme song of *Keeping Up with the Kitsune* before Ms. Genevieve could silence it.

Vivian could feel the apology forming on her lips and forced it back. This wasn't going to be won by being polite and meek, not this time. "I talked to Banderbridge." She clamped her lips shut. That was too abrupt; she'd been trying so hard not to bite her tongue that she'd overshot and been too blunt. Too late now.

The headmistress froze. "I see. About?"

Vivian clutched her hands to keep them from trembling. Yes, Ms. Genevieve had the power to kick Aria out of the school. But if she couldn't manage this, the chances were that they were going to get kicked out anyway. "Initially, about the gap in the gala funds."

"Ah."

Vivian forced herself to look the headmistress directly in the eye. "I understand why the Shadow Council would want this to be kept quiet. But I need you to have a word with Cecily and the rest of the Parent Advisory Council. You know perfectly well that there's a good reason this year's funds are lower. And that it won't impact the amount the school receives in the end."

"Throw Banderbridge under the bus, you mean," Ms. Genevieve said, grimacing.

Vivian tried not to sigh in relief. "You know he'd do the same to you."

"Oh, he tried," the headmistress said. Her hand clutched at her phone, the knuckles white. "You wouldn't believe... well, you of all people might. Anyway, he's still got quite the reputation around here. People don't want to hear it."

"But a few words in the right ears seem more than enough to eat away at a reputation," Vivian replied.

"As you know?" Ms. Genevieve snorted. "Fine. I'll talk to Cecily, but I can't promise it will have the effect you're hoping for. As you might have noticed, this isn't a community that changes its mind easily. You said initially, though?" She glanced at Orphne.

"I might have found a solution to a different problem," Vivian said, sagging back in the chair. Somehow her life had gotten to the point that proposing a seance was less stressful than dealing with financial fraud. Then again, her clients had never accused her personally of perpetuating the fraud, and she wasn't the one who had to conduct the seance. "Banderbridge also mentioned that the head of Grimoire Grammar has certain privileges with Mistress Widdershins."

Ms. Genevieve sat bolt upright. "That is indeed the first I've heard. That unscrupulous, condescending"—she struggled visibly for an appropriate insult—"old snake. He probably buried all the documentation in the older records, knowing I'd be too busy cleaning up his messes to get that far."

She brought herself back under control, tucking a loose hair back into her chignon. "Thank you for bringing this to my attention. Was there anything else?"

"Mistress Widdershins was the school founder, and also the person whose records contain the most complete description of the Reckoning prophecy," Vivian pointed out. She could see Ms. Genevieve wasn't making the connection, instead focusing on Banderbridge's betrayal.

"I ought to be able to tap that to ask her personally," Orphne added brightly. At Ms. Genevieve's nonplussed expression, she shot Vivian an apologetic glance. "Sorry, we need to speed this up a little if I'm going to get Evander to Spell Scouts on time."

"You think she'll be able to tell us if the Reckoning is going to interrupt Field Day," Ms. Genevieve said slowly.

"Like it has every major school event this year," Vivian finished. "And *only* school events."

"*Only*…?" Ms. Genevieve said. "Oh. You're right. How interesting."

"I brought everything I need," Orphne continued, pulling a wickedly sharp dagger and a pomegranate out of her purse. "We don't even need a locus: you and the school will stand for that. Just three anchors. So we can wrap this up before pick-up, easy peasy!"

"Three?" Vivian kicked herself for not asking about the full requirements before coming in. "I'll duck out and see if maybe one of the teachers…?"

"Oh, I don't want to bother them. We're good with us three!" Orphne chirped.

"I'm not a mage," Vivian protested.

"But you can light a candle spell, right?" Orphne turned her full, wide-eyed attention to Vivian. She continued earnestly, "And unlock the gate down by the parking lot? That's good enough, you don't need to even cast anything yourself. Just be present. It's more of a formality than anything else."

Good enough. If it had come from Cecily or Moira, it would have felt like an insult. Orphne's enthusiasm and kitten sweater made it seem like a fact. Good enough. When had she last been good enough?

Ms. Genevieve glanced at her calendar on her phone and fired off a few rapid emails. "All right. Ms. Immacolata will have to retrieve the ice pops. I have half an hour."

"From what I've heard about Mistress Widdershins, we'll be lucky to get five minutes," said Orphne. "And don't worry, I signed up to bring watermelon slices tomorrow."

Ms. Genevieve pushed the desk against the wall, revealing the circle inscribed in the floor beneath it. She sat down with far more grace than Vivian could have ever managed while wearing a pencil skirt. Vivian sank down across from her, feeling grubby in her jeans. Orphne cracked open the pomegranate and grabbed the dagger. Vivian expected her to slice open her palm, but instead she cut a shallow slice on the top of her forearm where it didn't interfere with the use of her hands. The nymph squeezed several drops of blood into a dish and then slapped a Band-Aid emblazoned with cartoon dinosaurs on the cut. She mixed the blood and pomegranate juice, painting a symbol in the middle of the floor with a seriousness that contrasted with the sweater. The other two women joined hands and Vivian fumbled her way into her place. Orphne cleared her throat and then started to chant in what Vivian assumed was ancient Greek.

The hair on the back of Vivian's arms rose. Her scalp prickled. Across the circle, she could see Orphne's oiled curls lift like she was touching a Van de Graaff generator at a science center. The nymph's eyes began to shine with a silvery light.

In between them, in the center of the circle, the air took on a misty, moonlit quality. A sharp scent, like freshly turned earth and moldering stone, filled Vivian's nostrils. Then the air crackled, as if lightning had struck.

She blinked the afterimages out of her eyes and found herself staring through a semi-transparent back clothed in faded black homespun wool.

"This'd better be worth my time, children," Mistress Widdershins was complaining to Ms. Genevieve. "I thought the last set was enough to put you all off on this summoning nonsense."

"Nonsense?" Orphne asked, her voice taking on a sepulcher echo Vivian had never noticed before.

"I don't hold with all that ghost-knocking foolery," the old witch said, waving a hand dismissively. "Didn't when I was alive, certainly don't now that I'm dead. Now, give me one good reason why I shouldn't aura-shock the lot of you and let you sleep off your folly until Beltane?"

"I am the current headmistress of Grimoire Grammar School," said Ms. Genevieve with great dignity.

"Oh, are you, deary?" Mistress Widdershins said, turning from Orphne entirely. On one hand, it was a little worrisome that she didn't seem terribly concerned about keeping track of the person who summoned her, an immortal denizen of the underworld. On the other, it meant Vivian wasn't staring at the back of her coif anymore. "Did the old cockalorum totter off into retirement on his own, or did you give him a push? He hasn't shown up on our side of the veil yet, thank heavens."

Ms. Genevieve was developing a tiny bit of an eye twitch, and Orphne was starting to look strained. Vivian jumped in, as respectfully as she could. "We're terribly sorry to disturb you, Mistress Widdershins, but we need your help."

"You always need Mistress Widdershins' help, never can figure a blasted thing out on your own," she sighed. "What is it this time? Plague of frogs? Mold in rye have everyone hallucinating and reaching for torches again? Oh, I remember you from Samhain. Did the imps you lot trapped to run your scrying boxes finally get intelligent enough to take over and cause mischief yet?"

"We didn't trap any imps, Mistress," Orphne said reproachfully.

"Then why are you always asking them for things? Siri, do this, Alexa, do that. They'll take on over, you just watch," Mistress Widdershins snapped. "Well, out with it, girl. What terrible emergency frightened you enough to drag me back over again? I should have burned that diary rather than let it live on for people to keep a-reading it. An entire town was involved in that spell, you know. But you forgot everyone else's names and only remember mine because I was fool enough to write it all down. Do you ever bother Goodman Williams? Or young Abigail Walker? No. It's Mistress Widdershins this and Mistress

Widdershins that, and everyone else gets a nice rest but poor Mistress Widdershins."

"With respect, Mistress Widdershins," Vivian said. "We needed to know what to do about the Reckoning."

"Zounds, girl, why?"

Vivian swallowed as the ghost's full attention rounded on her. She glanced at Orphne and Ms. Genevieve, and neither seemed likely to speak up and rescue her. "Because... because it's... here?"

"Blatherskite!" Mistress Widdershins rolled her eyes. "Every fifty years or so, one of you ninnies decides it's the End Times a-coming, and then 'Oh, Mistress Widdershins, it's the Reckoning' you cry. There ain't nothing wrong with your world that a little less watching scrying tablets and a little more mucking out pigpens wouldn't cure."

"But the prophecy," Vivian tried again. "Things have been going wrong—explosions and shadow wolves, and the eye in the stormcloud symbol appearing everywhere."

"I tell you, Minerva Vondelshank couldn't prophesy a thunderstorm if the raindrops were hitting her nose." Mistress Widdershins sniffed. "If there was such a thing, it would be rolling through the spirit world like a black tempest afore it ever reached you folks, and I can tell you, we haven't had so much as a wisp."

"You mean the Reckoning is not arriving?" Ms. Genevieve asked carefully, to be sure.

"No more than the Second Coming, hallelujah," the ghost declared. "Now if you're all done statin' the obvious, I have things to do on my side of the veil. And if you could make those rapscallions stop fiddling with symbols and casting ripples, that would be just fine by all of us!"

"But who is it?" Vivian begged as the witch began to fade out.

"How should I know?" she said, her voice getting tinny and faint. "If they ain't dead, I don't know 'em!"

Vivian's ears popped. All of a sudden, the light was back to normal.

"Well," said Orphne, cracking her neck. "She was a fizzy one."

"I don't understand," said Vivian. "If it's not the Reckoning, then what's going on?"

"Maybe someone wants us to think it is?" Orphne said.

"I'm afraid I have a great deal to do to prepare for tomorrow," Ms. Genevieve said, smoothing back her hair.

"I'm sorry, what?" Vivian said.

"Thank you for bringing this to my attention," Ms. Genevieve continued, rising to her feet. "I assure you the proper authorities will be notified."

"I don't want someone notified, I want to know what they're going to do," Vivian protested. "That's my kid they're targeting."

"I'll see you both at Field Day. Have a good night."

"But—" Vivian and Orphne found themselves shoved by a firm gust of wind out the door, which closed with a firm click.

"Was she in a different meeting than I was?" Vivian turned to Orphne.

"She isn't about to involve us in Shadow Council business." Orphne bit her lip and gave it serious thought. "I think we need cookies."

"We do *not* need cookies," Vivian snapped. "We need answers."

"You're right," Orphne sighed. "Cookies won't solve this. We need pizza."

As annoying as it was, Orphne was right. Pizza *did* help.

They had gotten into their separate cars, which gave Vivian time to think. She called Daniel from the road (briefly wondering if Alexa was indeed an imp that was going to take over eventually, then deciding that there wasn't that big a difference between imps and Big Tech, and setting that entire mess aside). He made some more calls for her, and by the time she'd made it home with all the pizzas she'd picked up on the way, there were already a few extra cars in the driveway.

"Aria, Evander, and the twins are doing something complicated with Lego in the basement. I pulled some beer and soda from the garage fridge and stuck a bottle of wine in the freezer to fast chill, which I need to pull before it explodes," Daniel said in a low tone as he helped her set up the pizzas in the kitchen. "But I'm still not clear on what everyone's doing here?"

"I've been trying to tackle this all on my own," Vivian said. "And I suck at it. We're all affected by this Reckoning thing: it's time to get everyone on the same page."

"Moira and Cecily aren't coming, are they?" he said, looking a little alarmed.

"If I thought they'd show up and help, I'd consider it," she said seriously. "But I figured I'd stick to the people who wouldn't put a curse on our kid."

"Good." He kissed the top of her head. "I'll be in the basement supervising, I guess."

"No, I need you, too," she said.

"I don't know anything about this magic stuff."

"But you do know money, and people, and I think that's what this all comes down to." She grabbed his hand and squeezed it. "And we're partners. I can't do this without you."

He smiled. Then he looked at the pile of pizzas. "Honey, exactly how many people are we expecting?"

The doorbell rang.

"The anchovies are for Raidne," she called over her shoulder, "and the bottom three are the extra-extra Meat Lovers."

The wolf pack bounded in or prowled in with stately grace, depending on generation.

"It took you long enough," Mrs. Fairhair remarked, accepting a paper plate and a slice of pizza piled high with bacon and pepperoni with only a twitch of an eyebrow. "But better late than never. We are her family, too, after all. I don't suppose I could trouble you for a fork and knife?"

"What's the situation?" Madhuri asked, hanging up her call as everyone found places to perch around the living room.

Vivian bit her lip. Who was she, out of all these people, to declare anything? But she was the one who had been there. She remembered how one of her senior managers had coached her on presenting to clients; that if she was feeling the imposter syndrome and didn't think people would listen to her, she should pretend to be someone they would listen to. She wasn't a mage or a werewolf or anyone else who had been born to this world. But auditors were the objective outsiders people brought in because they needed the unbiased perspective to prove things were being done correctly. She could do that.

"I thought we had two different problems," she said with a great deal more confidence than she felt. "The more concerning one for everyone, of course, was the Reckoning bringing doom to us all. And then somewhat less existential but still concerning was the apparent embezzlement of Parent Advisory Council funds."

She took a breath. "But from what we've found out, it appears that neither thing is happening. There is no Reckoning; there is no embezzlement."

She couldn't get the next thing she was going to say out over the hubbub. Madhuri waved her hands excitedly while Steve demanded answers and Orphne tried to explain something no one else could hear. Daniel was asking her something, but the younger werewolves were all talking too fast. Vivian raised her palms, trying to quiet people down, but a room full of excited mages and werewolves were a little too much to break through.

Mrs. Fairhair set down the knife and fork with which she had been elegantly dismantling her pizza. Without even standing up, she swept her gaze across the room, catching each person's eye. Silence followed in the wake of her gaze. She didn't even pause as she came to Vivian, but all the hairs on the back of Vivian's neck stood up anyway.

"Thank you," Mrs. Fairhair said. "Now. One at a time?"

"Let's start with the Reckoning, since that has the most potential for damage," Raidne said. "What do you mean that there's no Reckoning?"

"We spoke to Mistress Widdershins," Vivian said.

"Really? She's a hoot at Samhain. I'm impressed no one's in a coma." Madhuri raised her eyebrows. "What did she say?"

"That nothing's echoing through their side of the Veil," Orphne supplied. "And she's right. I've been asking my cousins—if there was some kind of backlash washing through time to engulf us all, they'd feel the currents over there."

"And what is the Shadow Council proposing to do with this information?" Mrs. Fairhair tilted her chin at Steve.

Steve sighed. "They have Orphne's report, of course, but since she's not an official Council member, all they'll say is that they're taking it under advisement."

Orphne pouted.

"So can an official Council medium talk to her, then? Verify what we said was true?" Vivian asked.

Steve rubbed the back of his neck, looking embarrassed. "Apparently Mistress Widdershins was not pleased about being asked the same question twice. They do think he'll stop speaking in Aramaic in twenty-four hours or so, though."

"You said that originally you thought there were two different problems," Raidne said, tapping a finger on her silk pants, which somehow she'd managed to eat anchovy pizza over without destroying. "I take it you think this is related?"

Vivian took the segue gratefully. "Banderbridge was very quietly fired because he was the center of an admissions scandal. Parents were paying large sums of money, laundered through the gala, to have their children accepted into prestigious schools. This is the first year that outlet isn't available. Here's what I'm finding suspicious. We have what appears to be a series of ominous warnings about a disaster that is not, in fact, happening. There's no prophecy about to come true, there's no Chosen One about to save us all. And if there was, it should be happening to the entire town. So why are all the omens only happening at school events? Especially school events related to the admissions Trials? And why this year specifically?"

"You think someone's faking this," Steve said slowly.

"Well, shit," said Madhuri. "The first one did cancel the results from the Talent Show entirely."

Daniel raised a hand tentatively. "Is Ms. Genevieve going to cancel Field Day tomorrow?"

"Apparently not," Vivian said. They were taking her seriously. Her legs suddenly felt wobbly and she sat down on the piano bench. Daniel put a supportive hand on her shoulder.

"She's new to the position," Mrs. Fairhair observed. "New pack leaders cannot afford to show weakness."

"They're humans, not wolves," Raidne reminded her.

"Go to the next PAC meeting and say that again with a straight face," Madhuri muttered.

"From the way Viv talks about those, people raised by wolves have much better manners," Daniel said unexpectedly.

"Thank you." Mrs. Fairhair favored him with a small smile. Then she turned to Steve. "What will the Shadow Council do?"

"I don't know," he admitted. "I was asked to recuse myself, since my kids are in one of the Trials classes, so they haven't been telling me much. They're watching, I know, but I don't know if they're watching for the right things. There were clearly a lot of sensitivities around the whole scandal last year—I didn't know any of the details, and I'm getting leaned on hard to stop asking. Gonna guess some real important people weren't confident their kids would get into the schools they wanted, and no one wants the full list of names to come out."

"Lovely," Daniel said, softly enough only Vivian could hear.

"It's no worse than some of the scandals in the non-magical world," she whispered back.

"What's the plan?" asked Thomas from the pile of younger werewolves. "The pack patrols the festivities and bites anyone who looks suspicious?"

"You know we're not allowed to bite people." Fiona elbowed him.

"OK, then we give wedgies to anyone who looks suspicious!" Rolando suggested, grinning.

"You're also not allowed to be on the field at all," said Madhuri. "Parents and friends have to stay in the stands."

"We're supposed to sit in the stands while our kids are out there and the next, what, explosion goes off?" Daniel objected. "If this is all connected, there's no way whoever it is will pass up another Trial."

"That's the part I can't figure out," said Vivian. "The Talent Show made sense. If someone didn't think their kid was going to place well, getting the results canceled buys them more time. But the judging was all done by the time the shadow wolf appeared at the Research Fair. And why bother with the hellhounds, or the gala, or any of the sigils getting burned into stuff?"

"The wolf part bothers me," Steve admitted. "I don't know if it's the pack or Aria, but it does feel like you're being targeted. Any idea why?"

"Most non-humans stick to themselves, or a few family members. Werewolves are some of the only shifters who work together closely enough to threaten the human mages," Mrs. Fairhair said, brushing a crumb off her tweed skirt. "The pack is powerful enough to make them twitchy, but too powerful to challenge directly."

"It's gotten kind of tense in town," volunteered one of the younger werewolves. "I tried to get a scone at the coffee shop yesterday, and it was like the whole room turned and stared at me."

Mrs. Fairhair gave them a sharp look that asked why this was the first she was hearing of it. The teenager cringed, body language expressing that if he had had a tail at present, it would be tucked between his legs.

"Also, Cecily's never liked you," Daniel pointed out.

"Cecily's a bitch." Madhuri rolled her eyes.

309

"But I'm not exactly a threat to her," Vivian said. "I mean, as much as I resent her at this point, I don't see what she has to gain. A couple of bad playdates don't seem worth this much trouble."

"Unless you're the scapegoat," Orphne pointed out, reaching over to gently pat her hand. "I'm sorry, but if someone's looking for a target, well. In the old days…"

"I'm the weakest goat in the herd," Vivian sighed.

"You are not weak," Mrs. Fairhair said unexpectedly. "You are the mother of a werewolf. If they think that means weakness, they haven't looked closely enough."

"Also, we're people, not goats," said Madhuri. "We're not going to leave you behind."

"Tell Aria to stay close to Evander tomorrow," Raidne said. "If nothing else, she can avoid the children who have been targeting her."

"We'll ask Shuri and Lucius to stick with her, too," Steve said. "I mean, they're kindergartners, there's only so much they're going to remember, but hopefully the four of them can help each out."

"The pack will be there, in strength," said Mrs. Fairhair. "Humans may not be good at scenting out miscreants, but whoever this is will find it a bit more difficult to evade us."

Vivian's eyes prickled. She had felt weird calling on the pack to even give advice; she had never expected them to involve themselves. And for the other parents to rally—she tried to remember a time she'd ever felt like a community had had her back before, and came up blank.

"Aria's one of our own," Mrs. Fairhair reminded her. "And, by extension, so are you. Neither wolves nor humans are meant to be on their own."

"I don't know what the Council is planning, but I'm sure they'll have representatives there," added Steve. "I might be sidelined, but I know most of the folks in the area who are in the field. Something goes wrong, we'll have friends on call."

"So that's it? We wait for whoever it is to make a move?" she said, frustrated.

"That's one of the things that sucks about being one of the good guys," Madhuri sighed. "We can't go around fighting random people. Sometimes all we can do is play defense. It's pretty shit-tastic."

"But this time, you won't be alone," said Mrs. Fairhair.

Orphne gave her a little thumbs-up. Raidne smiled coldly.

"Also, she's actually good at skirmedge," Daniel pointed out. "Well, not good, but no worse than any of the other kindergartners. Last practice, she even successfully stayed on the correct side of the field for the majority of the game."

"Maybe we're jumping at shadows," Madhuri said. "Maybe at the end of tomorrow, nothing will have happened, and you can all come over to our place for beer and dhoklas."

"And if not?" Vivian tried to give her a smile, but it wavered.

"Well." Madhuri shrugged. "Then maybe at the end of tomorrow, it will have been a total disaster, and then you can all come over to our place for beer and dhoklas. I sent Ajit out for chickpea flour and he brought back, like, ten times the amount I needed because it was on sale. Someone has to help us eat it all."

17

May 4 6:53 AM

It's Field Day! While we are all very excited to cheer on our young student athletes, please remember that air horns, fireworks charms, flash photography, voice augmentation spells, smoking, smoke machines, smoke monsters, and goats are all banned from the stands during today's events. Posters are permitted, but no larger than 18x24 inches, and any enchantments must not generate magical interference. Don't forget to hydrate! Have fun!

"What the hell is that?" Daniel muttered to Vivian as they made their way through the little carnival set up along the fence in between the athletic fields and the parking lot. There was only one gate onto the field, which made for excellent ticket collecting but seemed like a terrible fire hazard.

For a moment, she was too busy fretting over what might explode or who might attack them. She scanned for signs of eyes in stormclouds, but all she could find was a funnel cake vendor and trailer-sized shack selling school t-shirts and hot dogs. Then she saw the little petting zoo paddock.

The two mangy creatures lurching about inside were, without a doubt, the ugliest things she'd ever seen. They were like dogs, with the short coats and bone-protruding leanness of abused greyhounds, but with a crest of wiry hair that turned into six-inch spikes around their shoulders before dwindling down their spines. One turned beady eyes on her that glowed even in the daylight, and crouched to void its bowels, maintaining eye contact all the while.

Daniel managed to catch the sign before she did. "We've been getting address labels and offers of tote bags for months to get us to donate to preserve *that*?" he asked, watching with a mix of horror and fascination as the male chupacabra finally broke eye contact to begin aggressively licking its own crotch.

"Oh, yes, aren't they the sweetest?" Orphne bustled over. She was wearing an *Abracadabra, Chupacabras!* t-shirt with a cartoon of a chupacabra in a little top hat on it. The artist had taken an awful lot of liberties to make the cartoon more endearing, and only somewhat succeeded. "And increasingly endangered—it's so tragic. This breeding pair has gotten overly habituated to humans, so we're using them as part of our outreach efforts. 'Oo's got darling widdle murder-mittens? Is it you? Is it you? Just like big old Cerberus, you are. Show the nice people your widdle pawsies!"

Since the chupacabra's murder-mittens sported inch-long claws, Vivian was not particularly inclined to get close to see the widdle pawsies. "Have you seen anything? I mean… you know?"

Fortunately, Orphne caught on without Vivian having to bring up shadowy conspiracies while next to the lemonade stand. "I've been looking, really, I swear. Nothing so far. Although Frijolitos here didn't want his yum-yums, did he?" she asked, looking at the wrinkly monsters in the paddock.

A child dropped his cotton candy in by accident, and the female chupacabra leapt on it in a flash, savaging the paper cone into shreds and then looking around in confusion as the sugar cloud melted away into sticky patches on her snout. The kid burst into tears.

"They're very sensitive," Orphne added. "It wouldn't surprise me if they can tell something's wrong before we can. Can't you, cutie pie? You didn't even touch your goat blood!"

"Uh… huh," Daniel said. "We have to go find seats now."

"The left side of the stands gets more shade and you won't burn your behinds on the hot benches!" Orphne said, waving them off. "I'll see you up there!"

They wove their way through the other vendors, presented their tickets at the gate, and entered the field. A tall set of bleachers faced the field itself. The seats didn't go all the way to the ground. Parents were climbing the stairs to a deck a few feet wide that let the bottom seats still see over the heads of the volunteers setting up water stations in front of the stands. On the far side of the field was another fence and the woods where Vivian hoped the pack was patrolling. She and Daniel climbed the first little set of stairs and turned to face the stands.

"Did we underprepare?" Daniel muttered to her.

"Probably," she muttered back. "Story of our lives here."

It was easy to tell the families who had a kid in the Trials this year versus the ones whose children were just out for cockatrice egg races and potato sack relays. The ones whose kids were going to play a few awkward sports and then have ice pops chatted amongst themselves or fiddled with their phones, sporting a school crest t-shirt or maybe a ball cap. A few of the most obsessive, whose kids would face their Trials next year, clutched notebooks or tablets to take notes.

The Trials families, though, had gone all-out. There were bedsheets painted with encouraging messages draped over the railings, foam fingers and sparkling messages written in the air by wand tip, and three-dimensional rotating transparent illusions of children jumping in victory projected on top of hats. Parents clutched rattles and noisemakers along with their posters of varying levels of artistic ability or professional polish. Everyone talked with the exaggerated cheer of deeply anxious people determined not to show their trepidation, but she could see the stress in the pinched eyes and too-wide smiles.

As they climbed up the stands, Vivian had an irrational urge to stay down with the chupacabras. She was pretty sure that the chupacabras hated her, but she was also pretty sure that the chupacabras hated everything and everyone, roughly equally. The people in the stands hated her, specifically. She could see the whispers run down the rows like a wave, as eyes suddenly widened before the owners plastered neutral looks back onto their face. No one would meet her eye, of course, but as they approached rows with empty seats, bags and coolers somehow ended up at the end of the row, blocking their entry. They ended up on the far right, in the blazing sun, near the top of the stands and almost level with the announcer box.

"Something's going to happen, and we're going to be way up here and there isn't going to be a damn thing we can do about it," Vivian fretted.

"At least we'll have a good view," Daniel said gloomily. He took a deep breath and tried again. "Maybe nothing will happen at all. It's a clear sunny day, there are hundreds of people here. The werewolves are patrolling the woods on the borders of the field. There's a Shadow Council member or three lurking somewhere. We can contact the pack or our little circle on the

'We Hate Cecily' group chat Madhuri set up for us. Maybe we'll sit up here and watch our kid get distracted by clover or a bee or something and completely forget that she's supposed to be doing field sports, and then we'll all go over to Madhuri's house."

"Our best-case scenario here is that our kid flunks kindergarten?" she snapped. And then stopped herself. "I'm sorry."

He put an arm around her. "I am, too. I shouldn't have been flippant. I'm nervous."

She looked down at her hands, which had twisted her purse strap out of recognition. "Yeah, me, too."

Daniel suddenly lowered his voice. "Don't look up too fast, but Cecily's contingent is on their way up."

Vivian took the opportunity to take a deep breath before they could see it, and then looked up with her best smile pasted on. "Cecily, how very nice to see you."

"You've been dodging my calls," Cecily said coolly.

"I've said all I had to say," Vivian said, her heart beating faster. "I walked you through the math; you were there the whole time. The numbers are what they are. I've spoken to Ms. Genevieve about your concerns, and I'm sure she'd be happy to discuss with you potential reasons that this year's take was so much less than last year's, but she assures me that the total will more than adequately meet the expected budget."

She would have felt worse about throwing Ms. Genevieve under the bus if the woman had lifted a finger to help her. The headmistress had known all along what the problem was, and hadn't said a word.

Cecily's eyes narrowed. "I'd be terribly sorry if this were to affect your standing in the Parent Advisory Council. Still, I understand that your daughter has had some challenges in adjusting to Mandrake Room. I'm sure you'll be much more comfortable wherever you choose to go next year."

That bitch. Behind her, half a dozen other PAC members shifted from foot to foot. Feather-eared dad, still rocking the Bluetooth headset, flexed his hands and she suddenly wondered about his feelings on throwing rocks. Some glared straight at her, and she wondered who had been responsible for the rock through her window. Others looked less certain. Near the back, Moira refused to meet her eyes.

Vivian raised her chin, trying not to grind her teeth. "I'm happy to resign my position, if someone would prefer to step into the role. I have a full set of figures for the year, maintained at GAAP standards, that I would be happy to share. However, as I understand, where Aria ends up next year is between us and the school administration, not the Parent Advisory Council."

"This is a close-knit community," Cecily began.

"Yeah, yeah, I know people, too, Cecily," Vivian shot back. She was tired of playing nice—or playing stupid. "And it's not my fault your kid's a bully. How about you tell your child to leave mine alone and I promise not to darken your wine and cheese night again?"

Cecily looked shocked, and then murderous. "We'll see what the school administration has to say about that."

She wheeled about and headed back down the metal stairs. One of the other parents glared and hissed something about unnatural shifters and thieves in the night, and for a moment Vivian tensed, waiting for something physical. But they continued down. Moira paused for a moment, looking anxious and almost regretful.

"I thought we were friends," Vivian said, not trying to keep the hurt out of her voice.

"We all do what we need to do for our kids," Moira said. She opened her mouth as if to say something else.

"Friends and family, please take your seats." Ms. Genevieve's voice did not so much boom out as appear from the air, as if she were speaking from immediately in front of them. The amplification spell carried her words from where she stood in the center of the field. "We're about ready to begin. First up, our first graders will compete in the three-legged race!"

Moira turned and hurried back down to where her husband waited impatiently, holding banners for both Cara and Rory.

"It's no real loss," Daniel tried to comfort her.

"I can be glad I found out what she's really like, and still sad that she's not what I thought, can't I?" Vivian said, trying to decide what percentage wistful versus bitter she was feeling.

"You can feel as many things as you want," Daniel said. "But right now, we've got bigger fish to fry. Here, you take the binoculars, you've got a better idea what you're looking for."

"I have no idea what I'm looking for," she confessed. She scanned the field nervously. The three-legged race did not appear to involve tying the legs of two people together, but rather everyone individually growing a third leg and then attempting to run. In another context, it would be comical. But she was too busy looking for sigils or signs to pay much attention.

If only she could be sure she'd recognize a sign if she saw it.

Aria's class took the field and for a moment, she set aside thoughts of the apocalypse to jump up and down and cheer for her daughter. Aria scanned the stands, then caught sight of them and waved back madly. She was wearing a purple vest alongside half her class, with the other half of the class in gold. A whistle blew, and her whole tiny body trembled with focus.

She clutched her three-foot baton with more determination than many of her peers, some of whom kept whacking each other by accident every time they turned around.

Ms. Genevieve threw a ball up into the air, and when it hit the ground, it rolled off on its own. Aria ignored it completely, charging off towards the little glowing pyramid Ms. Genevieve had set in the middle of the field.

"Go for the baton change! Yes!" Daniel cheered. "You got this, Aria!"

Aria, along with a few of her classmates, tagged the pyramid with her baton, which suddenly contracted to a stouter stick only a foot long. She shoved the stick in her mouth.

"What is she—" Vivian started to say.

The ball rolled past the gold team, several of whom milled in confusion. Aria transformed into her wolf form, and vaulted off Evander's back to go chasing it, baton securely in her teeth.

Vivian sucked in a breath.

"No, this is great, we've worked on this," said Daniel, never taking his eyes off the game where their wolf cub now bounded in her oversized t-shirt, tail wagging from beneath a tennis skirt. "It's legal, and a great tactic."

Aria chased after the ball like mad, and then turned her head to tap it with her baton. Suddenly, iridescent wings burst out the sides of the ball.

"Avis form unlocked! That's my girl!" Daniel cheered.

The ball flew off, while kids scrambled back to the pyramid to reset their batons to flying mode. But Vivian could see that her daughter was doing relatively well, and her heart soared.

"I wonder what what's-his-face does for this event," Daniel mused. "I mean, I can see how you can write a kid's Fair poster for them, but how do you make a klutz any better at jumping through flaming hoops or whatever else they're going to do down there?"

"Who, the consultant?" She struggled to remember the name as she watched Evander try to make friends with a bird that frantically took to the air as Aria and Elowen dashed past him, trying to steal the ball from each other with only some deliberate success. "Lemere? Heh. He would probably try to glom onto the whole Reckoning thing somehow and milk it for sympathy points."

Daniel stared at her.

"Oh." Her eyes widened. "Oh, crap."

"What do we do? Can we call the werewolves and let them know?"

She was already trying, but Mrs. Fairhair's number went straight to voicemail. "Well, there's one disadvantage to having no thumbs."

She sent a quick message to the "We Hate Cecily" chat, instead. "Orphne and Steve say they'll keep an eye out for him. Wait, no, they don't know what he looks like."

"I got it," Daniel said, thumbing through his phone. "Here, I'll drop his LinkedIn headshot into the chat."

"There's got to be a way to warn the school officials." She bit her lip. "You stay here with the binoculars and keep an eye on Aria. I'm going to see if I can get anyone's attention down on the field."

Daniel nodded. On the plus side, being a virtual pariah meant people had given them a wide berth and she didn't have to climb over anyone's lap to get out of the stands. She tried to keep her pace to a brisk walk, purposeful but not panicked. She got suspicious glares anyway.

"Where do you think you're going?" Cecily stood to block her way.

"I need to talk to Ms. Genevieve," Vivian said, trying to stay calm.

"You're not going anywhere," Cecily said loudly. People turned in their seats, ignoring the kids careening around the field dangling from flying batons. "You're not going to bring your doom upon our beloved town."

"There is no doom, Cecily." Vivian spread her hands, exasperated. "There's no Reckoning."

"Do you think we're idiots? You were there, too, you've seen the signs. Just because you're too mundane to understand any of our traditions doesn't give you an excuse." Cecily's eyes narrowed. "I don't know whether you're that naive and your ignorance is going to curse us all, or if you're playing dumb and doing this deliberately. All I know is that I welcomed you with open arms and this is how you repay me."

Her voice had risen over the course of her speech until it was obvious that Cecily was talking less to Vivian and more to the angry mob of parents who were starting to drift near them.

"I don't mean I don't believe in the Reckoning," Vivian said, scrambling not to lose control of the situation. What if they didn't believe her? What if someone decided not to reserve rocks for windows? "I mean, it isn't happening right now. It's a hoax. Someone is trying to fool us."

"That's the bullshit excuse you're going to go with?" Cecily looked incredulous. "Maybe you mundane folks might believe an 'oh, it was all smoke and mirrors' excuse, but we're a little smarter than that around here."

"No, you don't understand—"

Columns of smoke erupted around the border of the field.

"Oh my god—Aria!" Vivian breathed.

Panicking parents swarmed down the stands. Vivian pushed

past a stunned Cecily. The smoke twisted in the air like a living thing, shot with glints of green light. People were screaming. In the center of the field, Ms. Immacolata shepherded the children together with her parasol. The smoke continued to swirl, billowing up from the ground to spin into a vortex. Overhead, clouds were gathering from nowhere, blotting out the sun.

Someone pushed Vivian, hard. Her shins connected painfully with the metal seat in front of her. Threads of the smoke had twisted into a spinning wall around the field. Through the closing gaps, she could see Ms. Immacolata sway and then fall, surrounded by hysterical children.

Vivian staggered to her feet, scrambling over someone's cooler, slushie soaking into the knees of her jeans. She was three rows from the bottom. Two. The gaps in the wall closed, creating a towering column of twisting smoke and ectoplasm that reached up into the stormclouds above. A black and green tornado that wavered but never shifted in place.

Parents who had been in the lower rows of the stands raced across the track onto the turf. Ahead of her, Vivian could see Raidne charge blindly into the smoke cloud. Green light flared and the siren's body flew back out, skidding across the track. Orphne smothered a scream with both hands and scrambled to her side.

People were smashed up against the railing. The crowd pushed, trying to get down the stairs on either side of the grandstand. Some parents scrambled up, trying to climb the railing and jump down. Vivian followed them, but nearly toppled as someone else crashed into her. She waved her arms wildly, grabbing the top rail right before she tipped over. She managed to get one leg over the railing. The other got stuck, her ankle twisting painfully. Two more parents tried to charge the storm tower. They, too, were flung backwards, twitching as if they'd been ejected from an electric fence. Vivian yanked her foot. It came free, her sneaker left behind somewhere. No matter. She managed to get two rungs down, but someone's chest pinched her fingers against the top railing. She kicked herself free and let go, praying. The shock of her feet hitting the ground reverberated up her legs, but nothing gave way. She staggered, but turned to face the cloud. She had to keep moving—not just to get to Aria but to avoid being crushed.

"Ms. Genevieve!" She saw the headmistress, whose arms waved in the air trailing sparkles and whose hair had finally escaped that perfect chignon. "Ms. Genevieve, I think I might know—"

"Not now," Ms. Genevieve said tightly.

"But—" Another surge of the crowd pushed Vivian away from the headmistress. She tried to struggle back.

"Hey, it's the mundane mom, the one with the werewolf kid!" The metal mage who had worn fairy wings at the gala pointed at her. "The Thief in the Night! This is your fault, you and your... your... spawn!"

"That's right!" The crowd started to turn towards her, murmuring angrily.

"Take it down!"

"You started this, make it stop!"

"What? I didn't... I'm not..." Vivian raised her hands, backing up. The crowd didn't let her get far. She swallowed, her mouth dry. "My daughter's in there too, I need to get to her!"

"So you can finish what you started? Not likely!" Cecily was pushing through the crowd towards her. Viv looked around frantically. There was nowhere to go. The whirling storm was on the left; the stands were on the right, terrified people pushing from all directions. This was how mobs started. This was how riots started.

A flash of lightning from the top of the stands stopped everyone in their tracks. Vivian blinked away afterimages, trying to make out a short figure standing on the roof of the announcer's box. It was Rory. Somehow Moira's son had managed to climb up onto the corrugated metal.

He was chanting something, arms raised, in a voice that occasionally cracked. From his fingertips, a light mist was starting to form and swirl.

While some people were still shooting threatening glares at Vivian, most had their attention captured.

"It's him, it's the one who saved us at the Research Fair!"

"The Winged Scholar!"

"I thought that was supposed to be the siren's kid?"

"Save us!"

"He's what, thirteen? What do you expect him to do?"

"It doesn't matter, the prophecy says he's the one!"

Vivian took the opportunity to slip away, dodging between people towards the cloud wall. Above, Rory waved his arms earnestly. He was glowing faintly, she realized as she glanced over her shoulder. The daylight had dimmed to near twilight with the thick clouds overhead, but Rory was faintly limned in white light.

"It's a counter ritual!" Kassie's mom exclaimed. "It's him! We have to crown him!"

"Please, save our children!" one of the other kindergarten parents begged.

Could he? Part of her wished so hard that this could be wrapped up neatly. The Winged Scholar would dissipate the Reckoning, the sunlight would flood the field, and everyone would go to Madhuri's house for beer and dhoklas. But that wasn't how the story was going to end, was it? If it did, if he was the Chosen One, then she was the Thief in the Night and Aria was the Stormbringer. The only way this ended neatly was if her family were the bad guys.

But they weren't, she reminded herself as she pushed through the crowd. There wasn't a Reckoning to dissipate. Someone was doing this on purpose, picking her kid for the scapegoat. And had picked Rory as the Chosen One. Rory, whose water magic wasn't strong enough and whose parents worried he wouldn't get into Pendragon Prep. Who had a Research Fair project that happened to be topical and clearly hadn't been written by an eighth grader.

Exactly how much had Moira paid? And how long ago had she singled out Aria to take the fall?

She was lucky that his increasingly impressive light show was pulling everyone's attention, or she never would have made it to the edge of the whirlwind. Everyone had shrunk back after the first couple mages had been knocked out. She nearly stepped on Raidne but pulled herself back in time.

Orphne looked up at her with tear-stained cheeks. "She's breathing, but I can't leave her or she'll be trampled. I can't get through to Evander and I can't get her out of here myself. Can you help me pick her up?"

"Of course," Vivian said, hoping that no one would see her and accuse her of trying to murder the siren or something.

They managed to edge along the whirlwind away from the crowd. Over Rory's head, an osprey was forming out of mist.

"There's no way that kid's doing that on his own, right?" Vivian muttered to Orphne. "He could barely train fish in a barrel in the fall."

"Fate has a way of making itself happen," was all the nymph could offer.

Mrs. Fairhair met them at the edge of the crowd, dressed in her robe. She did not look visibly stressed, but she had the terrifying intensity she had the first time Vivian had met her. Which scared Vivian even more.

"The cloud wall goes all the way around the field," she reported. She glanced at the unconscious Raidne as Vivian and Orphne set her down. "Astrid and Pilar each tried to break through and got knocked back for their troubles. They came to, but neither wants to repeat the experience."

Steve trotted up. His eyes flicked across the crowd, never settling. His hands were out, a little away from his sides, fingers flexed. "Y'all alright here?"

"For the moment," Vivian said tightly. "Until they remember I'm here and decide getting rid of me and the werewolves will make the Reckoning stop."

Steve inhaled sharply. He flicked his hands out, sketched an arc with his arms, and said something that immediately removed itself from her memory. "There. We're under a shield—for the moment, no one can hear or see us."

"Thanks." She swallowed. "Where the hell is the Shadow Council?"

"Reinforcements are on the way, but we've got ten, twenty minutes before they get here," he said, his eyes still moving constantly. "There should have been reps here already. There aren't. I'll be asking questions later, but there's not much I can do about that now."

"But you can get in, right?" Orphne looked up at him pleadingly.

For a moment, fear flashed across his face, and then cool

professionalism descended again. He knew how to handle near-rioting crowds and unexplained magic, Vivian realized. But not his kids being where he couldn't get to them.

Above them, the silvery osprey spread wings half the width of the sands and screamed silently in defiance at the swirling smoke wall. They ignored it.

"The winds are repelling any magic that tries to cross it," he said. "And that includes the magic in people's bodies. We've all absorbed enough into our bloodstreams over the years. It just kicks us all back out."

"But who's doing this?" Orphne asked, limpid eyes huge.

"Did you get Daniel's text? We think it's the consultant," Vivian said urgently. "Lemere. Moira is paying him to help get Rory into Pendragon Prep."

"Moira?" Steve looked skeptical. Vivian gestured at Rory on the roof, looking half terrified but waving his arms gamely as his osprey avatar crouched for takeoff and the crowd chanted about the Winged Scholar. "Huh."

Vivian scanned the crowd that was drifting back up the grandstand, looking for Daniel. He would be OK, surely? He barely went to school events: maybe they wouldn't recognize him.

"Can you find him?" she asked Mrs. Fairhair urgently. "Lemere?"

"I've never met the man, nor smelled him." The werewolf matriarch narrowed her eyes. "I don't know what scent to track."

"I'm not sure how much it matters right this second," Steve said. "For this to be repelling everyone, it can't be controlled from the outside. There must be a locus hidden somewhere on the field that the spell is tied to, at least until certain conditions are met."

A thought flitted across her mind, one that simultaneously

filled her with wild hope and desperate fear. "People with magic in their blood, you said? How much do you have to use magic before it's in your blood?"

His brows knit. "Usually a couple of years before it starts to stick, although if you've personally cast something recently, the residue clings to your skin... oh. Oh, Vivian, don't."

She swallowed. "Can anyone else get in? Who's here?"

Orphne's eyes got even wider, if that was possible. "But you use magic."

"Not much and not for long. I haven't even cast a spell myself in the last couple of days—can you think of anyone else here who can say that?" She wanted to let them talk her out of it. She didn't want to touch those swirling winds with their malevolent green underglow. But Aria was all by herself, except for some other terrified kids. Some of whom hated her. Vivian had to get to her. "What's the worst that could happen? It knocks me out, too?"

"What are you going to do when you get in there?" Steve said.

"Protect my kid," she said grimly. "Somehow."

He looked like he wanted to protest. But then he met her eyes and gave her a sharp nod. "If you see mine..."

"I'll do my best for them all," she promised.

"As soon as you step more than a foot or two away from me, you're going to be visible," Steve warned her.

She looked at the surging crowd that started only a few feet away. The osprey was tearing at the smoke, pulling clawfuls away to dissipate it. She didn't want to see what happened if Rory was allowed to win before she could get Aria out of there. "Got it."

She took a deep breath. And then she ran for the wall.

She almost made it. She stretched a hand out and her fingers brushed the smoke when an uncomfortable buzzing sensation traveled up her arm. Then someone tackled her midsection and she sprawled into the dirt.

"No!" Moira cried from on top of her. "I'm not letting you ruin his chance. We've tried too hard—it cost too much!"

"So you're going to sacrifice my kid instead?" she demanded, scrabbling at the grass, trying to get a handhold to pull herself up and out of Moira's arms. The woman was solid muscle under the layer of fat, exactly what one might expect of a seal. "I thought she and Cara were supposed to be friends!"

"Like you'd do any different for yours?" Moira yanked Vivian's arm back down. Her shoulder protested.

"I thought you were my friend," Vivian continued, trying to distract Moira enough that maybe she could roll over. Too much of the selkie's weight was on her arm. Vivian's joints screamed their refusal to bend that way. Where was Steve? If he helped her, would it put the Fairhairs in too much danger?

"Blood is thicker than water, and I know a lot about water," Moira grunted. "If it makes you feel any better, it wasn't the initial plan."

"No, Moira, that doesn't make me feel better!" Vivian managed to get an elbow into Moira's ribs. The selkie kneed her in the side and she gasped.

"You could have left it alone!" Moira protested, her voice sounding pained. "But no, you had to keep poking. At the stupid gala funds, at the stupid prophecy. You didn't give me any choice but to use the second to solve the first."

"You didn't have to make that choice. You could have chosen something else."

"I made the necessary sacrifices." Moira's tone had re-solidified into steel.

"There's a difference between making sacrifices yourself and sacrificing everything else!" Could she bite her? Vivian lunged and Moira twisted her arm behind her back in response. Vivian bit back a cry of pain. "You could give him up now, claim he went further than you authorized."

"Not when we're so close!" Moira grunted when Vivian twisted in her grasp. "Besides, he's got my skin as collateral."

For a moment, Vivian was confused, as she was very clearly trying to give Moira's very-present skin a rug burn. Then she realized what the selkie had given up.

"We all do what we need to do for our children," Moira repeated, although it sounded like it was as much to herself as to Vivian. "Would you stay down—augh!"

Moira fell off her back and Vivian scrambled to her feet, startled. The selkie was beating out her sleeve on the ground, which was somehow on fire. Daniel stood behind her, staring at his own hands in astonishment.

"I can't believe that worked," he said.

"Did you…?" She looked at him, equally astonished.

"Steve was trying to teach me," he said. "But it never worked before!"

A little giggle, verging on hysteria, escaped. "At least you left our curtains alone."

Moira made a grab for her ankle. Daniel flung himself on top of the selkie. "Go!"

There was so much she wanted to say to him, but now was not the time. Before Moira could stop her, Vivian turned and flung herself into the towering wall of smoke.

18

May 4 10:43AM
EMERGENCY ALERT
The school is currently managing a school-wide incident
related to Field Day activities. Emergency services are on their
way. We will continue to update you as the situation evolves.
Please follow any instructions from emergency services if you
are in the local area. We will advise you when the lockdown
has been lifted.

The wind scoured her skin, tugging at her hair and clothes
and bones and soul. She could feel the wall testing,
looking for magic and forcibly pushing it away. She
prayed the seance from yesterday didn't count—she'd been an
anchor, but Orphne herself had said she hadn't cast anything.
She could barely see her hands held out in front of her through
the black smoke, but the poisonous green light coiling over
them lit them through the darkness. She literally dug her feet
into the ground, grinding her toes into the turf and pushing
forward, one step at a time. Her teeth ached. She closed her
burning eyes and concentrated on the next step.

331

Suddenly the resistance vanished and she fell forward. Her eyes snapped open as she landed on her hands and knees inside the tornado. She looked up, expecting to see the sigil, but all she saw was clouds. Then again, if this was intended as a show to the adults outside, maybe the caster wouldn't bother.

It was even dimmer than outside the vortex, but she could see the kids huddled in the center of the field. She staggered to her feet and headed for them.

"Aaah, get him!" Three kindergartners ran towards her in a strangely familiar formation. She didn't have time to analyze it before they started kicking at her ankles.

"Wait! Ow! What are you doing?" she said, skipping backwards. They weren't very good at it, but every blow that landed stung.

"Wait wait wait! That's my mommy!" Aria bounded towards her, surprisingly back in human form.

Two of them backed off. "Sorry, Mrs. Aria's Mommy," one mumbled.

The third aimed one more kick before sulkily heading back towards the prone body of Ms. Immacolata.

Triage time. Vivian knelt down and wrapped Aria in a hug so tight she squeaked. She wanted to stay there forever, but there wasn't time. She pulled back to look her daughter in the eye. "Are you OK? Is everyone else OK? What's going on?"

"Ms. Immacolata fell down. She looks like she did the time Evander forgot he had garlic scapes in his tzatziki, and it smells all garlicky on the ground," Aria said, very seriously. "We need to move her but we tried dragging her away from the garlic and we didn't get very far. And garlic doesn't belong on the field so I thought maybe someone hurt her on purpose, and I told everyone we needed to do our skirmedge moves and defend her like she's the ball, but then you came through first and you weren't the one who hurt her so I guess we don't have to do skirmedge defense anymore. Also, Shuri got too close to the scary clouds and fell over and threw up but she's OK now."

Shuri gave a half-hearted little wave. Lucius patted her back.

"Wait, you organized your classmates into a skirmedge squad?" Vivian was taken aback.

"Only because she said it first," Elowen said sulkily. "I was about to say it."

"It was a good idea, kids," Vivian said. She had no idea who—or what—was going to come through the storm next. "You keep doing that. I'm going to check on Ms. Immacolata, OK?"

The kids nodded solemnly, and redeployed themselves. Aria watched them, biting her lip, and then readjusted the positions of the twins and Evander. She really had been working on her skirmedge strategies with the pack.

Vivian hurried over to the prone form of the kindergarten teacher. She reached down to feel her neck. At least the sun-repelling brooch was still in place. Ms. Immacolata didn't have a pulse and she wasn't breathing. But then again, she was a vampire. Did she ever? It wasn't like Vivian went around feeling the throats of her kid's teachers. She ran her hand along the turf. There were little white bits down near the roots of the grass. She pinched one and sniffed it—someone had rubbed what had probably been a couple of jars of chopped garlic into the ground covering a space several feet across. Aria seemed confident that getting her teacher away from the garlic would be enough. Vivian tried to heave the vampire into a fireman's carry. She did her yoga videos most days, but there was no way she'd developed the strength to lift someone from the ground. She tried to roll her into a stand and promptly fell over on her ass. The kids glanced at her nervously, already losing faith. She didn't have time for this. She grabbed the teacher under the armpits instead and started dragging her.

A few feet away and Ms. Immacolata suddenly started to stir. Vivian swallowed her own gasp of relief and continued dragging until the vampire's eyelids fluttered. Then she set her down gently.

"What…" Ms. Immacolata croaked. The teacher winced and started again. "Are the children all right?"

Vivian nodded. "For the moment, they're all OK. I need to leave you for a few minutes; will you be all right?"

"The garlic is gone?" Ms. Immacolata asked.

"It's still over there, but I dragged you away from it," Vivian said, her heart sinking. She'd lost her purse in the fight and didn't have the EpiPen with her this time. What was first aid for garlic exposure? Did it involve being bitten? Aside from the fact she'd forgotten to take an iron supplement this morning, she didn't have time to be bitten. Also, she really didn't want to be bitten.

"I am well enough for the moment," the vampire said as her eyelids started to drift shut again. "I must conserve my strength."

"You do that." Vivian fought down the stab of disappointment that getting her away from the garlic had not instantly cured the teacher. She could have done with another adult right now.

But she didn't have one. She had to find the locus, and then she needed to find some way to destroy it. But how? She looked around. The field was just that—a field. There were some lines spray-painted or magicked onto the grass, but that was it. If there was some object serving as a locus, where could it possibly be? How big would it be? Could it be buried? Or was it the size of a bead? There was no way she could possibly find it.

She glanced around in despair at the kids deployed in their little formation. Mostly. Some poked at the grass, distracted even in these circumstances. The twins clutched each other's hands for comfort. Aria looked around, watching her make-do pack, her nose twitching.

Vivian had a thought.

"Aria? Sweetie?"

Aria trotted over obediently.

"I need your help again, OK?" Vivian crouched back down to eye level. "Remember how when we were at the Research Fair, you said you smelled the same thing as when the auditorium exploded?"

Aria's eyebrows knit and she nodded slowly.

"Can you smell it here?"

Aria looked around. "I'd have to wolf out."

"That's OK, love. Go ahead."

Aria shivered all over and promptly sprouted fur. Her transitions were getting faster, Vivian noticed. She lifted her snout and sniffed the air, and then put her nose down to the grass. She snuffled about in a semicircle and then tentatively headed off away from Vivian, towards the far end of the field. Her pace picked up confidence and her tail wagged. She started to trot and then to bound. Vivian ran after her, limping in the one shoe. Suddenly she stopped and sat. She yipped once and stared expectantly at Vivian.

"Is there something here?" Vivian asked.

Aria yipped. This close to the storm wall, Vivian could feel the wind pulling at whatever magic residue remained on her. Aria's fur fluffed out and she laid her ears back.

Vivian knelt, running her hands over the turf, frantically looking for something out of the ordinary. The turf did seem a little uneven. Aria pawed at it urgently.

"You want to dig?"

Aria paused and then yipped again hesitantly.

If they were wrong, the grounds staff would kill them for destroying the turf. Figuratively. The storm or the mob might kill them for real first. "Go for it, kiddo."

Aria started digging with both paws, flinging dirt behind her to get swept up in the whirlwind. She hit something solid a few seconds later. Vivian reached in and pulled out a small golden casket.

It oozed slightly with green ectoplasm that matched the undertone of the cloud—this had to be the locus. But now what? She turned it over in her hands. There were hinges, but no lock. She tried to pry it open, but the lid stayed firmly shut. She glanced up. The wall of smoke remained as solid as ever at the bottom, but shreds were torn from the top. Through the ragged traces, she could see a giant osprey claw. She was running out of time.

She tried casting the opening charm from the gate in town. No change. Could she hit it with a rock? She glanced around at the immaculate playing field. The other kids had wandered over. They stared at her with big eyes. A few were sniffling.

She pulled out her phone. What were the chances? The video call went through.

"Vivian?" Steve's voice sounded level, but the tenseness around his eyes spoke volumes. "How are things in there?"

"Kids are OK," she said. Steve couldn't hide his relief. "Ms. Immacolata is sleeping off allium poisoning, but I think she'll be OK? I found the locus, but I have no idea what to do with it."

She pointed the phone at it.

"I don't suppose you know an opening spell?" Steve suggested.

"Tried it, no good."

Orphne pushed her head into the frame. "How about a rock?"

"No rocks."

"We could throw a rock in?" Orphne mused, off-screen again.

"What if it hit one of the kids?" Daniel replied, muffled. "Also, I don't see any rocks. What do we have?"

Steve bit his lip. "Dammit. I wish I could see it."

From off-screen, Daniel spoke up again hesitantly. "Could she maybe, like, bring it out?"

"I can't leave the kids in here, and most of them definitely can't make it through the wall," Vivian said. "Shit. I mean sugar. I tried to cast an opening spell a minute ago, so I probably can't make it through the wall anymore, either."

"The magic box thingy probably can't go through the wall, either," Daniel said.

"Actually, maybe it can," Steve said slowly. "The rules for people and inanimate objects are different. I could tell if I could see it, but…"

Behind them, she could hear the dull roar of a crowd. It didn't sound happy.

"What if I just hucked it out?" she said, desperately.

"It might come through, it might hit you in the face," Steve said. He was watching something off camera. A muscle in his jaw twitched.

"We're out of time, aren't we," she said.

"Just about." He glanced back at her.

"Fuck it, I'm throwing the damn thing," she said. The kids' eyes widened. "Uh, sorry, kids, don't repeat that."

Vivian cocked her arm back and let loose. At the last moment, she dodged to the side, in case the casket ricocheted back at her.

It passed through the wall and the storm collapsed.

Green ectoplasm splattered down, no longer holding the column of smoke aloft. The roar of the winds suddenly disappeared. She hadn't realized how loud it had been until the sudden silence descended. She stared up at the shocked stands full of parents, staring back down at her.

Above, Rory stood with outstretched arms, his osprey dissolving into mist. It suddenly occurred to her how very bad this could look, with her the only adult standing on the field. In front, Moira spun, raising a foam finger to point directly at Vivian.

Aria darted in front of her, growling, hackles raised. The crowd stirred angrily, looking up to Rory, who they believed had saved them all. She could feel the weight of their accusation.

A silver adult wolf skidded in front of Aria and faced the crowd. She howled once, and then visibly braced herself for a charge. Vivian held her breath. One adult wolf was not going to be able to hold off an angry mob. Some of the angry parents looked back and forth, clearly coming to the same conclusion. Hands gripped megaphones. The wooden stakes that held up *We ♥ Sara* and *Go Joon-Woo Go* signs suddenly took on a new menacing air. Vivian took an involuntary step backwards.

From the sidelines came an answering howl. A wolf bounded out of the woods, and then another and another. The pack converged, arranging themselves in a growling barrier between Aria and the mob in the stands.

Mrs. Fairhair glanced over her shoulder and gestured with her head unmistakably. *Run.*

Vivian looked around frantically. The cars were too far. There—Orphne was standing at the back door of the snack shack, jumping up and down and waving. Vivian scooped Aria up in her arms and ran down the field towards the dubious shelter.

Behind her, she could hear angry shouting about thieves and wolves, and snarling from the wolves themselves. Her breath hitched. Aria squirmed in her arms, whining. She didn't have the stamina for this. She could hear Ms. Genevieve pleading for calm. The mob at her back didn't seem calmed.

Behind her, someone screamed. A wolf yelped.

A bolt of energy crackled past her, scoring the turf to her right. She shrieked and nearly dropped Aria. Someone was shooting at her? The grass near her feet started growing and grabbed at her remaining shoe. She yanked her foot out and left it behind, running full tilt in her socks.

Someone came running from the side. She couldn't dodge them. She could only spare them a glance.

It was a Fae woman. She couldn't fight the Fae. Vivian tried to shield Aria with her body.

"Go!" the woman shouted. Suddenly Vivian realized where she'd seen the woman before. It was the mother of Rhiannon, the girl she'd used the EpiPen for all those months ago. "This balances the debt."

A haze shimmered around her, and she nodded and half-sobbed. Something exploded near her back, and the haze flared. She ran, praying the shield would hold.

Daniel was at the shack door, shouting something she couldn't hear. Her own breath filled her ears. She stumbled the last few feet, and he ran to meet her, supporting her. They staggered through the door and Orphne slammed it shut behind them.

19

May 4 11:02 AM
EMERGENCY ALERT
Please remain calm. Emergency services are on their way.
Please remain—

A ria squirmed out of her arms. Vivian dropped to her knees, panting and wishing she'd kept up with her Zumba classes. Her shoulder burned. She glanced down and realized there was a bright red streak on her arm, already puffing up into a massive blister. That bolt had been closer than she'd realized. She thanked her lucky stars she'd been wearing a sleeveless shirt and hadn't melted polyester to her skin. She poked the blister and hissed through her teeth.

"That's not going to keep them for long," Daniel muttered.

"Longer than you think," Orphne said.

"What did you do, love?" Raidne croaked. She was propped up against a wall, looking somewhat worse for wear. But mercifully awake. Evander clutched her, wide-eyed.

"Necro-aura." Orphne smiled sunnily and Raidne managed a weak laugh.

341

"Not up to speed here," Daniel said, raising a hand.

"Anyone who gets too close will suddenly have to deal with the overwhelming sense of their own mortality." Raidne shook her head and then winced. "Serves them right."

"We can't stay here forever," Vivian managed to gasp out, her breath only slowly coming back under control.

Aria shook herself back into human form. The pinny was somewhat worse for wear, but then again, no pinny was going to survive kindergartners in any form. "But, Mommy, you fixed it. Why are they still mad at us?"

She pulled her daughter into her arms, tears pricking her eyes. How could she explain? "Because people are scared, sweetie. And when they're scared, they want a villain to be mad at."

"We need to find their villain," Daniel said.

"Moira's got them wrapped around her finger, thanks to Cecily and Lemere," she said bitterly.

"Moira and Cecily aren't as popular as you thought," Daniel reminded her.

"That doesn't help when people want to be riled up," she countered.

"But Lemere's an outsider, too," Orphne said. "More than you. He doesn't show up to bake sales."

"An outsider who shows up to bake sales is probably the perfect scapegoat target," she said. Outside, angry voices blended together. "Right now, they're not going to be satisfied with some guy hiding in his fancy office in Manhattan."

"He can't be in Manhattan right now," Raidne said. "Not to pull off that osprey trick. He's got to be here, probably within line of sight. Under a shield like Steve's, most likely."

Vivian should have felt a sense of hope, but all she could muster was bone-deep weariness.

"Whoops," said Orphne. "We might have an itsy-bitsy problem."

Raidne closed her eyes and let her head thump back against the wall. Evander flinched. "Itsy-bitsy as in the time we were run out of Innsmouth, or itsy-bitsy as in the Atlantis debacle?"

"Oh, not as bad as either of those," Orphne assured her. "It's just that they've got a projective empath, and they're going to break through the aura soon."

Aria whimpered and buried her face in Vivian's neck. "But you'll tell them it's not our fault. It'll be OK, right, Mommy?"

"I'll fix it," she said, with no idea how to fix it. "It'll be OK."

She took a shuddering breath and steeled her spine. Daniel's hand fell gently on her shoulder.

"You don't have to fix it," he said. "It's not your fault."

"But it is my fault, again," Vivian confessed the dreadful truth. "I was the one who gave Moira the idea to fake the Reckoning. I was the one who went poking into the records and made them feel threatened. If I'd simply dropped it, maybe they would have done something less dramatic. If I hadn't kept asking, they would have picked something else, something that didn't target Aria. I put her in danger. Again."

"Oh, Viv," Daniel said. She turned away from his pity-filled eyes. She didn't want his sympathy.

"Those are the words of a fool," said Raidne. "If you hadn't been poking, as you say, would the gala funds still have been short?"

Well, obviously. And they still would have blamed her. Only in that case, she would have had no warning. Something in the back of her head started to stir. She'd tried. She'd tried so hard, and it hadn't been enough to keep this from happening.

She'd made friends with the right people, and it hadn't been enough to keep this from happening.

Because the people she was supposed to make nice to, the people her mother would have told her to befriend, were jerks. No matter how many favors she'd done them, it wouldn't have kept this from happening.

Because nothing she could have done could have kept this from happening.

Because it wasn't her fault.

Suddenly she realized that she was pissed. At Moira, and at Cecily, and at Ms. Genevieve for not listening to her, and at Cara and Elowen even if they were only kids, because she expected Aria to try to think about others' feelings, so why couldn't they? And at stupid smug Banderbridge, and at that slimy asshole Lemere, and Mrs. Fairhair's poor mad son for starting this entire mess, but mostly at Moira and Cecily. Because the rest of them hadn't been personal. But Moira? Moira had had a choice, and she had chosen to make a friend and betray her.

"We cannot control our fate, only how we meet it," Raidne reminded her.

"Fine," Vivian said, swallowing her tears angrily. "I'll see it. I'll fix it."

"No," said Daniel again. "We'll fix it. Together."

"All of us," Orphne added.

"It's my—"

"Not everything is your responsibility to fix," Daniel said, taking her hand gently. "We got this. Let someone else take it. You're not alone."

She wanted to protest. It didn't feel true. But she looked around the tiny shack, smelling of Fae candy and old hot dog water, too full of people who cared about her. Who weren't going to betray her. If it wasn't her fault, it wasn't entirely her responsibility. And she reminded herself of what Dr. Kumar kept telling her—that sometimes brains lied, and just because something didn't feel true didn't mean it wasn't true. She took a big breath. "OK."

"OK." Daniel nodded decisively. "So. Lemere isn't going to get his fees if Rory doesn't get into Whatchamacallit Prep, and if Rory's grades are as bad as you think, he's not getting in unless everyone officially declares he's the Wingy Scholar or whatever. What still needs to happen?"

Vivian tried to remember, and then thought to grab her phone and scroll back to the picture she'd taken in the library. "They have to crown him with laurels."

"So if we're right and Lemere's here, he can't leave until that happens."

Vivian wanted to groan. "If he's shielded, we'll never find him."

"But he's easy to find," Aria said. "Just follow the bad smell."

Vivian started to hush her and then stopped. "You can still smell the bad smell, sweetheart?"

"That's what I said!" Aria said, exasperated at grown-ups and their stupidity.

The grown-ups exchanged a startled look.

"Is it safe to let her out?" Vivian fretted. But Daniel was already texting. Vivian's pocket buzzed.

"Steve says the cavalry will be here any minute," Daniel read out.

"I can buy you that time," said Raidne, standing with effort.

"Will you be OK?" Evander looked up at her, eyes wide.

She smiled at him. "Beguiling is what I was made for, love."

The siren took a deep breath, the gills at her neck fluttering, and threw open the door.

The crowd surrounding the snack shack froze under the force of her song. Vivian blinked hard, trying not to sag under the lullaby of calm and peace. The sticks and megaphones drooped towards the ground. Step by step, Raidne made her way through the crowd, Orphne on one side supporting her, Evander on the other clutching her pant leg, his childish soprano rising in descant. The crowd parted before them. With a yip and a wriggle, Aria transformed back into a wolf and darted into the crowd. Vivian could only trust her daughter; she had no way to follow. Instead, she and Daniel stuck behind Raidne.

When they approached Ms. Genevieve, Raidne's song changed from soporific to suggesting that the crowd listen, consider, learn. She trailed off.

"The effects only last a few moments," Raidne warned her in an undertone.

Ms. Genevieve, at least, seemed to have an idea of where to go from here. "What happened inside the storm?" she asked.

Cecily, her arms full of Elowen, looked ready to interrupt. But before she could, Elowen piped up. "Aria's mommy saved us. She fixed Ms. Immacolata and threw away the evil box."

Cecily said, frustrated, "Sweetheart, I'm so glad you're safe. But we've talked about this before, how sometimes grown-up things are very complicated. And how people we think are our friends are not always our friends."

The crowd muttered. They'd calmed a bit under Raidne's song, but Vivian could feel them balanced on a knife's edge.

"Congratulations, sweetheart! We always knew you could do it!" From the top of the bandstand, Moira was leading Rory down by the hand. The crowd wavered, looking back and forth between Vivian and Rory. A few cheered for the middle schooler, who looked more frightened than proud. But the people farther away picked up the cheers.

"But, Mom—" Rory protested. "It didn't work like it was supposed to. She wasn't supposed to break the spell!"

Moira had a smile plastered on. "No, you did great, honey."

There was more murmuring in the crowd.

"What happened?" repeated Ms. Genevieve, her eyes narrowed.

Vivian raised her chin, and then raised her voice. "An admissions consultant who had been working with Banderbridge to get children into their school of choice if their parents paid enough has been faking evidence of the Reckoning the whole time. That's why the only signs have been at school events."

"Are you seriously expecting us to deny the evidence of our own eyes?" Cecily demanded. "We all watched Rory fulfill the prophecy."

"Mommy—" Elowen interrupted again, even as Rory protested, "But Mom—"

Daniel squeezed her hand. Vivian raised her voice. "The storm wall was a fake. It was created by Lemere, the consultant. It was only being held together by the locus."

"And what proof do you have of that?" Moira asked, more of the crowd than of Vivian.

Vivian opened her mouth. She didn't have any proof.

"This," said Steve from behind her.

She turned. He was trying to walk with a twin clinging to each leg. He held the golden box aloft. "I've got the locus right here—the one Vivian threw out of the storm."

"I told you," Elowen sulked.

"That's hardly proof," Moira said, but her knuckles were white where she clutched Rory's hand.

"It will be when the Shadow Council gets the full report, and the forensic magicians have gone over it," Steve promised.

From the other side of the crowd, near the parking lot, Vivian heard Aria's howl. It wasn't a howl of distress. It was a hunting howl.

Daniel was texting frantically. Vivian's phone started vibrating. As Steve spoke, continuing to elaborate on what he'd detected, she risked a quick glance.

He can't get far, there's a bottleneck by the parking lot, Madhuri texted back.

Aria yipped from somewhere near the fence.

Her phone continued to buzz in her hand, but she had no time to look at the messages. She left Steve and Ms. Genevieve and dashed after Aria, who was weaving through the crowd, many of whom were headed for the single gate. Something was blocking them, and people were piling up.

It was only a chain link fence. Could she climb it? Other people seemed to be contemplating the same, but no one had yet tried. As she got closer, she could see the hold-up. Officers in short robes with the Shadow Council logo had finally arrived, now that the worst was already over. They were blocking people from leaving, demanding information and papers. She pushed her way to the fence, barely in time to see Aria wiggle through and dash past the Shadow Council officers.

Aria flashed past the chupacabra enclosure as one of the Shadow Council officers grabbed for her tail and missed. Madhuri watched by the enclosure gate, a grin on her face. Vivian called to her, but couldn't make herself heard over the roar of the crowd.

Aria streaked through the fair and into the parking lot, barking her head off. She took a flying leap and suddenly a man in tactical gear stumbled out of literally nowhere. People gasped. Lemere turned, his face a mask of rage. He lifted a hand and opened his mouth. Surely he wouldn't hurt a child, in front of all the people? Only Aria didn't look like a child, she looked like a predator, her baby fangs bared and snapping at his pant legs.

Then the chupacabras slammed into him.

They snapped at his ankles, worrying and biting. Lemere's arms windmilled and he toppled over. The chupacabras attacked his shoes, which were stained red. Aria danced around, yapping up a storm. Two of the Shadow Council officers caught up, panting.

"You know, I seemed to have spilled the vat of goat blood over by the gate," Madhuri noted conversationally from the other side of the fence. "I do hope Orphne doesn't get too upset with me."

There was a large red puddle in front of the gate with footprints trailing out of it, Vivian realized. Steve had managed to push his way to the front and was having an urgent conversation with the remaining officers.

Orphne pushed her way next to them. "Oh no. When I asked you to feed them, I should have warned you. Those buckets can be ever so tippy. And the poor dears, they'd been off their feed all day. But you know predators, don't you, moving prey is always so much more appealing, they couldn't help themselves. I suppose I'd better go rescue them before that nasty man kicks the poor darlings."

She and Madhuri exchanged a smile. Orphne didn't seem to be in all that much of a rush, either, as the mangy monsters continued to gnaw at Lemere's shoes while the officers tried to haul him to his feet. Job well done, Aria pranced back towards Vivian, tail held high. Daniel elbowed his way in next to Vivian.

"Good girl," Daniel said with feeling. Aria wagged her tail proudly.

"So," Madhuri sidled up, wiping red off her hands with a wet nap, "dhokla and beer time?"

20

Raidne smiled as Vivian set down the tray of seedless watermelon slices. "I'm inferring you got to the potluck sign-up early, then?"

"Right up front, the only things already snagged were plates and spoons," Vivian said, smiling back. "I'm not baking again for a while, I promise."

"It's alright, I learned the lesson and wore less valuable shoes," Raidne said, turning an ankle to display shoes that still probably cost more than Vivian used to make in a month. But the effort was sweet. "Are you still available for the clam bake this weekend? Orphne has been planning for days."

"Wouldn't miss it for the world," Vivian said. "Although I

hesitate to ask—do you usually bake your clams?"

"Not typically," Raidne said, accepting a tray of exquisite tarts that sparkled in the sunlight from a nervous-looking mom with pointed ears. She paused, considering, and then deigned to place the tray near the front, and the elf-mom breathed a visible sigh of relief. Raidne had not changed. "But Aria was showing Evander videos again, and they are both most enthusiastic about the digging part. Humans apparently have been managing this for hundreds of years: how difficult could it be?"

Vivian made a mental note to bring a lot of purse snacks, and some hearty appetizers to share. "We'll see you there. Oh, the Fairhairs wanted to know if they should bring steaks?"

"No, no, Orphne already bought far too many. I hope. I must say, if Evander eats that much when he's a teenager, I may need to buy a share in a fishing boat." Raidne shook her head in disbelief. She could certainly afford it, if the money rolling in from Daniel managing her account was only a fraction of her holdings. "We can build a fire on the beach if they want to cook them."

"I doubt it, but I'm sure the kids would love to make s'mores."

"S'mores?"

"Oh, has Evander not had them? I'll bring the fixings," Vivian promised. They weren't quite the same without the chocolate, but Aria had pioneered a peanut butter version that was weird but half-decent. It wasn't a school event: they could have as many nuts as they wanted. She added extra wet naps to her mental list. Raidne turned to evaluate another nervous parent's baked goods offering, and Vivian waved as she headed off to mingle.

Cecily was holding court again over by the cheese tray. Steve shot Vivian a look, clearly begging for a rescue. She gave him a little wave; she'd get there, but she needed a little more fortitude before she could handle Cecily. Not Moira's alcohol-based fortitude—nothing wrong with a glass of wine, but she was trying to follow Dr. Kumar's advice and look for things that brought her joy instead of numbing pain. Not that Cecily was trying to actively cause her pain these days. Now that Aria and Vivian were the heroes of the semester, she was back to being overly chummy. But she was still Cecily.

Madhuri was chatting with some of the other eighth-grade parents, but pulled her into the conversation as soon as she drifted by.

"Is your daughter excited about next year?" she asked.

Madhuri waved her wineglass. "Well, Pendragon Prep didn't pan out, but fortunately Highwater did. And Gauri's already found some of her new classmates on social media. Sounds like I'm going to have to enchant another mirror if I want to make any calls this summer."

"I'll miss you at PAC meetings," Vivian said, fighting down a wave of melancholy.

"Text me the latest Cecily-ism," Madhuri said, winking. "I'm going to need something in my life to be catty about. And we should set up some kind of regular thing. Tea? Book club? Stitch-and-bitch?"

Vivian blinked. She'd assumed, with her daughter graduating, Madhuri was going to drift out of her life. She answered tentatively, "I don't know how to sew."

"Neither do I," Madhuri confessed. "But the bitching part sounds fun. It's all an excuse to hang out without the kids anyway. Good to have something in your life besides work and parenting."

"That would be wonderful. Aria ended up on the travel skirmedge team somehow, but maybe a weeknight?"

"Oh no, you poor thing," Madhuri commiserated. "Save us from the travel teams."

"I know, but I think Daniel's secretly happy. I caught him and Steve planning playlists for road trips in the Cunninghams' minivan. My kid's going to end up indoctrinated in some horrifying combo of dad rock and something called elfpunk?"

A few minutes later, buoyed by the regard of someone she liked, she felt sufficiently fortified to liberate other people she liked from people she no longer felt obliged to like. She headed over towards wine and cheese land.

Ms. Genevieve stopped her. "Vivian! Lovely to see you. Might I have a word?"

Sudden dread curdled in her stomach. Scenarios flashed through her head. Aria had bitten someone. They'd decided to rescind Aria's acceptance to first grade. They'd told Aria she couldn't be in first grade, and she'd bitten them.

"I appreciate the trouble you've taken with the PAC books this year," the headmistress said carefully. "And as you may have discerned, the parallel records on the school side may, perhaps, not have been what they should have been."

That was one way to put it. She dragged her mind back from worst-case scenarios and tried to figure out where this was going.

"After some discussion with the board, it's been decided that, while mage society schools have not typically operated with some of the oversights of registered mundane nonprofits, perhaps we should adopt some of the practices of our mundane counterparts," Ms. Genevieve continued. "That is, Grimoire Grammar finds itself in need of an auditor."

Vivian blinked. She answered cautiously, "You want me to recommend someone?"

Ms. Genevieve stopped fingering the tweed of her skirt and looked her directly in the eye. "We'd like to hire you part time to look over the school books."

She'd been braced for a reprimand to her child, not a job offer. She temporized. "You do understand that my experience is in corporate auditing for mundane enterprises, not small magical nonprofits, right? I mean, do you even follow GAAP? And I'm hardly independent, since my kid's at the school."

"It turns out that there are relatively few people who have experience in small magical nonprofits," Ms. Genevieve replied. "And while there aren't many regulations that apply to us, the Shadow Council is planning to send their own investigators next year to all the magical schools, in light of recent events."

"Ah. You want to know what's there before they find it," Vivian said, keeping her cynicism to herself. She hadn't forgiven the school for putting them through everything it had. The whole system was a mess. If they hadn't built it to require the high-stakes testing in the first place, none of this needed to have happened.

"Precisely. I suppose it would become more of a bookkeeper position over time, but initially, there is a bit of a mess to clean up."

"I'm not going to hide things," Vivian said, slightly alarmed. They'd gone through so much to keep their integrity. She had no doubt that, if she'd been Lemere's client, they would not have been targeted. She would play their games because she had to, but while she didn't have the standing to challenge the system, she wasn't about to turn around and do the same to someone else.

"I don't want you to," Ms. Genevieve assured her. "But I

imagine this will go better if we can show we're already making a good faith effort to self-report and fix any other, shall we say, *irregularities* when the investigators get here."

"Accountants aren't exactly the same thing as a bookkeeper," Vivian mused. Although, now that she thought about it with Aria increasingly out of the house, she needed something of her own. "But there's a lot of online education these days. I suppose I could learn. There aren't any other bookkeepers in the community?"

"I'm afraid the mages who are inclined towards financial pursuits tend towards high finance wizardry," Ms. Genevieve sighed. "We can only afford someone part time, and there aren't that many qualified people in the area."

She thought about Steve, doing his best to make things right from inside if he could, or at least protect his family if he couldn't. She could do what she could to keep things fair and reclaim a little piece of herself while she was at it. "All right. I'll do it."

Ms. Genevieve smiled, looking relieved, and Vivian realized suddenly that the shortage of mage accountants must be even worse than she'd implied. "Lovely. We can chat about the details sometime next week?"

After nailing down a time, she turned back to her rescue mission. Meanwhile, Cecily had managed to trap a wider circle. That was all right. She could handle Cecily.

"…and of course, with three different schools' admissions departments turning over, we'll need to completely change the approach to admissions night next year," Cecily was pontificating.

Steve sighed. "It's total chaos over in the Council. Three more resignations, and we haven't even gotten to the trial date yet. I swear, Lemere's dribbling out names slowly for the greatest possible PR effect."

"What does that mean for us non-Shadow Council folks?" Daniel asked, moving aside a little to let Vivian in. She glanced at him out of the corner of her eye—he could have asked about mundane families, but he'd chosen the group that included him in with everyone else. He glanced back and gave her a little smile, and then entwined his fingers with hers.

"Not much," Steve replied with a crooked grin. "Doesn't mean much for us lower-level Shadow Council folks, either, other than a lot of shuffling. It'll blow over."

"Well, I'm hardly one to cause drama, but I can't imagine what kind of example this is setting for all our children," Cecily said. "Why, in my grandmother's day, nothing like this ever happened."

"By the way, what ended up happening to Moira?" Sasha asked Cecily guilelessly. "You two were close, weren't you?"

"I would hardly let Elowen associate with a family who put themselves in such a position," Cecily said, suddenly stiff.

For a moment, Vivian was tempted to twist the knife. But she was going to have to continue to see Cecily at meetings for the next eight years. She decided to offer an olive branch instead. "I think Ms. Genevieve is going to do a little speech soon. Do you think it might be nice if someone from the PAC would say a few words? I saw her by the dessert table."

Cecily flashed her a look that might almost be gratitude but disappeared quickly. "Well, I'm not one to steal the spotlight, but if she needs an introduction…"

Vivian only felt a little guilty about siccing Cecily on the headmistress.

Steve cocked an eyebrow. "That was kinder than I would have been."

"Cecily is going to Cecily, she can't help herself." Vivian

shrugged. It felt good to take the high road, at least now that it didn't cost Aria anything. "I feel a little bad for her: she's stuck with herself all day."

"But what did happen to Moira?" Orphne asked.

The previous week, Vivian had found a pair of Cara's mittens mixed in with Aria's stuff while cleaning out her backpack. She'd debated with herself for a bit, trying to decide how much anyone would care about mittens, and how much she wanted closure. And then she'd texted Moira.

Moira had suggested meeting at a Starbucks out by the highway, outside of town. Vivian had been half surprised she answered at all. Maybe she'd wanted closure, too.

When she'd gotten there, the ritual of ordering got them through the first few minutes, but then the awkwardness had descended like a fog.

"How's Cara doing?" Vivian had finally asked.

"We're moving to Nova Scotia," Moira had said suddenly. "It will be nice to be closer to my family."

And away from everyone in town, and in a new school system. Vivian had nodded. Neither of them had met the other's eyes yet. She'd fiddled with her cup, labeled by the barista as *Bev* instead of *Viv*, which she supposed was still an accurate description of the contents if not the consumer. Since they seemed unlikely to ever see each other again and the conversation already consisted largely of non sequiturs, she had gone for it. "Why Aria?"

"It wasn't personal," said Moira, who had been turning a paper straw wrapper into a tightly twisted little rope. "But it was your idea. The Reckoning, I mean. If you'd left the whole accounting thing alone, none of this would have happened."

Vivian had told herself that too many times. And actually?

Dr. Kumar was right. It was bullshit. "No. It happened because you made choices. I didn't do anything that deserved that."

"Fine." Moira still hadn't met her eyes. "Bad things happen to good people and all."

"Did you get your skin back?"

Moira's laugh had lacked humor. "Yes, and it turned out in our favor, too. The Shadow Council tossed extortion on the pile of charges and let us off lightly." As long as they left, she left unsaid.

"Were we ever friends?" Vivian had pressed.

"I mean, yeah." She had started pulling the ends of the paper rope off, bit by bit, leaving a pile of twisted confetti on the table. "We were."

"Then how could you?"

Moira had looked up. "Can you tell me you wouldn't have made the same choice?"

"No," Vivian had said honestly. She'd spent some long nights thinking about it. They were too similar for easy sleep. She understood the desperation, and the willingness to do almost anything to protect her kid. But the difference was, for her, "almost" had never included hurting other people. "No, I really wouldn't have."

"Well," Moira had said as she stood up. "Then I guess we were friends, but we never had much in common. Have a nice life, Viv. Seriously. I'm not sorry about what I did. I'm sorry it didn't work. But I'm also sorry I had to do it."

Vivian had been sorry about that, too. "I hope things work out for Rory."

"Yeah, well, that's what we have wine for," Moira had said, a little bitterly. "Hope Aria enjoys the rest of Grimoire Grammar. It's all yours, now."

Vivian wrestled her thoughts back to the present. "They moved to Canada to be closer to family."

The others glanced at each other, mutually deciding to accept Moira's face-saving lie and let her pass from their lives. Vivian didn't think she would forget as easily. She deliberately shifted the conversation. "So, guess who's got a job at the school now?"

They followed her willingly, exclaiming and congratulating. Daniel picked her up and swung her around, whooping. She laughed, taking pleasure in his pride—in her twenties, this would have felt like a setback, but she wanted different things at the moment, and that was OK. Steve caught her eye and raised his eyebrows. She shrugged. There were big inequities Aria would have to face as an adult, and maybe she could help smooth that in a tiny way. Gotta get them there first.

"How's Aria doing after all this?" Steve asked, after the hubbub had died down.

Vivian turned to look where Aria was running back and forth with her friends. Ms. Immacolata was watching her former charges one last time so the parents could chat; she gave them a little wave. Evander had summoned a butterfly, and Aria and the twins were chasing after it, giggling. Aria leapt into the air, sneezed, and came down a wolf cub. The butterfly landed on her nose and she stared at it, cross-eyed in delight. The other kids tumbled over her, and she changed back to a human child, her loose dress and bloomers more damaged by grass stains than her transformation. The pack of children scrambled up again, following a flickering ball of light Shuri had cast, unperturbed.

"I think she'll be fine." Vivian smiled.

"How are the meds working out?" Sasha asked.

"Finally got a dosage that's working for her," Daniel said. "Thanks for the recommendation, the new doc is great."

"And thanks for the other recommendation, too," Vivian added. The couples therapist had turned out to be a bunyip and only did teletherapy from his swamp in Australia—apparently qualified couples therapists were fairly rare and in high demand in the magical community. But he'd had some very helpful insights and they'd been making real progress. The full-moon sleepovers with the pack had been going smashingly well; they were thinking of letting Aria stay with them for a few days so they could take a little romantic getaway sometime soon.

The conversation continued but Vivian only half-listened, watching her daughter play with her friends. They stayed until the kids were sleepy and the twilit trees full of will-o'-the-wisps. Daniel cast the family sigil, only a little wobbly, and Aria came trotting over.

"Ready to go home, Princess Fluffybutt?" Daniel asked as Aria's floof of a tail beat his leg with a tired wag. Aria nodded, her tongue lolling. He glanced at Vivian. "You, too?"

She smiled. "I think we're already here."

ACKNOWLEDGEMENTS

I have to admit, I'm glad I'd already had the better part of this written before *Dreadful* hit, or I don't know if I wouldn't have had the nerve to get it down. But once again, this book wouldn't be here without the contributions of so many other people.

Thank you to the Titan Books team, who have been amazingly supportive, both of my first book and this one, well beyond my wildest dreams. George Sandison's warmth, wit, and occasional tough love helped make this a much stronger book. Katharine Carroll, Kabriya Coghlan, Charlotte Kelly, Isabelle Sinnott, Katie Greally, Hannah Scudamore, Bahar Kutluk, Olivia Cooke, Kevin Eddy, Louise Pearce, and Claire Schultz have done so much to not only get this book into the world but also get it into your hands. Natasha MacKenzie turned out another beautiful cover. Thank you all so much.

Thank you to my agent, Sarah Fisk, who is taking the publishing world by storm. Super agent!

Before this draft ever got to these nice folks, though, it needed a couple rounds of major edits. Thanks to the Secret Cabal—Leonard Richardson, Tejal Kuray (K.S. Shere), Elizabeth Yalkut, Andrew Willet, and Cheryl Barkauskas. And thank you to Erica Kudisch, who let me lure her to a speakeasy and then pummel her with questions. This book is so much stronger for your feedback.

My husband and son continue to be the most supportive family a writer could wish for, even when I'm being an anxious mess. Sorry I keep disappearing for hours at a time, or staring blankly into the middle distance while listening to the people in my head. Thank you for buying all the garlic for the *Dreadful* launch party. Thank you even more for finding ways to eat all the garlic for the *Dreadful* launch party.

Finally, thank you to all the incredibly hard-working teachers and school administrators out there, and especially to the ones who have been supporting my child all the way. This was never an easy job, and it's only gotten harder in the more recent years. I hope you take the satire in this book in the way it was intended—as affectionate teasing. While the school supply list has sometimes been long, at least it usually comes with Amazon links and I don't need access to a hidden store to get everything. I'm pretty sure, given the incredible grace with which they've handled the challenges of the last few years, my son's school would have dealt with the Reckoning better than Grimoire Grammar did. Thank you for all you have done and continue to do.

ABOUT THE AUTHOR

Caitlin Rozakis is the *New York Times* bestselling author of *Dreadful*. After graduating from Princeton, she has had too many career changes, including mechanical engineering (cut short after the murderous robot incident), finance (amortizing tequila receivables is not as fun as drinking tequila), the American Museum of Natural History (who knew emus had birth certificates?), and a number of marketing positions, some at companies you may have even heard of. She lives in Jersey City with her husband and son. Visit her online at www.caitlinrozakis.com.

For more fantastic fiction, author events,
exclusive excerpts, competitions, limited editions and more

VISIT OUR WEBSITE
titanbooks.com

LIKE US ON FACEBOOK
facebook.com/titanbooks

FOLLOW US ON TWITTER AND INSTAGRAM
@TitanBooks

EMAIL US
readerfeedback@titanemail.com